Into the Wilderness

A novel by
Nicky Heymans

malcolm down
PUBLISHING

Endorsement

What a superb job Nicky has done of recreating the events after the parting of the Red Sea and before the forays of the Hebrew spies into Canaan. Telling the story from Joshua's perspective, she immerses us in a world of both otherworldly supernatural manifestations and everyday human squabbles. In the process, she makes the familiar feel unfamiliar, and she does this by deftly fusing the miraculous and the mundane. This kind of subtle storytelling could well see a revival of biblical fiction. And, as far as debut novels go, the storyteller herself shows that she has what it takes to attract a huge audience in the future.

Mark Stibbe PhD, Author of *A Book in Time*
(winner of the 2020 Page Turner Award for Fiction Writing).

First published 2023 by Malcolm Down Publishing Ltd.
www.malcolmdown.co.uk

27 26 25 24 23   7 6 5 4 3 2 1

British Library Cataloguing in Publication Data
A catalogue record for this book is available from the British Library.

ISBN 978-1-915046-64-2

Cover design by Esther Kotecha
Art direction by Sarah Grace

Printed in the UK

Dedication

This book is dedicated to my husband, Kingsley,
who believed in me and my abilities as an
author long before I believed in myself.

Acknowledgements

I have found the process of being a 'first-time author' incredibly exciting, but also quite daunting at times. The question that haunted me on a regular basis was, 'Have I really got what it takes to be a published author?' There are a few people who, throughout this process, have continued to tell me, 'Yes, you do have what it takes.' I am so grateful to you.

To my husband, Kingsley – the love of my life, my best friend, my rock. I can't put into words how much your belief in me has meant. Your encouragement and input over the last few years has been truly invaluable. Thank you for journeying with me through the ups and downs of our own 'wilderness' over the last 34 years. It is an absolute privilege to partner with you. The best is yet to come!

To my children: David, Caleb, Leanne and Talitha. You mean the world to me. I am unreservedly and unashamedly proud of each one of you, and so grateful to you for supporting me and encouraging me along the way. Each of you have been through your own 'wilderness seasons' over the years and yet, each time, you've come out the other side stronger and braver. I'm so excited to see what your futures hold, and blessed to walk with you into them. I love you so much.

To Mark Stibbe, my writing coach and mentor. What a gift you have been to me! I can genuinely say that, without your input, this book would not have happened. Thank you for recognising the storyteller in me and for pointing me in the right direction. Thank you for your incredible insight and creative input. Thank you for telling me the hard truths when I needed to hear them, but with such sensitivity that they didn't break me, but instead, motivated me to become a better writer. I could go on and on (as you well know!), but I won't. I'll do what you tell me to and 'strip it back'. So Mark – thank you!

Contents

1

Pursuit

A shaft of light, like a gigantic fiery arrow, hurtled down from the heavens, struck the earth, and exploded outwards.

Thrown to the ground, I lay there, panting with fear. Holding my hand up to shield me from the glare, I screwed up my eyes and blinked hard, watching what looked like two enormous wings of a flaming celestial being, unfurling sideways. Blasts of thunder echoed around the mountains – back and forth, back and forth, causing my ears to throb in pain. I ducked down and covered them with my hands, but my attempts to block out the onslaught of noise were futile. They did nothing to drown out the screams of my fellow Hebrew runaways, or the shrieks of those who were hell-bent on pursing us.

I lay on my side, frozen in shock, staring at the havoc unfolding before me. I couldn't breathe. My heart was beating so fast, it seemed to have lost all sense of rhythm. So I stayed, buried among the mass of bodies that littered the ground, and continued to watch in stunned silence. My position near the back of the multitudes of fleeing Israelites gave me an unhindered view of what was taking place behind us. It was a sight that would live in the recesses of my mind, continuing to haunt me, until my old age.

The Egyptian militia who, until that moment, had been relentlessly pursuing us, were now thrown into total disarray by the explosion of fire from heaven. Riders were flung from their horses as they reared up in terror, and the Egyptians' usually ordered array of chariots rammed into each other as horses skidded to a halt. Many were overturned in the ensuing chaos. The majority of foot soldiers were thrown to the ground, some thrust into the path of the jagged knives that jutted out from the wheels of Pharoah's plentiful chariots. Others were crushed to death by the sheer weight of the chariots as they drove over them.

The few who were lucky enough to be standing near the back, or on the outskirts of their formations, turned and fled from the blazing wall that loomed over them, without looking back. Most, however, were not so fortunate. Trapped among the swarming mass of chariots, horses, and men, they stared in terror at the mutilated bodies of their comrades who had been sliced in pieces or impaled on the jagged wheels of their own commanders' chariots in a gory bloodbath. Scrambling to their feet, they ducked and dodged, climbing on top of each other in their desperation to find an escape route out of that hellish corral.

As slaves in Egypt, we were forced by pain of death to line the streets and applaud the Egyptian militia whenever they returned from one of their military campaigns. As much as I despised their heathen ways and arrogant temperaments, I couldn't help but admire their military prowess as I watched row after row of chariots pass by, sparkling in the sunlight, their commanders decked out in full ceremonial dress, gold-edged cloaks rippling triumphantly behind them. Even their foot soldiers were majestic as they marched in perfect time through the streets of Egypt, their sandaled feet slapping on the stone slabs with striking uniformity. Eyes straight ahead, their leather helmet chin straps seemed to hide smug smiles, as if they knew how magnificent they looked.

I detested them.

But, despite my loathing, I could not deny that their formidable ranks were a thing of beauty.

This, however, was not that.

Gone were their flawless formations and intimidating attitudes and, in their place, I saw just men. Men like me. Men who feared. Men who screamed in agony as their bodies were hacked into pieces. Men who turned and fled from death, just as we had done.

Just men.

A vile smell filled my nose; I turned to see a man nearby vomiting as he watched the massacre of the Egyptian troops. Those near him retched and others joined him, spewing bile out of their mouths. I covered my nose and mouth to block out the smell, and watched breathlessly as the ever-widening fiery barricade continued spreading sideways, finally stretching the entire width of the valley, obscuring the Egyptians from our sight. As the rumble of thunder started to diminish, I became aware of the cacophony which it had been masking.

Children screaming.

Adults wailing, howling in terror.

Voices shouting out instructions.

The crash of waves breaking on the shore.

Tearing my eyes away from the wall of fire, I staggered to my feet and turned to look at the multitudes of people strewn across the shoreline as far as the eye could see. I took some deep breaths to try to slow my heart rate, watching my people cling to each other, gasping, staring first at the wall of fire behind them, then at the vast expanse of water in front of them.

The Red Sea.

'We're trapped!' A cry went up, rippling through the crowds. I could see panic setting in as they evaluated their options: to die in the towering flames, be killed by the Egyptians, or drown in the Red Sea.

They were not good odds.

'Why did we come this way?' a woman cried out, trying in vain to quieten her screaming child.

'Did Moses bring us here to die because there were no graves in Egypt?' her companion asked, the whites of his eyes revealing his fear. 'It would have been better if we had stayed in Egypt and died as slaves, rather than perish here in the wilderness.'

All around me, panic was turning to anger. I could feel it, a thread of dissidence that rippled through the crowds. They needed someone to blame, and who better than the man who had brought them here.

Moses.

A voice shouted out, over and over, cutting through the noise of the brawling crowd. I turned around to find the source of the voice. He stood near the water's edge; a man with a greying beard, not particularly striking or handsome, and not very tall in stature. In fact, you might be forgiven for disregarding him, were it not for the undeniable authority with which he spoke, and the staff that he held in his hand.

I knew that staff. I had seen what it could do – or what Yahweh could do through the man who wielded it.

My father, Nun, told me many stories about Moses. His parents had been friends of Moses' parents, so the tales of how they hid Moses from the Egyptians in a reed basket on the river Nile, how he was found by Pharaoh's daughter and became a prince of Egypt, were well known to me. My father had been newly married when Moses fled Egypt as a younger man but, when he returned to Egypt nearly forty years later to free our people from slavery, my father was among the elders. He and the other leaders met with Moses and, not only did my father's wisdom and leadership quickly gain him Moses' trust, but I believe the stories he was able to tell Moses about his parents endeared him to our new leader.

The elders' meetings were usually held in secret and only a select few were invited, so I never met Moses face to face. But, because my father and I were now all that was left of our family, he would tell me what was discussed at those meetings, and share with me his hopes and concerns for our people. I learned a lot about Moses through my father and now, looking at the man standing near the water's edge, I felt like I knew him.

I could see Moses shouting to the people, but I was too far away to be able to hear what he was saying. Whatever he said, it was clearly not well received, because scornful shouts began to echo through the throngs. Moses' brother, Aaron, stood by his side at the water's edge, looking decidedly agitated. He leaned in to speak to his brother, but Moses shook his head, holding up his hand to silence him. So Aaron stood fidgeting by his side while Moses stared at the sea, his back to us.

The crowds were getting more and more aggressive. A couple of minutes passed. I saw Moses walk to the edge of the water and lift his staff above his head. The words he spoke were lost in the noise of the crowds and the waves but, only moments after he lifted his staff, a fearsome wind rushed across the beach. All around me, headscarves were torn off, clothes flapped wildly, and the small of stature found themselves on the ground. I struggled to keep hold of my head covering. I couldn't turn away; I had to see what Moses was doing. Blinking repeatedly, I managed to pull my headscarf down enough to shield my eyes from some of the wind's impact.

Peering out through a slit, I watched in breathless silence as a ferocious wind surged towards the Red Sea; wind and water collided in an epic showdown.

2

The Cloud

The waters of the Red Sea started to peel back, as if an invisible knife was cutting a pathway through the waves. Weeping and complaining turned into gasps of amazement as we stood, dumbfounded, watching the spectacle unfold in front of us. The roaring 'whoosh' of the wind put a stop to any conversation, so we watched and waited in awestruck silence.

Minutes passed, and still the turbulent wind continued to force its way through the swells of water, driving them back inch by inch, creating rippling watery walls that rose higher and higher on either side of the rift.

Above the place where Moses stood was the cloud that had converged, forming a canopy over us as we left Egypt. It was vast, covering the beach and spreading out over the Red Sea. It was unlike any cloud I had seen before. It oscillated constantly, swirling and undulating and, from time to time, it shimmered with sparks of light, as if celestial beings were flying within its midst. A large section of the cloud plunged down to the earth, creating a billowing pillar near the water's edge that could be seen for miles around.

This was no ordinary cloud.

This was the cloud of Yahweh's presence, a sign of the holy covenant He had made with His people to protect us, provide for us, and lead us into the land He had promised, the land of our forefathers, Abraham, Isaac, and Jacob: Canaan.

The cloud was miraculous and, from the moment I first saw it, it ignited a raw passion in my heart. Embers of hope that had long been dead had started to stir in me once again. Despite the chaos unravelling around me, I couldn't help but smile to myself when the thought occurred to me that I had spent more time gazing up at the sky in the last couple of days than I had my whole lifetime.

Our lives as slaves had been characterised by back-breaking labour, our days spent hunched over under the weight of huge boulders in the quarries of Egypt. There had been precious little time for staring up at the sky.

Until now.

I closed my eyes and breathed in. Putting my head back, I breathed out and gazed up at the cloud. But something was wrong. Up until now, the cloud had moved forward with us at a steady pace. But, while the wind continued to move forward, forging a pathway through the waters of the Red Sea, the cloud now seemed to be moving backwards, towards the place where I stood by the wall of fire which separated us from our former slave masters. The cloud's appearance changed as it swirled overhead. Its iridescent form was darkening, and there was a murky denseness to it that I found disconcerting. I wasn't the only one who had noticed.

'Look!' said a young man nearby, pointing to the cloud. 'What's happening?'

'Why is it moving backwards?' his companion said to no one in particular.

'It's getting dark. Why has it turned so dark?' The first young man shivered, squinting in concentration. We watched the heavens with restless trepidation, huddling together as the cloud moved closer. Its massive form cloaked the hushed crowds in a shroud of darkness, like a thick blanket being pulled over a sleeping form. It moved closer and closer, the moody cloud dwarfing the rays of the sun, then extinguishing them from our sight altogether.

Darkness fell.

I held my breath, my eyes locked on the retreating cloud.

The silence was eerie and oppressive.

The cloud rolled over us and moved on towards the Egyptians amassed on the other side of the flaming wall. Out of the corner of my eye, I saw flickers of light – rays of sunlight glinting on the distant waters. The sun was once again shining down on those nearest to the sea as the cloak of darkness swept inland.

Now I understood.

Swivelling back to the fiery blockade behind me, I watched with bated breath as the cloud moved closer, creating a chilling canopy of darkness over the gridlocked Egyptians. The front edges of the thick cloud which usually formed the billowing pillar that went before us, cascaded down towards the ground, spreading out sideways and joining forces with the blazing wall to create an impenetrable barrier between Hebrew and Egyptian.

It took a matter of minutes for the cloud to complete its mission, and for me to feel the rays of the late afternoon sun on my back once again. I turned my attention to the sea as the wind continued its relentless assault on the waters. Once the chasm had widened to roughly nine chariots' width, by my estimation, it no longer pushed the boundaries further. Instead, it seemed content to concentrate its might on holding the watery walls in place so that Yahweh's people could cross over in safety.

But no one wanted to make the first move.

We waited and watched and, after a few moments, three figures approached the water's edge. Moses, his brother, Aaron, and a woman who looked like his older sister, Miriam. 'What are they doing?' I muttered to myself, staring at the three diminutive figures in the distance. They walked towards the dried-up seabed. Not looking back, and without any hesitation whatsoever, they picked up their bundles and strode into the immense canyon which the retreating waters had created. Every eye was focused on Moses and his siblings. No one moved, but the tension in the air told me that everyone was poised for action.

I was right.

As soon as they determined it was safe, people surged towards the water's edge, desperate to enter the canyon and get to the other side. It was like floodgates opening – floodgates that released not a flood of water, but a tidal wave of mankind. I grimaced at the mayhem that broke out as men, women and children swarmed towards the watery passageway, yanking their livestock behind them, or driving the reluctant animals in front of them.

Even those around me at the back of the multitude got caught up in the fresh wave of panic. Picking up their bundles, they ran as one, trying to force their way through the blockade of bodies in front of them. Shoving and pushing, they knocked each other over, some using their bags like battering rams to try to smash their way through the crowds. Children screamed, women were thrown to the ground and fists flew.

'*Stop!*' I shouted. 'Stop this! Be still!'

While some of them paused to look at me, eyes wide with fear, the more desperate among them continued trying to bulldoze their way through. At times like this, my stature was a great advantage, and I used it now to its full effect. Wading over to where the main troublemakers were, I used my body as a barricade to stop them. Grasping hold of a man's forearm, I shouted, 'Restrain yourself!' My voice stopped him in his tracks; he came to his senses, looking around him in confusion. I continued pinpointing disruptive individuals, confronting them with both my size and my voice. It worked. After a short while, it was quiet enough for me to speak again.

'There is no purpose in this,' I shouted. 'Fighting among ourselves will only make things worse. It will take time for our people to move through the waters, and we must be patient.' Speaking to the men in the crowd, I continued, 'Sit down. Let your families rest while they can. We have a long walk ahead of us and we must be ready when the time comes. Sit. Give the children some food. Drink. Quench your thirst.' I motioned to them with my hands and some sank gratefully down to the ground. 'Rest now. We must be patient and wait until it is our time.'

And so we waited. Bloody noses were dabbed, cuts and bruises attended to. Bundles that had been ripped open in the kerfuffle were retied, and many were used as makeshift pillows as the exhausted sojourners stole a few blissful minutes of sleep. I scanned the shoreline, studying the movement of bodies. From where I stood at the back of the multitude, they looked like a swarm of ants.

'Where are you?' I mumbled, searching the crowds. But the evening was drawing in and the rays of the late afternoon sun blinded my eyes, stopping me from finding the ones I searched for. I quashed my frustration. I couldn't start pushing my way through the people to try to find them now. I couldn't do what I had just stopped everyone else from doing.

I would have to wait, just like them.

3

Walls of Water

We waited and waited, and waited yet more. The afternoon passed into evening, and evening into night, and still we watched and waited. Droves and droves of our people had walked into the riverbed and yet the blockade of bodies in front of us did not seem to move. Night had fallen, and those around me at the back of the throng were getting increasingly anxious about the crossing.

Although we could no longer see our pursuers, we could still hear them, and the noise of the Egyptian forces behind us added to the stress of our waiting. Every few minutes, we would hear the jarring shouts of Egyptian captains, followed shortly afterwards by the muffled sound of hooves, the frantic whinnying of horses, and the screams of their riders. It seemed Pharoah was not content for his legions to loiter behind the thick barrier of fire and cloud, but was forcing them, time and time again, to try to break through it. Despite repeated failures, he was intent on persisting in that suicidal mission.

The sense of relief when we were finally able to move was overwhelming. Not to be confined in that space, not to have to listen to the screams that penetrated the curtain of fire, was liberating. I woke those who had drifted off to sleep and helped them ready themselves. But, although I felt such a strong sense of relief at finally being able to move on, I also felt an unusual reluctance to leave the cloud. Even in its present dark, forbidding state, I was strangely drawn to it, and felt an overwhelming compulsion to stay with it.

'Foolishness!' I thought. To stay behind would be a death sentence. 'And yet . . . I have no wish to leave you,' I muttered, turning again to look at it. 'Will you not come with us?' I had no choice but to continue on, but every minute or so I turned to stare at the cloud, willing it to leave its assigned place and return to us. My heart felt bereft, as if grieving for the loss of a loved one. It weighed heavily on me and, as I walked, I mused to myself how I could have come to love Yahweh's beautiful presence so profoundly in such a short time.

As we neared the water, those around me started to get increasingly agitated. From far away, the sight of the waters of the Red Sea held back by squalls of wind was wondrous and awe-inspiring. Up close, however, it was just terrifying. The walls of water which, from our vantage point near the fire barrier, had seemed just a few feet high, now towered above us, as tall as the edifices of Egypt which we had been forced to build.

Looking down at the fragile form of an elderly woman standing near me, I felt a surge of compassion. 'Come,' I said. 'Yahweh has not brought us this far only to leave us to the mercy of the Egyptians. Let us walk through this pathway that He has laid out for us, and such stories we will have to tell on the other side, *nu*?'[1] She hesitated, looked back at the blazing wall, then turned to stare at the Red Sea. I waited, watching the trembling of her body as she wrestled with her fear. After a few moments she swallowed, nodded and stepped forward.

It was agonising. The walk from our location near the trapped Egyptians down to the water's edge had been slow enough, but it was a gallop compared to this! On dry ground we could walk fairly steadily, albeit gingerly, while watching out for rocks that jutted out, or dips in the ground. Walking through the Red Sea bed, however, was far more precarious.

Our crossing took place within the late-night watches and, although the flaming wall behind us illuminated our way to some extent, the further away we went from it, the less we felt its effect. Some of us carried oil lamps or fire torches, but they only lit up a couple of feet around us and did little to help highlight the constant trip hazards. The ground was waterlogged, the slimy rocks and stones a constant menace.

The seabed had not dried out, as there had been no sun during the course of our crossing, and hundreds of thousands of our people had crossed over before us, as well as all their livestock and carts. By the time we made the crossing, the ground had been well

---

1. A Jewish expression.

and truly churned up and was more like a swamp-like bog than a seabed.

It took great strength and determination for the strong of limb to keep trudging on, but for the children and elderly, it was excruciating. Nevertheless, we plodded on, breathless and exhausted, slipping and sliding, our clothes splattered with mud and wet sand. We had no choice. The towering walls of sea water loomed on either side of us, an ever-present reminder of our predicament, and the flickering light of our lamps and torches illuminated strange-looking sea creatures that swam in the confined waters on either side of us. In the gloomy light, the fish, and all manner of creatures whose home was the sea, looked misshapen and hideous. Strands of seaweed transformed into monsters with tendrils that reached out to grab us and pull us into the water.

'Do not look to the sides. Look at where you are going, yes?' I urged a little girl after she had tripped again in fright after seeing a huge, distorted-looking fish flicking around the edge of the watery wall. Some of the children in our company cried out in fear of the sinister-looking sea creatures they saw, while others revelled in them, fascinated by this new phenomenon. Both groups stumbled on, regardless, until at last the shadowy figures we saw before us on the distant shores began to take shape.

As the last of the stragglers, we finally made our way onto solid ground, hugging each other in relief. But my eyes were instinctively drawn back to the cloud we had left behind. I drew my outer robe around me and rubbed my arms, suddenly aware of the cold breeze that surrounded us now that we were out in the open on the shore. I gazed into the distance, confused and not a little heartsore. The cloud of Yahweh's presence had been with us for such a short time.

'Why?' I thought to myself. 'Why will it not continue on this journey with us?'

As if to answer my question, the cloud's formation started to change. To my astonishment, the pillar of cloud which had plunged down to form the wall, now rose up to meet the rest of the cloud that had formed the dark covering over the Egyptians. I stopped rubbing my arms and leaned forward, frozen in anticipation. Narrowing my eyes, I peered across the dark waters of the Red Sea.

Yes! I wasn't imagining it!

The fire was dissipating, sparks flying left, right and centre; the mighty canopy was on the move again. The cloud's density was breaking up and, as it started moving towards the Red Sea, I saw the familiar flickers of light within it which I loved so much. My heart thrilled within me and I turned to those around me.

'It is coming!' I jabbered, pointing at the cloud. 'The cloud! It is coming back to us!' Turning to another group nearby, I shouted again, 'Look! The cloud! It comes! It has not left us; it is coming back!' 'Why are they not excited?' I thought, confused at the appalled expressions on their faces. Offence rose up strong in me, coupled with anger. 'Do they not *want* the cloud to come back to us?' Swinging round to look again at the object of my devotion, my face fell as I realised why they were not celebrating with me. The cloud was now well on its way back to Yahweh's chosen people, and the wall of fire had all but disappeared – leaving nothing to stop the Egyptians from resuming their reckless pursuit of their escaped slaves.

Yes, the cloud was coming.

But so were the Egyptians!

4

Shock

Silence, but for the sound of the waves and the eerie cries of circling gulls.

No one moved.

No one uttered a word.

The world seemed to hold its breath, paralysed by fear.

The screams of our oppressors still echoed in my ears.

Chaos.

Panic.

The cries of men in terror and the tumultuous roar of the waves had bombarded my senses as the waters of the Red Sea hurtled back into place, crushing everything and everyone in their path. I watched, horrified, as the God of Abraham, Isaac and Jacob annihilated the entire Egyptian army in one fell swoop. The waters of the Red Sea crashed down upon chariots and foot soldiers, and the might of Egypt disintegrated under the formidable hand of the God of Israel.

Then, there was nothing ... except the rapid beating of my heart in my chest.

Silence.

Undiluted.

Bizarrely peaceful.

Waves broke on the shore. I was mesmerised by the sounds of silence that assaulted my senses. Looking down, I noticed waves lapping at my feet, like small forest creatures nibbling at their food, scampering away, then coming back for more.

A kind of numbness took hold of me.

Shock.

I stood still, welcoming the naked simplicity of just breathing. I watched the frothy waves caressing my toes. Uncomplicated and innocent, they asked nothing of me but to be still and enjoy their ministrations.

And so I did.

In and out they scampered, nuzzling my toes with their foamy caresses, then withdrawing again. The gentle, rhythmic pattern of the waves worked its magic and I felt my heart rate slowing. As I came to myself again, there was one thing on my mind: the cloud of Yahweh's presence. Lifting my head from its downward focus, I looked up to the heavens and my heart leapt to see the object of my desire. It was as beautiful as ever, resplendent in glory. Gone was the thick, dark cloak that had covered the Egyptian army and, in its place, glimmering flurries of light once again ruled the heavens. Tears came to my eyes. I quickly wiped them away. I didn't like unnecessary shows of sentiment, especially at times when I felt I needed to be strong.

I gazed upward, noting the familiar sparks of light swirling within the cloud. The sun was rising and the underside of the cloud was tinged with light from the rays of the awakening orb. Its plumes were flushed with gold and pink, flecks of auburn and lilac that glinted in the light of the early morning sun.

A new day was dawning.

I looked down, captivated by the flashes of early morning light that glinted on the waves of the Red Sea. Revelling in the luxury of not having to do anything other than enjoy my surroundings, I stood for a while, just soaking it all in. We'd done it. We had actually done it. I felt those illusive tears come to my eyes again, and brushed them away impatiently. We'd made it across – or through – the Red Sea. How did this happen? My mind couldn't comprehend it and I was too exhausted to continue trying to work it out. Glancing away from the sea, I turned to look instead at the sea of people behind me. The shore was littered with families clinging to one another in a tableau of shock.

Shock, yes, but not fear.

Disbelief, certainly. But not fear.

Confusion, absolutely. But *not fear*!

The savage rod of fear that had broken our backs for centuries now lay at the bottom of the vast expanse of sparkling water behind us. For the first time since leaving Egypt, I smiled. A real smile.

A full-faced, eyebrow lifting, cheek-stretching smile! We had done it! Yahweh be praised, we had *done it*!

'Joshua!' I heard my name being called. I knew that voice! I scanned the crowds, and then I saw him. Indeed, it would have been hard to miss him! He ran towards me through the crowds, robes flapping around his legs, his tangled mass of dark hair bobbing up and down, headscarf trailing behind him and arms flailing as he yelled my name over and over.

Mesha. My closest friend, the brother of my heart. The brother I never had. He dodged clumps of people, jumping over bags that had been tossed on the ground, and hurled himself through the middle of a flock of rather bedraggled-looking sheep. 'Joshua!' he shouted again, laughing with joy as he flung himself into my arms.

'Mesha!' I laughed too, mostly with relief. We slapped each other on the back before kissing each other, first on one cheek and then the other. 'I did not think you would find me in this crowd.'

'Ech, it was easy,' he shrugged. 'All I had to do was look for a man who stood a foot taller than everyone else, and there you were! You will never be able to hide very easily, my friend.' We laughed, then his smile changed to concern. 'Are you well?' he asked. 'We lost you in all the chaos – what took place?'

'Forgive me. A young couple were struggling with their goats – they were frightened by the fire, bleating, and trying to run away – and their children were screaming . . . so I went to help them. When I turned back, you had gone.'

'We didn't realise you were not with us until we sat down to wait for our turn to go through the waters, but by then it was getting dark. We couldn't see clearly, we couldn't move, and the –'

'Mesha,' I put my hand on his chest and stopped him. 'All is well now, *nu*?'

He smiled and relaxed his shoulders. 'Amen. All is well. But . . . the waters?' His eyebrows shot up to the top of his forehead, eyes opened wide. 'The Red Sea! Did you see it? Never has Yahweh stretched out His hand like this. Never before! To witness this with our own eyes, it is . . . it is . . .' All of a sudden Mesha became aware of his surroundings. 'But come! Enough talk. We will have plenty of time to talk, yes?' Picking up one of my bags, he flung it over his shoulder, grabbed me by the arm and said, 'Let me take you back to the family – they are anxious to see you.'

We moved quickly through the crowds and, within minutes, I was reunited with my family – although they weren't actually my family, not the family of my birth.

My family were dead. Every single one of them had now passed through this world into the next. My father, Nun, had been the last to go. It still hit me with a jolt of pain each time I remembered that he was no longer with me. Over the weeks since his passing, I would find myself looking for him in a crowd, or waiting for him to return home. I longed to look into his warm, wise old eyes just once more, to put my hand on his shoulders and kiss his soft, wrinkly cheeks. But it was not to be.

The abuse that my *abba*[2] had suffered over his three score and ten years in Egypt had finally caught up with him, and his heart started to fail. He was not morbid about death, neither was he afraid of dying. He spoke with great certainty about going to be with his fathers' fathers, and was thankful that he had been given the privilege of meeting Moses and helping him with his mission to free our people from the tyranny of Egyptian oppression, before passing.

His only regret was leaving me without family, and so his last act on this earth was to rectify that. Mesha's father, Jesher, had been steadfast friends with my father since their youth, and our families spent much time together. It seemed only natural then, that my friendship with Mesha should follow the pattern of close friendship and brotherhood that our fathers had enjoyed. Jesher had shared many an adventure with my father over the years, so it was only right for him to be with him on his last adventure before leaving this earth.

He sat with me by my *abba*'s side, hour after hour, holding his hand or praying. It was during that time that it happened. My father reached out and took Jesher's hand in his, grasping mine with his other hand. Joining our hands together, he looked at me and said, 'My son, Jesher is now your father.' Turning to Jesher, he whispered, 'This is your son.'

Jesher's face crumpled and he fought back the tears as he whispered, 'I will embrace him as one of my own.'

Abba nodded, a gentle smile on his lips, still holding both our hands in his. One of the last things he heard was the sound of a

2. Hebrew word for father.

million or more frogs croaking as they launched a mass invasion of Egypt at the command of the Lord God. He looked at me with that familiar twinkle in his eye, and rasped, 'Pharoah has seen nothing of the reach of Yahweh's arm yet, *nu?*' Shortly after that, he slipped quietly through the veil that separates this life from the next, a smile still on his lips.

And so now I call Jesher '*abba*', and he is my father, for all intents and purposes. He is a good father, an honourable man who has loved me well through these first few weeks of my orphaned life.

Jesher was the first to greet me when Mesha and I returned. Striding up to me with a broad smile on his face, he held out his arms, hugged me fiercely, and kissed my cheeks. 'Joshua!' He looked at me with his dusky blue eyes. 'We thought you were lost to us.'

'I was, *Abba*,' I replied. Love for this noble man rose up strong in me as I returned his gaze. 'I was lost, but now I am found.'

5

Freedom

I could see the effect that the previous night's events had had on my family. Apart from Mesha, who had an uncanny ability to bounce back from traumatic situations with great dexterity, they looked as though they had been run over by a herd of stampeding oxen. The children's eyes were red from crying, their dusty faces streaked with tears and their clothes utterly dishevelled. The adults didn't look much better, although, instead of red eyes, they were mostly glassy-eyed, with vacant expressions. Our clothes were splattered with mud from the crossing, our hair windswept and matted. Even Jesher's wife, Shira, who would never usually have a hair out of place or a speck of dirt on her clothes, looked less than perfect.

And yet, it didn't matter. None of that mattered any more, because we were all here, together, sitting on a rocky beach on the other side of the Red Sea, our oppressors gone, and the glorious cloud of Yahweh's presence hovering over us like a glowing banner of victory.

It was true! What Moses had said was true!

This wasn't some cruel plot to entice us into the desert in order to kill us. It was true. We were free. *Free*! Free to go where we wanted, free to do what we wanted. Free to be who we wanted to be. Free! No longer slaves, but free. A whole nation of free people – the nation of Israel! I looked at the expanse of water behind us and realised there was no going back. This was it. There was only one way we could go now, and that was forward, towards the land of our forefathers – the land of Canaan.

All around me, people were starting to relax. The shock was subsiding and, for the first time in what seemed like forever, I breathed out; the full-bodied, unshackled breaths of a free man. The silence was broken as men and women, young and old, turned to each other in recognition of what had happened. Terror turned to relief and relief into joy, and cries of exhilaration started rippling through the throngs of those who had been, but were no longer, bondservants.

'They're gone.'

'We're free!'

'We did it!'

'They are gone. All of them ... gone.'

'We are free!'

Friends and strangers hugged each other, many sobbing with relief. Men slapped each other on the back while the women fell into each other's arms, all of us unashamedly shedding tears of joy. The sound of music started to reverberate through the crowds and God's own people started clapping, stomping their feet to the beat of the drums and tambourines. Twirling, kicking, dancing, we sang the praises of the God who had delivered us from our Egyptian oppressors.

Mesha's wife, Helah, took her daughters by the hands and swung them round and round, laughing as Mesha lifted their eighteen-month-old son, Shallum, onto his shoulders. Shallum giggled with delight, holding onto his father's hands as Mesha twirled round and round. The men formed circles and linked arms, kicking and shouting out, while the women formed their own circles and weaved in and out of each other, clapping and jumping in celebration.

'*Abba*, come!' I called to Jesher, who was standing nearby clapping his hands, watching the celebration. 'Come and dance with us!'

He hesitated, peering at me from under his bushy eyebrows. 'I do not know if that is wise, Joshua. My old bones ...'

'Today you are a young man, *nu*? You are free! Come! Come and dance with your family!' I broke out of the ring of dancers and clasped Jesher's hands, leading him towards the circle. The men cheered as he shuffled into place and linked arms with me on his right, and Mesha on his left.

'I am not a very good dancer, as Shira will tell you. I do not want to slow you down.'

Mesha laughed and gestured to his brother-in-law. '*Abba*, look at Hareph! If he can dance, then you can surely dance!'

Hareph frowned at Mesha and opened his mouth to protest. Seeing Mesha's cheeky expression, he thought better of it, laughed, and carried on stumbling around, trying to keep up with the other men. The shoreline of the Red Sea turned into a mass of hopping, jiggling bodies and, before long, neighbour danced with neighbour, and new friendships were formed in the most unlikely of circumstances.

The dancing continued for a long time and, as the morning wore on, we tired of dancing and sat, sweaty and exhausted, on the shores of the Red Sea. The lack of sleep the previous night caught up with us and we flopped on the ground, resting under the covering of Yahweh's cloudy canopy.

My mind was a blur. I lay on my side and raised myself up on one elbow to face Mesha and Helah. Gazing out across the glistening waters of the Red Sea, I muttered to myself, 'How did this happen?' I needed to harness my thoughts and bring some semblance of order to my restless mind.

'Hmm?' Mesha said.

'This all happened so quickly,' I muttered, more to myself than to him. 'Was it really only a few days ago when it all started?'

Helah sat up and sighed. 'It started with the Passover, didn't it? When they told us to put the blood of a lamb on our doorframes.'

'I remember that well,' Mesha said. 'I remember Hareph's reaction.'

'Why? What did he do?' I whispered.

'He argued,' Mesha replied, grinning at me. Looking over to where Hareph was dozing with his mouth wide open, he put on a slightly nasal tone, lowered his voice, and continued. '"But *why*? *Why* must we kill our lambs? We need to take them with us. We need them for the journey."' He giggled to himself and Helah nudged him.

'Mesha, shush. He might hear you.'

Mesha made a face, leaned over to me, and carried on. 'Abidan told him it was for Passover, so Hareph said, "What is that? What is this Passover? What is being passed over?"'

Turning to Helah, Mesha prodded her and whispered, 'Do you remember his face when Abidan told us to take some of the blood from the lamb and smear it on the doorposts and lintels of our houses? *"Put blood on our doorframes?"'* he said, once again mimicking Hareph's nasal tone and shocked expression.

I smiled at Mesha. Although I wasn't there when it happened, I could well imagine what took place. Abidan was an elder among our people, of the tribe of Benjamin, and he was generally quite a patient man, but Hareph's fastidious ways were enough to try the patience of even those as longsuffering as Abidan.

Hareph was Jesher's son-in-law, married to Jesher and Shira's daughter, Eglah. He was not a bad man and, in fact, I found him kind-hearted and intelligent. However, he was pedantic at the best of times, and people knew not to start a conversation with him unless they had plenty of time to spare, talking through the intricacies of any given situation. He was now middle-aged and somewhat pernickety, always needing to understand the exact 'ins and outs' of a situation before making a decision either way.

'But he obeyed, Mesha,' Helah said. 'He put the blood on the doorframe, even though he didn't understand.'

Mesha smiled at her and reached over to caress her cheek. 'He did, my beloved. You are right, as always. He put the lamb's blood on the doorpost. We all did, and we were safe.'

I noticed Helah shiver when he said that. A shadow passed over her face. She had not spoken of that night, the night of the death of the first-born, at least, not to me. I was alone that night, in the shack which I had shared with my father before his passing, when the angel of death had passed over us. Half of me had no wish to know what it was like for Helah, but the other half wanted to understand what it was that made Helah shiver at the very thought of it.

'Helah?' I asked. 'You have not spoken of that night.'

'It is not something I have been able to talk about,' she responded, keeping her eyes focused on the sparkling waters of the Red Sea. 'But,' she sighed, looking across at me, 'perhaps I should now.' I nodded and waited until she was ready. She looked over to where her children lay, to make sure they were all asleep before she began. Drawing her knees up to her chest, she put her arms around her legs, hugging them to herself.

'Mesha told me that all would be well, that Yoram would live, and no evil would come to us. I knew that in my head, but my heart could not grasp it. I did not want Yoram to fall asleep. I wanted to pull him close; to protect him from the threat of death that would stalk the land that night. But I could not make him stay awake.'

She shrugged and smiled. 'He was tired. He slept. Everyone slept, eventually. Except me.'

'Even Mesha?' I thought to myself, turning to him without thinking.

'Yes, I slept too,' he mumbled when he saw me glance at him. 'I have always been a heavy sleeper – nothing keeps me from sleep.' He turned to Helah. 'You should have woken me.'

Helah smiled at him. 'Why? So you could sit with me, staring at our son, not able to do anything but hope and pray? It was better that you slept. You needed your strength for the days ahead.' She turned her face forward again, focusing on the distant lands beyond the Red Sea. 'I tried to sleep,' she whispered, 'but I could not. So, in the end I gave up and sat up, waiting, and praying through the night watches.' Tears came to her eyes as she admitted, 'I watched the rise and fall of his chest as he slept, to make sure he was still alive. He looked so peaceful, just like when he slept as a baby – on his side, arms crossed as if he was hugging himself.'

Helah smiled as she recalled Yoram's early days, but then the smile faded and the shadow covered her face again. She looked down at the ground and whispered, 'It happened in the midnight hour. I felt a chill in the air, and the hairs on my arms stood up. I felt so cold.' She frowned. 'I remember shivering and drawing my shawl tighter around my shoulders. Then I heard a great wind blowing outside, whistling through the cracks in the doorframes and windows. Banging noises, like things being blown around.' Mesha put his arm around her and rubbed her shoulder, but she hardly noticed. She was back in that shack, feeling the terror of that moment. I didn't interrupt. She needed to talk. She needed to get free of that deathly shadow that had hung over her since that night.

'I leaned over him, trying to shield him from harm.' She winced and shook her head. 'As if I could have done anything – but I had to try to protect him. So I hovered over him, searching the darkness for any sign of danger. There was nothing to see.' She closed her eyes and whispered, 'I could not breathe. All I could do was wait, and listen to the whistling sounds and the banging. A dog started howling, then another, and another, railing against the wind. On and on, they howled.' Helah opened her eyes and looked across at me. 'It felt like an age but, in truth, I think it was over nearly as soon as it had begun.' Looking forwards again, she sighed. 'The wind died down, the dogs grew quiet and I could hear the sound of banging and rattling moving further down the street. I put my hand on Yoram's chest. I could feel his heart beating. He was alive.' Helah smiled through her tears. 'He was alive and still sleeping so peacefully. He was alive. My son was well.'

Helah stretched her legs out in front of her, looked at me and sighed. I could see the shadow lifting from her countenance as she continued her story. 'I left my hand on his chest for a while, feeling the steady beating of his heart. I just needed to be sure. That's when I heard it.'

'You heard what?' Mesha asked. It seemed this was the first time he had heard Helah's account of that night too.

'The sound of wailing, way off in the distance.' Helah put her arms around her torso and started rocking backwards and forwards. 'Shrieking and howling, echoing across the land, louder and louder. A lament for the dead. And I felt so guilty.'

'Guilty?' Mesha asked, frowning in confusion. 'Why?'

Tears rolled down Helah's cheeks, unchecked. 'Because my precious child was alive. But in homes all across the land, other mothers' children were not.'

6

Exodus

I didn't tell Helah, but I had also been awake that night, keeping a lonely vigil of prayer. I hadn't slept well since my father had died, and most nights I was still awake in the dead of night. So I had heard the haunting sounds of grief that echoed on the wind from the Egyptian quarters when the angel of death struck their first-born children. The lament for the dead had been part of our culture for generations, and during our time in Egypt we heard it on a daily basis. But not like that.

Never like that.

The sound of thousands of voices shrieking and wailing in anguish sent a chill down my spine each time I thought of it, and I hoped never to experience that again. That Passover night changed everything and, early the next morning, we heard the news: it was time to pack. We were leaving Egypt. Sitting here on the edge of the wilderness in front of the Red Sea, surrounded by thousands of sojourners, it seemed like it had happened years ago, not just a matter of days. It felt strange and surreal.

It felt strange back then, too. We had never packed before. We had never *been* anywhere before. Our fathers' fathers had been born in slave shacks with their mud walls; they had lived there and died there. We had all been born there and lived there all our lives, up until now – but we would not die there. No! We would die as free people, in our own homes, in the land promised to us by the Lord our God.

Frantic conversations had taken place as we rushed to prepare for our imminent journey. Trying to decide what to take with us and what to leave behind was almost impossible, because we didn't know what we would find there. We were not desert dwellers; we did not know the ways of the sojourner. How could we choose between taking precious family heirlooms passed down to us through the generations, or vital supplies like food and water? It was hard for all of us, but hardest of all for the women, who had a love of beautiful things which we men did not really understand.

The first time I ever heard Jesher raise his voice was the day after Passover, when we were packing to leave. Jesher listened and watched more than he talked, and loathed raising his voice. But, when it was necessary, he did, and when he did, it was awe-inspiring. This was such a time. I was helping Mesha in the next room when we heard Shira's shrill voice raised in objection.

'Jesher, I will not leave this bowl behind. It was part of my inheritance, handed down from my grandmother's mother. It cannot be left behind.'

'Yes, I know it was, but we cannot take it with us. It is far too heavy and too large. We cannot carry it.'

'Then one of the children can take it for us. Azriel can pack it with his belongings – it will be passed down to him and Leora one day, so they can look after it on the journey.'

'They will not be able to take it, Shira. They have enough possessions of their own to carry, as well as the children. They do not have room for a heavy bowl.'

'Well, then, we must leave behind something else, and pack the bowl instead.'

'There is nothing else that can be left behind. We have packed only what is necessary for this journey, and a large, heavy bowl is not necessary.'

'Not necessary? How can you call my grandmother's mother's bowl "not necessary"? It is part of our family's heritage.'

'Shira, it is not my intention to besmirch your family, or your grandmother's mother. The bowl is beautiful, but we cannot take it with us.'

'So what do I do with it, then? Leave it here for these heathens to use for their abominations? Or for them to smash into pieces? Would you have my grandmother's mother's bowl treated such?'

'I know not what will happen to it, but it will not be coming with us.'

Mesha looked at me, wide-eyed, lips pursed in anticipation. We stayed as still as possible, not wanting to draw attention to ourselves. There was silence for a few moments, and then Shira spoke again. 'Ech. Mesha will take it. I will talk to him now. He and Helah will be glad of such a beautiful heirloom.' Mesha looked at me, pulled a face and shook his head.

'No, Mesha will not take it. He has five children, and enough to carry.'

'Jesher, I will not leave – '

'*You will leave it behind, or you will stay behind with it!*' he thundered. There was no reply. Jesher's outbursts happened so infrequently that they took Shira by surprise, and I imagined her standing there, eyes wide open, and speechless (something that rarely, if ever, happened). Moments later, Shira swept out of the room, slammed the precious bowl down on the rug, muttering to herself about heathens and the abominations they would use the bowl for.

Looking around me now, I knew Jesher had made the right decision. The wilderness was no place for large, heavy, fragile possessions. I was lucky in that I didn't have a lot of possessions, and the things that were most precious to me were small and easily transportable. My father's ring was my most precious possession, passed on to me the day he died. I had not taken it off my finger since he put it on me and I did not intend to take it off until the day I passed on.

Everything I valued was right here with me: my father's ring, my new family. All my worldly belongings were rolled into two bundles. I shivered as I looked around at the vast expanse of land, sky and sea that now surrounded us, remembering what happened as we left Egypt. The tension that hung in the air that day was tangible, as was the outright hostility shown to us by the Egyptians as we walked out of the boundaries of the township, towards the open plains. Many of them hurled venomous insults at us, spitting at us as we passed by.

'Go! Get out.'

'Leave, and take your God with you.'

'Murderers!'

'Go! Die in the desert like the rats that you are!'

But, while some mocked and reviled us, there were plenty who looked on with what could only be described as naked fear. Egyptian mothers pulled their children behind their skirts to protect them from the unknown terror that was the God of Israel. They were in deep mourning for their first-born children, and I could still picture the devastated faces of the women as we passed by. Although I knew it was not true, I couldn't help but feel responsible for the grief I saw etched on the faces of the women who stared at us, willing us to take our God of death and leave.

That had been just a few days ago and now, as I sat on the shores of the Red Sea, I looked around in a kind of haze. Staring back across the vast expanse of water in front of me to the land of my captivity, the enormity of what we had done started to dawn on me. I felt restless. I couldn't just sit there, waiting for something to happen. I needed to do something. So I rose to my feet and stretched. 'I think I will go and see if I can help,' I said to Mesha and Helah. 'There must be many who are in need of help right now.'

'Truly. I will come with you.' Mesha started to stand up, but I put my hand on his shoulder and stopped him.

'No, Mesha. You have a family to look after. Stay with them. I will come and find you later.' Helah smiled at me gratefully as I turned to leave. I walked among my people, helping out where I could, but there was one question that kept rolling around and around in my mind: 'What do we do now?' Slaves don't make decisions; they just do what they are told. They don't get to choose; their choices are made for them. We had been slaves our whole lives – that's all we had ever known – so we didn't know how to plan for the future, only how to survive the present. Slaves don't have dreams, only masters; and our masters were gone. Our daily routine was also gone; demolished by the same waves that destroyed the Egyptians.

I realised as I stood there on that beach, surrounded by a never-ending expanse of people, that we were like children; utterly ill-equipped to enter the tantalising but terrifying new world of freedom.

By the time I returned, the sun had started its downward journey and, on the surface of the sea, flecks of gold glinted, shimmering in languid rhythm with the gentle movement of the waves. I had timed it well – the family were just sitting down to share the evening meal. They had been busy while I was away, erecting a tent covering using long wooden sticks, brought with us for that purpose. The sticks were tied together with thick twine to create a basic frame, and large pieces of woven woollen material were draped over it, their edges hanging down on all four sides. Our flight from Egypt could not have taken place at a better time. Winter was ending and, with it, the heavy rains. Warmer days had come; our makeshift shelters would serve us well in this weather.

Our few goats and lambs were tethered to a rod driven into the ground next to the tent and a firepit had been dug in front of the tent. Large, flat, smooth stones were placed in it, and cakes of dough were baking on them. I smelled the bread before I saw it. I loved the smell of fresh bread baking on the coals. It smelled like home. Inviting. Comforting. There were many things I admired about my father, but his culinary efforts were not one of them, so I relished the opportunity to eat the delicious food which the women in my new family provided.

'*Shalom*, Joshua!' Mesha called out when he saw me. 'You are back just in time! Come, break bread with us.' He moved to the side to make room for me and I sat myself down, crossed-legged on the ground between him and Hareph.

Jesher greeted me with a smile. '*Shalom*, Joshua. We thought we had lost you again.'

'*Shalom*, Jesher. I am sorry I have been gone for so long. Ah, thank you, Helah. *Shalom*,' I said, holding out my hands as she poured water over them. The water trickled into a basin which she placed on the ground and, after I dried my hands with the cloth hanging over her arm, she took the basin, pitcher of water and cloth away. A long reed mat was spread on the ground, where the women laid out dishes of food. At each end of the mat was a dish containing a stew of beans, lentils, garlic and onions. A dish of dates and figs was also on the mat, along with pitchers of water, pottery cups and a basket of freshly baked barley bread. I only had eyes for the bread – the smell was making my mouth water – but I waited for Jesher to pronounce the blessing.

'Yahweh be praised for bringing us through the mighty waters, to this place. Blessed be His name, who causes bread to come forth from the earth to nourish our bodies.' Calls of 'blessed be His name' echoed around the table, then Shira passed the basket of bread to Jesher. He broke one of the thin flatbreads in half and placed the other half back in the basket, which was then passed around the table, starting with Azriel who, as Jesher's first-born son, usually sat next to him.

'Oh, this smells so good!' Mesha used his piece of flatbread to scoop up some stew. Chewing enthusiastically, he dipped it straight back into the dish and stuffed it in his mouth.

'Mesha, slow down! There is no rush. Let everyone eat, *nu*?' Helah said, sitting down next to him and reaching for the breadbasket.

'Ech!' he blurted, looking at her in frustration. 'There is plenty, look! They have arms, they can reach, yes?' he said, gesturing at the rest of the family. She gave him a warning frown, but couldn't hold back a smile. Mesha had been blessed with a natural charm and could wheedle his way out of tricky situations with very little effort, using just a smile. Whenever Shira was in one of her moods, Jesher would send Mesha to talk to her and, before long, she would be restored. Mesha was her favourite child, and he could coax a smile out of her when no one else could.

'So, Joshua, where were you this afternoon?' Jesher asked me. 'What were you doing?'

'Well,' I paused. I felt a bit embarrassed, and found myself stuttering when I replied. 'I . . . uh . . . well, I've been with Moses.'

'Moses?' Yoram blurted, eyes wide with excitement. 'You have been with Moses?'

I nodded and took a surreptitious look around the table. No one was eating. Every hand was frozen in mid-air. Even Mesha had stopped eating and was staring at me, eyebrows raised.

'How did that happen?' Helah asked in amazement.

'Well, I was helping people to set up their tents when I bumped into Abidan. He was on his way to see Moses, so he invited me to go with him and, well . . . Moses asked me to walk with them. So . . . ' I looked down and busied myself with taking a mouthful of bread, 'I did.'

'This is unbelievable!' Hareph looked at me in astonishment. 'Among all the multitudes of our people, *you* stumble upon Abidan and spend the afternoon with Moses! In his presence!'

'Yes. It was . . .' I looked down at the ground, feeling awkward. I could see that Hareph was preparing to launch a full-scale interrogation, so I added, 'As surely as I live, it was not something I planned.' Mesha guffawed and raised his eyebrows at me.

'Yoshi, what's he like?' Yoram asked, gazing at me in wonder, as if I'd just told him I had encountered the Angel of the Lord. Yoram was Mesha and Helah's first-born son. I loved all Jesher's grandchildren and felt privileged to be part of their family, to be able to call his children my brothers and sisters, and his grandchildren my nieces and nephews. But Yoram was special to me. He was like me in a lot of ways – in fact, although I never said it, I thought he was a lot more like me than Mesha. He was a deep thinker and a feeler. I understood how he felt about life because, most of the time, I felt the same. When he went through the passage of time and changed from child to adult, it was me he talked to about how to navigate life as a man.

As a toddler, Yoram couldn't pronounce my name properly, so he called me Yoshi, and the name stuck. In return, I called him Yori. Yoram still calls me Yoshi. Mesha feigns contempt when he hears him but, deep down, I believe he likes it. At times, he and Helah also call me Yoshi, although that is generally a slip of the tongue.

I looked at Yoram and frowned in concentration. 'What is Moses like?' I repeated. 'Well, he is . . .' I paused, staring up into the sky. 'He is . . . quite reticent. He knew my father, so Moses said what a good man he was and how sad he was when *Abba* passed on. Apart from that, he did not say much to me, other than to give me a few instructions or ask me what I thought about something.'

A smattering of conversation broke out around the family circle as they discussed the significance of my involvement with Moses. This could reflect well upon the family, and they all seemed excited by the possible ramifications of our meeting. All except one. It took a lot to impress Shira, who just sniffed (which was her way of showing that she disagreed with whatever was being said), and got up to kindle the fire. I took the opportunity in her absence to speak to Jesher. 'I may be wrong,' I muttered, 'but I got the distinct impression that Moses is not very joyful about being the leader of an entirely new nomadic nation.'

Jesher nodded and scratched his bearded chin. 'Mmm. Why would he be?'

'Well, some men grasp at the slightest chance of being in charge, being able to tell everyone what to do. But I do not think Moses is like that. He is quiet and . . . has no wish to be in the forefront.'

'Yoshi, are you going to see Moses again tomorrow?' Yoram asked.

'Yes. He has asked me to go to him at sunrise. We are to break camp at daybreak and travel as far as we can before the midday rest.'

'Oy! He must have favoured you, then, if he asked you to help him again tomorrow,' Yoram said, looking at me in awe.

I laughed. 'I think he is just in need of all the help he can get and, since I do not have a wife or children, I am able to assist him.'

Mesha's eyes narrowed and he pursed his lips. 'I do not think so. I think he sees that you are a man of integrity, a true follower of Yahweh, and servant-hearted.' He grinned and added, 'And he sees that you are *strong*! Look at these muscles!' He prodded my biceps and I pushed his hands away.

'Mesha!' I said, reaching for the bowl of figs and dates. I offered them to him, trying to distract him. It worked. He took a handful of fruit and popped a date in his mouth straight away. Just then, Helah and Mesha's daughters, who had been whispering among themselves, scampered over to them, almost knocking Helah over in their eagerness to ask a question.

'*Ima*, can we go and play by the water?'

'Well, if *Abba* or Yoram go with you,' Helah said, 'then it should ...'

'No,' I said quickly, looking at Helah. Not wanting to appear too severe, I put a smile on my face and said to her and Mesha, 'That may not be wise today, but perhaps tomorrow, *nu?*'

'Aah, *Ima*? *Abba*?' they whined, looking at Mesha and Helah to see if they would overrule me and give them permission. Mesha looked at me, his brow knitted in confusion, but Jesher, seeing the look on my face, spoke to all of his grandchildren. 'Not now, my little ones. We have had a long day. The sun is going to sleep and so must you, *nu?*'

'Come, wash and get ready for bed,' Helah said, as Hareph's wife, Eglah, brought the basin and pitcher of water. The children dutifully washed their hands, feet, and faces, sulking in protest.

While they were occupied, Jesher leaned over to me and whispered, 'Why did you not want the children to play by the water? What is wrong with the water?'

I leaned closer to him. 'Nothing is wrong with the water itself, but ...' I lowered my voice, 'the bodies of the Egyptians are washing up onto the shore.'

'Hmm,' Jesher said, frowning and nodding again. He sat, scratching his beard for a while, and then turned to me. 'Come,' he said. 'Stir up the fire, my son, and let us sit together and watch the sun while it sets. Yes?'

7

Pillar of Fire

The sense of restlessness had increased. I didn't like it. Why did I feel so distracted, so disconnected with what was happening around me? I hugged my discontent to myself and crouched over the firepit, prodding the embers with a wooden stick.

Mesha and Helah, along with Azriel and his wife, Leora, were settling their children down in the tent. Shira was busy sorting out their belongings, while Eglah tried to calm Hareph, who seemed very agitated about something. It might have been to do with the sleeping arrangements, but I had no desire to know what was bothering him, and no intention of getting involved.

I sat by the firepit with Jesher as the twilight faded, and played at tending the fire. All around us, families were settling down for the night, doing the best they could with makeshift shelters and campfires. I poked the embers and blew on them, watching bursts of sparks fly upwards, when I heard Jesher's silver-toned voice.

'Where are your thoughts?' he asked me. 'What do you ponder?'

'Uh . . . my thoughts are as scattered as these stars above us, *Abba*,' I mumbled, staring at the fire, purposely not making eye contact with him. Jesher was not a man of many words, but just because he spoke only a little didn't mean he thought only a little. He listened and watched, and there was not much that passed him by. He had the eyes of a sage. They were a dusty blue colour – unusual in our people, most of whom had brown eyes – and when he looked at you, he seemed to look into your very soul. I found it disarming, especially when I was trying to hide something from him. I could feel his eyes on me and, when I did eventually look at him, he raised his eyebrows, smiled, and said, 'Mmm?'

I sighed and stood up, crossing my arms in a pitiful attempt to appear strong and in control. Looking up at the pillar of cloud that billowed in the middle of the camp, I mumbled, 'It's just . . . meeting Moses today, being in his presence, listening to what he said, it was . . . I mean, my father did . . . but I never thought that I would . . .' I cringed and uncrossed my arms. 'Oy! What is wrong with me? I cannot even talk properly.' I felt like a child, awkward and confused, and yet I knew there was nothing but love in Jesher's heart for me. He sat there, nodding his head, and waited. I took a deep breath before continuing.

'I could not speak of it to the others, but it was . . . wondrous, really. So strange, and yet it felt as if it was meant to happen, as if my meeting Moses and being with him was by Yahweh's design.' Turning towards Jesher, I made a face and said, 'Does that sound foolish?'

He shook his head. 'Not at all.'

I joined him on the ground again and turned my attention back to the cloud. Silence fell as we reflected on the day's events. '*Abba*?' I turned to look at him. 'I know not how but, after today, I have a sense that my life is about to change. That I am walking a new path.'

'Hmm.' He looked at me, his wise old eyes brimming over with emotion, and whispered, 'I believe you may be right.' Silence ensued, apart from the muted sounds of families talking around campfires near us. We were left to our own thoughts as the sun continued to slip down over the waters of the Red Sea and, by the time the rest of the family joined us, a calm sense of peace had descended.

I gazed up at the cloud, then sat bolt upright. '*Look*!' I pointed at the cloudy pillar.

'What?' they asked, turning to see what I was pointing to. 'What are we looking at?'

'The cloud! Look at the cloud,' I urged them. 'It's changing!'

'Is it?' Mesha asked, scrunching his eyes up. 'Are you sure?'

'Ech! Mesha!' I frowned at him and pointed again. 'Look at it!'

'I am looking, I am looking.' Mesha continued staring at the cloud, but none of them were as familiar with its form as I was, and it took a little while before they saw what I was trying to show them.

'There! Did you see that?' I leapt to my feet, shouted with excitement. 'Did you see that? Sparks! Sparks in the cloud.' By now they were beginning to see – and not just them, either. Word was spreading and, throughout the camp, people stood to their feet to get a better view of the pillar of cloud. Their shouts of excitement and pointing soon gave way to an awestruck silence as Yahweh's people witnessed for the first time ever, the transformation of the cloud of His presence into a pillar of fire.

It started with the sparks that I had first noticed. A handful sprinkled here and there, flashes and spurts of light. As we watched, the sparks increased in volume until it seemed that a million fireflies had converged on the cloudy pillar, dancing and quivering, aglow with light. Sounds of crackling and whirling filled the air as we watched with bated breath. Then, from within the belly of the cloud, embers began to glow – softly at first, but increasing in ferocity, they glowed brighter and brighter until, one by one, they burst into flame, as if coerced by the breath of a giant set of bellows.

The billowing plumes of cloud dissipated and, in their place, we saw sparkling fingers of fire in a spectrum of colours which we were totally unfamiliar with. I knew the shades of yellow, red and orange which we saw in our campfires, with occasional hues of white or blue, but the colours in the fiery pillar were unique and utterly enchanting. Flames of azure, indigo and scarlet swirled in magnificent partnership with rippling tendrils of amber, magenta and gold.

I was convinced I saw angelic beings flying in the midst of the embers, spiralling, swooping upwards and then plummeting down in an exquisite dance, their wings tipped with glints of gold and red. But I could not speak to ask anyone else and was content to keep my revelations to myself. The sparks continued to flicker and shimmer within the flaming pillar; the complexity of colours was mesmerising. It was glorious, a spectacle unlike any other; we were caught up in a cosmic show of fire and light and all eyes were on this dazzling display of Yahweh's beauty and glory.

Those who had been camped nearest to the cloudy pillar hastened to move their shelters back, away from the reach of its fiery fingers, although I noticed that the sparks that shot out from its midst did not seem to burn that which they touched. By now, the sun had set. I hadn't even noticed, because the icy chill that usually descended in the desert evenings had been eclipsed by a surge of warmth that spread through the camp.

Still, no one moved.

Conversation was irrelevant, all else forgotten.

No one wanted to do anything but gaze at the pillar. It was immensely beguiling – a celebration of warmth and light and life that compelled us to forsake all else but this glorious mystery before us. Compelled by the beauty of what I was witnessing, I knelt down, staring at the blazing pillar in wonder. I felt like a child gazing at their first sunrise or a newly birthed lamb.

'He is here,' I whispered, not taking my eyes off the billowing column. 'Yahweh is here with us. Among us. He is here.' This was Yahweh. He had promised to come with us, to lead us, guide and protect us – and here He was, in the form of this glorious, shimmering tower of fire.

God with man. His presence, right there, with us.

8

New Day

The next morning dawned bright with the promise of new beginnings. I awoke to the sound of desert sparrows, cheerful little birds with pale grey plumage and creamy chests. Their persistent chirps chivvied me, goading me to wake up. Putting my hand up to shield my eyes, I yawned and looked around, squinting at the glare of the early morning sun reflecting off the sea. I saw a mass of bodies and tents stretching the length of the shore, as far as the eye could see. Drowsy families were being roused from sleep by the rays of the rising sun, like golden fingers reaching out to confront their lethargy.

'It has gone,' I whispered, looking towards the centre of the camp where the fiery pillar had kept watch throughout the night. In its place, the pillar of cloud towered over us once more, its billowing arms outstretched over the expanse of the camp.

'I wonder if . . .' I mumbled to myself. Would the pillar of fire return again tonight? I closed my eyes, remembering the glory of last night, and a sense of warmth flooded me. But the sound of twittering interrupted my musing and I opened my eyes to see a desert sparrow perched on the edge of the wooden tent frame. He peered down at me with inquisitive eyes, tilted his head and warbled another melody.

'Ech! Yes, yes, I am coming!' I whispered.

Yoram was still sleeping soundly on the ground next to me, so I pushed the blanket off my legs and stood up quietly. Opportunities for time alone were few and far between, especially when travelling. Although I loved my new family, I had become used to living a quiet life with my father and so, at times, I found the hubbub of family life overwhelming. I stood and looked around me, trying to take in the immensity of our situation and surroundings, but my moment of solitude didn't last long. Within minutes, the whole family was awake, and we gathered for prayer. From Jesher right down to little Shallum, who stood unsteadily on his chubby little legs holding onto Helah's hand, we recited the morning prayer together.

'Blessed art Thou, King of the universe. I am thankful before You, living and enduring King, for You have mercifully restored my soul within me. Great is Your faithfulness.' As soon as we finished, a flurry of activity began. We dismantled the tent, repacked our bundles, milked the goats, prepared food and readied ourselves for the journey ahead. By the time the shofar sounded its piercing call, we were packed and ready to go.

'Are you ready, Hareph?' I asked, noting his fumbling attempts at organising his bags. Hareph was slight of frame and his health was not robust. He was frequently assailed by various maladies, the intricate details of which he would share with anyone who took the time to listen. I had learned some time ago not to ask him, 'Is it well with you?' His eyes had a disconcerting habit of wandering at times, which made it hard to know how to look at him when talking. Menial tasks always seemed to get the better of him and, clearly, sorting out their bundles was no exception.

Eglah heard me and turned her attention to Hareph and his fumbling attempts at trussing their luggage. She sorted their belongings into manageable bundles, tied them together, and threaded the smaller ones through a stick for Hareph to carry on his shoulders. I admired Eglah. She was a woman of valour. Not what I would call a beauty, but her calm, peaceful disposition gave a lovely countenance to her otherwise plain face. Eglah was Jesher and Shira's second-born, a patient woman who was devoted to Hareph, despite his trying ways. They had been married for thirteen years but had not been blessed with children, so she dedicated herself instead to looking after Hareph and making sure that his life went as smoothly as possible. That in itself, from what I saw, was a full-time vocation.

Eglah loved her nieces and nephews, and was a great help to her brothers and sisters-in-law. She never complained about not having children – at least, not to me. But, from time to time, especially when she was watching her nieces and nephews play, I saw glimpses of immense sadness in her eyes, and I wondered why it is that so often, women who would have made such wonderful mothers were found to be barren. Nevertheless, her nieces and nephews loved her dearly, and would jostle to hold her hand or sit in her lap whenever the opportunity presented itself. Today, Mesha and Helah's daughters, Shua and Serah, reached her first, so she tied her bundle onto her back and took them by the hands. They gazed up at her in adoration.

Helah lifted little Shallum onto her hip and the women shouldered their bundles while we men picked up the larger bundles and swung them over our shoulders. Because he was now considered a man, according to the ways of our people, Yoram was also given the responsibility of shouldering larger bundles. He was proud to be 'one of the men', and carried his burden willingly, along with Azriel and Leora's eldest son, Joel, who was a couple of years older than Yoram.

'Joel, are you ready?' Azriel asked him.

Joel nodded. He never talked much, preferring to keep to himself. Even though he and Yoram were of a similar age, Joel never shared the adventures with him that young men of their age usually do. Something about Joel disturbed me deeply. It was as if the lamp of his heart had been snuffed out. He was there, with us, but he was not there. Not really. I had never had the opportunity to talk to him alone and, even when I did try to engage him in conversation, he only ever answered with one word. At first, I thought it was because he didn't like me, or perhaps resented me being included in the family. But I soon came to realise that it wasn't just me he didn't want to talk to – he didn't talk to anyone. He didn't smile at anyone either and my heart was aggrieved for him, wondering what had caused him to shut himself off from his family in that way.

We set off together, trudging on through the rocky wilderness terrain with little relief from the relentless heat of the desert. Although shafts of sunlight would pierce Yahweh's cloud from time to time, for the most part it shielded us from the direct rays of the sun. But it could not shield us from the thick mugginess of the air and, when we heard the sound of the shofar resonate throughout our throngs near midday, we sank down with relief to rest.

'*Abba*? Is it well with you?' I asked Jesher. His face was red and shining with sweat, and he was hobbling.

'I am well, my son, thank you,' he said, taking a big swig of water from his waterskin. 'But these old bones are not used to walking such long distances, not in this heat, *nu*?'

Our journey had begun during the change of seasons. The winter rains had come to an end and we were entering the summer season, characterised by warm breezes and sultry air. Although we were familiar with the weather patterns of Egypt, I don't think we had fully anticipated the effect that the heat would have on us, out here in the desert. We knew how to find shelter in Egypt; our mud shacks had roofs, albeit leaky ones, and we knew where to find the best shade trees. But, out here in the desert, there was little relief from the relentless heat and it seemed to draw the life out of us.

I lay on my back, hands behind my head, and stared up at the sky. A shadowy figure flew in the canopy above us, followed by another and another. Vultures. Their rasping cries were an unwelcome reminder of the perilous position we found ourselves in. I turned to lie on my side, closing my eyes to block them out of my sight. I was not the only one who had noticed them.

'I cannot abide vultures,' Mesha muttered, turning his nose up in disgust. When the sun peaked and started its downward journey, the shofar sounded. We roused ourselves and set out again. The day continued on in much the same way and, by the time twilight came and we made camp, everyone was exhausted. There was no singing or celebrating in the camp that evening, only a growing sense of uncertainty as we grappled with the reality of what our new lives might look like.

The evening meal was quieter than usual. We were all busy with our own thoughts and, when the meal was done and the children were being settled down for the night, I went to sit by the firepit. Yoram joined me and, after a while, Joel came too, although he sat away from us, on the other side of the fire, closer to the tent. I poked the fire. Yoram and I sat staring hypnotically into the flames as the logs spluttered and crackled, sending sparks flying up into the air like a swarm of tiny fireflies.

We both knew that this was a rare moment to contemplate and be still, so we sat in companionable silence. My attention was divided between gazing into the fire and staring up at the pillar of cloud, which had positioned itself near the middle of the camp.

Being in the centre made it the focal point for all the sojourners, but none more so than me. My heart was no less enamoured of its billowing form than it was yesterday – in fact, more so. The longer I stared and wondered at its beauty, the more captivated I was by what I saw and sensed.

I sensed Yahweh.

It was as if Yahweh Himself was there, reaching out to me through those undulating plumes, causing my soul to ripple in time with their motions. I yearned for more, closing my eyes to capture the moment, holding it close in my heart. Everything else ceased to exist. Nothing else mattered. My aching body and tired mind faded into the background of my consciousness. All I knew was the mystery of the presence that overshadowed me.

'Well, the little ones are settled now.' Mesha's loud, cheery voice shattered the beauty of the moment. He plonked himself down next to me by the fire, with Helah close behind him. Yoram and I gave each other a knowing smile and lowered our heads again. The moment was over. There was a tangible sense of anticipation in the camp as the sun began to set and nightfall approached. Instead of sitting in a circle around the firepit, as was our habit, we unconsciously formed a semicircle. No one wanted to sit with their back to the pillar of cloud. Everyone kept one eye on what they were doing, and another on the cloud, in the hope that the mystical fiery pillar would once again appear.

Our hope was not disappointed!

The tell-tale sign of sparks flickering within the cloud created a buzz of excitement in the camp. Within minutes, chores were either finished or laid aside, and the hum of conversation stopped. Every face looked up in awe as the glory of Yahweh was made manifest and the billowing pillar of cloud transformed once more into a glowing tower of fire.

My heart was so relieved, I could have leapt for joy. Yahweh was truly with us! He had not abandoned us to the perils of the desert, to be food for vultures or grim stories to be relayed to future generations. He was here, with us, in this sparkling beauty of glory!

9

Sojourners

It had only been a few days, but already we were settling into a routine of sorts. Our morning started before dawn and, by now, everyone knew their designated tasks, so we were able to pack up camp and be ready to move within a considerably shorter time than when we first set out from Egypt.

That morning, Yoram made the unfortunate mistake of asking his uncle whether he had slept well, so Hareph launched into a full-blown exposition of everything his body had endured since leaving Egypt, and was busy regaling Yoram with a long, and rather detailed, description of his various bodily ailments. After a short while, Yoram threw me a look, begging to be rescued. I walked over to them, put my hand on Hareph's shoulder, looked into one of his roaming eyes, and said, 'Forgive me, my brother, but with your permission, may I take Yoram to help me pack the tent frame?'

'Oh, yes, yes.' Hareph's shoulder twitched. 'Please, go,' he said to Yoram. 'We will talk later.'

Yoram smiled at his uncle and bowed his head in acknowledgement. Walking over to the tent with me, he muttered, 'Thank you, Yoshi!' I grinned but said nothing, and we set to the task of packing up the tent.

During our travels that morning, Eglah seemed troubled. Her head was downcast and she was even quieter than usual. It concerned me, so I waited for an opportune moment to walk alongside her, a little behind the others.

'Eglah, is all well with you?'

She looked up at me and hesitated. Her brow creased and I could see her struggling to decide how much to say. 'Yes, yes, I am well, Joshua, thank you. But Hareph is . . . uh . . . not altogether used to travelling and is not . . . taking to it very easily,' she said, choosing her words carefully. 'This heat wearies him . . . greatly.'

'Ah,' I nodded. 'I see. Is there anything I can do to help? Can I carry some of your bundles?'

'No, no. Thank you,' she said, eyeing the considerable amount of baggage already strung over my shoulders. 'You have enough to carry. We will manage. But,' she looked at me, and I treasured the purity reflected in her eyes as she said, 'thank you, Joshua. Thank you for asking. Thank you for . . . seeing.' I smiled, and we continued on in our travels. Of all Jesher's children, to my mind, Eglah was the most like him. I saw in them a lot of similarities, such as their perceptive minds and caring hearts. It endeared her to me.

Once again, we rested when the shofar sounded in the heat of the day and continued on as the afternoon became cooler. We set up camp at twilight, made our firepits and assembled the tent covering. Thankfully, the nights were not so cold now that the season was shifting, so we were able to let the sides of the tent hang free without having to bind them to stop the cool evening breeze from blowing through the tent.

Later that evening, when the children were settled and we had once again witnessed the transformation of the cloud, we gathered around the fire to relax and talk before going to our beds. Jesher was a captivating storyteller who loved to sit around the fire and tell his grandchildren stories about our descendants. The story of Joseph, how he was sold into slavery and subsequently raised up to be Egypt's leader, second only to Pharaoh, was one of Jesher's favourites. Even though the children had heard it many times, they had not yet tired of it. Narratives about heroes like Abraham, his son Isaac, and those from centuries back like Noah and Melchizedek, were taught to the children around the family circle. But Jesher was finding his new life as a sojourner very tiring, so we would have to wait until his body adjusted to the new daily regime before we could hear more of his stories.

Yoram joined us, slumping down next to his father, and I could see he was already feeling the effects of carrying the baggage. Mesha also noticed the way Yoram grimaced as he sat down, so he knelt behind him and began massaging the top of his back, manipulating the muscles around his shoulders and neck.

'Ah!' Yoram gasped as Mesha pushed down hard. He closed his eyes, putting his hand over his mouth to stop any further noises from escaping.

'You worked hard today, my son,' Mesha said to him. 'I am proud of you. But perhaps tomorrow you should not carry so many bags, *nu*?'

'No!' Yoram protested. 'I'm strong, *Abba*. I can carry them. Joel carries heavy bags,' he said, gesturing to his cousin who sat, as usual, away from the rest of us next to the tent wall. 'I can carry them too.'

Joel glowered at Yoram and said nothing, lowering his head and staring at the ground. Mesha looked over Yoram's head at Helah. She frowned and shook her head, so Mesha shrugged and said, 'Joel is older than you and has done more physical work than you have. But we will see how you are tomorrow.'

'Joel,' Azriel called out to his son. 'Come, fetch your reed pipe and play for us.' Joel looked at Azriel and frowned, but didn't move.

'You have such skill with the pipe,' Jesher said, smiling at his grandson. 'Come, play for us, *nu*?' He raised one eyebrow and peered up at him from beneath his bushy eyebrows. Joel sighed, shrugged, and got up to fetch his reed pipe from the tent. Jesher was right, Joel was skilled at playing it. He had made the pipe himself out of a thick reed from the bullrushes that grew on the banks of the Nile river, and taught himself to play. But his playing brought no joy to my heart. Beautiful though it was, when I listened to the melancholy, minor tones that he played, it evoked only sorrow in my heart.

Joel slumped on the ground by the tent, raised the pipe to his lips, closed his eyes, and started to play. A ripple of velvety notes flowed out of the pipe. The haunting melody had a mesmerising effect, so I lay down, closing my eyes for a moment. I heard Yoram grunt as Mesha continued massaging his back, this time with a gentler touch. Then I heard Hareph clear his throat nervously, and opened my eyes to see him sitting down next to me.

'Joshua?' he whispered.

'Hmm?'

'Do you know where we are going? Or when we will get there?'

I sat up, looked into the fire, and sighed. 'I am not sure anyone knows that. When I asked Moses this morning, he said we must keep going until Yahweh tells us to stop.'

'Hmph,' Hareph snorted. 'That is not very helpful.' I raised my eyebrows and continued staring at the flames that were dancing in the firepit to the rhythm of Joel's soul-stirring music. 'The thing is . . .' Hareph started fiddling with his fingers, and his shoulder twitched, as it usually did when he felt nervous or uncomfortable. 'We, uh, we do not have much water left,' he whispered. 'I fear that I am at fault in this matter.' He looked down at his feet. 'It has been so hot, I needed to keep drinking and . . . uh . . . splashing my face with water. But now . . . well . . .' His head moved from side to side as he deliberated silently with himself. Glancing at me sideways, he blurted, 'I did not think. I did not know that . . . well . . . that we would not . . . I just did not think . . .' his voice subsided into a mumble. He lifted his head and met my enquiring gaze. 'We are on our last skin of water, and – we only have a few mouthfuls left,' he muttered quickly.

I could feel my eyes growing wide, and I turned to Eglah to see her reaction. She must have known what Hareph was telling me. Clearly it was not a surprise to her, because she met my gaze, calm and unflinching, then lowered her eyes to stare at the fire.

'That will only last you half a day, at most,' I whispered back to Hareph.

'I know. I know,' he chattered nervously, his head bobbing from side to side again, and his shoulder twitching in response. 'That is why I was asking where we were going and, uh, when we would arrive, you see. Yes . . . hmm.'

'Well, we must talk to – '

'No!' Hareph grabbed my arm. 'Do not tell anyone. Especially not Azriel. I beg of you, do not tell him of my foolishness.'

I stared at him, surprised by his passion. A surge of compassion for this kind-hearted, somewhat bumbling but often misunderstood man rose up in me. I lowered my voice and said to him, 'As you wish. All will be well, Hareph. You and Eglah will not go without water. We are family – sojourners, journeying together, and we look after each other. You are not alone.'

He swallowed hard, and I glimpsed tears starting to form in his erratic eyes. He quickly blinked them away and, without looking at me, mumbled, 'Thank you.'

Azriel took his responsibilities as Jesher's first-born son very seriously and Hareph often found himself on the other end of

Azriel's sharp tongue. Of her four children, Azriel was the most like his mother in character. Although he wasn't as outwardly overbearing as Shira, he definitely had strong opinions about the way things should be done and was not shy about sharing them. Hareph was not the man he would have chosen for his sister to marry and, although I never heard him say it in so many words, I think he felt that Jesher had failed in his choice of a husband for Eglah.

'All will be well. We journey together.' Pausing for a moment to think, I added, 'But perhaps no more splashing your face with water, *nu*?' Hareph smiled sheepishly and nodded. We sat in contemplative silence for a while, listening to the sorrowful strains of Joel's reed pipe, and thinking through the various scenarios that might play out the next day if we did not find water.

10

Bittersweet

'I never thought the day would come when I would be sorry that Hareph had stopped talking,' Mesha whispered to me as we trudged on through the wilderness.

'Mesha!' I said, trying to frown at him, but unable to stop a smile from sidling onto my face. We had set off early the next morning to avoid travelling in the heat of the day; a rather subdued company, with not much talk or banter as we journeyed. Even the children were quiet, apart from a few complaints about the heat or their tired legs. It was as though there was an unspoken pact among us to reserve all our energy for what was most important – for living; for surviving, making it through another day in this unforgiving heat, with no guarantee that there would be water at the end of the day.

The heat was intense and we had not come across any wells or springs since leaving the Red Sea. Thanks to the Nile river and its tributaries, we had always had a supply of water in Egypt. It was not the best tasting water, but we had never been without it for long. This was a new experience for us. Mesha was right, though, Hareph was unusually quiet, and myself and Eglah were the only people who knew why. Normally he would have kept up an incessant stream of commentaries and chatter, but not today. I thought about trying to start up a conversation, but decided against it. Once again, before midday, we heard the sound of the shofar, signalling the time to stop and rest. We laid our bundles down, passed the waterskins around, and everyone gulped eagerly. I turned my back to the rest of the family and offered my skin to Eglah and then to Hareph, then drank a little myself.

Mesha, who came and lay down on his back next to me, mumbled, 'Why are you giving your water to Hareph and Eglah? You need it for yourself.'

I didn't realise he had noticed. I wondered who else had. 'I have half a skin left still, there is plenty to share,' I replied.

'Yes, but that is not going to last you long in this heat.' He yawned. 'No more sharing, see? They have their own skin.' Silence. Mesha turned and stared at me through narrowed eyes. 'Yoshi? They have their own skin, don't they?'

I sighed. 'Yes, but . . . their water has run out.'

His eyes widened. 'Run out? They have nothing left?'

'Shh,' I whispered, putting my fingers on his lips to silence him. 'No, nothing. But – ' I continued, 'I have given Hareph my word that Azriel will not know. So you will say nothing.' Mesha tilted his head and looked at me in disbelief. 'Mesha.' I stared at him. 'You will say *nothing*. Give me your word.'

He looked at me, incredulous, then rolled his eyes. 'As you wish. I will say nothing. But,' he murmured, pointing his finger in my face, 'if we do not find water by this evening, we will have to say something.' I closed my eyes and laid my head down, trying to block out his penetrating stares.

Another weary afternoon of trudging through the desert followed. It was monotonous. Every corner we turned revealed the same dry, stony landscape; it seemed to stretch on forever, with the occasional clump of trees dotting the horizon. A cloud of dust surrounded us, kicked up by the thousands of weary feet that tramped on through the brown landscape. Conversation had all but stopped and the sound of rasping coughs became our desert lullaby. The stench of sweaty bodies was becoming more and more prevalent; even the women now reeked of the stale smells of damp perspiration. Just when we were beginning to resign ourselves to another fruitless day in our quest to find water, we heard a shout rippling and echoing through the crowds.

'Water!'

Drooping heads suddenly shot up. 'Water? Is there water?'

The reply came back strong and clear, 'Yes! There are flowing streams! Plenty of water for everyone!' The news spread through the ranks of our fellow travellers and I found a new strength flooding my body. We picked up the pace and Mesha, who was walking next to me, turned to Helah with a grin. 'Come, wife!' he said, 'Let's get to the stream quickly before the crowds get too big.' Turning to the children, he said, 'Who wants to splash in the stream?'

'Me! Me!' they cried, jumping up and down in excitement. It didn't take long for us to make our way to the water's edge. The children ran as one towards the stream, grasping the hands of their smaller brothers or sisters and dragging them forwards. Mesha dropped his load and ran with them, laughing with delight as he pushed his way through the crowds in hot pursuit of his little flock.

'Mesha, wait . . .' said Helah, frowning with concern as he ran past her. She cradled a sleepy Shallum in her arms, and looked at me in exasperation. I just smiled and shrugged. The whole family followed in my wake as I pushed through the crowds, but it was only when we reached the stream that we saw the devastation on everyone's faces.

'What is it? What's wrong?' I asked, already knowing the answer as I watched person after person taste the water and spit it onto the ground. 'What is it?' I asked again, more insistently.

'The water – it is undrinkable,' a young mother replied, tears in her eyes as she cradled her screaming baby in her arms.

'What? It cannot be!' I responded. Helah stayed with the family as I waded down to the edge of the stream and watched Mesha lean down, cupping his hands to bring some water to his mouth. Smelling it suspiciously, he wrinkled his nose, then sipped some. Immediately, his face wrinkled in disgust, he spat it out on the ground and wiped his mouth.

'Eeugh!' he said. 'The water – it is bitter. We cannot drink it.'

I had to try it. It wasn't that I didn't believe him, I just had to taste it myself. I gathered some water in my hands, sipped it and spat it straight out, just like Mesha had. No one believed the word of anyone else and, like me, each person seemed to feel the need to test the water for themselves. A steady flow of people came down to the brook, tasted the water and spat it out on the ground. Crowds formed all along the banks of the streams. Fights and arguments broke out as they debated what to do, shouting at the tops of their voices.

We huddled together with the children in the shade of a tree, pale-faced and silent. 'What do we do now?' Hareph muttered to no one in particular. 'What now?' No one answered. No one knew what to say. What could we say? Less than two small skins of water between eighteen of us – that would not last even a day in this heat – and then what?

'Why?' I thought to myself. This did not make sense. I turned to the others and asked, 'Why would Yahweh bring us out of bondage with such a mighty hand, only to let us die of thirst here in the wilderness? Why would He do that? If He wanted to kill us, why not do it in Egypt? Why bring us all the way out here to kill us?' Hareph, usually so eager to debate the ways of Yahweh, just shook his head and stared at the mass of angry, desperate bodies thronging in front of us.

'Look! Over there – is that Moses?' Azriel asked, squinting in the late afternoon sun.

Mesha muttered, 'It looks like him, but what of it?' The crowds quietened down and fighting was temporarily suspended as we watched the man of God make his way down to the water. Some rabble rousers started to jeer, shouting out threats, but Moses ignored them. He was carrying a large blade, which he used to hack at a tree growing near the water's edge.

Azriel put voice to what we were all wondering. 'What is he doing?' We stood up to get a better view.

'Why is he chopping a tree down?' Hareph said, eyes wide in disbelief.

A fight broke out downstream of where Moses stood and a crowd was quickly forming, so I said to Mesha, 'Wait here, I will be back soon.'

I stepped into the water and waded downstream towards the rabble. Striding into the middle of the group, I held my arms out to separate two aggressive men whose argument had rapidly escalated into a fight. Thankfully, my size and demeaner had the desired effect and I was able to reason with them. They stood down, glowering at each other, before stalking off in opposite directions. I turned towards Moses who, by now, had finished chopping the tree and was pulling it, slender trunk and branches intact, towards the water. His brother, Aaron, was helping drag it, but Aaron was a skinny man and not particularly strong, so Moses was definitely doing the lion's share of the dragging.

'*Shalom*, Master, *shalom*, Aaron,' I greeted them, and gestured to Aaron, 'May I?' He nodded gratefully. I took the tree from him and asked Moses where I should take it.

'Into the water, thank you, Joshua,' he responded, as if it was a normal everyday occurrence to cut down a tree and drag it into the middle of a stream. Moses and I waded into the water up to our thighs, hauling the leafy tree behind us. We laid it down in the middle of the stream and I stood there, enjoying the refreshing sensation of cool water around my legs. Moses smiled at me, closed his eyes, and started mumbling in prayer, rocking slightly as he stood in the water. I was fascinated, but didn't want to appear rude, so I lowered my gaze and waited as he prayed, wondering to myself why someone would drag a tree into the middle of a flowing brook and then start praying. As I stared at the water, it seemed to gain momentum. Whereas before it had meandered with a lacklustre trickle, it now rushed past my legs, bubbling with merriment.

Shortly afterwards, Moses stopped praying and turned to the elders who stood nearby. 'Come, drink,' he said, smiling benevolently. They looked at him, askance and, to their astonishment, Moses gathered some of the water in his hands, lifted it to heaven in thanks, and drank of it.

'Master, no!' I spluttered. 'It is poisonous!'

He looked at me with a mischievous grin and swallowed. 'It was, yes. But it is not poisonous now.' He gazed at me with his piercing eyes. 'Now, it is *blessed*!' As if to confirm his prognosis, he dipped his hands in the stream again and drank deeply, laughing with delight when he finished. The elders looked at each other, clearly not keen on the idea of drinking from the stream, until Abidan, one of Moses' most trusted advisors, walked up to him, dipped his hands in the stream, and drank without hesitation. A huge smile broke over his face and he turned to Moses. They embraced, slapping each other on the back and lifting their hands in praise to Yahweh, before drinking again and again.

I looked at Abidan, then at Moses, then at the stream. 'Well, why not? If Moses can, I can,' I thought to myself. Plunging my hands into the cool liquid, I drew it up to my mouth. Hesitating slightly, I couldn't help but sniff the water first, before taking a tiny sip. I licked my lips and dipped my hands back in the water a second time. This time I took a large mouthful, swallowed and went back for more. The faces of those around me echoed my own, turning from confusion into sheer delight. Those near us at the water's edge started drinking, then those near them, and so on. A ripple of excitement worked its way along the banks of the now fast-flowing stream as, one by one, Yahweh's people tasted the water and drank to the full.

Looking upstream to where my family was sheltering, I turned and waved, shouting at the top of my voice, '*It is sweet*! The water is sweet! *Come*! Come and taste it!' I stood in the middle of the stream, enjoying the sensation of the water surging against my legs. Mesha and Yoram came down to the water's edge to drink. Azriel helped Jesher down, followed by a reluctant and somewhat suspicious Shira, then the rest of the family. The children were ecstatic, splashing each other, giggling and shrieking with joy. I watched my precious family delighting in the miracle that Yahweh had wrought for us, threw back my head, held out my arms, and laughed with utter abandon. All around me, chaos was breaking out, but this was the best possible kind of chaos, and we revelled in it!

Hareph and Eglah took their turn at drinking by the water's edge and, once she had tasted of the stream's delights, Eglah turned to look at where I stood, upstream of them. She placed one hand on her heart and her face filled with immense gratitude as we shared a moment of relief. Hareph, once he had drunk his fill of water, also turned to me. His eyebrows shot up into his brow and he gawked at me.

'Joshua!' he called out, making sure he had my attention. 'Joshua! I am splashing! Look! I am splashing!' he shouted, filling his hands with water, and splashing it all over his face, over and over again. 'It is a miracle!'

We frolicked and splashed in the waters of Yahweh's joy, drinking and laughing until our stomachs hurt and we could drink no more.

11

Servanthood

A sleepy haze settled over the camp as the sun slipped slowly out of sight behind the horizon of rocky landscapes. Families gathered around their campfires, and the smell of roasted herbs and warm bread permeated the air as the women prepared the evening meal. A buzz of conversation filled the camp as the adults congregated to discuss the events of the day, while the children played on the ground around them.

'So, did Yahweh tell Moses to put the tree in the water?' Jesher asked me as we sat around the fire, our bellies full of food, our thirst satiated by the sweet waters of the streams.

'Yes.'

'He said nothing else? Only "put it in the water"?'

'Yahweh told Moses that if we listen carefully to Him, do what is right in His eyes, and keep His decrees, He will heal us.'

'Heal us by putting a living tree into bitter water?' Hareph interrupted.

'It seems so.'

'But why a tree? Why did Yahweh tell him to put a tree in the water?' Hareph asked me. 'And why that particular tree?' Now watered and refreshed, he was back to his usual pedantic self, and was ready for a long and detailed discussion about the complexities of the day's events.

I smiled to myself. Turning to Hareph, I said, 'I do not know. The more I think I understand the ways of Yahweh, the more I realise how little I understand them. We have seen His hand move powerfully.' I numbered them on my fingers. 'The plagues in Egypt, the cloud of His presence, the pillar of fire, His hands holding back the waters of the Red Sea, and now this – a miracle of bitter water turned sweet and fresh.' I looked around the circle and smiled. 'I think perhaps it would be foolishness on our part to try to understand why Yahweh does these things. Our portion is to obey. To listen to Him and obey His voice.' Turning to Jesher with a cheeky grin, I said, 'Or at least, that is what Moses told me!'

They all laughed, then Mesha turned to me. 'So, it looks as if we might not see so much of you now, *nu*?'

I shrugged. 'I am sure nothing will change.'

'Oh, so has Moses not asked you to come to him in the morning, then?' Mesha knew I wasn't comfortable being the centre of attention so, whenever the opportunity presented itself, he would tease me.

'Well, yes, he did,' I mumbled.

'You see!' Mesha shouted, pointing his finger at me. 'I knew it! I knew he would esteem you highly once he saw your uprightness of heart.'

'He did not say that. He only thanked me for my help and asked if I could come back tomorrow. It may not continue – he may not have need of me for much longer. There are many men standing with him, advising him, like Abidan and Hur.' I paused to think for a moment. 'Hur is older and not strong enough to do too much, but he is a man of great wisdom – and there is Moses' brother, Aaron,' I added.

'It will continue.' Mesha stared at me long and hard. It made me uncomfortable, but he went on, despite my obvious discomfort. 'I know it. I feel it in my bones.' Reaching out to put his hand on my shoulder, he muttered, 'You will serve Moses for many days to come.'

I lowered my eyes, embarrassed. Wanting to change the subject, I turned to Shira and the other women. 'This is delicious, thank you.'

Shira just raised one eyebrow and sniffed, but Helah smiled at me. 'Yoshi, you will always be welcome around our fire . . .' She gave me a cheeky grin and continued, '. . . no matter how important you become!' I cringed and shook my head. Thankfully, Azriel changed the subject.

'So! Has Moses told you how long we will be staying here at . . . uh . . .' he looked at me, 'What is the name of this place?'

'Moses has named it Marah,' I replied, 'because of the bitterness of the water.'

Mesha raised his eyebrows and looked at me, surprised. 'Marah? Ay, ay, ay. I would not name it "bitter". No, I would name this place

Zis – because never have I tasted water so sweet.' Touching his fingers to his lips and opening his hand with a flourish, he said, 'Like nectar dripping from my tongue!'

'Amen, amen!' I agreed, raising an arm to heaven. 'But Moses has named it Marah, so there it is.'

'So be it,' said Mesha.

'So, do you know how long we will be staying here?' Azriel persisted.

'Moses has not told me but, if I hear something, I will tell you what I know. But he did tell me where we will journey to next. It is a place called Elim.'

'Elim?'

'Yes. Moses knows of it from his shepherding days. He took his flocks there every year at the beginning of the dry season, about this time. It has lots of palm trees and an abundance of springs – an oasis for the soul and the body.'

'Ooh, that sounds good.' Mesha sighed, relieved. 'That is good to know, is it not, Hareph?' he said, turning to him. 'Plenty of water, so we can splash our faces as much as we like!' Hareph grimaced, embarrassed, and we chuckled among ourselves.

'Well,' Jesher said, reaching for his stick. 'These old bones need to rest, especially after a day like this, *nu*? So I will bless you with deep sleep, my children, and take my leave of you.' I jumped up and helped Jesher to his feet, walking with him to the tent. Shira went before us to prepare Jesher's bed roll, but Jesher leaned in closer to speak to me. 'Joshua,' he asked. 'Have you seen Zivah and Seled in the camp, or any of their family?'

Zivah was Jesher's third-born child. She married Seled many years ago and lived with him and his rather extensive family. Although Seled was a good man and a worthy husband for their daughter, Seled's father did not see eye to eye with Jesher on various matters, and disapproved entirely of Shira's forthrightness. As a result, discord developed between the two families, so it was not often that Jesher and Shira were able to spend time with Zivah, or see their grandchildren. 'I was hoping they would journey with us, but I think perhaps Seled's *abba* did not share the same hope. But it would be good to know that they are well, and the children.'

'Yes. I will make enquiries tomorrow.' Clasping his hands in mine, I said, 'Do not fear.'

'Thank you, my son. But,' he whispered, peering at me, 'do not tell Shira of this matter, *nu*?' I nodded.

Jesher walked towards the tent, then stopped and turned back to me. He gave a long, pleasurable sigh. 'Elim, mmm? Now *that* sounds like a good place to camp. I look forward to seeing it.' He chuckled to himself, winked at me, and shuffled into the tent, shaking his head.

12

Free

Elim was everything we had hoped it would be. Nestled in a long valley between two ridges of mountains, our greatest joy on arriving there was finding not one, not two, not even three or four, but twelve springs of water spread out over the length of the valley. The springs were surrounded by an abundance of palm trees providing shade, palm fronds for weaving baskets and mats and, most importantly, delicious dates!

The dry season was beginning and the palm trees were loaded with huge clusters of plump, juicy dates. We spent much of our time gathering these reddish-brown, wrinkly fruits. The children picked them off the smaller palms and put them in baskets, but many of the palm trees were as tall as three men, so their fruit hung in tantalising clumps out of reach way above our heads. We laid mats on the ground underneath the taller palm trees and shook their trunks as hard as we could, so the ripe dates would fall onto the mat. Sometimes we climbed up the trunks and tried to knock the clusters down with a stick. The girls weren't very good at climbing, but Yoram and Arad, his younger brother, harvested many dates for us during our time at Elim.

There were palm trees in Egypt, but Hebrews were not permitted to pick their fruit. So, apart from the odd one which we found on the ground and managed to conceal, we had not been able to enjoy the delights of these sweet treats until now. I sat on the ground under the palm trees and fingered some of the wrinkly fruit in my hand, noting the ones that had tiny grains of white on them – granules of crystalised sugar! These were the sweetest, most flavoursome dates. I picked one up and sniffed it, surprised at its mild fragrance, considering the intensity of the flavour hidden within. Anticipating the burst of sweetness that would fill my mouth, I bit into it.

A syrupy, sticky sweetness tantalised my tastebuds; I shuddered with delight, savouring the sensation before eating the other half. I had never tasted anything so sweet and succulent!

I laid back, closed my eyes, and listened to the rustling of the palm fronds blowing in the wind. It was soothing, stroking my mind, infusing me with peace. The palm trunks were solid, deeply rooted and yet, the higher they grew, the more willowy and flexible they became. The top of each palm culminated in a waterfall of fronds which flowed down, dancing gracefully to the tune of the wind.

'I would be like that,' I thought to myself. 'Solid, rooted in Yahweh and His ways, but not so stiff as to be stubborn or unmoving when He bids me go.' I lay under the palm thinking on that until Yoram called me; it was time to take our tasty treasures back to the tent.

We never told the womenfolk how many of the dates that we picked did not find their way back to the family tent. It was an unspoken pact between those of us who harvested them – the secret reward for our labours! The dates that we did take back were added into stews, baked into cakes, or placed in dishes to be eaten fresh and whole. Not all of the dates that fell from the taller trees were ripe, so the unripe fruit was laid out in the sun – although we learned very quickly to tether the goats far away from them!

Elim was a time of celebrating, of enjoying the fruits of our labour and of resting. Compared to some of the places we had camped, it was paradise. However, not everyone was enjoying Elim. Over the weeks since leaving Egypt, Joel had grown more and more sullen. He was withdrawn. Anger lurked inside him; the kind of anger that churns round and round inside of you, turning your gut to bile. The kind of anger that when it's time comes, strikes without warning, like a turbulent sandstorm, stinging everything in its path. Joel's anger found its release early one morning, soon after we had arrived at Elim.

Shira had gone with the girls to fetch water from the well, and Yoram and Arad had gone to climb some palms in search of more dates. Since we were staying at Elim for a little while and had no need to be packed and ready to move at first light, I made the most of the opportunity to rest a little longer. I could hear scuffling, a branched broom sweeping the ground outside, then Azriel and Leora's voices.

'Joel, what are you doing here?' Leora said. 'Have you spent the whole night out here?'

Joel grunted and yawned.

'Did you sleep, my boy?' Azriel asked.

'No,' Joel muttered. 'I never sleep.'

Joel's younger brother, Naim, bounded out of the tent. 'Joel, come with me. I'm going to see Mati's new lamb.'

'I don't want to see his lamb.'

'But it was only born yesterday, it's – '

'I said I don't want to see it. I have seen lots of lambs; I do not need to see another one. Besides, Mati is not my friend, he is yours.'

'He used to be your friend too.'

'I don't have any friends.'

'I wonder why,' Naim responded but, before Joel could retaliate, Azriel interrupted.

'Naim, you can go and see Mati's lamb, but be back soon to break fast.' I heard Naim's footsteps pounding as he set off running. 'Then take the goats out to pasture,' Azriel shouted after his son. I sat up, reached for my outer robe, and fastened my shoes on my feet as the discussion continued. I should not have listened, but I had no choice. Nothing is private in the lives of nomads.

'Why do you not want to go with your brother?' Leora asked Joel.

'They are just children. I have no wish to spend my time with children,' he muttered. Besides, I have seen new-born lambs many times.'

'Hmm. It might do you good to go for a walk. Still, it is up to you,' she muttered. 'We need more dung for the fire, and you look like you could do with a walk. Come, up you get, and go and collect some. It will dry quickly in this weather.' I peered through the gap in the tent walls and saw Leora chivvy Joel with her bundle of sticks.

'There is no need to shout, I'm going,' he snapped, glaring at his mother.

Azriel swung round. 'Joel, do not speak to your *ima*[3] like that. You must honour your mother – repent at once.'

---

3. Hebrew word for mother.

'Why?' he asked. 'She treats me like a child. Do this, do that, go here, run there. I am not a child. I am a . . . a . . .'

'You are right, you are not a child. You are a young man and, if you want to be treated with respect, then you must behave like a man.' I peered through the slit in the tent curtain and saw anger on Azriel's face. 'What is afflicting you? You are not yourself. I do not understand you at all. We are free now, free from Egypt, free to live our own lives, to come and go as we please.' Azriel opened his arms and swung around, looking at his surroundings. 'We can do what we want. We are in this beautiful place, surrounded by palm trees, springs of water. You should be happy, but instead, all you have done since we left Egypt is complain and sulk.' Turning back to Joel, he said, 'You are like a . . . a . . . a donkey with no tail!'

Joel launched to his feet and stood face to face with his father. 'What does that mean?'

I stood up. I had never heard Joel speak to anyone like this before; I knew I could hide no longer. Pushing the curtain aside, I stepped outside to see Azriel standing in front of Joel, red-faced, with his hands on his hips.

'What do you mean, "What does that mean"?' Azriel asked him. 'What does *what* mean?' He turned to Leora and lifted his arms as if to ask her for help. Jesher, Mesha and Helah had also come outside and were standing around, concerned but unsure what to do. I could see Hareph and Eglah lurking behind their tent curtain.

'*Free!*' Joel shouted. His hands were by his sides, fists clenching and unclenching, his body shaking. 'What does it mean to be free? I do not know what that means. I do not know how to be free.' His voice cracked with emotion, and the arrogance on his face turned to confusion. 'I do not know who I am now. Who am I, *Abba*?' He looked up at his father, then his eyes darted to his mother. '*Ima*? Who am I?' By now, neighbours from the surrounding tents had come out to see what the noise was about. They were staring, whispering among themselves.

'Please, tell me.' Joel was unaware of everyone except his parents. 'I have always been a slave. I know how to be a slave, but I do not know how to be free. What do I do now?' Tears started to form in his eyes. His shoulders hunched over, arms now hanging at his sides, head sagging. He whispered, 'I do not know what to do.'

Azriel stood, bewildered, but Leora stepped forward and took Joel in her arms, murmuring, 'Peace, peace, Joel. I know, my boy. I know.'

'*No!*' He shoved her away. 'You *do not* know!' Helah gasped. Mesha and Jesher stepped forward and stood next to Azriel and Leora. Joel backed away. 'You *do not* know because you were not there. None of you were there. You do not know what it was like.' His face crumpled into a portrait of pain, and he spoke through racked sobs. 'You were not there when they were beating him. You did not see what they did. You did not see what they did to him. You did not have to stand there and watch him die.' We stared at Joel in shock.

'Joel.' Azriel reached out, but Joel backed away from him.

'No,' Joel said, shaking his head. '*No!*' he yelled and, without another word, turned and fled.

Azriel went to go after him, but Jesher put out his arm and stopped him. 'No,' he said. 'Let him go.' I stared at Jesher, wondering why he had stopped Azriel from going after Joel. But, as Azriel turned to talk to Leora, Jesher stared back at me and gave me an imperceptible nod.

I nodded back, slipped out, and disappeared into the early morning mist.

13

Strangled Heart

I followed Joel from a distance as he fled through the jumble of tents towards the outskirts of the camp. Once outside the camp, he ran towards a grove of acacia trees, their widespread branches creating a thorny, leafy canopy. Joel went to a large tree and sank down onto the ground at the base of the trunk, sobbing and retching.

I couldn't disturb him. Not yet. I stayed out of sight and waited as the anguish that had been buried deep inside of him for so long poured out. It left him gasping from his exertions until he lay, spent, on the ground. It was then that I made myself known. The minute Joel saw me, he sat bolt upright and put his hands either side of him, like an animal getting ready to flee the hunter. I held my hands out to stop him.

'Wait!' I said, standing still. 'I will leave if that is your wish.' He sat, poised and ready to run, his bloodshot eyes wide with fear. 'But, with your permission,' I said, 'I would like to stay. I would like to help.'

Joel stared at me, trying to discern if I was trustworthy or not. 'You cannot help me,' he said, unblinking. 'No one can help me. There is nothing you can do.'

'I can listen. I have been told I am a good listener.'

Joel frowned. I could see the desperate struggle that was taking place within him. I waited, not moving and not talking and, after a while, he spoke.

'I . . . I do not know what to do.'

I took that as a sign of consent, so I walked towards him and sat next to him. 'You do not know what to do about what?'

'Everything!' he said, staring at the ground. 'I do not know what to do. I cannot eat. I cannot think. I cannot sleep. I cannot stop them!'

'You cannot stop what?'

'The dreams,' he said, looking at me. I saw fear in his eyes. No, not fear – terror. Raw, naked terror. 'They come, night after night, and I cannot stop them. I try not to fall sleep but sometimes I do, and then they come . . .' He panted, his chest rising and falling noticeably.

'Do you want to tell me about your dreams?'

Joel shook his head vigorously and turned to stare at the ground again. I could see his hands trembling, so I waited and wondered what could have caused such horror in such a young man. He closed his eyes.

I waited.

He shuddered and wrung his hands.

I waited.

He spoke with a whisper.

'They start with hands . . . long bony fingers reaching for me, stretching out, longer and longer. They pull me down, hold me on the ground. Hard, stony ground; the jagged edges of the rocks dig into my back. I try to fight them off, hitting out with my fists, and then I am running and running. I am so tired, I am panting . . . gasping for air . . . my chest is pounding, but I cannot stop running because they are always there. I look behind me and I see their eyes glowing in the dark . . .' He opened his eyes and stared at me. 'I tell myself, "Do not look back! Do not look back, just keep running . . . keep running", but I cannot. I trip and I am down.' Joel grimaced and closed his eyes again, talking faster and faster. 'And then they are on top of me, dragging me down, down, further down, and there are rocks everywhere, flying through the air, hitting me over and over, pinning me down under their weight.'

Joel put his hands on either side of his head and started rocking.

'I cannot breathe. I cry out, "Help me! Help!" But they just laugh, and their mouths are like caves, and their laughs sound like an animal shrieking, echoing round and round inside my head, and rocks and stones are everywhere, covering my body, pressing down on my chest, on my neck, my face, and I am paralysed . . . I cannot move, cannot breathe.'

Panic had set in. Joel started gasping, his eyes squeezed shut, his body shuddering. 'Dust and stones pouring onto my face, filling my mouth . . . I am choking on it. Please . . . please . . . no!' Joel shrieked, sat up and stared at me, panting heavily. Drops of sweat glistened on his forehead.

I reached out to touch his shoulder, but he recoiled like a viper under attack. I took my hand away, holding it up to show him I was not a threat. He stared at me, his breathing ragged and uneven. Gradually, his breathing slowed and the trembling stopped. He looked away and wrapped his arms around his slim body.

'How often does the dream haunt you?' I whispered.

His voice was dull, as if weary to the point of death. 'Every night.'

I had never felt as useless and ill equipped as I did in that moment. To be plagued with this terror every night, and he had kept this to himself, not told anyone? How was it that he was still alive? I desperately wanted to help him, but how? Nothing in my life experience so far had equipped me to deal with this. My heart broke for this young man. I knew I could not leave him in that place. I had to do something. But what? Out of the blue, Jesher's face flashed into my consciousness. The look he gave me when he nodded to me to go after Joel. He knew I was the right person to help him. He knew it. So I would not disappoint him.

'Joel,' I asked, 'when did the dreams start?'

'When he . . . the day he died. I could not stop thinking about it. He was my friend. My closest friend.' He looked up at me, his face a mask of pain. The tap to the deep places of his soul opened up again and another torrent of pain poured out. 'I tried! I tried to stop them, but I was powerless. I could not stop them. They kept on beating him, again and again. I carried as many of his rocks as I could, but I could not take them all. I could not save him. I tried, but I could not save him.'

He broke down into heart-wrenching sobs again and, this time, there was no hesitation. I put my arms around him and held him tightly. He didn't pull away. I knew now. I knew what was tormenting this young man. I knew well the pain of a loss like this. After some time, Joel's sobs subsided and his breathing evened out into spasmodic gasps. Still, I held him close. His head rested on my chest; he didn't pull away. 'My heart grieves for you, Joel, that you had to endure that. What was his name, your friend?'

'Jacob.'

'That is a good name, a strong name.' We sat in silence for a while, then Joel sat up and wiped his face on the sleeve of his robe.

I gazed off into the distance, recalling the day my heart had been severed. 'I had a friend like that. His name was Jezrel. He was my close friend.' Putting my hand over my heart, I thumped my fist on my chest and looked at Joel. 'He knew my heart and I knew his. Just like Jacob knew yours, and you his.' Looking out over the palm trees and bushes that were dotted over this landscape, I whispered, 'Jezrel was a good man, a man of honour. He did not deserve to die like that, so young.'

Joel stared at me, frowning as the realisation dawned on him that someone else did actually understand what he had gone through. Silence descended and our hearts were welded together in mutual grief. He stared at his feet, trying to make sense of the conflict waging war in his mind. After a while, I put my hand out and clasped his arm. 'Joel, Jacob's death was not of your doing.' He looked at me out of the corner of his eye, his head still hung low. I persisted. 'It was not of your doing. We both know the cruelty of our taskmasters. We lived with it every day. You could not have saved Jacob, just like I could not save Jezrel. You are not guilty of his death.'

Joel shook his head. Shuddering as he wiped away the last of his tears, he uttered a deep sigh. 'I grieve for him. I grieve for him so deeply.' A few more errant tears rolled down his cheeks. This time, Joel didn't try to wipe them away, but let them fall, unhindered.

'Joshua?' Joel whispered. 'What can I do?' My heart ached at the vulnerability I saw on Joel's face. What could he do? I stared at my feet and thought a while, and then I knew.

'I know what you should not do. Do not do what I did. When Jezrel died, something in me died as well. I was overcome with anger.' I looked up at him to make sure he understood me. 'There was such rage within my heart; evil found its home in me and I turned to fighting.' I grimaced. 'Even as a young man, I was tall and strong for my years. There were few who could prevail against me. I was so filled with rage, my hands meted out violence because I did not know what to do with my rage – my pain. So I turned away from Yahweh.'

Joel looked at me, bemused. 'I did not know that. No one told me.'

'Not many people know. Your uncle Mesha knows, and your saba,[4] because he and my father were like brothers. He stood with

---

4. Hebrew word for grandfather.

my *abba* during those dark times. I know not if they told the family but, if they did, no one has said anything. It is over. I put it behind me. It is not something I am proud of.' I looked at Joel. 'Do not do what I did, Joel. Do not turn away from Yahweh. Do not turn your back on Him. Hear my words: that is a crooked path that will only lead you into darkness.'

Joel stared back at me, his eyes swollen from weeping. 'So what must I do, then?'

I paused and stared at him, trying to gauge whether or not he was ready to hear what needed to be said. 'You must move on. Just like we all must. Keep living. Do it for Jacob. Remember him. Remember Jacob.' I stretched out my hand and put it on Joel's chest. 'Hold him close, here, in your heart, but do not hold the pain close. Let go of the pain, Joel. Let it go, or it will strangle your heart. Let go of your pain, and live.'

'I cannot remember how to live.' Joel's voice was dull. 'I know not what to do with my life. Every day is the same as the one before. Full of . . . nothing. I have no friends. My brothers and sisters hate me, my *abba* and *ima* do not understand me. In truth, I think they do not even like me.'

'Once you let go of the pain, your heart will be free to love again,' I encouraged him. 'You will make new friends. I did. It took a while, but I found a friend – your uncle Mesha. He helped me through my dark times, although I did not make it easy for him.'

'Mmm,' Joel muttered to himself. 'But who would want to be a friend to me?'

I shrugged. 'I can think of someone: Yoram.'

'Yoram?' Joel scrunched up his face in disgust. 'My cousin Yoram?'

I laughed at the expression on his face. 'Yes, your cousin Yoram. Is that such a foolish thought?'

'Well, no, but . . . ' he huffed. 'He is not the right friend for me. He is so . . . happy. He is always smiling, and . . . and he is younger than me.'

'Not that much younger, only a year or so,' I said. Seeing the hesitation in Joel's eyes, I added, 'But one step at a time, *nu*?' Joel nodded. 'You are a free man, Joel, no longer a slave. You can do anything you want. You are your own master, free to make your own decisions. You choose what path to walk on.'

Joel frowned. 'I do not know how to choose. I have never had to choose anything before. I just did what I was told to do, tried not to get beaten. I learned how to do that.'

Something in me burned when he said those words; a fierce desire to protect this broken young man. I sat up on my haunches and turned to face him, putting my hands on his shoulders. 'Joel, no one is going to beat you now. Those days are over. No one will beat you ever again. *No one.*'

He struggled to look at me. I knew he desperately wanted to believe me, but trauma had kept him locked in a cage for so long, he hardly dared believe it was possible to be free. I knew the demons he was battling with. I remembered them well from my own dark days, especially when Mesha had come alongside me. He tried to free me from my self-inflicted prison, but I had been locked in my reclusive cage for so long and, although it was a lonely, fearful place, it was familiar. I knew what to expect. I knew who I was in that cage and I knew what to do to survive. When freedom beckoned, although I had longed for it with a desperate passion, the fear of what was outside that cage – so many unknowns – held onto me with an iron grip for many moons before I finally made the decision to step out of captivity.

I knew Joel was asking the same questions that I had asked myself, all those years ago. I could see the immense battle that he was fighting. His eyes were darting all over the place, his brow furrowed, shoulders hunched. 'But what if I do something wrong?' he blurted out. 'What if I make the wrong decision? What if I walk down the wrong path?'

'You will!' I smiled at him. 'Joel, you will make wrong choices because you are human. That is part of being human. But no one will punish you or beat you for that. Not now. Not ever.'

Joel frowned, and I could see he was longing to believe what I was saying. 'So, tell me what to do,' he said. 'Tell me what to do and I will do it.'

I smiled, and shook my head. 'No, Joel. The time of being told what to do is over. You must now decide what you want to do. You choose your path.'

'But what? What path?' I could see his mind was racing with the threat of new possibilities. 'I must do something – or so my *ima* keeps telling me – but what?'

'Your *ima* is right,' I chuckled. 'Search your heart. What lies within? What do you want to do?'

'I do not know.' Joel's brow furrowed in concentration. 'I have never thought about what *I* wanted to do, only what I had to do.'

'Well, your father followed in the footsteps of his father, working at the potter's wheel. You are old enough to learn a trade.'

'Mmm.' Joel made a face.

'Does your heart not lead you down that path?' I asked, although, judging from his distasteful expression, I already knew the answer to that question.

'No. When I think about sitting at the wheel, my heart turns cold. I know not why, but . . . something about the wheel . . . the cold, hard stone, going round and round in the same motion. I cannot . . . I cannot do that,' he muttered.

'Well, how about becoming an apprentice? You could be a stone mason?'

'No!' Joel snapped, his head shooting up, eyes angry. 'Forgive me,' he apologised. 'Not stones. No more stones. Or rocks.'

'Yes, of course,' I nodded. 'I did not think.' I needed to think of something quickly before he retreated into the darkness of his cage again. Then a thought occurred to me. 'What about wood? I have heard that Bezalel is looking for apprentices to train in carpentry.'

Joel raised his eyebrows and tilted his head to one side. 'Carpentry? I wonder what it would be like to create something out of wood. Rocks are so hard, so unfeeling and . . . dead. But wood . . .' He looked at the acacia trees that surrounded us, stood up and walked to the nearest one. Looking at it curiously, he put his hands on the trunk, running his fingers down the grooves in the wood. He leaned back and peered up into the thorny branches, surrounded by sprays of leaves and bursts of tiny yellow flowers.

'Trees are full of . . . life. They give us shade, and their leaves feed our goats. My *ima* uses them to make poultices – they restore life to us. They are a gift to us from Yahweh.' He turned to face me and smiled. A real smile. A peaceful smile. It was the first time I had seen him smile like that, and I marvelled at the change it made to his countenance. The sullen lines that usually drew his face downwards were gone. His eyes lit up; the smile gave him an air of strength and confidence.

'I think I would like to be a carpenter, Joshua,' he said, still smiling. 'My heart is stirred at the thought of crafting wood.'

I leapt to my feet, lifted my hands in the air, and shouted, 'Amen! Yahweh is good!' Joel laughed, his fingers still tracing the threads that ran through the tree bark. He gazed at it as if it was a length of the finest silken cloth. 'Shall we go and take counsel with your *abba* and *saba*, then?' I aske

The smile dropped off his face as quickly as a knife cuts through a sheep's fleece. Fear once again shadowed his face. 'He will not allow it,' he mumbled. 'My *abba* will not let me walk this path.'

'Why not?'

Joel sighed, looked at the tree and stroked it one last time before turning towards me. 'Because he is Azriel ben Jesher, the first-born son, and because I am my father's first-born son and as such, it is my portion to walk in the ways of my father, and his father and his father's father. His heart has always been fixed on my sitting at the potter's wheel, continuing the inheritance handed down to him by his father's father.' He looked at me with a sad smile that touched the edges of his mouth but did not reach his eyes. 'My *saba* was a skilled craftsman, Joshua. He crafted beautiful vessels on his potter's wheel, until the time when his hands became unsteady and he could no longer mould the clay. I have seen some of the vessels he made – the workmanship was magnificent.' Joel stared at me with a vacant expression. 'My *abba* is a good potter, and the vessels which he makes on his wheel are sturdy. But he is not the craftsman that his *abba* was, and I think his hope has always been that I would, be the potter that he cannot be.'

A solitary tear formed in Joshua's left eye, and rolled down his cheek.

'I have been a disappointment to him. I am not the first-born son that he had hoped for, because there is no joy in my heart at the thought of sitting at a potter's wheel.'

'Has Azriel told you this?' I asked him. 'Has he said you are a disappointment to him?'

Joel looked at me, his brow wrinkling with concentration. 'No, but I know it. I can see it in his eyes each time he looks at me and sighs. I know it within my heart.'

I put my hand on his shoulder. 'Joel, the heart is easily deceived. I believe Azriel is steadfast. He will not hide his face from you. Come. It is time to go back.'

Joel frowned. We made our way through the grove of acacia trees towards the outskirts of the camp and, as we walked, I talked. 'Your *abba* is a good man, Joel, and there is much love in his heart towards you. Tell him what you desire, then turn your ear to him and listen.'

'Mmm.' Joel was deep in thought. I thought he was dwelling on his fear of speaking to his father, but I was wrong. 'I have dishonoured them, Joshua. My parents. What I did this morning; I know my words were like daggers to them. I must humble my heart and repent before I speak of anything else.'

'Yes. You speak great wisdom. That will bring rest to your soul, and then you can talk to them about being a craftsman of wood, *nu*?' He looked at me and nodded. 'And when you have done that, we can break fast.' I grinned at him, laying a hand on my grumbling stomach. 'I am in need of some food!'

14

Driftwood

'So, you are not displeased?' Joel asked, his face a picture of bewilderment.

'My son,' Azriel replied, 'I would not be displeased if you asked to spend your life sweeping up dung in the sheep pens, if that is what you really wanted to do.'

'But . . . but I thought you wanted me to be a potter, like you and *Saba*, to carry on our family trade throughout the generations.'

Azriel looked over at Jesher, who was sitting next to me on the ground, glowing with contentment as he watched their discourse. Shira and the girls had not yet returned from the well, Yoram and Arad were still picking dates, and Naim was still with Mati and his new-born lamb. The rest of the family were gathered outside the tent.

The tension when I arrived home with Joel in tow was palpable. Hareph's shoulder (which was usually a fairly good barometer of atmospheres) was twitching at a rapid rate, and Leora had clearly been weeping for some time. But, true to his word, Joel went straight to his parents and knelt before them, asking their forgiveness for his outburst that morning. Once they had cleared the air, the conversation naturally progressed to him asking Azriel and Jesher about being apprenticed to Bezalel as a carpenter.

'Your *ima* and I want you to be happy, and if carpentry will make you happy, then that is what you must do. Besides,' Azriel added, cocking his head to one side, 'carpentry is a good trade. There is always work for a carpenter in Israel, *nu*?'

Joel, still looking dumbfounded, muttered, 'But . . . forgive me, *Abba* . . . if you are not disappointed in me, why is it that you sigh so often when you look at me?'

Azriel stared at Joel, his eyebrows high in his brow. 'Disappointed? Ech, my son. I do not sigh because I am disappointed in you. I sigh because my heart sorrows for you, for the pain that had plundered your heart.' Joel stared at his father as if seeing him for the first time. The veil of deception was lifting; his father was not who he thought he was. Father and son continued to stare at one another, neither of them sure of what to do. Then Azriel put his hands on both Joel's shoulders and spoke a blessing over him.

'May the Lord be between you and me, my son, and between our descendants, forever. May you be like an olive tree flourishing in the desert, planted by streams of water.'

The calls of 'Amen! Amen!' sounded out as the family voiced their agreement. Azriel held out his arms to Joel and, somewhat self-consciously, drew him into an embrace. It lasted quite a while. Clearly, Azriel had decided that since it was so long overdue he would make the most of it, and he revelled in the joy of being able to hold his son. Leora started crying again, this time with tears of joy, and mopped her face with her headscarf. Eglah gave her a hug and then turned to embrace Hareph, who was crying unashamedly, muttering to himself, 'So beautiful . . . yes?'

Jesher watched his family with a heart that overflowed, then looked at me, his eyes misting up. 'Thank you, Joshua,' he whispered. 'Thank you.'

After a while, Azriel drew back, kissed Joel on each cheek, and wiped his eyes with his headscarf. 'This is good, *nu*?' he said. 'This is very good.' Joel nodded and gave his father a watery smile. Jesher clambered to his feet, clapping his hands in delight. He embraced first Joel and then Azriel, then turned to Leora. All at once, the whole family were celebrating, hugging each other, and thanking Yahweh for His goodness. In the middle of it all, Shira arrived back at the tent with the girls, buzzing with some news.

'I'm sorry I was so long; Jesher, I bumped into Zivah at the well! She is well, and the children . . . but . . .' she paused, apparently annoyed that her announcement was being eclipsed, and that no one was paying much attention to her.

'What has happened?' she asked Jesher. 'Why are you embracing one another? Jesher, tell me, what has happened?' Jesher gave her a brief summary, and Shira frowned when she heard that I had been the one to go after Joel, and bring him safely home. 'Why did Joshua go to find him?' she demanded.

Jesher paused, then replied, 'Because he was the right person.'

Shira sniffed and turned away, muttering something inaudible. Jesher held out his arms to his family. 'Come! Come, let us eat, *nu*? Helah, bring some of those fresh date cakes. Leora, fetch the bread from the coals! Eglah, some goats' milk, dates and figs, yes? Today we feast as we break fast. Today we celebrate, yes?'

The boys returned as the family were sitting down around the mat, and were told the news. Blessings were pronounced and plans formed as we feasted together. Azriel raised his voice and declared, 'So! My son is going to be a carpenter!'

'Well, I hope so, *Abba*,' Joel said. 'We must speak with Bezalel first.'

'Ech, of course you will be a carpenter!' he responded, slapping Joel on the back. Pointing up to the sky, he declared, 'Yahweh has ordained it so, *nu*?' Everyone laughed.

'Although, I do not understand why I feel so excited about working with wood,' Joel said. 'It makes no sense to me.'

'Aah.' Azriel stared at him thoughtfully. 'I think I might know. Do you remember when you were just a little boy, you found that piece of driftwood by the river?'

Joel frowned. 'No. How old was I? What happened?'

'You were about this high,' he said, holding his hand about 2ft off the ground, 'only five, maybe six years old. You brought that piece of driftwood home to show your *ima*,' he said, shaking his head and smiling broadly. 'I remember it well. It could have been the Pharoah's jewels; you were so proud of it. To you, that piece of wood was a priceless treasure – you even kept it with you each night as you slept!'

There was a smattering of laughter around the family circle, and Naim took the opportunity of teasing his older brother about sleeping with a piece of wood.

'Wait! I remember that!' Joel exclaimed, ignoring Naim. I could see his mind slowly peeling back the protective layers that had covered his precious memories for so many years. 'Yes! It was about this long,' measuring roughly a foot with his hands, 'and had so many different colours and grains in it.' He gasped as the memory became clearer. 'I remember the way the wood curved – so smooth, and yet so strong and well defined – it seemed to have a life of its own, a soul. I remember it! It was beautiful, was it not?' he asked, turning to face his father, excitement flooding his face.

'Well, you certainly thought so,' said Azriel, chuckling with delight.

My heart caught in my chest when I saw the way he looked at his son. There was a sense of awe in his countenance as he watched Joel. I felt privileged to witness it. Would that I could have a son to love in that way. Joel's transformation was like the unveiling of a priceless masterpiece that had been shut away for years in a dusty chest. Truly remarkable.

Tears came to Azriel's eyes. He leaned closer to Joel and said, 'You saw in that piece of wood what none of us could see. You saw beauty. You saw life.' Turning to me, he explained, 'Even as a child, Joel would notice details and intricacies which the rest of us never saw. He moulded clay into shapes and carved patterns into it, created beauty from the most ordinary things – from the dust of the earth! Ay, ay, ay,' he exclaimed, raising his hands to the heavens. 'Such a gift Yahweh gave him.' Turning to Joel, he took his hands in his and said, 'These hands were made to create. Not just to labour, or make common vessels like your *abba*, but to create beauty, to bring forth life. Yes?' He looked at him expectantly.

Joel stared at his upturned hands, as if seeing them for the first time. He moved his fingers, touching them reverently, a cautious smile forming on his lips. 'If Yahweh gives me the skill, I think I could do that.'

'I know you could – but only if your heart desires it,' Azriel said earnestly, waving his finger in Joel's face. 'Only then, yes?'

'Yes, *Abba*.' Joel turned to me and grinned, stuffing a date cake into his mouth. I saw fresh shoots of hope pushing through the soil of trauma in his heart, steadily dismantling the fear that had gripped him for so long. '*Abba*,' he said, turning back to Azriel. 'What happened to my driftwood?'

Azriel's smile faded. 'You do not remember?' Conversation around the circle suddenly petered out and a tense silence gripped the atmosphere. I turned to Mesha, who was seated next to me, and tilted my head as if to ask him to tell me. He just looked away.

Joel shook his head. 'No, I only remember having it with me.'

Azriel sighed, looking at him nervously. 'Ah. Well. The first day you joined the workforce – you had only seen seven winters, but you were tall and strong for your age, and they said you were ready . . . They told me to bring you the next day to work with the other children collecting straw and mud for bricks.' Azriel paused, and I could see he did not want to continue.

'What happened?' Joel glanced around, aware of the silence that had fallen. Azriel looked at his son, and then at Jesher. '*Abba*? Tell me,' Joel said calmly. 'I must know what happened.' Azriel continued to stare at Jesher, searching his eyes for guidance. Jesher met his gaze and, very slowly, nodded at his son.

Azriel looked down at his hands and sighed. 'You took your driftwood with you on that first day, tied to your belt. I had not seen it, but they saw it and they took it from you.' He swallowed hard. He leaned forward. 'They . . . they used it to beat you when you tried to take it back from them. When it broke, they threw it into the fire and stood there laughing as you wept.'

Joel looked down at his hands. 'I do not remember that,' he whispered.

'I am glad,' Azriel said. 'I watched as they dragged you away to the brick compound, weeping as you went. I could do nothing. Yahweh forgive me, I could not help you,' his voice cracked with emotion. Silence. All eyes were focused on Joel, waiting to see how he would react to this news. Would he retreat back into the darkness where he had hidden for so long?

'Don't go back,' I begged him silently. 'Do not go back, Joel. Stay. Stay with us.'

'So you see,' Azriel said after a while, 'I know what it is like to stand by and watch someone you love being beaten; not able to do anything but watch while their heart is broken and their hope is trampled into the mud.'

'I never knew.'

'But now you do, *nu*?' Azriel nodded his head slowly. 'That day . . . you changed. When I fetched you that evening, my happy little boy was gone. They took your creativity. They took your smile. They took you away from us. You never moulded clay again. You no longer played with wood. You hardly played at *all*, any more. They broke not only your stick, but your heart also.' He hung his head in silent defeat. I wanted desperately to say something, to do something to stop the flood of desolation from rising up in Azriel's heart. I wanted to make this right, to bring Joel back again. But how? Then I heard his voice.

'No, *Abba*.'

'Hmm?' Azriel looked up, frowning in confusion.

'They did not destroy me.' Joel's voice was calm, his face peaceful. I was struck at how much more grown-up he looked. A man. Not a boy. Joel smiled at his *abba* and then shrugged his shoulders. 'For a while, maybe, I was hidden. Hidden, but not gone. They did not destroy me, *Abba*. I am still here.'

Tears formed in both their eyes; pain was supplanted by joy, as father and son seized each other and hugged, long and hard. There was no hesitation this time. Tears became laughter as they rocked backwards and forwards, smacking each other on the back, then kissing each other on the cheek.

Azriel turned to me next. 'Joshua, thank you. Thank you for bringing my son back to me.' I smiled and gave a small nod. I couldn't speak. The lump in my throat would not let me. I felt as though I should be the one thanking them for giving me the privilege of being part of such a redemptive moment.

Conversation resumed once again; a babble of voices chattered in relief, the feasting and laughter resumed. In the midst of the buzz of conversation, Joel sat, looking across the circle at me. Reflected in his eyes was a deep, inexpressible gratitude.

No one would ever know what really happened in that acacia grove today. No one would know the depths of agony that Joel had suffered, or the pain that had ripped into my heart as I watched him labour in it. No one needed to know.

But we knew.

Yes, we knew.

15

Tumbleweed

Something within me had been exposed. Like a wineskin that ruptures due to age and much use, I found leaking out of my heart a bitterness that had long been buried, and I felt helpless to stop it.

The whole family rejoiced at the deliverance that Joel had experienced that morning. We feasted and celebrated, offering prayers of thanksgiving to Yahweh. Even Shira was smiling! She laughed at the stories that Jesher told us from his youth, and smiled at Hareph's jokes. There was a sense of harmony among us that was fresh and unspoilt. I felt it. We all felt it. It was beautiful.

After we had broken our fast, I made my way to Moses' tent. My thoughts turned inward and what they unmasked was not fresh and unspoilt, nor was it beautiful. It was bitter and rancid, and I was ashamed to be thinking such thoughts on a day like this. I pushed them deep inside of me and turned my attention to the tasks Moses had me do. But the thoughts lurked beneath the surface. Like cankers in a man's mouth, unseen by the human eye, they festered, throbbing, calling for attention.

The mood that evening was a continuation of the morning, light and celebratory. Azriel and Jesher had gone with Joel to speak to Bezalel, and he had agreed to take Joel on. They retold the story around the dinner mat, celebrating the start of his apprenticeship, but I found little pleasure in it. I felt disconnected, as though I was sitting on the outskirts watching what was happening instead of being there, in the family circle. I tried to smile and join in the conversation, but my heart felt false.

I continued in my falsehood, thinking I had succeeded in hiding my inner struggles, until Jesher said, 'These old bones are stiff. Joshua, come, walk with me.'

He had seen through my pitiful performance. When Jesher asked someone to walk with him, even though his tone was inviting, it was never a question. Declining was not an option. So I helped him up, gave him his walking stick, and we set off on the pathway that snaked in-between the clusters of tents, leading to the outskirts of the camp. We gazed up at the pillar of fire, talking of its magnificence as we walked, and I knew he was giving me time to unburden myself. I didn't know how to. So, after a while, he spoke.

'Joshua, what ails you?'

I knew better than to say that nothing was wrong, so I muttered, 'Why do you ask?'

'You have been quiet this evening. You hardly said a word when we broke bread, and you did not eat much.' He smiled at me. 'Something must be wrong. So what is it, my son?'

'I have been pondering.'

'Pondering what?' Jesher had a disarming way of drawing information out of people. It was extremely hard to resist his gentle, persistent prodding and so, despite my resolve not to, I found myself talking.

'I have been thinking about Joel.'

'Mmm?' He waited for me to continue.

'What happened this morning. I cannot recall when I last saw pain like that in a young man. He laboured in such anguish.' Jesher frowned and nodded in sympathy, but said nothing. 'I did not know what to do, or how to help him, other than telling him my story.' Jesher looked at me and raised his bushy eyebrows. 'I told him about Jezrel. How he died . . . and what happened to me after he died. I think it helped him to know that, in truth, I did understand what his heart suffered. Such pain in such a young man, locked up for so long. He was overwhelmed with dread, but then . . . it was as if the gates of his soul opened up. He poured out his heart to me, and now . . .' I paused, trying to think of the words to describe what I witnessed.

'Mmm.' Jesher stopped walking and turned to face me. 'His soul has found rest, yes?'

'Yes.'

'It is a thing of beauty. You have done a wonderful work today, Joshua. I knew you could do it.' I loved the simplicity of Jesher's heart. He didn't need to know the details of what had happened that morning. Although I knew he would listen to whatever I wanted to tell him, he would never demand to know the tasty morsels that gossips so often crave. He only knew that Joel had been captive and was now free. That was enough for him. 'But?' he prompted me. By now we had reached the edge of the camp and, without thinking, I made my way towards the same grove of acacia trees that Joel and I had visited that morning.

'I have not thought about Jezrel or that time in my life for so long. Talking to Joel brought it all back to me.' I could taste the bitterness of that canker in me as it rose to the surface. I knew I could not hold back. I had to spew it out and find peace again. 'There I was, telling Joel what to do, how to make the right choices, even helping him find his path in life, when I . . . I do not even know my own path,' I blurted. 'Joel knows now what his path is, and you saw how his countenance changed. He is made new! I helped him to find his path – and yet I cannot find my own.' By now, we had reached the grove of acacia trees. I slumped down with my back against a tree trunk and Jesher sat next to me, still silent, still listening.

'What path am I on? Where is my path leading me?' I shrugged. 'I have no trade, no wife or children, no blood family, nothing before me. I cannot see my way. *Abba*, I cannot see my way forward and, although my heart condemns me for saying it, there is jealousy in my soul towards Joel, because he can see. He can see his path, and it is a good path. And yet I, who helped him find his, cannot even see the next step on my own pathway.'

There it was. Out in the open, exposed for the bitter canker that it was. I breathed in and turned to face Jesher, ready to face the disappointment and judgement I knew I would see in his eyes. There was none. He looked at me with such love, such compassion, it pierced me like a knife. I would rather he had judged me, scourged me with his words, so I could bow my head and castigate myself. But he spoke not a word, although his eyes spoke much.

'*Abba*, what does Yahweh want of me?'

'He will tell you Himself, Joshua, then you will know your pathway.'

'When will He tell me? I am not such a young man any more. When will I find my path?'

Jesher looked away from me and pondered awhile, focusing on the fiery pillar in the distance. I waited for him to speak, fiddling with some stones that lay on the ground around me until he was ready to respond. 'Yahweh holds the times and seasons in His hand. He knows when it is right for you to take the next step and He will show you when you are ready.'

'But when will that be?'

He ignored my question, still gazing off into the distance. Then he looked up at the acacia tree that we sheltered under. A strong, broad trunk formed the base of the tree, and from it spread a crown of bright yellow blossoms, clustered together and interspersed with long grey thorns. 'Look around you. These trees do not blossom during the winter rains. But when the rainy season comes to an end and the dry summer months begin, they flower. We enjoy their beauty through the summer months, but they die before the rains come. Why? Why do these blossoms die? Hmm?'

I wasn't sure if he was waiting for me to reply, but my mind was so stupefied, I couldn't think of an answer. So I said nothing. Jesher smiled at me. 'They die so that new buds can form in the next season. They die in order to bring forth new life.' Putting his hand on my arm, he continued, 'Joshua, for every beginning, there is an ending. A new beginning follows that ending, and so forth. So it is with us. Joel's winter season has come to an end, his summer has come and he will start to blossom. So it will be with you. When the winter rains have come and gone, new shoots will push their way through the bark of your tree, and clusters of bright yellow blossoms will begin to form. New life will come, my son. But you must wait on Yahweh; He alone knows the right time, *nu*?'

I sighed. 'It is not easy to wait, *Abba*.'

'It never is, but everything precious is worth waiting for. That is how we learn patience – by having to wait, yes? A man cannot say he is patient unless he has faced a time of waiting.'

I grunted and gestured to a clump of tumbleweed in front of us, tossed around by the evening breeze. 'My life is like this tumbleweed – rolling around aimlessly. How could I help a young man like Joel find his path in life, when I do not even know what my own path is?'

'I know not, but you did help him!' Jesher chuckled and punched me on the arm. 'This tumbleweed was once a living plant.' He reached out and picked it up. 'But, when it's season was over, it dried up and broke off here, at the base of its stem. Now it is blown wherever the wind takes it, scattering its seeds as it goes.' He peered at me, one eyebrow raised, checking to see if I was understanding his point. 'Joshua, you must go wherever Yahweh's mighty wind blows you. And you will. You will. Yahweh will show you your path.' He stared into my eyes for a few moments, as if searching for something, 'And I think you will be surprised at where it leads you.'

'I do not understand.'

'You will. Keep serving Moses, let wisdom enter your soul, and the Lord will show you.'

Another tangle of tumbleweed blew in front of us and settled, quivering for a while as if unsure of which direction to go. Jesher looked at it, smiled at me again and raised his eyebrows. With that, the tumbleweed was whisked up into the air, borne away on the wings of an invisible breeze. We watched it being blown further and further away, until it became a mere speck on the horizon, and finally disappeared from our sight.

16

Womenfolk

I had missed my opportunity and now I was trapped! Jesher had gone to talk with some of the leaders and Azriel, Mesha and Hareph had joined him. Yoram and the boys had taken the goats and lambs to graze and Joel was working with Bezalel, leaving the women alone at the tent.

With me.

I should not have been there but, when I arrived at his tent that morning, Moses asked me to deliver a message and said he had no need of me until later in the day. I delivered his message and went back home to find Mesha. Helah told me where he and the others had gone and I debated whether to join them, or make the most of this rare opportunity to lie down and rest. I poured myself some water from the pitcher, still pondering what to do, when I heard Saadia's jarring voice. Ducking back inside, I pulled the dividing curtain down, hoping that she had not seen me.

It seemed the decision had been made for me. I was trapped.

Saadia was a friend of Shira's, although I was never convinced that she was a particularly good friend, or a particularly good influence on her. She was just as strong in her opinions as Shira, but she also had an insatiable appetite for gossip, and an 'all-knowing' attitude to go with it. There were not many people who I felt the need to avoid, but she was definitely one of them. Each time we met, she would demand to know the latest camp news – what Moses had been doing, what decisions the elders had made and what Moses had me do. Her husband, Yacob, had not been blessed with leadership qualities and, to compensate for that fact, Saadia busied herself trying to leach information out of anyone who had anything to do with Moses or the elders.

I had been the focus of her steely gazed interrogations before and I was not willing to go through that again. Not today, and definitely not when no other men were around to stand with me. So, I unrolled my bed and lay down, closing my eyes, even though I knew sleep would not come to me – not with Saadia's shrill voice piercing the morning air. But at least my body could rest for a while. I was content to do that. Anything to avoid facing Saadia.

'Sixteen?' Saadia's voice cut across the mumble of women's voices outside. 'It seems like only yesterday he was a little boy hiding behind your legs, too scared to chase a lamb! He cannot be sixteen.'

Helah responded. 'He is. He is nearly as tall as his *abba*.' I could hear the pride in her voice. I smiled to myself. Yoram was a son to be proud of and I knew he would bring honour to his family.

'He is an excellent young man! You and Mesha must be so proud of him.' I recognised Abigail's voice. She was another friend of Shira's, but quite opposite to Saadia in character. Friendly and kind-hearted, she loved nothing better than to sit with her friends, discussing the latest goings-on in camp. Her conversation consisted mostly of agreeing with everyone else – which is why, I believe, Shira and Saadia invited her to join them. They did like to be agreed with! However, it seemed to me that Abigail told people what she thought they wanted to hear and, because of that, I never felt I could trust her. Her words were like buttermilk; sweet to the taste, but without much substance to them.

'Thank you, Abigail. We are proud of him. He is a good boy,' Helah responded.

Eglah spoke up next, her smooth tones bringing a sense of calm to the group. 'You should be proud of him, Helah. He will bring great blessing to you and Mesha!'

'Amen! Amen!' Clearly, the women all agreed. Of course they would – how could they not? I smiled to myself, content to lay there with my eyes closed, thinking on the many good qualities of my adopted nephew.

'Oy! Where did the years go?' Abigail clucked in commiseration. 'When my Shaul was young, he grew like a lamb in springtime! Every time we measured him he had gr – '

'Ah yes, I remember those days.'

I frowned. It irritated me when Shira monopolised conversations. It was dishonouring. 'My Mesha grew so quickly, people thought I was secretly feeding him portions of meat!' Small bursts of polite laughter broke out among the group. 'And now my Mesha is a man, with his own children, and *his* first-born is now a man.' She tutted to herself. 'Such a man, my Mesha.' There was an awkward silence; I imagined the looks that were being passed among the other women. Quick to agree, as ever, Abigail spoke up.

'True, true!'

Jesher and Shira had four children: Azriel, Eglah, Zivah and Mesha. But a stranger who was not well acquainted with the family might well be forgiven for thinking that Shira had only one child. Mesha was her pride and joy and she would seize any opportunity that presented itself to talk endlessly about his many outstanding qualities. Nothing was too good for Mesha, no one could possibly outdo him, and if Yahweh Himself needed a helper, Mesha was the one most suited to the task.

Mesha was my close friend and I loved him like a brother. He had many good qualities; he was loyal and faithful, a hard worker, friendly, kind, a risk taker and an eternal optimist. If there was tension in the air, Mesha could nullify it within minutes, and his most useful quality (as far as the family was concerned) was his unique ability to charm Shira out of her 'dark moods'. He was a good man with a great many strengths, but I was not blind to his weaknesses. He could be reckless and displayed a lack of wisdom, often rushing into situations without thinking them through first. He could also be quite insensitive, usually without realising it, and he lacked patience. Waiting was Mesha's least favourite pastime!

'Helah, what are you weaving?' I heard Abigail ask.

'A new breadbasket,' she replied. 'Mine is old and starting to break. I picked these palm fronds from the palms at Elim before we left. They are strong and thick and will make a good basket.'

We had moved on from Elim a few days ago, continuing our journey south, although the decision to leave was not a popular one. Many of our people objected to leaving the lush vegetation and fresh springs of Elim, but Moses was adamant. Yahweh told him it was time to move; the cloud of His presence moved, so we moved with it. We filled every waterskin that we had, picked as many dates, figs and fruit as we could carry – as well as a supply of fresh palm fronds which Helah used for weaving – and we moved on.

'That is a beautiful design you are weaving. Shira, you are blessed to have such a skilled daughter-in-law,' Abigail gushed.

Shira muttered, 'It will be a good, strong basket, I am sure.'

I shook my head as I lay there listening. It was not that Shira disliked Helah, it was just that, in her eyes, no one was good enough for Mesha. Helah was a devoted wife to Mesha, although she was also not blind to his faults, and had no problem telling him so! She grounded him and brought a much-needed balance. It never ceased to amaze me how he allowed her to reprimand him (although she never did it when Shira was present). Helah was small, petite in stature, but he would listen to her rebukes in a contrite manner and, when she was finished, he would usually kiss her on the forehead and comply with her requests.

Helah was a do-er. She struggled to be still; in fact, I can't recall a time when she did not have something in her hands. She was always busy. Good home-making skills were important to Shira, so Helah's excellent work ethic, along with her cooking skills and agility in weaving, earned her Shira's begrudging respect. For Helah, that was enough.

Saadia's shrill voice blared again. 'Leora, is that a new weaving frame?'

'Yes, it is. Joel made it for me. Did you know that he is apprenticed to Bezalel?'

'I had heard. I was very surprised that Bezalel took him on.' I could tell that Saadia was trying to hide the fact that she was impressed. Very few were chosen to study under Bezalel's tutelage. 'He must have *some* skill then, I suppose.' I grimaced. How could she be so brash? But before I could ponder Saadia's insensitivity, Shira joined in the discussion.

'I was surprised too, especially in light of Joel's . . . afflictions. But he has taken him on, so we will have to wait and see if he is able to walk this path or not.'

Shira's obvious favouring of Mesha created problems within the family and, were it not for Jesher's frequent interventions, there would have been ongoing conflict among his children and their spouses. Azriel was the one who spoke out the most, usually with the undesirable result of being on the receiving end of Shira's sharp tongue. It was due to Shira's interfering that he was regularly cheated out of his privileges as first-born son and, as a result, he had a fairly turbulent relationship with his mother. Azriel was a man of strong opinions, much like Shira, although he was more understanding and did not feel the need to control people like his mother did. However, because they were similar in a lot of ways, they clashed on a regular basis, especially when it came to the children.

Shira favoured Mesha's children and, in her eyes, Yoram (as Mesha's first-born) could do no wrong, just like Mesha. Joel, however, was not one of her favourites. Shira liked doers, not thinkers, and her opinion of Joel and his behaviour due to the trauma he had encountered was firmly set in stone.

'Bezalel is very happy with Joel's workmanship,' Helah said. 'In fact, Mesha told me that Bezalel said Joel's skill already rivals that of his own sons, who have been apprenticed to him for years.' I could hear Shira sniffing – I would recognise that sniff anywhere! It was her way of showing her disapproval without actually voicing it.

Eglah joined in the conversation in support of Joel. 'Leora, that frame looks so sturdy. Joel has fashioned it well. You must be so proud of him; he is bringing blessing on his family.'

I could hear a smile in Leora's voice as she responded. 'I am. He said Bezalel is teaching him how to craft tent poles and pegs now and, when he has mastered those, he will learn how to craft wheels. His desire is to make a cart for the family.'

'Yahweh be praised!' Helah joined in. 'That would be a great blessing!'

'Yes, Azriel is very happy!' Leora replied. 'To pull his potter's wheel on a cart instead of carrying it would greatly ease his burden.'

'True, true!' Abigail agreed.

'Yes, yes. A cart would be a blessing, but we must first see if Joel can craft it before we allow ourselves to rejoice, hmm?' Shira's icy voice cut through the conversation, silencing any further discussion on that topic. I closed my eyes.

Then Saadia spoke, but her voice was much quieter than usual. 'Yacob has gone to talk to the elders this morning, you know. A lot of the men are going to speak to them today.'

'Why?' Abigail asked.

Saadia whispered, 'Because there is *trouble* in the camp.' I opened my eyes. Trouble in the camp? My mind started racing.

Helah echoed my thoughts. 'Trouble? What do you speak of?'

'They are not happy,' Saadia replied.

'Who is not happy?' Abigail interjected.

'Everyone! Oy! What do we have to be happy about?' Saadia sounded exasperated at their apparent ignorance of the facts. 'Wandering around from place to place in this heat, not enough water, and now we are running out of food. And you know what *that* means,' she said.

'What? What does that mean?' Abigail was clearly getting flustered.

'*A man must eat!*' Saadia screeched. I frowned to myself. What? Food? That's what the 'trouble' was about? Surely not. But, according to Saadia, it was. I lay still and continued listening. 'If a man cannot eat what he needs to, to keep himself strong, there is trouble. I can only cook with what I have. I cannot do miracles . . . although,' Saadia paused, and I readied myself to listen to the self-aggrandisement which I knew was coming, 'considering I have so little to cook with, it could be said that the food I produce is nothing short of miraculous. My mother taught me well, peace be upon her. My Yacob always says he chose me because of my food. He says my food is worthy of Moses himself, although there is only so much even I can do with what we have to cook with now.'

There was a general mumbling in response, then Leora changed the conversation. 'Do you remember the little vegetable gardens we had in Egypt? Oh, how I long for some cucumbers and melons.'

'And the leeks! Do you remember the leeks? Oh, they were so tasty.' I smiled. Eglah had a particular fondness for leeks.

'Barley bread, still warm from the coals . . .'

'Oh, yes! Cabbage leaves, wrapped around onions, garlic and dates, baked with sweet tomatoes . . . I have almost forgotten what they taste like.' Helah sighed. I could picture the wistful expression on her face.

Shira agreed. 'Fish is what I long for the most. Stewed, baked on the coals, cooked on hot stones . . . oh, what I would do for some fish!'

'Amen! Amen!'

Saadia's voice cut through the conversation like a jagged knife through softly spun wool. 'We had everything we needed there.

Leeks, cucumbers, melons, fish, onions, garlic . . . we wanted for nothing! We should never have left Egypt.'

'But Saadia, we were slaves in Egypt,' Helah said.

'Yes, yes, but life was not that bad, was it? At least there we had homes, we had food and water. I do not know why we left there. We were deceived.' I sat up. Complaining about food was one thing, but insulting my master was entirely a different matter. 'Moses led us, with nooses around our necks, into this desert to die!'

Saadia was a woman with strong opinions and a marked lack of tolerance for those who didn't agree with her. I knew Abigail had learned that lesson a long time ago, which was why she now mumbled, 'True. True.'

I didn't know how much more I could bear. I could feel my face growing hot, and my heart beat faster. The urge to confront Saadia was burning in me. There were a few mutters in response, but clearly not enough to satisfy Saadia, because she continued her tirade.

'What do we have to cook with now?' she snapped. 'A few vegetables, dates, grains . . . it is enough to cause anguish in the heart of a good woman! This morning, Yacob said we should slaughter the goat, because he wants meat to eat. Slaughter the goat? Where will we get our milk from then? No!' she shouted. 'It is enough now, yes? They must talk to Moses and tell him. It is time for the truth to be spoken!'

'But what will they say? What can they do about it?' Helah sounded agitated.

'They will tell Moses and Aaron what must be done, that is what they will do!' Shira joined in. 'They will tell Moses what is right. We never should have left Elim. Such a place that was! When I think of those springs of water, the palm trees, the dates, and figs . . . ay, ay, ay.'

'We should *never* have left there,' Saadia voiced her agreement vociferously. 'I told Yacob. I told him, many times. "Yacob," I said. "We must not leave Elim."'

Shira agreed. 'I told Jesher too. I told him!'

'But . . .' Helah interjected. 'I thought we were going to Canaan. Is that not the land that Yahweh has promised us?'

'Canaan! Psshh!' Saadia dismissed her. 'What is Canaan? Why go to Canaan when we have everything we need in Elim?'

'But Yahweh said – '

'But *did* He?' Shira interjected. 'Did Yahweh say? Did we hear Him? Did you hear Him?' With only a momentary pause, she continued. 'No! Of course not. We did not hear Yahweh say anything; we only have Moses' word for it, *nu*?'

I stood up.

'But Moses is – '

'Aah, Helah,' said Saadia in a patronising fashion. 'You are young, yes, but you will learn. Your mother understands what I talk of. You will learn in time.' That was it. I had heard enough. I would rather risk the threat of interrogation by Saadia than listen to any more of this shameful foolishness. I flung the dividing curtain back, and strode outside just as Saadia was starting another speech.

'No, the men will tell Moses, you will see. They will – '

I stepped outside the tent, greeted the circle of women, then stared directly at Saadia. '*Shalom*, Saadia.' She looked up at me and, for once, was speechless. I had the element of surprise and took full advantage of it. I stared hard into her eyes before turning to Shira.

'With your permission, I will take my leave of you.' Looking back at Saadia, I said, 'There is much that I need to discuss with Moses,' before striding off in the direction of Moses' tent.

17

Shameful

The sun had long since set by the time I arrived back home. My anger had not abated. In fact, what I had witnessed that day only succeeded in fanning the embers of my anger into a raging fire.

After I left the women, I went to find Moses, hoping to warn him of the trouble. I was too late; the mob arrived at his tent just before I arrived. I stood with him, barely managing to hold my tongue while they complained, on and on, maligning his character, condemning his decisions and rebelling against the instructions that Yahweh had given him.

I stayed with Moses all afternoon in case they came back. My rage burned hotter, but I said nothing. The man of God had much to think on and my raging would not have helped him. When the night drew in, he thanked me and sent me home. By the time I arrived, my family were finishing the evening meal, and the force of my anger could no longer be contained.

'*How can they defy Yahweh like that?*' I ranted, plonking myself down next to Mesha. 'How could they speak so shamefully to Moses? Their words are like the venom of a cobra and their feet run to do evil, spreading a net for the righteous. They spoke words of falsehood and deceit – it was shameful!' I looked up to see startled faces staring at me from around the mat. All conversation was suspended. This was a side of me that not many of my new family had been privy to before. Yoram stared at me, wide-eyed, and even Hareph was shocked into silence at my outburst. After a pause, Jesher thanked the women for the meal and gave them permission to withdraw inside the tent with the children.

'Jesher, I would like to – ' Shira started to object.

'Shira!' He did not look at her, but his tone of voice was resolute. There would be no discussion. It was not often that Jesher silenced his wife, but he did so now. She stared at him, fuming, then, realising she would not win this argument, swept into the tent with the other wives. Jesher waited until the women and children were inside the tent before turning to me. 'Speak your heart, Joshua.'

'You saw what happened, did you not?' I asked. 'You were all there when they arrived at Moses' tent, yes?'

'No, my son,' Jesher replied. 'We were talking with Abidan and some of the leaders when we heard the noise of a mob. It took us a little while to find out what was happening, and to decide to follow them.'

'So you were not there when they called him out, then?'

Jesher shook his head. 'No.'

I snorted. 'Their arrogance was unbelievable. To summon Moses, like he was some . . . some faithless heathen!' I clenched my fists. 'I wanted to show them what happens to people who show such insolence to Moses, but he stopped me.'

'Mmm.' Jesher nodded, then passed me the basket of bread. 'Eat. You need your strength.' I broke off a piece and stuffed it into my mouth, continuing to rant as I ate.

'I know not how Moses could be so calm. He stood there and listened as they poured out grievance after grievance. "We have no food", "our wives are unhappy", "there is not enough water", "we want to go back to Elim".' I raged on, forgetting that they had been there and heard it for themselves, apart from Yoram and Joel. Thankfully they were wise enough, and kind enough, not to remind me of that fact, and even Hareph stayed silent while I railed on. 'And then they say he is not a good leader. Not a good leader! And, if he didn't take us back to Elim, they would choose a new leader.' I slammed my bread down on the mat and shouted, '*Who*? Tell me, who? There is not *one* among them who could do what Moses does. They are deceitful, greedy, arrogant . . .'

'Joshua, calm down,' Mesha urged me. 'You will grieve the children.'

'Forgive me,' I said, lowering my voice, 'but how could they turn on him like that? Some of them were elders, the same ones chosen *by him* to help lead this people!'

Azriel, who up until now had been quiet, asked, 'Were all the elders there?'

I thought for a bit. 'No, I think not. I did not see Abidan there, or Elishama, and Hur was standing with Moses, so clearly was not with them. But you saw the crowd – there were so many people. Many were just there to watch, so it was hard to know who stood with Moses, and who stood against him.'

'Mmm.' Jesher nodded, his dusky blue eyes watching me with concern.

'Ech!' Hareph's shoulder was twitching a lot, and he mumbled to himself. I bit into a fig, ate a piece of cheese and poured myself a cup of water from the pitcher, drinking eagerly. I hadn't realised I was so thirsty. As I glugged it down, Jesher spoke.

'Moses is a wise man. His feet will not rush into evil.' He looked at each of us in turn, and an unexpected smile broke out on his face. 'My heart was stirred when at last he spoke to his accusers, *nu*?'

I looked at him and, for the first time that day, allowed myself to smile. 'Yes, mine too. Did you see their faces when he said, "I will seek Yahweh on this"?'

'Yes.' Mesha chuckled. 'And then he just walked through the crowd, head held high, staff in his hand. It was like the parting of the Red Sea all over again,' he said, using his hands to show how Moses had walked through the middle of the mob.

Jesher smiled and shook his head, and then his expression turned serious again. 'What did Moses do after that?'

'He spent the rest of the afternoon in his tent, praying. I stayed with him – I thought they might come back again, but they did not.' I sighed. 'He may have looked calm on the outside, but he was full of anger!' I glanced at them. 'You should have heard his prayers.'

Silence fell as we contemplated the day's events and the possible consequences of the rebellion. After a while, Hareph spoke. 'You do not think Moses will consider going back to Elim, do you?'

I snorted. 'No! Yahweh did not promise us Elim. He has given us the land of Canaan as our inheritance and that is where Moses is leading us. We will not be going back to Elim; I bear witness to that.'

'True, yes. Canaan. Mmm,' Hareph nodded and his shoulder twitched.

'So what will happen now?' Mesha asked.

'Moses has called all the elders to meet with him tomorrow morning. He will speak to them then. That is why I returned so late;

it was my task to tell them.' I knew I had said enough. Peace was returning to our gathering, so I did not tell them about the words I exchanged with the rebellious leaders that evening when I gave them Moses' message. He made me swear an oath not to retaliate or harm them and I honoured his request. But only just. Never had I yearned to outwork the force of my anger on men like I did that day. I would willingly have crushed the heads of my master's enemies for the wicked words that they spoke of him.' Many of them said they would not come to meet with him the following morning, but I knew that they would. They would not stay away. The curiosity in their wicked hearts would not let them stay away. So I would have to face them again after the rising of the sun, and listen to their taunts and insults.

I wrestled with my thoughts and looked up to see Jesher watching me, a gentle smile on his face. I could not help but return his smile. I lowered my eyes and spoke. 'Brothers, forgive me for my anger. I was not myself.'

A jumble of understanding noises and manly acknowledgements echoed around the circle. I was forgiven. Jesher stood to his feet and walked over to the firepit; I followed him.

'*Abba*,' I mumbled. 'My heart fears for what may happen tomorrow. Moses is a gentle man and humble in heart. His desire is not to lord it over Yahweh's people but, when they disobey Yahweh and rebel against Him, he . . . he changes. I have seen what happens when zeal for Yahweh overtakes him.' I looked at Jesher. 'He is only one man. I am only one man, and I am not sure I can protect him against such a multitude.'

'Mmm.' Jesher nodded, as was his way, and thought for a while before responding. 'Come,' he said, gesturing to the glowing fire in the middle of the camp. 'Look at this magnificent fiery pillar. The Lord is mighty. His arm is strong, Joshua. Why should we fear those who cannot hurt us? Moses is Yahweh's prophet and Yahweh will protect him. You will see.'

I gazed up at the rippling tower of fire before us. 'I hope so, because I do not believe I can.'

18

Falling Bread

It was everywhere. I could feel it. I saw it in their eyes and heard it in the whispered conversations that were taking place all over the camp. It was as though a ravenous wolf had escaped the shadowy confines of its cage. Free of its shackles, it was stalking us, out in the open for all to see. We could deny it no longer. It gripped our hearts and fuelled our anger.

Fear!

I rose early and was outside Moses' tent before sunrise. I had hardly slept at all, though my body had longed for it. I understood what Jesher said about Yahweh protecting Moses, but I could not shake the overwhelming sense of responsibility that weighed on me, and the sense of dread I felt whenever I thought about Moses' meeting with the leaders. Aaron was with Moses already, along with Eleazar and Ithamar, Aaron's third and fourth-born sons. His first and second-born sons, Nadab and Abihu, were conspicuous in their absence, and I wondered why it was that they never seemed to stand with their uncle during times of conflict. I didn't have long to think on that before Moses spoke.

'Ah, Joshua, *shalom*.' He greeted me with a kiss on both cheeks. 'Thank you for standing with us.' I was relieved to see that Moses looked calm. I could see no sign of the rage he had displayed the day before. 'Come, let us not keep them waiting, *nu*?' He picked up his staff and walked out of his tent. There was no conversation as we walked to the Meeting Tent. Moses walked briskly with Aaron by his side; Eleazar, Ithamar and I walked behind them. Moses didn't look at people or greet them like he usually did. There was no exchanging of pleasantries today and no greetings offered. He was a man on a mission, focused on the path ahead. Conversation stopped as we walked through the camp. Hushed voices muttered as we passed, but no one tried to stop us. Perhaps they saw my hand, poised over the hilt of my sword. I would take no risks today. I was ready to protect my master at all costs.

The leaders were already gathered by the Meeting Tent. The cloud of Yahweh's presence hovered over them, but I saw in it a turbulence which unnerved me. Its billowing folds were dark and angry and, instead of the iridescent flickers of light which never ceased to thrill me, I heard rumbles of thunder. It seemed heavy laden, like the storm clouds that gathered in the rainy season before a downpour.

Moses wasted no time. Walking to the front of the assembly, he turned to face them and shouted, 'The Lord God has heard your complaints. For your complaints are not against us, but against the Lord Himself.' He lifted up his staff and roared, 'And *He has heard you.*' I positioned myself on one side of Moses and scanned the crowd. I saw the same angry, arrogant faces that I had seen the day before, plus a lot of new faces, some of which did not look angry, just concerned. Abidan was one of these, Jesher with him. He caught my eye and nodded at me in greeting, and I returned the nod before continuing to scan the growing crowd.

Moses paused to look at the people. I knew he detested conflict and avoided it wherever possible. However, I also knew that as prophet to the Most High, when confronted with the sins and rebellion of these people, Moses transformed from a humble, mild-mannered man into a formidable leader with a commanding sense of authority.

He stood before them, eyes ablaze with passion. 'Why do you tempt the Lord your God?' he shouted. As soon as Moses said those words, the swirling cloud of Yahweh's presence in the sky above us glowed, and flashes of lightning burst from the cloud. Even though I knew there was no falsehood in my heart, I ducked down with the rest of the crowd. Our cries were swallowed up by the noise of thunder crashing in the sky above us; we cowered before the Lord's presence.

'Tomorrow morning,' Moses continued when the noise had lessened enough for him to be heard, 'you will see the glory of the Lord, for the Lord God will rain bread from heaven.' I steadied my shaking legs and stood up again, watching the crowd for any signs of dissent. But the force of Yahweh's cloud had quashed any signs of aggression and there were none who stood to confront Moses. He continued, 'Go out and gather the bread from heaven early in the morning, and you will know that Yahweh is the Lord your God, who brought you out of Egypt.'

Blank faces looked at each other in bewilderment. Yahweh would rain down bread from heaven? What foolishness was this? Ignoring their confused expressions, Moses went on, 'You will gather it according to each one's need, one omer for each person. None shall be left for the following day. You will eat and be filled, and you will know that He is the Lord. Yahweh has spoken.' Without another word, Moses turned his back on them and strode away in the direction of his tent. Aaron, Eleazar, Ithamar and I followed close behind. A stunned silence fell and, as we left, we heard a buzz of voices all asking the same question: 'How can bread rain down from heaven?'

Eleazar and Ithamar went back to their wives and children, while I escorted Moses and Aaron back to Moses' tent. 'Thank you for standing with me, Joshua. It was good to know that you were there.' Moses patted my shoulder. 'I think you should go and rest now – you look like you could do with some sleep!' In a matter of moments, the awe-inspiring, confrontational leader was gone, and my mild-mannered mentor had returned.

'Yes, Master. Will you have need of me later?'

'No. I will spend the rest of the day in my tent, but I think there might be some interesting things to see in the morning, *nu*?' he said with a twinkle in his eye. '*Shalom*, Joshua.'

'*Shalom*, Master. *Shalom*, Aaron.' I put the tent flap down as I left but, once outside, I paused, unsure of what to do. I felt the need to stay on guard outside Moses' tent for a while, to make sure he was safe, but I didn't want to disobey his instructions. As I stood there, debating what to do, I heard Aaron ask, 'So, how is Yahweh going to rain down bread from heaven?'

'I have no idea.'

My head shot up. I listened to Aaron's confused response. 'But you told them that Yahweh will rain bread from heaven tomorrow morning.'

'Yes, He will.'

'But you do not know how?'

'No.' I heard Moses chuckle. 'As Yahweh's prophet I speak what He tells me to. But that does not mean I always understand what He tells me. I know not what the "bread from heaven" will look like, but I know that Yahweh will fulfil His words.' After a pause, Moses chuckled again and said, 'And I look forward to seeing it.' I could imagine the confusion on Aaron's face – no doubt the same confusion that was etched on my own, and on the faces of those who greeted me when I arrived back at the family tent. Jesher was sitting outside in the sun, his family gathered around him. They had obviously been discussing what had happened and the question on everyone's lips was, 'How will this bread fall from heaven?'

I told them I didn't know.

'But what did Moses say? Did he not tell you what would happen?' Hareph asked.

I hesitated. A surge of loyalty made me reluctant to tell them the truth but, try as I may, I couldn't think of a way not to. 'No,' I said, pouring myself a cup of water to avoid Hareph's stare.

'So, what did he say?' Hareph persisted.

'He said . . .' I sighed. 'Moses does not know what the bread from heaven will look like, or how it will come.'

'Moses does not know?' Hareph wrinkled his nose in disbelief. 'But he was the one who told us that bread would rain down from heaven, yes?' I nodded. 'So how can he not know?'

'I know it sounds like foolishness, but we must trust him.' I felt a strong compulsion to defend this man who had started to occupy such a huge place in my life and heart. 'Moses speaks what Yahweh tells him, but that does not mean he always understands it. The ways of Yahweh are a mystery; His ways are not our ways. Moses obeys, not because he understands, but because he honours Yahweh. Brothers, do not treat him with contempt. Do not reproach him. We must stand with him, and trust that Yahweh will do what He said.'

'But . . .' Hareph continued, but Jesher put his hand up to stop him.

'Joshua is right. Moses is Yahweh's chosen leader. Counsel and sound judgement are his, and we will trust him.' Jesher frowned and cleared his throat. 'Even if we do not understand how this will happen.' We sat in silence, trying to picture in our minds what that could look like. Hareph's shoulder twitched a lot and he muttered under his breath. Azriel stared up at the sky, scowling in concentration, probably trying to imagine how the heavenly bread would appear. Mesha looked at me, shrugged and grinned, and Helah continued weaving palm fronds, her brow creased.

'So . . . bread raining down from heaven,' Mesha broke the silence. 'Hmm. I wonder what that will be like.'

'Will it fall from the skies?' Helah asked, looking up at the blue expanse above. 'How will we catch it, then? In baskets?'

'If it comes with the rain it might be wet,' Leora added. She turned to me. 'Will we need to dry it?'

'I don't know.' I shrugged my shoulders. 'It sounds like foolishness to me. Water from heaven, yes. But bread?' I looked around the circle. 'But if Yahweh has decreed it, then it will be so. I will hold my peace and wait to see what miracle He performs.'

'Mmm,' Jesher nodded, smiling at me.

'I think there is only one thing to be done,' Helah said. 'We need to be ready early in the morning – Moses said so, did he not?' she asked me. 'We must take baskets, and bring the children to help us catch the bread as it falls.'

Shira snorted and rolled her eyes. '*If* it falls,' she muttered but, noting the warning in Jesher's expression, said no more.

We fell quiet, each wrestling with ludicrous images of cakes of bread falling down from the heavens.

19

What is It?

A restless night followed. Sleep was not to be had by many and there were lots of bleary-eyed faces poking out of tent flaps the following morning. Wearily, we dressed and, just before sunrise, we picked up our baskets and traipsed outside into the chill of pre-dawn.

All except Shira.

She refused to stand outside with a basket ready to catch the bread, and made it very clear that she wanted nothing to do with 'this foolishness'. Jesher decided on this occasion not to oppose her, so we left her tidying the tent and went to stand outside, intermittently looking up at the sky, trying not to make eye contact with each other.

'I feel foolish,' Helah whispered, rubbing her arms, and stamping her feet in an effort to try to get warm. 'I must look like a crazy person.'

'You are not the only one, *Ima*,' Yoram whispered back. 'We all look a bit crazy, don't we?' Yawning, he asked me, 'Yoshi, how long do we have to stand here for?'

'I do not know,' I said, shrugging my shoulders. 'Until something happens?'

'*Ima*, do I have to stay?' Arad asked Helah, shivering in the cool of daybreak. 'It is so cold.'

'Yes. We must all be here to help ... uh ... catch the bread. Go and put your mantle on. That will keep you warm while we wait.'

Arad plodded back into the tent. Just then, we heard shouts coming from the outskirts of the camp, sounds of a disturbance.

'What is taking place?' Hareph asked, turning to me with big eyes.

'I will go and find out.' Even though the announcement about the 'bread from heaven' was not of my doing, I couldn't help but feel somewhat responsible. Standing outside our tent waiting for bread to fall from heaven was one thing, but if there was to be any trouble, I did not want my family anywhere near it.

'I will come with you,' Mesha said. Yoram, Joel and Helah joined us, still carrying baskets to catch the bread in.

'Helah, no. Stay behind with the other women,' I protested, but she had one of her stubborn expressions on her face, and I had no time to stand and argue. 'Mesha?' I turned to him for help.

Seeing the expression on his wife's face, Mesha came to the same conclusion. 'I will watch over her,' he said, putting his arm out and bringing her close. We followed the noise and made our way to the outskirts of the camp. To say the scene that greeted us was unexpected would be a gross understatement. It was inexplicable and astonishing and alarming, all at the same time. We saw what looked like a lumpy, cream-coloured rug on the ground, stretching the length of the camp. It was covered with dew and glistened in the light of the rising sun.

We stared in disbelief, mouths gaping. Those who lived on the outer fringes of the camp had seen it first and were already picking some of the 'rug' up, fingering it cautiously. Yoram was the first of our family to pick it up. 'What is it?' he asked.

Mesha looked at it suspiciously, took it from him and sniffed it. 'It looks like snow-capped mountains, but it smells like . . . coriander . . . and honey!' he said, childishly pleased with himself for recognising those flavours. 'Here!' he said, thrusting it at Helah, who backed away as if it was going to bite her. Then she leaned forward tentatively and smelled it.

'Oh! You're right,' she said. 'Coriander and . . . yes, honey!' she said, intrigued. Joel bent down next and picked a piece up, examining it. Unsure what to do, we looked around. People were eating it, just as it was, straight off the ground. I grimaced, shrugged and reluctantly broke a piece off Yoram's portion. It had a slightly flaky texture; I rubbed it between my fingers and watched it crumble and fall to the ground.

'It is a little damp underneath, perhaps from the dew,' I said.

'Yes,' Mesha mumbled. He looked up to the heavens. 'So – not from the sky, but from the dew on the ground, which . . . comes from the heavens?' he said, trying to make sense of what Moses had said, and what he saw before him now.

'Well,' I said, looking around at the masses who had not only started eating it, but were gathering it up with unbridled enthusiasm, laughing among themselves. 'It looks like it is safe to eat. Shall we?' Without hesitation, Joel and Yoram immediately took an enormous bite out of their pieces. Helah nibbled hers, and Mesha and I broke off a small piece and put it in our mouths.

'Oh! It is . . .' Mesha's face lit up in delight as he chewed a second piece.

'Extraordinary!' said Helah. 'The flavours! Mesha, you were right! I can taste honey and coriander and olive oil and . . . some other spices, but I cannot think what they are.' Yoram wasted no time on talking. He gathered more and stuffed it into his already overflowing mouth.

'Whoa, Yoram, slow down!' said Mesha, laughing.

'But it tastes so good!' Yoram said, spitting crumbs out as he talked.

'It is wonderful!' Joel agreed, shoving more in his mouth. He and Yoram had become firm friends over the last few weeks since our talk, and it brought much joy to my heart to see them laughing together. Joel had not only come out of the cage of his captivity, but was reclaiming the years which he had lost during that time, and there was a sense of childlike fun and spontaneity about him which was endearing.

'Yoram! Joel! No! You will make yourselves sick,' Helah said, looking around self-consciously. She needn't have bothered – no one was looking at us. They were all far too busy gathering up the flaky substance by the handful, stuffing it in their mouths and loading their baskets with pieces of the 'creamy rug'.

I watched what was happening. Although I was as thankful as the next person for this unexpected blessing, my heart was troubled when I thought of the events of the last few days. It never ceased to amaze me how quickly Yahweh's people turned from anger and rebellion to celebration and devotion. 'We are false-hearted,' I thought as I watched them laughing and chatting among themselves. 'We are a false-hearted people, running this way and that, like a wayward goat that turns its back on its master and runs to the one who offers it food. Teach us to honour Your name, my Lord. Unite our hearts to fear You. Teach us not to cast off restraint, but to walk in Your ways.'

Helah was also watching the people around her, a smile plastered all over her face. Turning to a woman near her, she asked, 'What is this called?'

'I do not know.'

'So what should we name it?'

The woman shrugged, intent on gathering it up. 'What is it?'

'Well, it is . . . uh . . . I do not know. What is it?'

'Truly!' replied the woman. 'That is what it is! "What is it?"' she said, laughing.

'But . . .' Helah looked at her, confused. 'We cannot call it "What is it"!'

'What would you call it, then?' the woman asked.

'Well . . . I know not what it is.'

'There you go!' The woman roared with laughter again, put another piece in her mouth, and turned away to continue gathering more of the 'What is it?'. Helah turned to me and pulled a face, shrugging before bending down to gather some more 'What is it?' (or 'manna', as it came to be known in the Hebrew tongue).

That day was one I would not forget. I would always remember the sight of that creamy rug covering the desert floor, nestled on a blanket of dew, sparkling in the light of the early morning sun. Even in my last days, as an old man living in Timnath-Serah, I still remember the taste of the manna on my tongue, and the flavours of coriander and honey still make my mouth water.

I looked up at the cloudy canopy overhead. It seemed brighter than usual. Spears of sunshine pierced it, glittering shafts of light that beamed down from the heavens. I soaked up the uninhibited beauty of that moment and, as I watched, I saw the movement of wings in the canopy, like a flock of birds playing a game of catch within the cloud's form. It must have been my imagination, but I felt sure I heard the faint sound of laughter echoing within the clouds. It made my heart glad.

'Yahweh, You are faithful to Your people,' I prayed silently. 'You have not forgotten us. You will never forsake us.'

I spent time with Moses that day and told him how conflicted my heart was. My joy at seeing the miracle that Yahweh had wrought felt tainted by the knowledge of how fickle our people were. His heart suffered the same. It was good to know I was not alone in that struggle and, by the time I left his tent, I felt lighter. Our evening meal was a culinary adventure! The women experimented with different ways of cooking the manna; they ground it and crushed it, mixed it with dates and spices to make cakes, and formed herb-encrusted bread loaves with it. We feasted to our hearts' content and the sounds of merriment echoed throughout the camp that night.

I watched Joel as he ate, delighting in what I saw. Gone was the sullen, withdrawn captive, and in his place was a young man full of hope and joy. I pondered the ways of the Lord as I watched him laughing and joking with Yoram, and talking with Azriel. His relationship with his father was restored and the whole family had witnessed the effect that it had on both of them. I thought back to that day in the acacia grove. I had been part of a miracle, as if the hand of Yahweh had reached down through me and pulled Joel out of darkness and into a place of hope and light.

Joel looked up and saw me watching him. 'Joshua? There is something you would say?' I hesitated. There was something I wanted to ask, but I was unsure whether I should. I decided to risk it. 'I was wondering if you still have the dream that used to come to you each night.'

Joel paused and then smiled at me. 'No. I have not been haunted by fears in the night since that day we talked at Elim.' His countenance was clear and unclouded; I could see no trace of his former anguish. Truly, this was a miracle! *He* was a miracle!

'Joel, will you play for us?' I asked. 'Surely, this is a night for music and celebration, *nu*?' The others sitting around joined in the call for music, so Joel jumped up and went to fetch his reed pipe. Within minutes, the sounds of celebration rang out as Joel put his pipe to his lips. I had heard him play before, but never like this! When he played in times past, he sat hunched over with his eyes closed, and the tunes were melancholy and mournful, as a lament for the dead.

This was no lament for the dead, it was a festival for the living! Joel stood, tapping his foot in time to the music as he played. The notes were crystal clear, jubilant, and their sound was an unmistakable call to merrymaking. As part of his apprenticeship with Bezalel, Joel had fashioned a sturdy wooden frame for an animal skin to be stretched over, so Yoram played along on the hand-crafted drum as Joel piped. The joyful beat of their music was a summons we could not ignore. One by one, we stood and joined in the dance.

Clapping and whooping, we formed circles around Joel and Yoram, leaping and kicking, interlocking arms and joining hands. Even Shira joined in the dance, and Hareph, with his two left feet, managed to keep in time – almost! Jesher was persuaded to join in, despite his usual protestations about old bones, and I smiled to see him hopping and waving his arms in the air. Our neighbours stood up and started clapping along to the beat and, within moments, they joined us. Two circles turned into six, seven, then eight, and we feasted and celebrated together into the night.

For me, it was a double celebration. I rejoiced with a thankful heart in the miracle of the manna that Yahweh had provided for His people. But I also celebrated the miracle of the young man who stood before me, utterly transformed. When our dancing was over, Joel came to me, breathless but elated, and said, 'Once my music was a cry of pain from my heart, but now Yahweh calls forth songs of joy from me!'

20

Shabbat

The next morning, the whole nation of Israel was up early to greet the dawn, in the eager hope that there would be more manna; sure enough, there was! The glistening, creamy carpet was ready to be harvested, and this time there was no hesitation. Baskets full of the 'what is it' were collected in no time, and the sounds of laughter and celebration reverberated through the camp once again.

Moses had me walk through the camp with him that morning on his way to meet with the elders. Now that their bellies were full and their wives happy, they were quite amenable to Moses' leadership, so the meeting was harmonious and uneventful. Moses was able to tell them Yahweh's instructions for the new laws about the keeping of Shabbat and they, in turn, would communicate them to the leaders of families in their tribes. I was given leave to tell my family the news, so I returned home. However, as soon as I neared the tent, Helah and Eglah ran to greet me.

'Were you there?' Helah asked me, grasping my arm. Her eyes were wide and she wore a mischievous grin on her face.

'Where?' I asked.

'With Moses – this morning.' She looked around to make sure no one was near, and lowered her voice. 'Is it true? You know ... what happened this morning, when Saadia met him?'

'How is it you know about that?' I was astounded at how fast news travelled, but then, I shouldn't have been surprised. After all, nothing is private among the tents of the nomad.

Helah and Eglah looked at each other and giggled. 'We just met Abigail and she told us what happened. She said Saadia did not want to waste any of the manna that she and Yacob collected yesterday.' Raising her eyebrows, Helah whispered, 'They collected a *lot*, far too much for two of them to eat – you know Saadia, she is not one to scorn an unexpected blessing, is she?' Eglah rolled her eyes in response; Helah continued, 'Abigail said Saadia made some cakes with her leftover manna, put them in a clay pot and wrapped it in a cloth to keep them airtight overnight. She wanted to give them to Moses because,' she cleared her throat and put on a nasal tone, 'everyone knows I bake the best bread cakes, and I am sure Moses does not get to eat good food like mine very often, *nu*?'

I frowned and bit my lip, struggling to keep a straight face. Helah's imitation of Saadia was very accurate! Eglah put her hand over her mouth to suppress a giggle as Helah told me what they had heard. It was true. As Moses and I walked through the camp this morning, Saadia (who had obviously been waiting for us to pass by), stopped us and told Moses she had 'something special' for him. She handed him a pot but, when he opened it, he found odorous cakes that were full of maggots.

The older I grew, the more I found that people seemed to want to tell me their troubles and share the secrets of their heart. It was not something I encouraged. The more secrets you know, the more they weigh you down, like the pack donkeys that the Bedouin traders used to carry their goods. Their beasts were always loaded down with bags and bundles, and looked so weary. No, I had no wish to be loaded with other people's burdens, and yet they seemed to share them with me anyway. I was not a man who longed to know the details of other people's lives and I detested tongues that wagged in the way of the talebearer. Perhaps that is why people shared their hearts with me – because they knew their secrets would be safe?

Saadia's story, however, was not something I had been told in confidence, or happened to hear about – I was there. I saw it. Helah and Eglah seemed to know the details already, so I wouldn't be telling them anything they didn't already know. I didn't see how I could deny it.

'Uh ... yes, that is true,' I mumbled.

'No!' said Helah. 'Oh, the shame,' she said, covering her mouth with her hand to try to stop the giggles from escaping. 'Poor Saadia!'

'Poor Moses, in truth! Oy!' Eglah shook her head in sympathy. 'What did he do?'

'He did not know what to do.' I could no longer hide my smiles. 'He thanked Saadia, muttered something about already having broken his fast that morning, gave the pot back to her, and we went on our way. He was much discomfited.' I grinned at them. 'We have not spoken about it since, and I doubt we will.'

'Word will spread, though,' Eglah told me. 'Abigail saw the whole thing, and you know what *that* means.'

Helah made a face and nodded her head slowly. 'Everyone is going to know about it before very long. I wonder if Shira knows.'

'Do not tell her!' I urged, grabbing Helah's arm. 'I beg of you – Eglah, you too. We must keep silent. Shira must not hear it from our lips, *nu*?' I could see Helah weighing up the satisfaction of telling Shira about Saadia's shame, against the unfavourable outcome of being the one to tell her. She had been on the other end of Saadia's sharp tongue before and an opportunity like this was obviously very tempting. She and Eglah exchanged glances, then she sighed. 'Be at peace, Yoshi. She will not hear it from us.'

'But why did she keep the manna overnight?' Eglah asked. 'Moses told us only to take what we needed – and now we know why.'

'You know Saadia. She always thinks she knows better than everyone else. Even Moses!' Helah chuckled to herself, then turned to me. 'Joshua, why have you returned so early? Has Moses no need of you today?'

'I was with him this morning when he met with the elders. Yahweh has given Moses a new law which he taught them. They are to explain it to the leaders in their tribes, they to their families, and so on. He gave me leave to come and tell the family.'

'What is the law about?' Eglah asked.

'Shabbat.'

'Rest? Yahweh has given us a law about rest?'

'He has,' I replied, 'and it is a good law. It will bring health and life to our people.' I gestured to the tent. 'Come, gather the family and I will make known what Yahweh has commanded.' We sat under the shady covering of our tent, from Jesher right down to little Shallum, who sat in Helah's lap, playing with some strands of her hair. I told them what Yahweh had commanded: that we should work for six days but, on the seventh day, no work was to be done. The seventh day was holy to the Lord, and it was to be a day of rest.

'A day of rest?' Hareph's shoulder twitched and he cocked his head to one side.

'Yes.'

He screwed his face up in confusion. 'Every seventh day, we are to do no work?'

'Yes. From sunset on the sixth day to sunset on the seventh day, we rest.'

'Mmm.' Jesher peered at me from under his bushy eyebrows and scratched his beard. Blank faces with furrowed brows stared back at me. The Egyptians held various religious festivals throughout the year where they feasted and celebrated, but we were never allowed such luxuries. As slaves in Egypt, we worked day in and day out. Every day was like the one before: we rose with the sun and worked until midday, when we were allowed a short break. We continued in the afternoon, finishing when the sun started to set. The next day we rose with the sun and the cycle was repeated. The concept of having a whole day off with no work was incongruous and, for some, almost disturbing.

We had never had a day off. Ever.

We didn't know what that was. We didn't know how to rest.

'So ... what do we do, then, on the seventh day?' Mesha asked.

'We rest.' I waited for smiles and signs of excitement. None came.

'Uh ... so ... how do we ... ?' Mesha looked at me, bemused.

'Mesha!' I blurted. 'We rest!' I looked around the circle, hoping someone had understood and could help me explain. Nothing. I struggled on. 'We sit and talk, tell stories, sleep, break bread, make music, take time to ponder and think.'

'What do we think on?' Mesha asked.

'Whatever you want to think on!' I snapped.

'What about the women?' Azriel asked, glancing at his wife. Leora raised her eyebrows and shrugged. All eyes were back on me.

'What about the women?' I repeated the question.

'Yes. Must the women rest too?' He looked at me with suspicion. I felt like I was on trial, being charged for a crime I had not committed. This was not how I thought the conversation would go.

I smiled at Azriel and Leora. 'Yes, the women must also rest on Shabbat.'

Shira sniffed. 'We cannot rest,' she announced. 'There is always work for women to do. We must cook and clean, wash the clothes, fetch water ...'

'Cooking and cleaning are forbidden, and there is to be no gathering of wood or carrying of burdens on Shabbat.'

'That is foolishness,' Shira glared at me. 'What kind of a law is it which forbids a woman from looking after her family?'

'It is the law of Yahweh,' I replied. Out of all my adopted family, Shira was the only one who had never welcomed me or accepted me into the family. When we disagreed on certain matters, I would usually defer to her, but on this matter of Shabbat, I could not. 'Yahweh has spoken,' I said, looking directly into her eyes, 'and anyone who profanes the Shabbat will be cut off from among His people and put to death.'

There was a stunned silence. Shira gawped at me. 'You . . . you . . .' she stuttered. 'You dishonour me in my own home?'

I held her gaze. 'It is not my desire to dishonour you; the Lord forbid that I would stretch out my hand against you. But I must declare the words of Yahweh. He will not be mocked.' Silence fell. Hareph's shoulder twitched, but he said nothing. Even the children were quiet; most of the family looked down at the ground. None of them looked directly at me, or at Shira, apart from Jesher. He gazed first at his wife, and then at me. After a while, he cleared his throat, and spoke.

'So be it. We walk in the ways of Yahweh. We will learn how to rest and we will honour the Lord, and keep the Shabbat.' Muffled calls of 'amen' echoed around the circle. Shira bristled, but remained silent. 'Tell us more about Shabbat, Joshua,' Jesher said. 'What did Moses say?'

'That it is a sign between Yahweh and the children of Israel throughout the generations, a perpetual covenant between Yahweh and His people. Shabbat is holy unto the Lord.'

'Oy!' Hareph looked up at me, his eyes alight with revelation. 'Yes! Remember the account of creation! Yahweh created the heavens and the earth in six days and on the seventh day he rested. So . . .' he turned to Jesher, 'when we keep Shabbat, we will be walking in the very footsteps of Yahweh?'

'It seems so, yes,' Jesher smiled at his son-in-law. 'We will be walking the ancient paths, *nu*? We must not despise the ancient ways.'

'But this . . . this knowledge is wonderful! Our hearts must make diligent search for the thoughts of Yahweh on Shabbat, yes, *Abba*?'

'Yes indeed, my son,' Jesher agreed, looking at Hareph with great fondness. Hareph had not been Jesher's first choice of husband for

Eglah but, when his offer of betrothal had been received, Eglah begged her father to accept it. It seemed she saw something in Hareph that others could not see. She saw beyond his awkward exterior to the kind, intelligent heart within. Jesher had spent days pondering what to do and, after nine sunsets had come and gone, he gave his consent – not because he fully believed that Hareph was the right choice of husband for Eglah, but because he trusted his daughter. In time, his trust in her was rewarded, and Jesher began to see the treasure that lay beneath the surface of his son-in-law.

Shira never did.

'Does this mean we cannot mould clay at the wheel on Shabbat?' Azriel asked. He did not usually see things in the way that Hareph did.

'Yes,' I replied.

'Or gather wood for the fire?' he continued. I nodded. 'Pick fruit or vegetables, or take the flock out to graze?'

'None of these are permitted, and we are not to walk long distances on Shabbat.'

Leora joined in the discussion. 'But, if we are forbidden to cook on Shabbat, what will we eat and when will we milk the goats?'

'Everything must be done on the sixth day, in preparation for Shabbat. Extra water is to be fetched, the goats milked and livestock fed, fuel gathered for the fire, and food prepared for the following day.'

'What about the manna?' Helah asked. 'Are we permitted to collect manna on the morning of the seventh day?'

'No, that is counted as work. But Yahweh has instructed us to collect twice as much manna on the morning of the sixth day, enough for the following day.'

'But it would be rotten by the next morning, would it not?' Helah said, then, avoiding Shira's narrowing eyes, added, 'At least, that is what I have heard.'

I moved on. 'Yahweh is good. Every day, the manna must be eaten on the same day, or it will spoil, but the manna that is gathered on the sixth day will stay fresh until the end of Shabbat.'

Hareph stared at me in awe. 'Yahweh's ways are truly a wonder. Blessed be His name!' He raised his arms up to the heavens and declared, 'Blessed be the name of the Lord forever!'

'And blessed be His children gathered here!' Jesher joined in. 'May He satisfy us with long life and withhold no good thing from His people. And . . .' he added, leaning forward, and pointing his finger at us one by one, 'may He teach us all how to rest and cause us to delight in Shabbat!'

21

Ima

'So, how was your first Shabbat?' Eleazar asked me. 'Did you and your family rest?'

Eleazar and I had spent a fair amount of time together in recent weeks and I enjoyed his company. As Moses' nephew and Aaron's son, he was frequently with Moses, who must have thought we were a good partnership, because he had started sending us out together to speak to witnesses of a fight, find out the truth behind a dispute, or convey messages. Initially, our conversations had been about camp life, or the business of the day. More recently, however, I had begun to trust him with the deeper issues of my heart. I knew him to be a fervent follower of Yahweh and there was a warmth in his brown eyes that hinted of a hidden depth. He had become something of a confidant to me.

We had been walking all morning, delivering messages to various leaders, and it was nearing midday, so we drew aside to refresh ourselves and sit in the shade of a large acacia tree.

'Yes, we did rest,' I said, taking a mouthful of water from my skin and swallowing it with relish. 'Although not all of the family embraced Shabbat like I thought they would.'

'No?' Eleazar seemed surprised. 'I would have thought that a day of rest would be a blessing for our people.'

'I thought likewise, but it was not so. She . . . uh . . . said it was foolishness, making a law that forbids a woman to look after her family.'

'She?'

I hesitated, reluctant to speak ill of any of my family, but angst had been building in me for some time and it would be a relief to talk of it. I knew I could trust this man with the gentle eyes who sat by my side, so I told him. 'Shira.'

'Ah, your *ima*.'

'I must confess, I do not call her that. I cannot call her that. I have never called her my *ima*. She is not *ima* to me.' Eleazar's kind eyes looked at me and he nodded, but didn't speak. 'On his deathbed, my *abba* joined my hands with Jesher in covenant, and I called him *Abba* from that time onward. He has been a good *abba* to me, embracing me as part of his family – as his son. He is my *abba* now. But I cannot bring myself to call Shira *ima*. I do my best to honour her for Jesher's sake, but she will never be a mother to me.'

'Tell me of your *ima*. You never speak of her. What was she like?'

He was right. I never spoke of her to anyone. It was as though to speak of her would besmirch the memories I had of her and lessen their worth. But I found that, for the first time in a long while, I wanted to talk about her. I wanted Eleazar to know who she was, to hear her story – and mine.

'She died in childbirth when I was still young. My father told me when I was older that she had not been able to carry a child through to birth. Four children had been lost to her in the womb before I was born, so great was their rejoicing when my mother carried and gave birth to a baby boy.' I looked at Eleazar and smiled. 'My father shared with me several times over the years his joy at hearing my first cries; loud, lusty cries from strong lungs, he said. Apparently, not only was I a healthy baby, but I was also a hungry one! I thrived at my *ima*'s breast and grew quickly. They named me Joshua because the Lord God had saved me. I was the first fruit of her womb, the fulfilment of their union.'

Eleazar looked down, rubbing the fingers on one hand with his other hand. 'Your story gives me hope, my friend.'

'How so?'

'We lost our first child. Just before we left Egypt. Bathshua was unable to carry past her fourth month.' He looked up at me. 'But perhaps Yahweh will smile upon her womb, as He did with your mother, peace be upon her.'

'I pray so. I will beseech the Lord God on your behalf.'

'Thank you. I would like to have children . . . lots of children, to carry on my great name!' he grinned at me. 'Were there others in your family?'

'No. A little over two years after I was born, my mother was found to be with child again. She carried the child well, but the birth was a difficult one, and both she and my baby brother died.'

Eleazar's face filled with pain. 'I am so sorry. That must have been grievous to your *abba*.'

'It was. I was too young to understand very much, but Jesher was my *abba*'s companion and brought much comfort to him during that time. It was expected that he would marry again, but he never did. He never recovered from losing my mother; his love for her was so strong, he could not contemplate the thought of taking another wife.'

I sat up and leaned my forearms on my bent knees. 'So there were only two of us. Father and son, left alone to navigate life as slaves in Egypt. And we did. My father gave me the love of both a father and a mother. There was much love in his heart for me; I believe he saw in me the likeness of his wife. He taught me the ways of Yahweh and I learned that to be a son of Nun was to be associated with honour and dependability. He was held in high regard by all who met him, and for that I was grateful, especially when I found myself alone after his death.'

Eleazar spoke in earnest. 'Your *abba* lives on through you, Joshua. You are his legacy. You have been greatly blessed to have had such an *abba* to teach you the ways of Yahweh. And now, you have an *abba* in Jesher. He is a man of upright heart and great wisdom. I have seen how he looks at you – there is much love in his heart for you.'

'And in mine for him.' I sighed. 'I only hope that one day it will be so with Shira. I have tried to keep the peace, honour her, even show love to her, but she sees me only as another mouth to feed, an imposter. Never as her son.'

'Do not give up hope, my friend! One day she may see the heart inside of you. Your hearts may yet be joined together!'

I did not hold much hope in my heart for that. Even though I had not known my own mother for long, I still remembered her beautiful, big hazel eyes brimming over with love, and I could still recall the feeling of being held, safe in her arms.

Whatever Shira was to me, she was not that. She would never be that. She could never be my *ima*.

22

Darkness

My favourite time of day was fast approaching – twilight! We had delivered all the messages and the sun was setting, casting its golden glow over the camp. Shortly, the alluring cloud of Yahweh's presence would begin to sparkle with tendrils of flame, and the billowing pillar of cloud would transform into a breath-taking tower of fire. A sense of anticipation filled me. I increased my pace, lengthening my strides as we walked through the camp on our way back to Moses.

'Oysh! Joshua, slow down!' Eleazar panted, struggling to keep up with me. His strides were not as long as mine. 'What is your haste?'

I turned to him. 'Forgive me, I did not realise I was walking so fast. My thoughts were elsewhere.'

Eleazar stopped for a moment, grabbed my arm, and bent over, trying to catch his breath. 'Are you late for something?' he gasped.

'Yes,' I said, then immediately second guessing myself, turned to Eleazar. 'Well, no.'

'So, which is it? Yes or no?' Eleazar looked up at me, screwing up his eyes in confusion.

'Well . . .' I hesitated. 'It's just that . . .' I looked at Eleazar, trying to decide how much to say. Realising it would be pointless and probably rather difficult to avoid the truth, I breathed out and looked back towards the direction we had come from. Placing my hands on my hips, I said, 'There is no one waiting for me as such, but I . . . I long to watch the cloud transform into fire. I have not missed a night yet and I do not want to start now.'

I turned to face Eleazar. 'I like to be alone when Yahweh's cloud transforms, to look upon the cloud and fire and be still. I am . . . I am jealous of that time, Eleazar. It is holy unto Yahweh. It is when

I sense His presence the strongest. It has been so ever since the first night and my longing for His presence does not lesson – it grows stronger each time.' I studied his face for any signs of ridicule or derision. 'Does that sound foolish?'

He returned my gaze in silence before responding. 'No.' He shook his head. 'It does not sound foolish.' His face broke into a smile. 'My friend, my heart bears witness with yours.'

I breathed a sigh of relief. 'It does? You understand my heart in this matter?'

'I do.' Eleazar nodded. 'I feel the same. I feel the touch of Yahweh in the cloud and fire. He reaches into my very soul and I know Him there.'

'Amen!' I agreed. 'It is good to know that you also sense Him in the cloud. I have had to guard my mouth and restrain my lips, because other men cannot fathom it. They cannot understand what I see. Jesher's son, Mesha, he is a good man, and my companion since we were young. He knows my heart and I trust him, but he cannot comprehend my longing for Yahweh's presence.' I gave Eleazar a lopsided smile. 'He says I am obsessed with the cloud and maybe I am.'

'What better obsession can there be?' Eleazar asked, grasping my upper arm. 'I too have longed to find a brother who shares my passion for Yahweh. So, we will be obsessed together, *nu*?' I grasped Eleazar's arm in return and we nodded in agreement. Turning back to the pathway through the camp, we walked for a short while, sharing our experiences of the presence, all the time looking up to the cloud. After only a few minutes, however, we noticed the first familiar flashes of flame flickering within the cloud.

'No!' I groaned. 'It is starting! We will not make it back in time, even if we run all the way.'

'You speak true,' Eleazar responded. 'There is still too far to go. Shall we tarry here and watch?' He pointed to a nearby clearing. 'We can rest over there, be still, and let our prayers come before Him.'

We walked over to where a rocky outcrop stood proudly amid the mural of tents and campfires, by a grove of trees. We sat, each on our own rocky seat, and fixed our gaze on the cloud, soaking in the wonder of Yahweh's creativity and the glory of His Presence. Neither of us said a word. I felt comfortable with Eleazar and my heart was at peace sharing this moment with him. My attention was focused solely on the evolving cloud until I felt an icy chill down my back. I shivered. A strange sense of darkness shadowed my soul, then I felt them.

Eyes.

Watching me. Boring into me, drilling into my thoughts.

From out of the grove, a sinister voice sliced through the sweet stillness of the moment. 'Why do you stare at it? It is just a cloud.'

I spun round, my heart thumping in fright. Peering into the deepening gloom of dusk, I saw a man slumped against the side of a tree on the edge of the grove. One leg out in front of him and one knee drawn up, he lay slumped on his side, his sizeable belly protruding over the leather belt that strained against it.

'*Shalom*,' I muttered, swallowing the lump that had materialised in my throat.

The man didn't move or return my greeting. Continuing to glower at us, he repeated his question. 'Why do you stare at it like that? It is just a cloud.' One corner of his mouth lifted up in a sneer as he scanned our faces for a reaction.

I frowned and shook my head. 'No, my friend. It is not just a cloud; it is the cloud of Yahweh's presence – the sign that He is with us and leads us on our journey towards Canaan.'

The man grunted and pointed to Eleazar. 'You – do you believe this too?'

Eleazar, who up until that moment had been staring at the man, put his shoulders back and sat up straighter. He stammered a reply. 'Yes. Yes, I do.'

The man stared at us, his piercing eyes boring into us, before grunting and hauling himself to his feet. Wheezing and coughing, he brushed the dust and twigs off his robe and stood, arms crossed, still staring. We also stood up and stared back at him in silence, unsure of what to say or do. I was painfully aware that this unexpected, and very unwelcome, encounter was robbing me of the joy of seeing the cloud's transformation. My limbs seemed to have lost their strength; I felt unable to move, like an animal trapped in the presence of a hunter with no means of escape. The man lumbered towards us and stopped a couple of feet from where we stood. Leaning forward, he leered at us and said, 'There are other powers, you know . . . besides Yahweh. So many mysteries that you know nothing of. But I know.' He pointed to himself, prodding his chest several times. 'I saw much during my time in Egypt.'

I looked into the man's eyes and saw only darkness. They were dull and dead, and yet they seemed to have a hypnotic power which pulled me towards him. I blinked and looked at the ground in an effort to break eye contact, but I found it hard to resist the lure of the man's gaze, and glanced up. 'How do you know of such things?'

The man smirked at us and replied, 'I worked in the household of a very influential Egyptian, from a young age. I worked my way up through the ranks of his household, year after year, until I became the master's personal manservant.' Looking at us to make sure he had our attention, he continued, 'My master served Pharoah himself as priest of the gods of Egypt.' The man stepped back and crossed his arms again, watching to see what impact his announcement would have on us. I knew I should say something. I tried to speak, but words would not form on my tongue. My mind was in a fog.

'Moses is not the only man who can perform signs, you know.' Pointing his finger in our faces, he growled, 'My master did wonders in the courts of Pharoah. I was there when Moses and Aaron came before Pharoah. I stood by my master's side and watched Aaron throw down his rod. I saw it take on the form of a serpent . . . and my master, with the other holy men, performed the same magic in the sight of everyone there.' He watched us closely to see our reaction.

I could stay silent no longer. 'Yahweh, give me the words to say,' I prayed silently. Stepping forward to take up the challenge, I looked the man in the face. 'Moses and Aaron do not do magic tricks like Egyptian sorcerers. They perform miracles in the holy name of Yahweh and by His power alone.' Before the man could rebuff me, I pressed on. 'And if you were there, then you will also know that Aaron's serpent swallowed up the serpents of Pharoah's sorcerers before changing back into the staff that Moses now carries – the same staff which he used to separate the waters of the Red Sea so Yahweh's people could cross over into this land.'

The man glared at me, then shrugged and sniffed. 'I did not say that Yahweh had no power. I said He is not the only one who has power.' Changing the subject, he went on, 'They conjured fire, you know – my masters. I saw it with my own eyes. Out of nowhere, fire appeared – they held it in their hands, but it did not burn them.'

I smiled. My mind was clearing. Words were quickened to me, so I turned towards the centre of the camp and pointed to the fire. 'My God creates a tower of fire every night, to bring warmth and light to His chosen people.'

Eleazar had been watching the sparring match between the man and I, but before another challenge could be thrown out, he turned to him and said, 'May we ask your name?'

The man paused. His eyes narrowed and he whispered, 'My name? You want to know my name?'

'Yes. My name is El . . .'

'I know who you are,' the man barked, 'and you,' he said, jabbing his head in my direction. 'My name . . . my name is Chisisi.'

'*Shalom*, Chisisi,' I greeted him.

'Chisisi?' Eleazar repeated, his lips pursed. 'That is not a name I am familiar with. What tribe are you from?'

'I am of the tribe of Simeon. My ancestral name is Shimea, Shimea ben Ani, but my masters changed my name to Chisisi after I had been in their service for some years.' Leaning forward, he whispered, 'It is an Egyptian name meaning "secret". They named me so because I became the keeper of many, *many* secrets.' Shimea leered at us and we drew back. I felt a shudder go through my body, and was overcome by a sudden yearning to bathe, to cleanse myself of what felt like an invisible slime covering both my body and soul.

Shimea continued. 'I was well thought of in the priest's household, despite not being an Egyptian. They treated me well and showed me favour, even teaching me their ways. I was given many privileges that others did not have. I ate good food and had my own quarters, away from the other slaves. I had no wife – that was not permitted – but I had no need of one. I had everything I needed.'

I was about to respond when Eleazar interjected, 'Shimea . . .'

'Chisisi!' he barked, glaring at Eleazar.

'Yes.' Eleazar acknowledged him, but proceeded without calling him by his Egyptian name. 'If you were so contented with your life in the priest's house, why did you leave Egypt? Why did you not stay in his service?'

'I would have if it had been my choice. I wanted to stay, but they would not allow it. The night when the first-born died, my master's son was taken by your God. His grief and rage were terrible to behold.' He shook his head. 'When the dawn broke I was called into his chambers and told to leave. They no longer wanted any of "my kind" in their service. I left within the hour, taking with me as much as I could carry.'

He spoke with raw emotion and, for the first time since our conversation started, I saw in Shimea's eyes a glimmer of heartfelt vulnerability. Pain and rejection flickered briefly but, within seconds, the dark veil was once again drawn over his countenance and the arrogant, mocking persona returned. Crossing his arms in a defensive pose, he scowled. 'And that is how I now find myself traipsing across this accursed desert wasteland in the company of a pitiful displaced people, forced to journey with them to who knows where for who knows how long.' Shimea scowled. 'Well, I must not keep you, must I?' he said, feigning obeisance. 'I am sure men of importance like yourselves will have lots of . . . important things to do, hmm?'

We stared at him, then glanced at each other.

'It has been . . . enlightening talking to you, but now I must take my leave.' He mimicked an indiscernible bow of the head, turned and skulked off. Looking back over his shoulder, he hissed, 'I'm sure our paths will cross again,' and disappeared into the darkness.

23

Evil Eye

'Master, I have not encountered darkness like this before. In the Egyptians, yes, I saw it many times, but never in one of our people. How can this be?' Eleazar and I had come straight to Moses after our encounter with Shimea. We were troubled and shaken, so he sat us down, gave us a drink, and listened without interrupting as we told him what had happened. Only when we had finished telling him our story did he ask questions.

'What did you say the man's name was?'

'Shimea ben Ani, of the tribe of Simeon,' I answered, 'but he goes by the name his Egyptian masters gave him – Chisisi.'

'It means "secret",' Eleazar added. 'He said they named him so because he was the keeper of many secrets.' He grimaced. 'Do you know of him?'

'No. No, I have not heard of him, but that is hardly surprising, since it sounds like he lived a life very separate from our people.' Moses leaned forward and rested his forearms on his legs, looking down at the ground. Silence fell. 'Tell me,' he said, after some time. 'Tell me about Shimea's eyes.' Lifting his head, he looked directly at me. 'What did you see in his eyes?'

'They were . . . dead. Dull and so dark. Like looking into a bottomless pit from where there is no return.'

Moses nodded.

'They were also strangely hypnotic – mesmerising, shrouded with evil,' I explained, struggling to find the right words to describe what I had felt. 'I struggled to look away. It was as if his eyes were pulling me deeper into that thick darkness.' Moses looked at me intently and I realised how foolish my words must seem. I shrugged. 'I probably sound like a madman but, in truth, that is what I saw.'

Moses spoke with a clear, even tone. 'You are not a madman, Joshua. I have seen what you describe. I saw it every day, as a young man growing up in Egypt. I saw it in the eyes of the priests and those who served in the temples, in the eyes of the "holy men", and even in the eyes of my own Egyptian father.' He looked first at me and then at Eleazar. 'It is a darkness that fills those who worship the gods of this world, those who prostrate themselves before idols made with human hands. It is a darkness that comes upon those who do all manner of evil in the name of their gods. It controls them, takes over their soul. It is seen through their eyes.'

Moses leaned forward and stared at me. My heart caught within me and I held my breath, fearing what he was about to say. I wanted to look away, to stop him from seeing the sin that must surely be laid bare before him. But I could not. So I stared back at him as he spoke on. 'If you want to know what is in a man's heart, look into his eyes. Our eyes mirror what lies beneath. They expose the deep desires of his heart.' What could he see? Could he see iniquity in me? Did he see the failings and shame of my past?

Moses sighed, then, and muttered, 'I had hoped never to see that darkness reflected in a man's eyes again, but it seems it has followed us.' Was he referring to Shimea? Or me? Or both of us? I felt lightheaded and made myself breathe out, then in, out and in, slowly but steadily. Moses spoke again. I wished he wouldn't. I wished I could walk out of his tent, away from this talk of evil and darkness. But I couldn't. 'Where it is found in one, there is always more. That darkness spreads, like a plague upon the earth . . .'

It was unbearable. I felt beads of sweat on my forehead. Why did he not just say it? Why not just accuse me and be done with it? I could not wait any more. I could hide no longer. I had to speak out. But, before I could find the words, Eleazar spoke. 'Moses, how did you stay free from that darkness? How is it that this evil did not grip your soul when you lived in Egypt for so long?'

Moses thought for a bit and then smiled at his nephew. 'Forty years in the desert looking after sheep goes a long way to clearing the debris from a man's heart.' Eleazar and Moses shared a welcome moment of humour. I faked a smile and looked at the ground again. 'My father-in-law, Jethro, helped me through that time. When I first met him, and his daughter Zipporah, I was . . . uh,' Moses snorted, 'anything but a prince of Egypt. I was a desert wretch – no home, no possessions, no idea who I was or what I was supposed to do with my life. But he took me in, embraced me as one of his own. I owe much of who I am to him – to his patience, his loving rebukes, and his teachings.' Moses smiled to himself. 'Jethro is a man of pure heart and such wisdom! He became a father to me. The father I never had.' Standing up, he stretched. 'Then, of course, he become my father by marriage when he gave Zipporah to me, and she bore me sons.' A wistful expression came over Moses' features. 'Aah, I miss them more than I can say. But, when the time is right, I will send for them. What a day that will be, *nu*?' He bent forward and grasped us both by the shoulder, nodding and smiling. I was so confused. He hadn't judged me. Had he? Or perhaps he hadn't seen falsehood in my heart.

'So what do we do about this darkness?' Eleazar asked. 'About Shimea?'

'Mmm. We watch and wait – and we pray. Yahweh will show us what to do.'

'Amen,' we agreed. We stood up and made ready to go. I couldn't wait to leave.

'*Shalom*, Moses,' Eleazar said.

'*Shalom*, Eleazar. God be with you.'

'*Shalom*, Master,' I said.

'Joshua, can you stay for a moment? I have something to ask you.' I froze. He had seen it. I braced myself for the accusation. I would not deny it. I could not deny it. 'Sit,' he said. I would rather have stood and faced it like a man, but I sat down and focused on my hands.

'Joshua, what happened today changes everything.' I nodded, but said nothing. 'Our enemy is among us and we must be vigilant. I have heard many rumours over the past few days of trouble brewing in the camp, and now this darkness that you and Eleazar have told me about. There are troublemakers among us and they are stirring the people up, turning them against me. Joshua . . .' I braced myself and stared directly into his eyes. 'I must have good men around me if we are to defeat this darkness. Men I can trust. Men whose eyes are full of light. Men who can discern the darkness that has come among us. Men who hunger after Yahweh and His righteousness. Men like you.'

'Me?' I stammered, surprised.

Moses smiled. 'Yes, you. Do you doubt that you are a man like that?'

'I . . . uh . . . well, I . . .' I avoided Moses' gaze. My heart started thumping loudly. It was time. This was the moment I had been dreading. The moment when I had to tell him about my past, and see the disappointment in his eyes. The moment when my tenure of serving the prophet of God would come to an abrupt end. Taking a deep breath, I looked at him. 'I have not always followed Yahweh fully, Master. When I was young, I turned away from Him.' Now that I had started, I found I could not stop. My confession rolled off my tongue, unrestrained. 'My friend died – killed by the taskmasters. His name was Jezrel and he was a good man, a kind man. He was betrothed to be married. He did not deserve to die and . . . I blamed Yahweh for his death. I was so filled with anger, I turned away from the Lord. I dishonoured my parents and defiled my father's name. I brought shame on our family and was a companion of fools, violent and aggressive – fighting became my daily vice.' I muttered, 'I have done evil in my time. I am not the man that you think I am. I am not worthy to serve you.' I stared at the ground and waited for words of condemnation to whip me.

They never came.

Moments passed, heavy with anticipation. I lifted my head to look at him, preparing my heart for the disappointment and accusation I knew I would see. Moses sat before me, looking at me with what could only have been described as immense compassion. 'Is there anything else you would tell me?'

'Uh . . . no.' Wasn't that enough?

'Thank you for being honest about your past and not hiding this from me. That in itself shows me that you are a man of integrity.'

'But I am not, Master! I was a violent man. I caused harm to many, and brought shame on the good name of Nun!'

'Joshua, I *killed* a man, not in self-defence or in battle, but out of anger! I too was violent, and I followed the gods of Egypt for many years, but Yahweh still chose me to lead this great people out of bondage and into the land He has given to us.' He smiled at my confusion. 'Yahweh does not choose us because we are worthy. He chooses us because of what is in our hearts.' I sat in silence, my brow furrowed in confusion. 'Joshua, when I look into your eyes, do you know what I see?'

I shook my head. I didn't want to know.

'I see strength and purity and compassion. I see a hunger for Yahweh and a love for His people. I see a heart of service, a heart that is humble before God. I see a man who has a past, but who has not let that past define his future. I see an honest man – a man who I can trust and rely on. That is who I see.'

I stared at him, hardly breathing.

Moses stood up and walked to the other side of his tent where his staff stood, propped up against a wooden box. He fingered it, touching the contours of its shape. 'I want to thank you for your service so far. You have come whenever I have had need of you. You have proven yourself to be faithful and trustworthy, and you have done everything I have asked of you.' Picking up the rod, he turned around to face me. 'And now I must ask of you one more thing.'

I stood up and took a deep breath. 'Anything, Master. I will do anything you ask of me.'

'Will you give your life over to serving me – to walking by my side every day, going where I go and doing what I command? Will you be my trusted manservant?'

He wanted me! He knew of my past shame and rebellion, and still he wanted me to serve him. To be his manservant, no less! Moses was surrounded by men of great ability who supported him in different ways, but to be his manservant was a considerable responsibility, and a great honour. It was a position of trust and intimacy, of knowing your master as others did not, sharing his life and walking with him on his path.

And Moses had chosen me?

I couldn't believe it. As I made my way home, I looked across at the blazing fire that shimmered off in the distance. 'Truly, Your ways are not our ways,' I said. 'Blessed is Your name.' I felt as though I had wings. I wasn't walking, I was floating. Like a beast of burden relieved of a heavy load, I skipped with delight, chuckling to myself. Realising how foolish I must look, I quickly composed myself and looked around to see if anyone had seen me. I couldn't see anyone. The sun had set some time ago, and the camp was quiet. The evening meal was long over and families had settled down for the night, ready to awaken with the dawn the following day. There were still a few firepits scattered here and there around which people still sat warming themselves, discussing the day's events, or staring off into the distance to where the fiery pillar glowed with ethereal light.

It was so peaceful. Too peaceful! I wanted to leap up and down and shout out loud, but instead, I had to content myself with a small skip every now and then. When I arrived home, I was surprised to see Jesher, Mesha and Helah still sitting around the firepit, talking in hushed voices. Concerned at how late it was, they had decided to wait up for me to make sure all was well. 'Have you broken bread this evening, Joshua?' Helah asked as soon as I sat down to join them.

'Uh ... no, I haven't,' I replied, putting my hand on my grumbling stomach. 'Moses tends to forget about mundane things like eating!' Helah brought me some water to wash my hands, and fetched some bread, cheese and figs. I spoke in between mouthfuls, telling them of my conversation with Moses when he asked me to be his manservant.

'So? What did you say?' they asked, eyes wide with anticipation. 'I said yes.'

'Yes!' Mesha shouted, punching the air and then, remembering how late it was, whispered, 'I knew it would be so! I knew your path would be one of greatness.' He leaned over and grabbed hold of me, locking me in a bear hug.

'Yoshi, that's wonderful news!' Helah said. 'Yahweh be praised! Moses' manservant ... ay, ay, ay!' She clapped her hands in excitement and reached out to me.

'Thank you,' I smiled and clasped her little hands in mine.

Jesher sat there nodding, his dusty blue eyes twinkling as he watched me. 'Yahweh honours you, my son.'

'Moses' manservant ... oy!' Mesha grinned and punched me in the arm. 'So! What will you be doing all day, with Moses?'

'I'm not sure. More of what I have been doing, I believe – delivering messages, fetching and carrying, but also ...' I lowered my voice, 'I think Moses will be in need of some protection.'

'Protection from who?' Mesha asked.

'Well ...' I hesitated, reluctant to tell them what had happened that evening when Eleazar and I met Shimea. Some things were for Moses' ears only, and I realised with a surge of sadness that I would no longer be able to share with my adoptive family everything I saw and heard. 'I have heard there are troublemakers stirring people up against Moses.' Jesher's keen eyes watched me. I realised he knew I was holding back.

'Ech! There are always people making trouble, especially in a throng this size, *nu*?' Mesha said, grasping my arm. 'But they will not withstand the reach of your arm, my friend. Moses will be safe with you at his side.'

We laughed, Helah yawned and said, 'The night deepens. I must go to my bed. I bid you a good night. Peace be upon you.'

'Joshua, come and help an old man up,' Jesher said to me. Mesha walked into the tent with Helah, while I helped Jesher to his feet and gave him his stick. He held my arm and whispered, 'Are you at peace? Is all well with you?'

'I am, *Abba*,' I replied. 'My heart is full; I can hardly find the words to speak of what stirs within me.' Jesher smiled at me, but didn't move. Still holding onto my arm, he looked at me, inviting (or perhaps compelling?) me to say more.

'Do you remember when we talked about my path in life?' I asked him.

'Mmm,' he nodded.

'Well . . . I know what it is now – my path. My pathway has led me to serve Moses. To serve him as manservant, but also to protect him. To fight for him, and fight *with* him against the forces of darkness in this land. I believe this is what Yahweh would have me do.' Looking back to where the pillar of fire glowed in the middle of the camp, I whispered, 'Something changed in me today, *Abba*. All that Moses said to me, what he saw in me – my eyes have been opened.' I turned back to Jesher and smiled. 'Just like Joel's were. I see the battle that is raging and I know my part in it. I know in my heart what I must do, and I bear witness to you today that, as Yahweh wills it, I will do it.'

24

Betrothal

It had been a few weeks since we had left Egypt, and we were becoming accustomed to our new life as sojourners. By now, we were into the summer months, and the days were getting longer and hotter. We had just passed through Dophkah, and made our way through narrow rocky canyons towards Alush, where we made camp. Alush was an inhospitable territory surrounded by mountains, with little vegetation and no wells or pools of water. We could not stop there long; we would only be passing through.

Our days slipped into a routine of sorts, starting at daybreak when we rose with the sun, and finishing soon after sunset. Ours was a simple life and, on the whole, it was peaceful and harmonious. I relished equally the opportunities for fellowship and discussion with Moses, as well as the chaos and community of my new family. We had celebrated two Shabbats since the new laws had been passed and were learning how to rest, although it came easier for some than others! Today was our third Shabbat; Moses always released me early on Shabbat so I could go and prepare for it.

I arrived home to find the usual pre-Shabbat hustle and bustle. The women were busy preparing food for the evening meal and the following day, the men were sorting out wood and dried dung for the fire, and the youngsters were trying (somewhat unsuccessfully, it seemed) to milk the goats. Everything had to be readied before sunset and, once all the chores had been done, we all had to wash before the evening meal. Shira reigned supreme during times like this, barking out orders which were usually obeyed without question.

Joel arrived back at the tent at the same time as me, but I knew the moment I saw him that something had happened. Without stopping to greet those of us who stood nearby, he rushed straight over to his father. '*Abba*!' he blurted in excitement. 'I have found a wife!'

Azriel looked at him in bewilderment. 'You have what?'

'I have found her! The woman I would take as my wife.' We all froze, staring first at Joel and then at each other. Mesha looked at me and shrugged. Joel was still a young man, not yet twenty, but permitted by law to marry.

'Who is she? What family is she from?' Azriel asked.

'Her name is Alya – her father is Eliphalet, of the tribe of Simeon.'

'Simeon? So she is not a Benjaminite?'

'No,' Joel frowned, 'but she is of our people.'

'And where did you meet this Alya of the tribe of Simeon?' Azriel looked suspiciously at his son.

'I met her on my way to Bezalel's workshop. We talked.'

'You talked to her? You spoke to a strange woman?' Azriel was appalled. 'Were you alone with her?'

Joel was clearly getting frustrated at Azriel's interrogation, and his lack of focus on what was really important. 'No, *Abba*, I was with Dahn.' Before Azriel could ask who Dahn was, he gabbled on. 'He is another apprentice; we work together and he walks with me to the workshops. We have met her several times. Her tent is near Bezalel's tent, on the east side of the camp.'

By now, Jesher, who had been washing inside the tent, heard raised voices and came outside to see what the commotion was about. Azriel turned to him, lifted his hands, and said, 'He wants to marry! He says he has found a wife.'

'I have, *Saba*,' Joel said, rushing up to Jesher. 'Her name is Alya and she is so beautiful. She has green eyes and she loves wood! She has seen some of my work and admires my craftmanship. I asked her if I could take her to be my wife, and she said yes!'

'What?' Azriel exploded, grabbing Joel by the arm and swinging him around. 'You did what?'

'I asked her if I could take her as my wife. She said yes.' Joel glared at his father and, for a brief moment, I was reminded of the dark days before his redemption, when he and Azriel were divided by anger and misunderstanding. My heart feared for them both.

'Joel, you know our customs – the father chooses a bride for his son. You cannot just decide you want to marry someone! There are traditions that must be followed. You must abide by our customs.'

'Why?' Joel scowled at his father. 'Why must you choose who I spend my days with? I have chosen Alya and I will marry her.'

'Tst, tst, tst.' Jesher stepped forward to divide father and son. 'Stop now. Peace, be still,' he said, putting his hands up to stop the barrage of words that was about to explode from both sides. 'We will take counsel together, yes? But not now. Shabbat is nearly upon us.'

'But *Saba*, I told her we would go to her *abba* today to ask his permission.'

'Not today, Joel, it is nearly Shabbat. There is no time.'

'Tomorrow, then? Will you go with *Abba* tomorrow to speak with her *abba*?'

'No, Joel. It is our day of rest tomorrow. It must wait until – '

'But we cannot wait! We must speak to – '

'Joel!' Jesher spoke sharply. 'You are not yourself. Hold your peace.' Joel stared at Jesher in shock. His grandfather was not a man who raised his voice often but, when he did, he inspired awe and respect. Jesher had spoken, so that was the end of it. Joel stalked off. We went about our business and, by the time the sunset came, we were all washed and ready. Shabbat started with a time of prayer while the cloud's transformation took place. It was usually a peaceful time, a time to stop and think on what we were thankful for, a moment when our thoughts centred on Yahweh and His blessings.

Not so tonight.

We were all acutely aware of the conversations that were yet to come, about Joel and his desire to take Alya as his wife. I closed my eyes in an effort to block everything else out and focus on Yahweh, but it was fruitless. The air was thick, laboured with tension. We shared our Shabbat meal, but the usual sense of celebration and festivity was missing. Jesher refused to discuss Joel's situation any further that evening, so it was put off until the next day. Our day of rest.

It was not a very restful Shabbat.

Lots of discussions took place, mostly led by Jesher. None of us could go out or work, so we stayed by the tent and, because nearly everyone had their own opinion on the matter, the discussions continued in sporadic bursts throughout the day. Nevertheless, by late afternoon, Jesher and Azriel had agreed to go and visit Alya's father the following day to ask about her betrothal to Joel.

I set off early for Moses' tent the morning on the day after Shabbat, eager to escape the nervous tension that hung in the air. Joel went to work in Bezalel's workshops, as was required under the terms of his apprenticeship, so he would only find out what happened when he returned home that evening. Bezalel must have had pity on Joel and let him leave earlier than usual, because he arrived home before me. I could hear the raised voices long before I reached the tent, and saw clusters of nosy neighbours standing around, watching the drama unfold. The whole family stood outside, gathered around Joel and Azriel. Both were red-faced – Azriel with anger, Joel with passion. No one greeted me or paid any attention to me as I arrived, so I slipped in next to Mesha and whispered, 'What has happened?'

He grimaced and whispered back, 'Her father did not give permission for the betrothal.' I was surprised. Although ours was not one of the larger or more affluent families in the tribe of Benjamin, we had a good reputation, and a family trade. Besides which, the fact that Joel was apprenticed to Bezalel was a great honour, so he should be considered a good match.

'Why?' I asked.

Mesha lifted his eyebrows. 'Because Alya is already betrothed to another.'

'What?' I was stunned. 'Why did she not tell Joel?'

'Because she had no knowledge of it – until today.'

As the argument raged on, Mesha filled me in on the details. Apparently Alya's father had arranged her betrothal to a man named Jamin a short while ago, but had not told her. Jamin and Alya's families were closely aligned, and the purpose of the marriage was to unite the two families. The betrothal ceremony had been set, and the preparations well underway when Jesher and Azriel had arrived at their tent. They were not well received. Alya's father, Eliphalet, was not an easy man to talk to, and had not taken kindly to the disclosure that his daughter had been talking to another man. He hauled her up in front of Azriel, Jesher and his family, and castigated her in front of everyone.

'Azriel said her *abba* struck her before sending her away in shame,' Mesha added. My heart constricted and I felt anger rise in me. If there was one thing I abhorred, it was men who struck women just because they could. I pushed down my anger and we turned our attention back to the argument between Azriel and Joel.

'She cannot marry him! She does not love him,' Joel shouted. 'She loves me! I know it, *Abba*, I know she feels for me what I feel for her.'

'It matters not what you feel for each other,' Azriel shouted back. 'Alya is betrothed! It is done, Joel! You cannot take her as your wife.'

'I must have her!'

'She is not yours for the having!'

'Then I will go and speak to her and we – '

'You will not go to her and you will not speak to her, or you will see my wrath!'

Joel froze for a moment and stared at his father. When he spoke again, his words were laced with ice. 'I say this to you in truth. I will surely have Alya as my wife, and if it proves not to be so, I will cut off my right arm.'

Jesher stepped forward, 'Joel, no!' I could see that Azriel had come to the end of himself. The fight had gone out of him and he stared at his son in despair. I wanted desperately to help – to stop Joel from going down this road of pain and hardship. He had listened to me once before. I was sure he would listen to me again. I stepped forward and put my hand on Joel's shoulder.

'Joel, please, turn your ear to me and heed my words. If you walk down this path, it will bring only pain to both of you. You must restrain yourself! Let Alya go. You know our ways. She is betrothed to another; she cannot be yours. You must let her go.'

Joel's eyes filled with fire. He shook my hand off his shoulder and yelled at me. 'You know nothing! You speak to me of our ways, but you cannot talk to me of love. You know *nothing* of what it is to know the passion for a woman that burns within a man's heart! *Nothing!*'

I felt a dagger enter my heart. I staggered backwards. Mesha's arms steadied me. A violent flush of rage filled me, spreading up through my body, until it reached my face. Heat overwhelmed me and my hands clenched into tight fists. 'Let me strike him,' I prayed silently. 'Yahweh, let me strike him.'

My breathing came hard and fast, but I heard Mesha whisper, 'Joshua, no . . .'

Silence.

I raised my head to look into Joel's eyes.

'You know nothing of my heart,' I said through clenched teeth. 'It would be better for you to remain silent about things you know nothing of.' Without another word, I turned and walked away, leaving behind me a stunned silence.

25

Death Hole

The following morning, there was no time for further discussion. The shofar sounded early, we broke camp, and continued on the next leg of our journey. I was relieved that we were moving on. I think we all were. Alush was not a place where anyone would want to stay for very long and we needed to find water. Our supplies were once again running dangerously low.

There was not much conversation as we trudged on in the heat. The unresolved conflict which had taken place the previous day hung in the air like the foul stench of soiled clothes. Azriel's face bore a look of pain and defeat. The despair that he and Leora felt was laid bare for all to see; their son, who was found, was once again lost. He had gone from them.

Joel reminded me of an exotic bird I had come across at Elim one afternoon when I sat down to rest by an oasis. A bee-eater flew down and perched on the branch of a palm tree by the water's edge. Its colouring was exquisite: a turquoise breast, flecked with shimmers of azure blue, golden wings and a head the colour of burned orange, with markings of gold and turquoise. I had never seen a bee-eater before – it was magnificent! I sat in stunned silence, holding my breath. Its bright eyes surveyed the surrounding trees and then, as quick as a flash, it swooped down and snatched up a dozy bee that was buzzing around the yellow palm flowers. The bird disappeared in a flurry of gold and blue, as quickly as it had arrived, leaving me struck with wonder, and longing for more.

After Joel was restored to us, he was like that bee-eater. We saw vibrant creativity, colour, life and joy in his music, his manner and his smile. He was a wonder to behold, a miracle which had unfolded in front of our eyes. But, just as quickly as the bee-eater left, so had Joel. He disappeared, and with him went the colour and life which he brought to the family. Normally, Joel walked with Yoram when we journeyed, but today he kept to himself, his face like the gathering storm clouds of winter. Mesha moved to walk next to him; I overheard his fruitless efforts to try to initiate conversation and lighten the atmosphere.

'So, I hear you are working on some wheels for a cart now, yes?' Joel just grunted and didn't even look at Mesha. 'That will be a great blessing to us in our travels – a cart to carry the heavy loads. Such a gift you have, such a blessing.' Normally, Mesha was able to draw people out of their dark places, but not today. He tried for a while longer, and then left Joel to come and walk by me.

'Yoshi?' He lowered his voice so that the rest of the family could not hear our conversation. 'What Joel said last night, he did not mean it. He would never intentionally cause you pain. He knows nothing of . . . what took place. If he did, he would never have said those things.'

'I know.' I kept my head down and continued tramping on, kicking up the dust and dirt as I walked. I didn't want to look at Mesha. I didn't want him to see the pain and rage that still burned my eyes.

Mesha probed a bit more. 'Will you tell him?'

'No.'

'I could tell him. It might help him to know . . .'

'He will not be told.' I looked Mesha in the eyes. 'Joel does not need to know. No one needs to know. Do I have your word on this?'

He sighed and nodded. 'You have my word.' He walked with me for a while and then went to take Shallum from Helah. After some time, Yoram came and walked with me. He said nothing but, out of the corner of my eye, I saw him look at me every so often. His concern for me was palpable. He and I were so alike, he knew I did not wish to talk. He stayed by my side, like a faithful shadow, until we stopped to rest at midday. As we took a mouthful of water, Yoram looked at me and whispered, 'Yoshi? Are you at peace?'

I knew I could not throw out some meaningless platitudes or falsehoods. Not with Yoram. He knew me too well for that. So I looked at him and mumbled, 'No, Yori, my heart is not at peace.' Seeing the anxiety on his face, I smiled and said, 'But I will be. Soon.' Yoram needed no explanation and he asked no questions. Like Joel, he didn't know what caused me such pain, but it seemed he didn't feel the need to know. He stayed with me the rest of the day, silent but attentive.

We moved on together. The heat hung in the air, mercilessly sapping our energy hour after hour. Although we were grateful for the covering of Yahweh's cloud, the heat was so extreme that rather than relieving us of its effects, all it seemed to do was trap the heat under its canopy. The sweat poured off us, dampening our hair and our spirits. Normally, in weather like this, we would splash water on our heads, necks and faces, and drink liberally from our waterskins to refresh ourselves. But splashing was out of the question.

'How much longer, Jesher?' I heard Shira ask her husband. It was unusual for Shira to look dishevelled. But today, her immaculate appearance had vanished, and she looked as unkempt and bedraggled as the rest of us. 'Are we nearly there?'

'I don't know, but I am sure it will not be long now,' Jesher said, wiping the sweat off his forehead with the back of his hand, giving her a weak smile.

'Water.' Shira's voice rasped. 'Please . . .' Jesher nodded and put his bundles down on the ground, signalling to the family that it was time to stop for a quick drink. Every man took the waterskin from around their neck or shoulders and gave it to their wife and children. Jesher took a waterskin off his shoulder, where it hung from a strap made of twisted twine, and held it out to Shira. She took a mouthful, holding the precious liquid in her mouth for as long as she could, savouring the sensation, before swallowing.

I took a large swig of my water and looked at Jesher as he raised his own to his lips . . . to no avail. He tipped it up higher and shook it gently. A few drops trickled into his mouth. He turned the waterskin upside down and Shira, who looked at him at that moment, gasped when she saw no liquid flow out. Before Jesher could say anything, I stepped forward and offered him my waterskin.

'No, Joshua. Thank you, but we cannot take your water. It is so precious,' Jesher muttered hoarsely.

'As are you, *Abba*,' I said. 'Please, drink.' He hesitated. 'I have only myself to look out for. Drink.' I turned to Shira. 'There is enough for both of you.' Jesher took the skin from me and swallowed a small mouthful, and another after I prompted him. He passed it to Shira and she took one more mouthful, closing her eyes when she swallowed. They were misty as she passed the precious liquid back to me.

'Thank you, Joshua.' I don't recall her ever saying that to me before and, in all the time I had known her, I had never once seen her cry. It felt good – not that she was crying, but because I knew now that there was a heart in her; that she did feel; that she could be grateful, even to one such as I.

We regrouped and continued walking. By now, every step was an effort, but we had no option but to keep going, stoically trudging through the arid desert wasteland. We dragged one tired foot after another, stumbling and tripping over the never-ending expanse of dirt and stones. My mouth was dry and cracking, my swollen tongue sticking to the roof of my mouth. I repeated a mantra over and over in my mind. 'Keep walking. Just keep walking . . . we will be there soon . . .'

Just when I was starting to lose all hope, I heard the blast of a shofar in the distance and a cry went up. 'The cloud is still! Make camp!' Shouts of, 'We've arrived!' and 'Yahweh be praised!' echoed through the crowds. Eyes wide with anticipation, hearts flooding with emotion, Yoram and I stared at each other, exhausted. I looked up and pointed. 'Look! The cloud is still!' Feet that had been heavy and laboured just minutes before somehow found the strength to walk the last part of our journey to find that precious, life-giving water.

But something was wrong.

The faces of those that greeted us, having arrived first, were not smiling but frantic. This was not the welcome we had expected. What was wrong? And where was Moses? I could see panic setting in as word spread from mouth to mouth, family to family: 'There is no water. The streams of Rephidim are dry.'

Shira looked at Jesher, her eyes full of fear. 'Jesher? There is no water? But the cloud has stopped, how can there be no water? There must be water.'

Jesher turned to me, his shoulders stooped. I gave him my waterskin. 'Sit, rest. I will go and find out what is taking place.' I walked towards the middle of the camp. The cloud of Yahweh's presence was still; I could see it clearly – it had stopped, which meant we were to make camp. But why would Yahweh have us make camp if there was no water? As I made my way through the multitudes, I saw children howling in pain and frustration, their tears making dirty streaks on their dusty faces, as parents looked on helplessly, trying unsuccessfully to comfort them. Soon, I came across a crowd of men arguing about what to do. I recognised many of them as leaders of families, and tribal elders. I stood on the fringes of the group and listened.

'Perhaps we should keep travelling through the night to try to find water?'

'Or we could send a scouting party ahead to find water?'

'How long would that take? What if they did not find any?'

'There are too many ill and frail, and the children are too weak to go on without water.'

'We could leave the weak in the camp and move on with those who are strong enough.'

'Oysh! What would your mother-in-law say to that?'

'We cannot move on. The cloud had stopped. We cannot move on until the cloud moves.'

'Why not? Why must we always follow this cloud?' My head shot up, and a shiver ran down my spine. I would recognise that voice anywhere! I craned my neck to try to see whose voice it was but, even before my eyes settled on him, I knew who it was. Shimea! 'We are not foolish men. We have minds of our own – so let us use them! Why must we wait for this?' He pointed upwards to the cloud. 'It is just a cloud. Can we not decide for ourselves how to lead our families, our people? Why do we not turn back to Elim? We had everything we needed there.' The seeds of discord which he planted immediately took root in the fearful soil of the men's hearts. Voices shouted and volume levels escalated as they tried in vain to agree on a plan of action.

'We should have turned back to Elim. We would be there now if we had just turned back when we first talked about it.'

'We should never have left Elim in the first place. We had everything we need there.'

'But we follow the cloud. When the cloud moves, we move. The cloud moved, so we moved, yes?'

'But why would it lead us here, to a place where there is no water? The streams are dry. We cannot stay here.'

'I said it before but I will say it again: we cannot move until the cloud moves.' On and on they argued, voices steadily rising in conflict. Then the inevitable happened. They turned their attention from seeking a solution to finding someone to blame. The malignant, icy tone of Shimea's voice threw the first accusation.

'Moses! This is his fault. *He* brought us here. He has led us to our deaths. He told us we were going to "a land of brooks of water, of fountains and springs", not this death hole in the desert.' He needed to say no more. Accusations filled the air, fuelled by fear. The deliberations turned abruptly from what to do about the lack of water to thoughts of stoning Moses and, equally as swiftly, to arguments about who would be his successor.

As the dispute continued and they fought over who would lead them out of this death camp to find water, I slipped quietly away and went to find Moses.

26

The Rock

'Moses must pay for what he has done! He has led us out here to die of thirst!' I recognised Shimea's toxic tones. He was now standing in the middle of a huge crowd, holding court with an air of absolute command. 'We need a new leader! A strong leader!' he shouted, lifting his arm and shaking his fist. The crowd had grown significantly in the short time I had been gone. It was now a mob, an angry mob, fearful and desperate, bent on destruction, and increasing in both size and volume.

I stood panting for a moment, letting my heart rate slow while I took it all in. Drawing a deep breath, I exhaled before making my way through the crowd. In times past, I often wished that I was shorter and slimmer, so I was not such a focus of people's attention. But, at times like this, my height and strong build were a great asset, and I was able to push my way through the wall of men fairly easily.

'Quiet!' I shouted, lifting my arms up to silence the unruly throng. 'Be still! I have a message from Moses.' Shimea swung round and his menacing eyes narrowed when he saw me. I hoped my calm demeanour would bely the frantic beating of my heart. To my relief, the noise died down long enough for me to relay the message. 'Moses says you are to assemble immediately at the rock in Horeb. He will meet you there.'

Shimea tried to stop them from listening to me. Many of his followers did go straight back to their debate about who should take over leadership of our new nomadic nation. However, for most, curiosity got the better of them, and the news that Moses had called them to assemble spread like wildfire. The huge crowd started to make its way the to the massive rocky outcrop. Many others joined them, swept up in the momentum, being stirred up into a rage. But the majority sat on the ground, watching hopelessly, too exhausted to join in or object.

I was desperate to get there before them, so I shoved my way through the crowds, stumbling and falling over the rocky terrain, until I reached the front where Moses stood waiting. I turned to face the crowds, poised and ready for action. I glanced up at the cloud of Yahweh's presence which swirled in the heavens above us. 'Yahweh is angry,' I muttered to myself, noting the dark denseness of the cloud, and the flames which flickered within it. Moses stood before them, silently watching the tableau of fear playing out before him.

Aaron and Hur stood a little behind him, like silent watchmen and, as the mob raged against him, Moses stood tall and still. At times like this, my respect for my master knew no bounds. He showed no fear. In fact, he closed his eyes, concentrating intensely, which seemed to anger the mob even more. Shimea picked up a rock and shouted, 'Stone him!' Immediately, the men standing with him picked up rocks and joined in the chant. 'Stone him! Stone him!' they bellowed, shaking their arms, stones clenched in their fists. I leaped in front of Moses, arms outstretched. Out of the corner of my eye, I saw a man move towards me. I swung round, ready to confront him – a man of similar age to me, also of strong build, and with the same passionate look in his eyes.

But he didn't attack me. Instead, he came and stood next to me, turning to face the crowd, ready to defend Moses. I stared at him, trying to discern whether this was a trick, or if the man was genuine in his desire to join me in my quest to protect Moses. Moses held out his arm, instructing both of us to stand down. I frowned, but stepped to one side, turning my attention back to the crowd, ready to tackle the first man who made a move. My fellow defender looked at me, nodded, and followed suit. The rock-wielding men were quickly joined by others and soon, a great number of them held rocks in their hands, ready to hurl at the man of God standing silently before them. Looking at each other with wild eyes, they shouted and egged each other on.

But no one was willing to make the first move. No one would throw the first stone.

I watched Shimea. He heckled and stirred up the men around him, but it seemed he also was unwilling to throw the first stone.

He was nothing but a bully – a coward. He reminded me of the heavy-set clouds that came at the end of summer, bringing the promise of rain, but which moved on without watering the land. Shimea was all words and no action. He wanted others to do his dirty work for him. I homed in on him, feeling contempt for this worm who had the audacity to try to take on a giant like Moses.

Seizing the moment, Moses opened his eyes, took a deep breath, and shouted, 'Why do you quarrel with me? And why do you put the Lord your God to the test? Do you not know that He is mighty? His arm is not short. Why do you tempt Him?' The noise of the mob dulled down at his words. Moses stepped forward and took his rod, the mighty symbol of his authority, in his right hand. The crowd gasped and shrank back.

'You want water? Then you shall *have* water,' he cried. Grasping the rod with both hands, he lifted it high above his head and, with a ferocious roar, struck the huge rock with all of his might. There was an ear-splitting crack, followed by a deafening rumble as the ground beneath our feet began to shake. The mob covered their ears, cries of terror on their lips, and many turned and fled. Those who were trapped in the middle of the crowd could do nothing but watch helplessly as pandemonium broke out. Stones quivered where they lay and many of the mob were thrown to the ground by the juddering of the earth beneath their feet.

The man with me fell down, as did I, although we stood back up as soon as we were able. The whole congregation watched in astonishment as a torrent of pure, sparkling water burst from the crevice where the mighty rock had fractured. With a deafening roar, shafts of water exploded out of the rock, creating a division right down the middle of the assembled mob. Cries of fear turned into gasps of wonder, and thereafter into shouts of celebration as the crowd realised what was happening. The fickle voices that only minutes before had cried out for Moses' death, now shouted in jubilation and sang his praises.

They rushed to stand under the flow of water, drinking eagerly and splashing each other, laughing and crying all at the same time. Jostling to stand under the showers of water, they stood fully clothed, arms outstretched, soaking in the wonder of that moment. They collected water in their hands or filled their water pouches, and drank deeply. Within minutes a watercourse formed, flowing down through the rocks, creating large pools on its way. People flocked to the pools of water and spontaneous dancing broke out; voices raised in laughter as songs of celebration, with prayers of thanksgiving, echoed throughout the countryside.

'Blessed are you, Lord our God, King of the universe, who brings forth water from the rock to refresh Your people Israel!'

I watched in amazement, not only at the extraordinary flow of water that poured out of the rock, but also at the instantaneous change of mood that I witnessed in the crowd. I turned to talk to the man who had stood with me against our aggressors, but he was gone. I searched the crowds for him, but he was nowhere to be seen. Moses stood alone near the top of the rock, leaning on his staff, watching Yahweh's people as they splashed and played in the water. Aaron and Hur had gone to investigate the pools, so I climbed up onto the rock and stood with Moses, smiling at their playfulness, and laughing out loud when the children shrieked with delight. Turning to Moses, my smile faded. I saw no joy on my master's face, only sadness.

'Are you not pleased, Master?' I asked him. 'Yahweh has saved us. Another miracle – water from a rock! Never have I even heard of such a thing. Truly, His arm is not short.' Puzzled, I asked, 'Is this not something to rejoice in?'

'It is, Joshua.' He turned and smiled at me. 'Yahweh is kind and has compassion on His people.' He turned back to the pools of water and silence fell again.

'Forgive me, Master, but why then are you downcast?' I asked, bemused by Moses' melancholy demeanour. 'If Yahweh has shown Himself to be kind and compassionate, the people are happy and we have plenty of water, why are you still sad?'

Moses sighed. 'They are only happy because they have what they shouted for. They are like children, Joshua; joyful when they have what their heart desires, but stubborn and rebellious when things do not go their way.' I stared at the frolicking people again, this time with a frown. We watched in silence for a while, and then I glanced sideways at Moses.

'Master, the man that confronted Eleazar and I – the one we told you about ...'

'Shimea.'

'Yes.' I was impressed Moses remembered his name.

'What of him?'

'He was here today, among the crowds, inciting the mob to violence.'

'Yes.'

'You saw him?'

'I saw a man who fitted the description you gave me,' Moses replied. 'But more than that, I saw his eyes and I knew it must be the same man. You were right, there is great evil in him. Darkness has gripped his soul and turned his heart from Yahweh. He could be a formidable adversary.' His face broke into a confident smile. 'But not to Yahweh.'

I nodded. 'What will you do, Master?'

'About what?'

'About Shimea. Will you meet with him? Talk to him, or challenge him?' Moses stared up at the cloud which, by now, had lost some of its denseness. The dark swirling spirals had dissipated and the familiar flickers of light were returning.

'I would imagine that Shimea uses words like weapons; twisting people's thoughts and provoking them to action through his persuasive speech. Yes?'

'Yes. He moulds them with such skill, it was like watching a potter at the wheel. They were clay in his hands.'

'Mmm. I saw this many times with the "holy men" of Egypt, but words have never been my strong point, Joshua. I speak when Yahweh commands me to, but I prefer to let Him show His power and the strength of His arm without my help – or interference,' he said, with a familiar twinkle in his eye.

'You will not speak to Shimea, then?'

'No. Not yet. Not unless Yahweh instructs me to do so. I will come before Him and seek His face on the matter.' Moses looked at me with great solemnity. 'Shimea does not stand alone, Joshua. There are others like him and their poison will spread among our people. We must be vigilant and ready to move against this darkness, as Yahweh commands.'

Silence fell for a time as we pondered the ways of Yahweh and the great darkness that had infiltrated our ranks. Then I remembered the man who had stood with me. 'Master,' I asked, 'who was the man who came and stood by me, when the crowds threatened to stone you? Is he known to you?'

'Ah, yes,' Moses said, smiling. 'That is Caleb ben Jephunneh. He is a Judahite, a man who follows Yahweh closely, just like his father. His father is a good man and a strong leader, and Caleb is following in his footsteps, although he is somewhat . . . impetuous at times,' he said with a chuckle. 'He is one to watch, Joshua. He would be a good man to join your heart with.'

I nodded and muttered to myself, 'Caleb, son of Jephunneh, of the tribe of Judah. I will seek him out later. I want to thank him for standing with me.' Thinking back to what had happened, I asked, 'Master, do you think they would have stoned you? Would they do such a thing?'

'Perhaps,' Moses said, shrugging. Staring down at the families crowding around the pools of water, he continued, 'I do not presume to understand the hearts of this people, Joshua. They continue to tempt Yahweh, to rebel against Him and reject Him. They want only to follow their own desires. They think they reject me, but they do not. They reject the Lord God Himself.'

'Perhaps they will believe Him now, Master, after today – after seeing what the Lord has done. Perhaps now they will believe in Him.'

Moses was silent for a while, and then spoke with a quiet certainty. 'No. They will continue to rebel against the Lord and turn from Him.' He drew a deep breath and sighed. Turning to me, he smiled and put his hand on my shoulder. 'But it is good to hope, my young friend.' Looking out over the land, he whispered quietly, 'Yes, it is good to hope.'

27

Falsehood

Yahweh's miraculous provision of water lifted our spirits and, for a few days afterwards, there was peace in our household. At least, that's what it looked like. Joel's brooding had lessened; although he was distant and distracted, he was fairly amenable. He joined the family to break bread, he smiled and responded when asked a question. Azriel and Leora seemed relieved, and I overheard Azriel telling Jesher that they were glad we could 'put it all behind us'.

I wasn't so sure. I didn't believe it was behind us.

As much as I wanted to, I didn't believe Joel's smiles, or his polite attempts at conversation. His smile was false and there was a gleam in his eyes that had the look of rebellion. He was planning something. I knew it – and Joel knew that I knew it. I studied him as we sat around the family circle to break fast one morning and, when he looked up and saw me watching him, he flushed and looked away. After that, he avoided me and would not look me in the eyes. There was falsehood in him, and my heart was sick within me for what I feared would happen.

As it turns out, I was right to fear.

A few days after Joel's outburst about Alya's betrothal, I arrived back home late in the afternoon to see three men leaving. They stomped out of the tent, glared at me as they passed by, and did not return my greeting. Jesher, Azriel, Hareph and Mesha all stood outside the tent, watching them go. Their expressions ranged from anger and sorrow to disbelief and confusion, and Hareph's shoulder twitched every few seconds. That was always a bad sign.

I asked, 'Who was that?'

'Alya's *abba* and her two brothers,' Mesha said, looking uncharacteristically serious.

'Why were they here?'

'They discovered that Joel and Alya have been planning to flee this place together.'

'No!' My mind was reeling. I knew Joel was planning something, but this . . . this was beyond my imaginings. To leave his family, his people, and run away with a woman – what madness was this? I asked how they came by this knowledge.

Mesha grimaced. 'Alya's sister told them. Alya asked her for help, but she betrayed them to her father.' He frowned as he watched the retreating figures of the three men. 'I can understand why. Her *abba* is a man to be feared, and her brothers are of a similar heart.' He glanced at me. 'I would not wish to cross them. There is anger in their hearts and venom in their words.' Just then, Joel came into view, thankfully approaching from the opposite direction. All five of us froze and he slowed his pace when he saw the looks on our faces.

'What is it?' he asked. 'What has happened?'

Azriel walked towards him, his face a mask of pain. 'How could you? How could you even think of doing that? Deserting your people, stealing another man's woman – leaving your family?' Joel's face paled and he stared at his father, like a rabbit caught in a hunter's snare. 'Why?' Azriel whispered. 'Why would you do that? I thought you were happy. I thought you had come back to us.' Joel's lips moved, but no words came out. 'Why, Joel?'

'I had to!' he blurted. 'She does not love Jamin. There is evil in him. He is not a righteous man.' Azriel stared at his son in utter confusion. Joel continued his haltering defence. 'And . . . and her *abba* is . . . I have to get her away from him. He is not a good man. His soul feeds on violence.'

'I know,' Azriel said. 'We just met him.'

'You met him? How? Where?'

'He and Alya's brothers came here to find you.' The pain in Azriel's face lessened, replaced by a resigned sense of numbness. 'They found us instead. It was good that you were not here.'

'But how did they know?' Joel stuttered. 'How did they find out?'

'Alya's sister told them.'

Joel shook his head. 'I told Alya to keep silent. I knew we could not trust her sister.' He ran his hand through his tousled hair. Looking at the ground, he muttered, 'I must go to her. I must go and speak with her.'

Azriel's eyes opened wide and he stared at his son, incredulous. 'You must go to her? *You must go to her?*' He stepped towards Joel, his arm raised as if to strike him. Mesha and I held him back and, before he could do anything, Jesher stepped forward and took control.

'You will not go to Alya, Joel. Not now, not ever. You are never to see Alya again. You are never to speak to her again. Her *abba* has moved the place of their lodging and forbidden her to fetch water from streams, to pick fruit, to meet with her friends, to go anywhere. She is to be a captive in her *abba*'s tent until the time of her marriage to Jamin.'

Joel shook his head. 'No, he cannot . . .' but Jesher continued, unheeded.

'The only reason why Eliphalet has not brought charges against you is to save his family from shame. He does not wish to jeopardise the betrothal. He and his sons are not waiting here to bring grave harm to you, because we swore an oath that you would not come near her.'

'You swore . . . ?'

Jesher did not blink. He continued to stare at his grandson as he threw the final blow. 'If your own heart testifies against you, and you do try to find Alya, not only will you bring great shame upon your family and grievous harm to yourself, but you will bring about Alya's death. Her father has sworn an oath. If she is found even talking with another man while betrothed to Jamin, she will be taken to the edge of the camp and stoned.'

The cry of a wounded animal burst out of Joel's mouth.

Jesher sighed and broke eye contact to look at the ground. Lifting his gaze again, he put his hand on Joel's shoulder and spoke to him with compassion. 'So, if you truly love this woman as you say you do, you will never see her again.'

Pain erupted inside of me as I watched a shroud of desolation fall on Joel. I had seen anguish pour out of him only a few weeks ago, when his soul had been lost and broken. And now, I knew the devastation that he would have to endure, the agony of separation. I knew it all too well. Joel's knees buckled. He cried out, crouching on the floor, rocking backwards and forwards, his arms around his waist. He gasped and grunted, as though labouring to bring forth a child. No tears came from his eyes; his grief was too great for tears.

At last he stood up. 'Joel . . .' Jesher reached out to him, but he jerked backwards, staring at his grandfather as if he were holding a snake in his hand. He turned around and stumbled away as fast as he could, still hugging his grief to himself like an invisible cloak.

Azriel turned to his father, alarmed. '*Abba*, we must go after him. What if he tries to go to her?'

'No.' Sadness clouded Jesher's face. 'He won't,' he whispered, staring after the retreating figure of his grandson. 'He will not go to her. He will not risk her life. He truly loves this woman.'

Mesha turned to me and grabbed my arm. 'Joshua, go to him. Talk to him.'

'No. I cannot,' I muttered. 'Not this time.' Mesha frowned at me but I shook my head. 'No. Leave him be. No one can help him now. In time he will find his way through the pain . . . In time.'

28

Warfare

'*Me*?' The blood drained from my face. 'You want *me* to lead our warriors into battle against the Amalekites?'

'Yes. I can think of no one better.' Moses sat, waiting for me to respond. My mind was a blur, my thoughts like a swarm of bees buzzing around a dripping honeycomb. My heart started thumping so loudly in my chest, I wondered if they could hear it. Hur and Aaron glanced at each other, then at Moses. They waited in uneasy silence while I grappled with my thoughts. My mind was still reeling from yesterday's confrontation with Joel – this was the last thing I needed. War? Me? Lead the . . . ? No. No, no, no.

'I . . . it is an honour to be asked, Master, but . . . I do not believe I am the right person,' I stammered. 'I have never fought a battle and I have no training in warfare.'

'None of our men do, Joshua. But you are a strong man; strong in body and in heart, and the Lord is with you. There are plenty of men who are strong in stature, but I need someone I can trust.'

'That may be so, Master, but the Amalekites are a fearsome people, and their weaponry is more advanced than anything we have among our ranks. They have fought many battles and are well-versed in the ways of warfare. We cannot face them.'

'Yes, that is true,' Moses said. 'But they are here and we will face them, nevertheless. Remember, we have something that they do not have.' I frowned. 'What do we have?' I thought to myself. 'We have nothing.' Moses smiled at me. 'We have Yahweh. He will fight for us, just like He did when the Egyptians attacked us before the Red Sea. They are also a military people with highly trained soldiers, chariots, weapons, but remember their end. Think on what the Lord God did to them. Summon your power, Joshua! Yahweh fought for us then, and He will fight for us now.' I looked at the ground and breathed in and out a few times, trying to steady the frantic beating of my heart and the jumble of thoughts that still bombarded my mind.

After a while, Moses stepped towards me and put his hand on my shoulder. 'Joshua – will you do this?' I searched Moses' eyes and saw only trust and confidence. Neither of us blinked or looked away. There was only one answer to that question. He knew it and I knew it.

'I will, Master. If that is your will, I will do it.'

'It is not only my will, Joshua, it is Yahweh's will. He has chosen you for this task and He will be with you when you face the Amalekites.' Gesturing to a space next to him, he said, 'Come, sit. Let us discuss the battle plan. There is much to do before tomorrow.'

'Tomorrow?' My eyes widened in shock. 'We go to war tomorrow?'

'Yes, tomorrow.'

'But . . . but we need time to train the men and plan our attack . . .'

'There is no time to train, Joshua. The Amalekites are here and we must face them tomorrow. The night watchmen came to me early this morning. It seems the Amalekites marched through the night and have made their camp a few miles away, on the other side of the plain. They estimate a few thousand warriors.'

'A few *thousand*?'

Moses plunged ahead without allowing me the liberty of wallowing in fear or uncertainty. 'I suggest we choose 500 men from each tribe.' Turning to his right, he said, 'Hur, make haste, summon the elders and start the selection of warriors from each tribe. Tell them to choose men who are strong and able to wield a weapon. They must not choose young men who have recently married, those whose wife is with child or has recently given birth. The men are to gather by the tent of meeting after midday. Joshua and I will speak to them then.' Hur stood up, nodded to Moses, and went on his way without a backward glance.

Moses continued. 'Aaron, ask Eleazar to spread the word; any man who has sword or spear, shield, bow, or weapon of any kind, must bring it to the tent of meeting by midday today. All those with the skill of metal welding are to go to Bezalel's workshops and be ready to work all day, and through the night, to fashion weapons for our warriors.'

Moses turned to me next. 'Joshua, Yahweh has instructed me to stand on top of the hill overlooking the plain, with the staff in my hands. Aaron and Hur will stand with me. Go now and spy out the Amalekite camp, get the measure of our adversary. The watchmen are waiting outside, ready to take you to the best vantage point. I would suggest you take Caleb ben Jephunneh with you. He will stand by your side, like he did at the rock in Horeb, nu?' Moses grasped my shoulder. 'He is a brave man, and loyal – the kind of man you want standing with you in battle.'

Before I knew what was happening, I was on my way to the watchman's post. The rest of the day was a blur. I remember standing in front of thousands of our chosen warriors, trying to speak to them about bravery and courage, while my own heart trembled within me. I remember going with Moses to see the weaponry that we had amassed. It was pitiful. My heart sank when I realised we would be sending all but a handful of our warriors into war against the Amalekites, armed with nothing but rods or sickles.

I returned home that evening, my mind a fog and my heart numb. I went into my curtained-off section of the tent and pulled the curtain closed, but no sooner had I sat down then Mesha burst in and demanded, 'Why was I not chosen to stand with our warriors in the battle tomorrow?'

I was startled to see my friend looking so aggressive, but I suppose I should have expected it. I thought he would be angry. 'Mesha . . .'

'*Why*? I am young and strong, and ready to fight for my people and my God. So why was I not chosen to war against the Amalekites?'

'It is not because you are lacking in any way, Mesha. You are all of those things.'

'Then why have you spurned me?' Mesha stood in front of me, fists at the ready by his side. 'Was it you? Did you exclude me?'

'Mesha, come. Sit down and let us ta . . .'

'*Was it you*, Joshua?'

I hesitated. Holding my friend's gaze, I muttered. 'Yes. It was my decision.'

'*Why*? What have I done? Am I not bra – '

'It is not about you, Mesha!'

Confusion clouded Mesha's face. His fists clenched and unclenched as he said, 'How is that?'

'Sit.' He stared at me, unmoving, but I waited until he sat down before continuing. Staring at the ground, I spoke slowly. 'This will be my first battle. My *first battle*, Mesha, and it is against the Amalekites. You have heard the same stories as I have. You know they are formidable warriors, bloodthirsty and brutal. They show no mercy to their enemies. Their weapons are sharp and plentiful, and their armies are meticulously trained in the ways of war.' I looked up, so Mesha could see saw the fear in my eyes. I was past hiding it. He knew me better than most – I knew I could trust him. 'How do we fight them? We have no training in warfare and just a few crude weapons. Our warriors, brave though they are, will not be able to stand against the Amalekites. Not only must I face them myself, but I must also lead our army into battle tomorrow, Mesha. I am to lead 6,000 of our men into battle to be slaughtered.'

'So why not let me stand with you? Surely you need every man you can get. I will stand with you to the end, Joshua. I will not run.'

'I know. And that is why I cannot let you come.' I sighed at the confusion on Mesha's face. 'Mesha, I must have clear thoughts tomorrow. If I go into battle with my mind filled with thoughts of how to explain to Helah and the family that you have met your death, I will be distracted. I must be single-minded. That is why, as much as I want you there, I cannot have you stand by my side.'

Realisation flooded Mesha's face. Neither of us spoke for a while. I could see that he now understood my reasons for excluding him, but still did not agree with my decision. He wrestled with himself, trying to think of what he could do to change my mind. Before he could present his case, I spoke. I had to speak out what had been churning in my heart, sickening my gut, all day.

'Mesha . . . my heart is fearful about what we will face tomorrow. We have so few weapons, hardly any training and no armour. Moses offered me the use of his armour, given to him years ago, but I could not accept it. How can I go into battle clothed in armour, when my men have none?' I ran my fingers through my hair. 'How can I lead our warriors when I myself am fearful? I know not how to do this. I cannot lead an army. I am a manservant. I would gladly follow a captain into battle, but . . . I cannot be that captain. Why has Yahweh chosen me to do this? Why? Moses seems so confident.

He seems to have no doubt that we will be victorious. How can he be so sure?'

I was grateful for Mesha's silence. This was not the time for platitudes or insipid reassurances. 'Do you know what he said?' I laughed and rolled my eyes. 'You will not believe this! He said Yahweh told him to stand at the top of the hill overlooking the battle ground, with his staff in his hand. What will he do? Strike the ground with his staff and hope that water comes out and drowns the Amalekites?' I snorted. 'I know Moses is a great leader, but sometimes I fail to understand his ways. There is little sense in what he does.'

Mesha nodded and waited to see if I had any more to say. It was my turn to stay silent. I put my head in my hands.

'We saw no sound judgement when Moses held his staff over the waters of the Nile – but then the river turned to blood.' Mesha spoke with a calm certainty that I had rarely heard in him. 'For what reason did he strike the ground with his staff? Because Yahweh told him to. And when he did, the dust of Egypt turned into gnats, causing our enemies great discomfort. It seemed foolish for him to stretch his staff over the Red Sea, did it not? And to strike the rock at Horeb? But he did it, nevertheless, and look what happened when he did.'

Mesha bent forward to look at me. 'We may not understand His ways, but when we obey, we see Yahweh's hand move on our behalf – and He will move on our behalf tomorrow.' He reached out to grasp my arm. 'It is not wrong to be fearful in battle. You would be foolish not to fear. But Yoshi, let that fear cause you to rise up against this enemy. Let it provoke you to run headlong towards them! Yahweh was right to choose you. I know of no man better qualified to lead our warriors.'

I looked into Mesha's eyes and marvelled at what I saw. These were not the insincere platitudes of a man who thought our cause was lost; Mesha believed every word of what he was saying. He believed in me. I wondered what I had done to deserve it.

'Moses is right about one thing. Yahweh *is* with you – and He will be with you on the battlefield tomorrow.' Mesha stood to his feet. 'I will do as you ask. I will stay in the camp tomorrow and wait for your victorious return.' Holding the curtain open, Mesha turned to face me. 'Just this once, Joshua. Only this once. The next battle, I fight by your side.'

29

Wounded

It was very late when I finally made my way home, battle-weary and wounded, but alive. Yahweh's fiery tower still stood, like a majestic watchman, in the middle of the camp, but tonight, the peace that usually hovered over our camp at night was replaced by the shouts of those who celebrated the safe return of their loved ones, and the lament of those who bewailed the passing of the men who had fallen in battle.

'Yoshi!' Yoram yelled, leaping to his feet as soon as he saw me. He ran towards me and threw himself into my arms.

I yelped, clutching my chest.

'Yoram, no!' Mesha yelled from the entrance to their tent.

Yoram backed away. 'Forgive me, I did not know . . .'

'Peace, Yori. Peace to you,' I mumbled, smiling through the pain.

Jesher, Shira and all my brothers and sisters were sitting around the firepit awaiting my return. They all rose to greet me, but Mesha strode out to meet me first. 'You have returned. Did I not say that you would?' He put his hands on my shoulders, and kissed me on both cheeks. 'Forgive him,' he whispered, jabbing his head at Yoram, who had retreated into the background, mortified at the thought of causing me pain. 'He has been sitting out here for hours awaiting your return. While the children slept, he insisted on staying out here to wait for you.'

'Yahweh bless him,' I whispered. 'The hour is late. He must be tired.'

'Yoshi!' Helah joined us, tears in her eyes. 'Yoshi! You are safe!'

'Of course he is safe,' Mesha said.

Helah noticed the blood on my robes. 'You are wounded,' she said. 'Come inside and let us tend to your needs.' She led me inside, while Eglah poured hot water from a pot on the fire into a clay dish. Leora busied herself warming up some broth for me on the fire, and even Shira hovered around, plumping a cushion for me, and arranging my bed roll. I winced in pain as they sat me on it.

'Lie back and let us take a look at you,' Helah said.

'Helah, I am fine, I just need to sleep. I . . .'

'Joshua, *lie down*,' she said.

Mesha looked at me with a twinkle in his eye. 'Experience has taught me that it is best to obey. She is a fiercely determined woman!' I grunted and lay down, too exhausted to try to argue. Eglah and Helah sat either side of me. Yoram sat by my feet, my faithful shadow, watching everything that was happening, and the rest of the family gathered around. Helah drew back my outer robe and gasped when she saw a bloodstained rip in my tunic, revealing a jagged gash below my rib cage. Drawing the robe away from my shoulders and arms, Eglah saw another incision across my right arm, and bleeding gouges on my torso and arms.

'Hmm,' Helah said. 'We need to clean these and make a poultice to put on your wounds.'

'Helah, that's not necessary, I . . .'

'*Joshua, lie still!*' I was taken aback by her forthrightness. This was a side of Helah I had never encountered before.

I whispered to Mesha, 'Has she always been so ferocious?'

He looked at his wife with begrudging admiration. 'Only when it is necessary.' Eglah covered me with a blanket and Mesha helped her pull my tunic over my head while Helah went to the cooking area and fetched her mortar, some fresh herbs and a small clay jar of honey. She ground a selection of herbs using a smooth stone, then added some honey. While she was busy preparing the poultice, Mesha asked, 'So? How was it? What took place?'

I stared at him. How could I possibly convey to him the atrocities I had witnessed that day? The unbridled brutality of the Amalekites. The terror of warfare. Mutilated bodies falling all around me, hacked to death by razor-edged weapons. The blood . . . I put my hand to my face to wipe away the blood that I knew had splattered on me from the bodies of the men I had felled. How could I speak of the butchery and slaughter of war? I looked at the faces of those gathered around. How could I tell them?

I could not. I would not. I had no desire to speak of it. I wanted to wipe the horrors of that day from my mind, as we wiped the dew off our tent each morning. But I knew it would not be so easily erased. This day's events would stain the memories of my mind for much time to come. No. There would be another time to tell Jesher and my brothers about the horrors of war. I would not speak of it now, in front of the women, and not while Yoram was with us. But I could speak of the courage and bravery I had witnessed this day. I could tell them about the miracle that Yahweh had wrought, and the victory He had brought about as we made war in His name. Yes, I could speak of that.

I looked up and saw Jesher watching me. He knew. He had lived long enough to have seen the unspeakable brutality of men, and the lengths that they would go to, to protect those they loved. All I wanted was to sleep; to close my eyes and leave behind the terror of that day. To forget. But I could not. Not yet. So I drew in a breath, exhaled, and focused on Mesha's robe.

'The battle lines were drawn. Moses stood on the hill overlooking the battle, Aaron and Hur with him. He raised his staff above his head and shouted, and our warriors returned the rally cry, sprinting towards the Amalekites, shouting and screaming.' I shook my head. 'It was astounding. Most of them carried no weapon, but they ran headlong into battle, nevertheless. Their courage was . . .' Emotion welled up and I fought to hold it back. My mind searched for words to describe the courage I had witnessed that day. I found none. 'I was proud to stand with them on the battlefield.'

Eglah started washing my wounds with a cloth dipped in water. The pain ripped through me, and I stifled a cry. 'Forgive me,' she whispered, wiping as gently as she could.

'There is nothing to forgive, Eglah. Thank you for your kindness.' I could sense Mesha's impatience, so I continued. 'The Amalekites were just as brutal as we expected them to be, but our men were fearless. Caleb was . . . well, let's just say that the way he fought was . . . unusual, but very effective.' I smiled at Mesha. 'You would love fighting alongside him.'

'Yes? Why?'

'Well, he is not the most . . . masterful warrior, but his passion is unrivalled. As the battle raged, he found an Amalekite club – thick wooden handle, metal spikes all over it. He held it in front of him with both hands, leaned back and started spinning round and round, screaming at the top of his voice!' I laughed out loud, and then winced as stabs of pain shot through my chest. 'He slew many with that club.'

'He does sound like my kind of warrior,' Mesha agreed with a grin. 'What happened next?'

I refocused. 'The Amalekites had not expected us to lead the charge; their lines were in disarray, so they hastened to form ranks. I think they expected us to be animal fodder, but we were not. We drove into them, time and time again and, every time an Amalekite fell, one of our warriors took up his weapon.' I looked at my brothers individually, wanting them to understand the enormity of what I was telling them. 'Our warriors drove the Amalekites divisions back, little by little. We held the line and were winning, until . . .' I paused, unsure of how much to tell them.

'What?' Mesha asked. 'Until what?'

I frowned. 'They started to push us back.' I paused to thank Eglah, who had finished washing my wounds. Helah started applying the poultice. It was cool and refreshing, oddly comforting. 'I looked up at Moses, and saw that he no longer held his staff above his head – it was by his side. Yahweh told him to take his staff with him, and I knew there must be a reason for that.'

'What do you speak of, Yoshi?' Yoram asked.

'The staff. It is a symbol of the Lord's power. I brought to mind what happens when the staff is held out – Yahweh performs miracles! Remember when we were in Egypt, Moses stretched out his staff, and hail fell from the heavens on the Egyptians? The staff was stretched out over the river and it turned to blood! When Moses held the staff over the waters of the Red Sea they split asunder and, even here in Rephidim, he held it up and struck the rock – '

' – and water flowed from it! Yes!' Hareph blurted, moving closer to me, his face lit up with curiosity. 'But what does that have to do with warfare'?

'I felt certain that Yahweh's power would be seen through the staff. I entreated the Lord to strengthen Moses and, shortly afterwards, he held his staff above his head again, and shouted. Our warriors returned the rally cry, surged forward, and the battle turned in our favour. Each time Moses held up the staff, the same thing happened. But that was not all! I noticed that the Amalekites were watching Moses as well, and every time he lifted the staff, their hearts melted and they fell back. I saw it on their faces. *They were fearful of us*, not the other way around.'

'Whoa,' Yoram said, gazing at me. I closed my eyes and held my breath as Helah applied the poultice to the wound under my ribs. It felt like a knife slicing through my wounded flesh all over again.

'Forgive me, Yoshi.' Helah murmured. I opened my eyes, smiled at her, and nodded for her to continue, not trusting myself to speak.

'So then what happened, Yoshi?' Yoram asked.

'Every time Moses held up the staff, we triumphed, but when he put it down, the Amalekites triumphed. I thought Moses had realised that and would keep the staff lifted up but, the next time I looked up, he had lowered it again. I spoke to Hur after the battle and he explained that Moses could no longer hold the staff above his head – his arms shook from weariness, he was in anguish. So Hur found a rock and rolled it to the edge of the mountain. Moses sat on the rock, held the rod above his head, and Hur and Aaron stood either side of him, supporting his arms.'

'Oy! There is a battle plan that has never been seen before,' said Hareph, fascinated.

'Eish! The staff must be really powerful,' Yoram said in awe.

I looked at Yoram. 'The power does not lie within the staff itself, Yori. The power lies within the heart of the man who believes Yahweh and wields the staff at His command.'

Yoram looked at me, enthralled, but Mesha, impatient as ever, said, 'So? What happened after that?'

Eglah and Helah helped me sit up, and started binding the gashes in my arm with strips of cloth. I shrugged. 'It was done! We advanced steadily from then onwards. Moses didn't lower the staff again, and we continued to drive the Amalekites back until they were utterly defeated. The few who hadn't yet fallen in battle eventually dropped their weapons and fled from us.'

I bit my lip as the women wrapped my torso with the cloth and fastened it on the side, before continuing. 'We gave chase and felled many of them, but I decided to let some escape, so they could give account to their king of the slaughter of their army at the hand of the Israelites!' I shook my head again. 'I never would have believed that a throng of Amalekites would run from us. They *feared* us!'

'And so they should!' Mesha exclaimed. 'Yahweh is with us and He is greatly to be feared. The nations will see that His arm is not short.'

'Amen! But what is even more important – oh, thank you, Leora.' She handed me a dish of steaming broth. 'What is even more important is that *our men* saw that Yahweh's arm is not short. They saw Him move today through the rallying cry of a prophet holding up a wooden staff. What is more,' I said, taking some mouthfuls of broth, 'there was much plunder to be gathered up after the battle – weapons, armour, treasures . . .'

'Yoshi, what were the Amalekite weapons like?' Yoram asked.

Before I could answer, Jesher stepped forward. 'I think that is enough stories for one night. We must let Joshua sleep so he can recover, yes? He can tell us more in the morning but, for now, we are all tired. So let us thank Yahweh for this victory, for returning Joshua to us, and go to our beds.'

I don't remember finishing my broth, or who took the dish from me when it was empty. I don't remember saying goodnight to anyone. I don't remember the blessings that Jesher prayed over us. I only remember lying down, closing my eyes and sinking into the blissful darkness of the realms of sleep.

30

Reunited

'Master! Master!' I ran through the crowd, darting past people, zigzagging on my way. 'Master, they have arrived! They are here!'

Moses' head poked out of his tent flap, his eyes wide with anticipation. 'They are here? Where? Where are they?'

'On the east side of the camp. I told them I would fi – ' Moses had already taken off running, dignity cast aside like unwanted rags. People scattered left, right and centre, as he ran through the crowds.

'Ech! Forgive me!' he called out as he went, not looking back or stopping to apologise properly.

'Ay, ay, ay! Why such haste?' a man grumbled, thrown off balance when Moses rushed past him.

'Moses! What is wrong?' another shouted at him. Their questions were tossed to the wind, left unanswered as Moses hurried on his way. I followed behind him, but my wounds were still healing, and the one by my rib cage hindered me from running as fast as I usually would have. I was bombarded with questions as I made my way through the crowds.

'Joshua! Where is Moses going in such a hurry?'

'What is happening?'

'They are here,' I panted, holding the wound in my chest, but not stopping to talk.

'They are here? Truly?' Turning to his neighbour, the man said, 'They are here! No wonder Moses is in such a hurry!'

'Ah, yes. It has been a long time, *nu*?'

'I wonder what she is like,' I heard the man mumble.

'Well, she is not one of us, that much we know,' said his wife, raising an eyebrow.

'And the father? They say he is a priest, but a priest of what god?'

'It matters not. They are not one of us,' the woman replied. Nodding their heads in agreement, feigning disinterest, they all went back to their business, surreptitiously scanning the pathway through the camp for signs of the new arrivals. Many of the women decided the area outside their tents needed sweeping, and some of the men felt a sudden urge to go and collect firewood from the east side of the camp.

A crowd had gathered. I heard Moses shouting, 'Zipporah! Zipporah!' Pushing my way through the wall of bodies, I saw Moses plunge forward and lift his wife off her feet. He swung her round and round, laughing with joy. It was a transformation! I had never seen him so full of life, so vivacious.

'Moses!' Zipporah gazed at him in adoration, her eyes filling with tears as he set her down. 'I thought I might never see you again, but here you are! Alive and well and with all your people.' Moses drew her into his arms, holding her tightly, the tears in his eyes matching hers. It was a moment of such tenderness, I felt as though I was intruding, so I looked away and waited. My heart ached. To have someone who loves you that much, who knew you so completely . . . would that I could have that.

'Is it true, what we have heard?' Zipporah asked, stepping back a little to look at him. 'The Red Sea, the Egyptians . . . ?'

'Yes. It is true, all true.' He laughed with delight at the expression on her face and swept her into his arms for another embrace. The two boys who had been standing behind her now walked forward and gazed expectantly at Moses. 'Gershom! Eliezer!' He held out his arms and they bolted towards their father, almost knocking him over in their eagerness to hug him. He kissed both boys and stepped back. 'Let me look at you. Oy! What has your *ima* been feeding you? You have grown so much – look how tall you are!' Moses looked at them with pride, then pulled them close for another embrace. 'Oh, my heart has longed to hold you.'

My heart tightened some more. Sons. Sons to carry on your family line, throughout the generations – this was the way of our people. This was the blessing of God, the reason for our existence, our hope, our joy – our legacy. For some.

A large man stood watching their reunion, a satisfied smile plastered all over his face. He was tall and imposing, with a kingly bearing and, when Moses turned to acknowledge him with a bow and a formal greeting, he returned the courtesy. *'Shalom aleichem,* Jethro.'

'Aleichem shalom, Moses.'

Putting a hand on each other's right shoulder, they kissed one another on the cheek, then Jethro pulled Moses into a jubilant bear hug. Moses, trapped in Jethro's arms, laughed and returned the embrace as they slapped each other on the back. This must be Moses' father-in-law, the priest. A priest of Midian. Although Moses had spoken well of Jethro, of how he had been a father to him and helped him during his time in the desert after leaving Egypt, I was yet to be convinced. Jethro was a Midianite. He was not one of Yahweh's people.

Drawing back, Moses kept his hand on Jethro's shoulder and said, 'Thank you. Thank you for bringing my family to me.'

'It was my honour, Moses,' Jethro nodded his head in acknowledgement, 'and besides, you know what my daughter is like once she has made up her mind about something. I had no choice in the matter!' They laughed and Moses looked at his wife with admiration, shaking his head when she shrugged her shoulders in response. Jethro's expression changed from joy to concern. 'You look terrible,' he said to Moses, his eyes narrowing.

Moses grimaced. 'Thank you!'

'Are you unwell? What has taken place here?' Jethro persisted.

Moses hesitated for a moment. 'There is much to discuss.'

'Yes. Yes indeed,' Jethro responded. 'All in the course of time, yes?'

Moses, aware of the crowds standing around, signalled to his family, and said, 'Come, let me show you where your tents are.' He gestured to me. 'This is Joshua, my manservant and now, leader of the armies of Israel.' Jethro turned to look at me. Contrary to what I expected, I saw no guile in his face, only openness and curiosity. Greetings were exchanged and introductions made, before the small caravan of people and livestock moved through the crowds to find their new home. I left Moses to become reacquainted with his family, and went home to mine. They were very curious about Moses' family but, as I had just met them briefly, I could only answer their questions as best I could, with a promise to tell them more in time.

The following morning, when I arrived to accompany Moses to the Meeting Tent, I found him tired and unusually grumpy. He had been up late into the night talking with Zipporah and Jethro, and was not pleased at the prospect of spending a day sitting in the tent of meeting, listening to people's complaints. But he was a diligent man who knew his duty, so we walked there together. Later in the morning, when Moses was dealing with a case of suspected thieving, I looked up to see Jethro standing at the back of the tent. I found him a comfortable place to sit, so he could watch his son-in-law in action, and time passed by as Moses dealt with case after case of disagreements and disputes, from petty misunderstandings to issues of greater importance. Just before midday, Moses indicated to me that he would take a break, stood up and walked towards Jethro.

'*Shalom, Abba*,' he said, smiling at his father-in-law. 'Did you sleep well?'

'*Shalom*, my son,' Jethro said, rising and kissing him on each cheek. 'I did, thank you. You are quite impressive in your judgement seat there.'

'Hmm. It is not something I enjoy, but it has to be done.'

'Yes, indeed. A people as mighty as this need a strong hand to lead them.' Opening his arms wide, Jethro smiled and said, 'But now you are done, so shall we walk and talk?'

'Forgive me, *Abba*, but I only have a short break and then I must continue.'

Jethro raised his eyebrows in surprise. 'You are doing more?'

'Yes. But I will finish in time to break bread this evening.'

'Oh.' Jethro thought for a moment, then shrugged and said, 'Very well, we will talk then. Perhaps we can walk through the camp tomorrow and you can show me where everything is.'

Moses looked at him apologetically. 'Forgive me, *Abba*, I do not think you understand. I have to judge the people again tomorrow, and the next day and the next. I do this every day, except on Shabbat.'

'Every day? You sit there and judge the people *every day* from morning until night?'

'Yes.'

'Moses, this is not good. When do you have time to rest, and what about time with your family?'

'Well, my family was not here.' Moses ran his fingers through his beard. 'But perhaps I need to make some changes now that they have joined me.'

Jethro peered at him. 'Moses, you need to make many changes, and not just because your family is here, but because this is not good for you – it is not good for your people, either.'

'I suppose so,' Moses said, rubbing his temple. 'But the people come to enquire of God. I have to teach them Yahweh's statutes and make known to them His ways.'

'Moses,' Jethro said, taking hold of Moses' shoulders, 'you cannot do this on your own. Look at the multitudes that surround you! You will make yourself really ill!'

'I know, but what can I do?' Weariness and desperation were etched on Moses' face. 'They are like children, Jethro, always having to be told what to do, unable to make decisions for themselves. They must be given instructions, all the time. They know not how to live out here, in the wilderness – they are ignorant of the ways of the sojourner.'

'Just like you were, when you first came to be with us, yes? Well, they are blessed to have you to teach them.'

Moses sat down under the awning and rested his head in one hand. 'I can teach them, but there are so many of them and they come to me for everything. Endless queues of people asking, "How should I do this?", "Why must we do that?", "What must I do when my neighbour does this?"' Moses looked up at Jethro, frowning. 'They also *argue* like children, on and on. Why this, why that? I do not like this; I want that . . . *Abba*, I am brought low. It lies heavy upon me. I do not know how much longer I can continue.'

I was not surprised at his outburst. I had seen weariness assailing Moses over the past few weeks, and I had my concerns about how much he was doing, but I never felt it was my place to say anything. He had never voiced his struggles to me. Jethro studied Moses. I could see compassion for his son-in-law rising up strongly in his heart. 'You are only one man, Moses. An impressive man, yes,' he said, shrugging, 'but one man, nevertheless. You cannot do this on your own.'

'So, what should I do?'

Jethro thought for a while. 'Well, I know the first thing that needs to be done.' He lifted his hand and signalled to me.

'Jethro? Can I assist you?' I asked.

'Yes. Joshua, please tell the people that Moses will not be judging them this afternoon.'

'*Abba*, I cannot . . .' Moses protested, but Jethro put his hand up to silence Moses and ploughed on, regardless.

'Tell them that he will not be judging them tomorrow, either. Or the next day.' Frowning deeply, Jethro said, 'Yes. In fact, tell them that Moses will not be judging them at all, until we send word to them.'

I hesitated, my eyes darting between Jethro and Moses. 'Master, is this what you would have me . . . ?'

'Go, go, go! Tell the people!' Jethro said, waving me away. Then, seeing my concerned expression, he put his hand on my shoulder, leaned closer and smiled. 'All will be well, Joshua. All will be well. My son-in-law cannot continue in this manner or he will wear himself out, yes? We will take counsel together about how to help him. But for now, no more judging the people, yes?'

Moses stood up, caught my eye and nodded wearily. 'Let it be so, Joshua. Walk with us back to my tent, and then take that message to the elders.'

Jethro turned to Moses. 'Now, we are going to get some food into that scrawny body of yours, and then you are going to get some sleep, yes?' Putting his arm around Moses' shoulders, he led him away from the tent of meeting. I walked behind them.

'Are you eating properly?' Jethro asked.

'Uh, when I remember to.'

Jethro raised one eyebrow and peered at him intently before swinging around to look at me. 'Joshua, how often does he remember to eat?'

I hesitated. It was hard to hold back information from Jethro. He had such a commanding sense of authority and I could already see in him a discerning spirit – he would know if I was withholding information. There was nothing for it but to tell him the truth. 'Not often, my lord.' I gave Moses an apologetic glance.

'In truth,' Moses said, 'by the time evening comes, all I want to do is sleep. Sometimes I eat with Miriam or Aaron, but you must understand, I am in the company of people all day, every day and by the time the evening draws in, I can abide it no longer. I must be alone in the evenings, to be quiet, to think and pray. So I stay in my tent.'

'Hmph,' Jethro snorted. 'Well that explains why you are so thin, yes?' Moses gave him a wan smile, Jethro burst into raucous laughter and slapped Moses on the back. As they walked, Jethro talked to him, like a father talks to his son. My heart yearned for my own father and a fresh wave of grief washed over me. My *abba* would talk to me in the same way. But no longer.

'Moses, you are Yahweh's man, chosen to lead His people. You do this well, and you will continue to teach them the statutes and laws, showing them the way in which they must walk. But you cannot do this on your own. That is not good. There must be men of wisdom here; men who fear your God and hate unrighteousness. We will find these men and they will help you judge the people.' Moses, too tired to object, just nodded. Clearly pleased with himself, Jethro turned to me. 'Yes, that is what we will do.'

We walked away, an odd trio; one slender man, thin and hunched over, a fatherly giant towering over him, tall and sturdy, and me, their faithful watchman following quietly in their footsteps.

31

The God of Moses

The tour of the camp started with a walk first thing the following morning, to collect manna. I accompanied Moses and Jethro as they walked through the camp to the outskirts where the manna still appeared early every morning.

'So, this . . . manna,' asked Jethro, looking at the ground. 'It just appears, like this, on the ground, every morning?'

'Yes.'

'And you just . . . pick it up, and . . .' Moses nodded, picking some manna up and handing it to Jethro. He fingered it, fascinated by its wafer-like texture. 'How do you eat it? What do you do with it? Do you have to cook it?'

'The women grind it and make bread cakes with it, or porridge, or we eat it just as it is.'

'Intriguing,' said Jethro, holding it up to his nose. 'It smells of . . .' he concentrated, sniffing it, 'of . . . coriander!'

'Yes, it tastes like it too,' said Moses, laughing, 'with flavours of honey and spices. Come, let us take this back to Miriam. She is teaching Zipporah how to make manna cakes.'

Jethro cocked his head to one side spoke to me. 'Joshua, I love my daughter dearly. She has many outstanding qualities and is skilled at many things. But cooking is not one of them.' He turned back to Moses. 'I speak truly, yes?'

Moses smiled and nodded. 'But do not tell her I said that!' We walked on, and Jethro asked Moses about the thick cloud above us which hovered and swelled, yet never dissipated. Moses explained that the cloud was the sign of Yahweh's presence and His protection over us, that when the cloud moved, that was the sign that we were to move on, and that we follow His presence, His direction, His cloud.

'You follow His cloud,' Jethro muttered, eyes narrowed in concentration, trying to grasp the enormity of this fact. He stopped for a moment to study the billowing canopy and marvel at its form. 'I have never seen anything like this, in all my years. The way it shines, its movement, and the colours, they are like . . . like a rainbow within the cloud!' Jethro must have noticed the expression on my face, because he said, 'Your heart, it yearns for this cloud, yes?'

'It does, my lord.' Even though I had known Jethro such a short time, I knew I could trust him. I knew he would understand. So I told him how my heart yearned for Yahweh's presence more than the food I ate, that there were times during the day, or at night, when I had to take my leave of people, so I could be alone with Yahweh. I glanced at him to make sure he was not laughing at me. He seemed to be captivated by what I said, so I carried on. 'I go outside the camp to find somewhere where I can be alone, and there, I sense His presence. His power moves me, through His cloud – and through the fire. Did you see how it transforms at night into a pillar of fire?'

Jethro clutched my arm, his eyebrows shooting up into his forehead. 'Oysh! Moses brought me outside to look upon it. I thought my heart would stop! The sparks, the flashes of light – the glowing embers in the midst of it! My heart was so full of wonder, I could hardly speak!' I nodded. No words were needed. We stood for a while, gazing upwards in reverential silence, contemplating the complexity and wonder of Yahweh's presence.

'The cloud changes form sometimes,' Moses added after a while.

'Yes? How?'

'When Yahweh is angry the cloud grows dark and dense, and we have seen fire come from its midst.'

Jethro shook his head. 'Your people are truly blessed to have Yahweh's presence with you, to have the covering of this cloud and to witness the fire each night. None of our forefathers have witnessed anything like this! Your people are favoured, Moses, truly.'

Later that day, we took Jethro to the rock at Horeb which was now the camp's water source. He listened carefully as Moses told him the story of how Yahweh had instructed him to strike the rock.

'So you had the rod in your hands?' Jethro held an imaginary staff in his hands, looking at Moses to check that he was correct in his assumptions. Moses nodded. 'And you . . .' Jethro held his arms up, still looking at Moses, brought down the imaginary staff with great force. 'And the water . . .' Jethro made billowing motions with his arms.

'Yes.'

'And many people saw this, yes?' Moses nodded again and smiled. 'Did you see it?' Jethro asked me.

'I did. I was with Moses when he struck the rock.'

'Hmm.' Jethro frowned. 'Yes. Hmm.' Scratching his thick beard, he turned to find a rock to sit on. We sat in companionable silence for a while and allowed Jethro time to think. 'Ha!' I jumped as Jethro slapped his hand on his leg. 'Ha!' Jethro shouted again, this time even louder. 'Moses!' He clasped Moses to him. 'My son . . . I have no words. What can I say? I have never . . . in all my years . . . I . . . Moses . . .' He sighed. 'Truly, your God is God. He is the Lord. The one true God.' Looking at the water gushing out of the rock again, he clicked his tongue. Shaking his head and chuckling to himself, he muttered, 'Water from a rock. Yes, indeed. Cloud and fire, and. . . water coming from a rock. Hmm. Ha!'

That night, a feast was held in Jethro's honour. The elders gathered to eat with Moses' family, and I was invited to attend. In the firelight, the stories of our exit from Egypt, the plagues, the Passover, the parting of the Red Sea, the bitter water and the water from the rock at Horeb were told and retold, again and again. Jethro, Zipporah and her sons listened, enthralled by what they heard, asking questions about the ways of Yahweh and His power, which was so clearly displayed. I was given a seat near Jethro. It made me uncomfortable, especially when I saw some of the elders looking at me and whispering among themselves, obviously wondering why I had been given such a great honour. What had I done to deserve being exalted in such a way? I didn't know.

I asked if I could move to the outskirts of the gathering, but Moses would not hear of it. He told me it had been Jethro's request, and that to change places would be to dishonour him. So, I stayed there and tried to ignore the whisperings and envious looks. Jethro asked me about the battle against the Amalekites, so I told him how our victory came about.

'So, only when Moses held up his staff were your warriors victorious?'

'Yes. When he lowered the staff the Amalekites drove us back, but when the staff was raised, we drove them back, every time.'

'And there were many Amalekites?'

'Thousands – all of them fully equipped with weapons and armour.' I leaned forward. 'My lord, it was impossible for us to have won that battle without Yahweh. Our warriors are brave, but we had hardly any weapons and no armour. We had not been trained for war and had no skill in battle.' I looked up at the pillar of fire which blazed nearby. 'But Yahweh was with us and it was He who won the battle for us.'

Jethro shook his head. 'This is not a battle plan I have ever heard of before.' He laughed and punched me in the arm. 'But clearly it worked, yes?' Jethro continued questioning me for quite a while about Moses and our journey thus far. But, near the end of the evening, he was silent and seemed deep in thought. Turning to Moses, he said, 'I knew something of your God from the stories you told us at Midian, but now I know without a doubt that your God is greater than all other gods. I have seen it with my own eyes, heard it with my own ears.'

I caught Moses' eye and we shared a smile by the flickering light of the fire. Before either of us could respond, Jethro lifted his hands to silence everyone gathered round. He declared in a booming voice, 'Blessed be the Lord, who has delivered you out of the hand of the Egyptians and out of the hand of Pharaoh. He has delivered your people from under the rule of the Egyptians. He separated the waters of the Red Sea so His people could walk through on dry ground. He even made water flow from a rock, yes?' His face broke into a smile. 'Truly, He is greater than all other gods.' Jethro lifted his arm to heaven and declared, 'He alone is God.'

Voices were raised in agreement around the fire. 'Amen. Amen!'

Looking at the elders individually and holding their gaze where possible, Jethro solemnly proclaimed, 'Before all of you gathered together here, I make this solemn oath: that from this day I, with all my people, will serve the God of the Israelites,' he pointed to his son-in-law, 'the God of Moses – and we will worship Him only.' Cheers erupted from the group. Jethro waited until they quietened down and then went on, 'Tomorrow, as a sign of this oath, I will offer sacrifices to the God of Moses, and I will learn of His statutes and laws.'

Blessings were pronounced on Jethro and his descendants.

'Be strong and blessed!'

'Amen! Amen!'

'May abundant peace, and long life be upon you and your descendants!'

'May your strength be increased from this day.'

'Amen!'

'May Yahweh's great Name be blessed forever and ever!'

'Amen!'

The minstrels began to play their instruments and some of the elders rose to their feet, inviting Jethro to join them. They formed a circle around him and joined hands. I was not usually given to dancing, preferring to watch rather than join in but, on this occasion, I was not given a choice. Moses grabbed me by the arm and hauled me up. Ignoring my protests, he pulled me into the circle of men, laughing at my obvious discomfort.

Arms held high, we stamped our feet, shouted and danced, from the youngest to the eldest, who tottered unsteadily. The dancing started slowly, increasing in speed as the music got faster and louder. Jethro stood in the middle of the circle, clapping his hands, roaring his approval and singing along as best he could. My awkwardness dissolved in the face of the joy that permeated the atmosphere and, before long, I joined in with gusto, dancing along with the best of them.

The celebrations continued late into the night and the noise echoed all around the camp until, exhausted but exhilarated, we stumbled to our tents to tell our families the news. The report spread that the father-in-law of Moses, along with his whole family and all his people, were no longer unbelievers, but were now as one with our people; worshippers of the one true God, Yahweh.

Speculation was rife and many were unconvinced, but most withheld their ruling until such time as they could see and judge for themselves – and they were able to do this, for Jethro very quickly became an intricate part of the daily life of our wilderness camp.

32

Son of My Heart

Things were going well in the camp. The days that followed were more fruitful than all the previous weeks put together, and many changes took place under the watchful eye of Moses' father-in-law. Together, Jethro, Zipporah and I made sure that Moses ate regular meals and rested, and it didn't take long for Moses' strength to return, for some flesh to appear on his worn-out body.

As he met with the people to teach them the ways of God, his heart was encouraged and his strength returned. Leaders were duly appointed; leaders of tens, fifties, hundreds and thousands, and Moses passed on to them the wisdom and knowledge of Yahweh. Each day was a new opportunity to learn from each other and grow in wisdom and character. The people adjusted to the new system and balance was restored. I felt contented – more contented than I had felt for a very long time. It was good.

Before Jethro's visit, Moses and I had developed the habit of walking through the camp every day, in the cool of evening, before the cloud transformed into fire. I looked forward to it – it was a time where we talked, man to man, and our walks usually finished with a time of prayer and reflection as we watched Yahweh's cloud transform. However, since our battle against the Amalekites, I had become well known – a situation I was extremely uncomfortable with. I had not asked for the renown that came with being a military hero and I did not welcome it. The evening walks had become a struggle for me and, being a naturally reticent man himself, having gone through similar circumstances, Moses understood my dilemma. After Jethro arrived, he joined us on our evening walks. To my relief, a lot of the attention that had previously been given to me was now focused on Jethro. He greeted people and smiled in recognition when meeting those he had come to know.

'*Shalom*, Jethro. *Shalom*, Moses. *Shalom*, Joshua,' people called out as we passed by.

'*Shalom*, Ahlai,' Jethro responded one evening when greeted by a faithful follower. Ahlai had made a habit of waiting outside his tent about the time we went for our evening walk; it seemed he enjoyed talking with Moses' famous father-in-law. 'How is your family?'

'All well, yes, all well, Yahweh be praised,' Ahlai responded, raising his hands to the heavens. Then, sensing an opportunity, he went on to say, 'Moses, may I ask you a question? It is about my son and his apprenticeship. He is having troubles with Peleth and I thought maybe if you could . . .'

Jethro stepped forward before he could finish. 'Ahlai, have you spoken to your elders about this?'

'Uh, no, not yet,' he said, fiddling with his hands nervously. 'But I just thought, since Moses is here now, perhaps . . .'

Jethro was an imposing figure and he towered over Ahlai, who was a man of less than average height. The contrast was comical. Moses and I smiled to ourselves as Jethro firmly reminded Ahlai of the new rules that had been set in place. 'Ahlai, you know the new laws for judging disputes. You must speak to your elders first, not to Moses.' Invariably, every time we walked, there were at least one or two people who decided to one or two people who would try to sidestep the new process.

Most evenings, Jethro would discuss the day's affairs with Moses as they walked. Today, however, he was much quieter.

'Moses,' Jethro said, looking straight ahead. 'Moses, the time has come for me to return to my people.'

Moses said nothing. Turning his face forward, he concentrated on the pathway in front of him.

Jethro turned to look at him. 'I have been away for many days; I must return to my people.'

'Yes, I understand,' said Moses, avoiding Jethro's stare. Silence prevailed as we walked; the only sound was the scuffing of our footsteps and the laughter of children playing nearby in the sand. Then Moses stopped and swung round to face Jethro. 'Stay with us!' Watching Jethro's face for some sign of agreement, he entreated him again. 'Stay with us, *Abba*. Stay here and help me lead these people. You will have a place of honour. You will lack nothing and my people will be your people, as my God is your God.'

'Moses,' Jethro said, his brow wrinkled and his eyes full of understanding. 'You do me a great honour. Thank you. But I cannot stay.' Moses' face fell, and Jethro put his hand on Moses' shoulder. 'You know that. As much as I love you and your people, I must go back to my people. I must now teach them the ways of Yahweh and take back to them everything I have learned here. You must see that.'

Moses sighed. 'I do.' They continued walking, each grappling with their own thoughts in the heaviness of the silence that hung between them. I hung back a little, walking a little way behind them so as not to intrude.

'Do you remember the first time we met?' asked Jethro.

Moses smiled. 'How could I forget it? I did not make a very good first impression, did I?'

'No. You really did not,' said Jethro, laughing. 'You were filthy and skinny – even more so than now,' he said, poking Moses in the side, 'and you had the social skills of a trapped animal.' Moses grimaced, saying nothing. 'You knew not who you were, who your people were, or where you belonged. You were lost. But even right back then, I knew there was someone special in there, someone strong and powerful. Someone who would lead others. A man of significance. That is why I gave Zipporah to you. I could not have given her in marriage to a lesser man. But I could see that man through all the layers of pain and anger and confusion. I could see *you*, Moses. I could see who you would become.'

Jethro stopped in the pathway. I stayed back. 'Moses, you have become that man. You are a great leader. A *great* leader. Yahweh has chosen well. You lead your people with wisdom and strength. You do not need me to be with you. You have good men around you, strong men with noble hearts. And,' he turned and gestured to me, 'you have Joshua.' I looked at Jethro, startled that he would see me as worthy of mentioning, but his attention was already back on Moses. 'Yahweh has given you everything you need to take your people into the land He has promised you. So go!' Jethro's hand formed into a fist. 'Go and *take* that land! Take hold of what is yours, not for yourself, but for your people and for your God. Yahweh is with you, Moses. Never look back to where you have come from.' He gestured behind, then he pointed to the path in front. 'Fix your eyes on what is ahead and go and take that land. You are well able, Moses. You are *well* able.'

Moses stared at him and I could see a mixture of emotions in his expression. Pain, fear, faith, excitement – and love. 'You have been a father to me.' Tears clouded Moses' eyes – and mine, as longing for my own father welled up again.

'And I could not think of you any more my own son, even if you were my own seed,' Jethro responded. 'You are the son of my heart, Moses.'

It was twilight by the time we arrived back at the tent. We watched the transformation of the cloud in silence together and, when it was done, Moses asked, 'When do you leave?'

'There is no point in drawing this out. We leave tomorrow.' Jethro turned to me. 'Joshua, a word with you, if I may?'

I was mystified, but said, 'Of course, my lord,' and followed Jethro to his tent.

'There is something I would like to give to you,' Jethro said.

'To give *me*?'

'Yes. I want to thank you for serving my son-in-law so faithfully, and for – '

'My lord, there is no need to – '

'Ech!' Jethro said, holding out the palm of his hand. 'There is every need. I know there are not many who see all that you do for Moses, but I do. I have seen not only what you do, but how you do it and I am grateful to you, Joshua, for standing by his side, serving him so well. You are a man of honour, faithful and loyal, and your heart is steadfast.'

I struggled to maintain eye contact with him. Moses was a good man, and I knew his heart was pure, but he was not a man who was effusive with praise so I was not used to being honoured like this. I did not need to be acknowledged on a regular basis, and did not seek it. I felt uncomfortable being singled out in this manner.

'Your sword, where did you get it from?' he asked.

'I took it from an Amalekite warrior on the battlefield.'

'Ah, I thought so.' Jethro drew a sword out from the folds of his robes. I knew just by looking at it that this was no ordinary sword. It was enclosed in a scabbard of superior quality leather, encrusted with precious stones and, as he drew the sword from its ornate cover, I gasped at the workmanship. The blade gleamed in the firelight and there were patterns engraved down both edges. 'It is magnificent, is it not?' Jethro smiled with satisfaction at the expression on my face. 'It was given to me by a desert dweller who I came across a few years ago. He presented it to me as a thank you for helping him with a . . . shall we say, rather sensitive family matter.' Sliding the sword back into its scabbard, he held it out to me with both hands. 'And now I entrust this sword to you.'

'My lord, this is a very costly sword. I cannot . . .'

'Joshua!' Jethro barked. 'A warrior such as yourself deserves a fine sword like this. I have heard from others about what you did in the battle against the Amalekites, how you fought and the way you led the army. You will not dishonour me by refusing it, will you?'

I stared at him, looked down at the sword, and then back up to him. 'No, my lord.' I bent over at the waist in a full bow in recognition of the honour he was bestowing on me. 'It would be my very great honour to accept it.'

'Just as it is mine to give it,' Jethro said, his stern face breaking into a broad grin. Handing it to me, he drew me into one of his hugs and slapped me on the back, nearly causing me to drop it. 'Ha!' he roared, as was his way. Drawing back, he said, 'Now I know I can take my leave, because my son has a man such as you to stand by his side. Thank you, Joshua.' His voice clouded with emotion. 'Thank you.'

As I took my leave of Moses and Jethro that night, I turned back and saw them standing together, side by side, basking in the warmth and glow of the flickering pillar of fire. Their farewell was a private affair, in the early hours of the following morning, before the sun had risen. Moses, Zipporah and the boys walked with Jethro and his company a little way into the wilderness. Moses asked me to accompany them.

Jethro embraced Zipporah and the boys first, then put his hands on Moses' shoulders and looked deeply into his eyes. 'May the Lord uphold you and give you to drink of His goodness in abundance. May wisdom be a garland to grace your head. May you flourish like the acacia trees in the desert, and bear much fruit in your old age.'

Moses joined his arms with Jethro's. 'May Yahweh be your shield. May He withhold no good thing from you. May no evil befall you, nor plague come near your dwelling, and may the Lord be between you and me and between your descendants and mine, forever. Go in peace.'

They embraced one last time, then Jethro turned to look at me. He smiled and nodded once, then turned his face forward. The caravan of men and beasts made its way slowly towards the rocky hills. After a while, Gershom and Eliezer returned to the camp with their mother. Moses stayed, staring at the retreating figures until Jethro's caravan was just a speck on the horizon, and until the blinding rays of the rising sun prevented him from seeing any more.

I waited at the edge of the camp, keeping the few curious onlookers away. My eyes did not wander from the place where Moses stood. I stayed, as Jethro knew I would, a faithful sentinel keeping watch over his master.

33

Special Treasure

The dawn had not yet broken. I sat outside watching the fiery pillar finish its nightly vigil, enjoying the last threads of quietness before the sun rose and the camp burst into life. I had always been an early riser, and found great solace and contentment in the quietness of early mornings. I gazed at the flickering fingers of flame as they dissipated, and was preparing myself for the day ahead when the piercing blast of the shofar erupted, shattering the peace.

I heard Jesher shouting out in fright, so I leapt up and bolted inside the tent to find him struggling to free himself from his blanket, which seemed to have wrapped itself tightly around his skinny frame during the course of the night.

'Shira!' he bawled. 'Shira! What is it? Are we under attack? Is it the Amalekites?'

'Of course not,' she said, rolling her eyes. 'Oy! When will you learn the different shofar calls, hmm? That is not the call to arms, it is the call to assemble.'

'At this time in the morning?' Jesher peered at her, his nose wrinkled in confusion. 'Joshua? What could be so urgent they must wake us before the birds with this noise?'

'I do not know, *Abba*.'

'Of course he does not know,' Shira muttered. 'Why would he? Jesher, you must go and find out. Quickly. Get up.' She ripped the blanket off his body.

'Ay, ay, ay, let a man wake up first, *nu*?' he glared at her, eyes bleary with sleep, pulling the blanket back to cover himself. He rubbed his arms and shivered. 'A drink and something to eat, then I will go.'

'There is no time, Jesher,' Shira said. You must go now and be one of the first to find out what is taking place.'

I reached out, helped him to his feet, then escaped to safety outside the tent. I could still hear him muttering to himself. 'Can a man find no peace in his own home?' He stumbled outside, blinking in the light as Shira handed him his sandals. 'Here, put these on – and tidy your hair,' she said, looking with irritation at the tufts that stuck out at right angles on the top of Jesher's head. 'You look like a camel that has been through a sandstorm.' Jesher licked his hands and tried to smooth the rebellious tufts down. Shira looked at him in disgust.

Jesher grabbed his head covering and threw it over his ruffled hair. Intertwining the ends of the cloth, he tossed them over his shoulders in a gesture of defiance, his bushy eyebrows dipping down as he glared at his wife. He straightened his back, lifted his head, said, 'Joshua, shall we walk together?' and set off without waiting for a response. I bowed my head in acknowledgement to Shira, who stood shaking her head, then ran to catch up with him. Jesher mumbled to himself as we walked, 'There is only so much a man can deal with, so early in the morning.'

'I wonder why they have called us,' I mused. 'Moses said nothing of this to me yesterday. It must be important.'

'Nothing is so important that it cannot wait until after I have broken my fast,' Jesher grumbled as we trudged on together to the assembly point. As it turned out, it was important. Very important.

The family gathered around when Jesher and I returned later that morning to give them the news: Yahweh would meet with His people!

'But how will that happen?' Hareph asked.

'The cloud of Yahweh's presence will come down upon Mount Sinai, and He will speak with His people.'

'He would speak with us?' Hareph's eyes lit up. 'In truth?'

I smiled at his response. There was something almost childlike about Hareph's enthusiasm. 'Yes. We are to consecrate ourselves, wash our clothes and be ready at the foot of the mountain on the morning of the third day. Then Yahweh will come and meet with us.' Sounds of amazement and apprehension broke out as the family all started asking questions, talking at the same time, deliberating about what might happen. Jesher was standing with his back to us, staring at the outline of the mountain and the clouds that enveloped its craggy peaks. He was making noises and appeared to be talking under his breath.

'*Abba*?' Azriel asked. 'Are you well?'

'Yes, yes. I am well,' he murmured. 'I am pondering the words of Moses.' Jesher turned to us and looked at us with his dusky blue eyes. One by one, we stopped talking. Once we were all silent, he spoke slowly, and there was a sense of awe in his tone. 'Moses told us that if we obey Yahweh's voice and keep His covenant, we would be to Him a special treasure above all people – a kingdom of priests, a holy nation.' Jesher reached up and scratched his beard. 'A special treasure . . . us. Yahweh's special people. A holy nation, a whole kingdom of priests . . . hmm.' He bowed his head and rocked slightly on his toes. A reverent silence fell as we feasted on the hidden depths of his words. A shiver ran down my spine. To meet with Yahweh! To have Him talk with us . . . with me! The thought thrilled my heart – it was what I had longed for, for so long.

It also terrified me.

What if Yahweh found me wanting? What if iniquity was found in me? What would He do? I had seen the reach of His arm. I had witnessed first-hand his wrath outworked on the Egyptians and I saw the darkness and fire that consumed His cloud when He was angered. What would He do if He found evil within me? My mind ran, unrestrained, through the various scenarios of what might happen, and my heart started thumping. But, as terrifying as that thought was, it could not eclipse the desperate yearning of my heart to hear His voice and be in His presence. My heart raced out of fear of what might happen if I was not pleasing to Him but, simultaneously, with an irrepressible expectation of what could take place if I was. I closed my eyes and let myself imagine the glory of that moment.

'Hmph! That is foolishness!' Shira snorted in derision, shattering the holy moment into jagged shards. 'A kingdom of priests? We cannot all be priests, can we? Moses spoke falsehood – he must have heard wrong.' I glanced at Jesher. His face was filled with disbelief and sadness, which turned to anger. As he continued to stare at his wife, I saw in his eyes what looked like pity. She was the foolish one, not Jesher, and definitely not Moses. She could not even recognise, let alone begin to understand the priceless treasure hidden in these words of Yahweh, spoken through Moses.

Jesher opened his mouth to speak to her. Then he closed his mouth. Lowering his gaze, he walked away from the tent in the direction of the tent of meeting where Yahweh's cloud plummeted down into a pulsating, glistening pillar.

34

Mount Sinai

It started long before the sun rose. Usually, we woke to the chirping of desert sparrows, but not today. Today, the babbling of voices chattering excitedly overshadowed the sweet warbling of the birds. A noisy buzz of conversation filled the air: the day had arrived and Yahweh's people were assembling at the foot of Mount Sinai to meet with Him.

The previous night when we sat down to break bread together, Shira had made her intentions very clear: she wanted to stand near the front of the crowds, so she could see and hear everything clearly.

'Shira, Moses said we are not to go near the foot of the mountain,' Jesher told her. 'It is dangerous. We cannot get too close.'

'Ech! Saadia told me that Abidan and the other leaders will stand at the front. We can stand with them.'

'Abidan is an elder.' Jesher frowned at her. 'I am not an elder and it is not our place to stand at the front with them.'

'Joshua will be at the front, and he is just a manservant,' she declared. 'If he can be there, so can we.' Jesher looked at me apologetically. I smiled at Jesher to reassure him that no offence had been taken. Mesha changed the subject, and the decision of where to stand was left hanging.

Jesher was probably hoping that Shira would forget about it – but that was a barren hope. I accompanied Moses, Aaron and his sons early that morning, and stood with them watching the multitudes make their way to the mountain. The pressing of the crowds was intense but, despite all the pushing and shoving that was taking place, it didn't take me long to locate Shira. She was a force to be reckoned with as she elbowed her way through the throngs of people, beating a pathway to the front. She dragged Jesher in her wake until they reached the place where the elders and their wives stood waiting. She turned to Jesher with a triumphant smirk, but he ignored her, pulling his head covering down over his forehead.

I made eye contact with Jesher, but he just shook his head and rolled his eyes. I couldn't see the rest of the family, so they must have decided not to join their mother on her arrogant quest to reach the front of the congregation. We watched in anticipation as the thick canopy of cloud that covered the top of the mountain expanded and spread down the sides of the mountain, swelling and swirling as it moved. The buzz of conversation came to an abrupt end and, in its place, a growing sense of impending danger hovered over the waiting crowds.

I stayed at the foot of the mountain, near the elders and their wives, watching with bated breath as Moses walked towards the mountain and stepped into the swirling mass of cloud. Flashes of lightning lit up the mountain, cutting through the air like a dagger, closely followed by deafening claps of thunder that reverberated above us. Cries of terror filled the air; all around me, people fell to their knees or crouched down low, covering their ears to try to escape the onslaught of thunder. My heart pounded like the blows of an ironmonger's hammer but, although my legs were shaking, I managed to remain standing.

Just then, the ground beneath our feet began to shudder, as if the earth itself were labouring to bring forth life. Those of us still standing were thrown off balance and found ourselves bowing low before the might of Yahweh. Not one person could stand before Him.

A shout went up. 'Fire! The mountain is on fire!' Another bout of screams erupted and, to my horror, the mountain burst into flames. Smoke engulfed it, fiery tentacles reaching up into the sky, stroking the rocks that jutted out. It was difficult to see where the cloud ended and the smoke began. I pulled my scarf over my nose and mouth to stop the acrid stench of smoke from overcoming me. I lifted my head to check whether Jesher and Shira were still safe, but my scarf slipped, and I breathed in the smoky air. Instead of choking on pungent fumes, however, the air around me was fragrant and pure. I glanced around in astonishment and breathed in some more air. How could this be? I blinked. My eyes were not stinging from the smoke. In fact, it was as though I was seeing everything more distinctly than before. I looked up at the mountain, gasping in disbelief.

'Look!' I shouted, pointing to some shrubs on the lower parts of the mountain. 'They do not burn!' Turning to those around me, I cried, 'The bushes – they are on fire, but they do not burn!' Some of the elders near me lifted their gaze, faces still covered, and studied the bushes and trees at the base of the mountain through the slits in their head coverings.

'The air, it is sweet! Breathe the air! It is the breath of Yahweh!' I encouraged them, throwing my head covering back as proof of my claim.

Abidan, ever-courageous leader of the tribe of Benjamin, was the first to pull his face covering down. He took a deep breath, a smile formed on his face and he dropped his scarf, shouting back to me in excitement. 'You speak truth! The air – it is . . . fragrant!' he stuttered. Jesher was near him and quickly followed suit. His response was the same: astonishment and wonder. He turned to Shira, who was still crouched down on the ground. He tried to get her to sit up and breathe in the air, but she refused, clutching her scarf tightly around her face.

Just then, I heard the sound of a horn, blasting over the heads of the multitudes. Louder and louder it sounded, over and over again and, just when I felt like my ears would explode from the pressure, I heard a voice.

It was like thunder. Reverberating, rich and melodious. The sound of many waters, flowing, bursting with harmony. 'I am the Lord your God, who brought you out of the land of Egypt, out of the house of bondage. You shall have no other gods before Me.'

No one moved.

All eyes were transfixed on Mount Sinai, where the voice came from. He spoke again. 'You shall not make for yourself a carved image or any likeness of anything that is in heaven above, or that is in the earth below. You shall not bow down to them, nor serve them. For I, the Lord your God, am a jealous God . . .'

Jesher was sitting outside the tent waiting for me when I arrived home that evening. As soon as he saw me, he clambered to his feet and came to meet me. 'Joshua, I must talk with you.'

'*Abba*? Is all well with you?' I asked.

He looked agitated and unsettled. 'Yes, yes, most assuredly. But there is much to discuss.' Glancing back at the tent where Shira and the other women were busy preparing the evening meal, he scratched his beard and said, 'Come, let us walk.' We walked back the way I had come. 'The fire, and the smoke and the bushes that were on fire but did not burn. You saw them?' He continued without pausing. 'Did you smell the air? Joshua, the . . . the sweetness of the air . . . The smoke, it was not smoke, it was . . . it was not smoke . . . and . . . and the sound of Yahweh's voice, like thundering waters . . . you heard that too?'

'I did.'

'It was . . . wondrous, was it not?' he asked. 'But . . . but how can it be?' Without waiting for me to respond, he ploughed on, pouring out the overflow of his heart, lifting his hands to the heavens. 'It is too much for the soul to contain, *nu*?' His eyebrows dipped down in his forehead. 'I marvel at Yahweh's works, but my heart fails to understand all that He said.'

'How so?'

'The words that He spoke – I cannot get them out of my mind.' Jesher stood still for a moment and closed his eyes. 'We are to be His own people . . . His special treasure . . . a holy nation.' The words washed over him and, when he opened his eyes, they were filled with tears. Clasping hold of my arm, he whispered, 'Never have I experienced such a thrill. Never before have I sensed the seeds of life that now stir in my heart.' His voice cracked with emotion and the tears overflowed.

I looked at him in amazement. Jesher chuckled. 'Oh, do not fear for me, Joshua. These are just the broodings of an old man. Yahweh's words are simply too wonderful for my heart to conceive.'

'In that case, I must be an old man too, because I have similar "broodings".'

'Truly?'

I nodded. My bond with Jesher had deepened over the months since my father had died, but I had never felt it more keenly then at that moment. I knew in my heart that he would understand my own 'broodings'. 'I long for Yahweh's presence, more than anything,' I admitted. 'I hunger for His holiness, *Abba*. It consumes me. Sometimes I cannot sleep at night.' I looked up at the cloud that hovered over us. 'There are times when I go outside in the middle of the night, just to gaze upon His fiery presence. And in the day – I spend so much time looking at the cloud, it is my constant distraction! So you see,' I smiled at him, 'I also am a brooder!'

Jesher put his hand on his heart. 'We are of the same heart, then.' He shook his head, smiling to himself and we continued walking. 'Moses said Yahweh is a jealous God. We are to be His own people, His special treasure, a holy nation. But how can that be? A whole nation, holy? Not just the priests and the prophets, but all of us, holy unto the Lord? How is this possible?'

'I cannot fathom it either, *Abba*. I do not know how it will happen, but I know this is Yahweh's will for His people. He has spoken clearly. Moses talks of this often, how we must walk in Yahweh's ways and keep His covenant – that is how we will be a special treasure to Him. That is what will make us different from the other nations that surround us. Our God is not a mute idol made of iron or stone, or wood. Our God is the Creator, the God of all gods; the God who talks to us, protects us, who *knows* us. We must keep His commands. Yahweh has called Moses to come up the mountain to meet with Him. Perhaps He will tell him more about this then.'

'Joshua, if you hear anything, I beg you, tell me. I must know the ways of Yahweh. I must know how we become this special treasure, how we can be His holy nation. These questions plague my mind constantly – I can find no relief from them. You must bring me word as soon as you hear something, *nu?*'

Love for Jesher welled up in me. This was a man humble in heart and steadfast of spirit. A man who yearned to walk in Yahweh's ways. A man who was prudent in speech, whose words were graced with wisdom. This was a man worthy of eldership. I thought of Abidan, of Hur, Elishama and the other elders of Israel, and I could see nothing in them that I could not see in Jesher. Surely, he could stand with his head held high in the company of these men. So why had he not been made an elder of our people?

35

Esteemed

The following day I returned home late in the afternoon to find that Jesher had been summoned to attend a meeting for the heads of families. 'I know of no leaders' meeting,' I told Mesha. 'Moses was with Aaron and his sons this afternoon. He did not meet with the leaders, nor did he call such a meeting. Who brought the message?'

Mesha shrugged. '*Abba* did not say, but he has been gone for some time.' He turned away to speak to Helah, and left me to my own, uneasy thoughts. Why were leaders' meetings being held without Moses, without his knowledge? My heart was troubled. Should I try to find out where the meeting was being held? Should I go and tell Moses about the meeting? Should I go and find Jesher, or wait until he returned? When would he return? The evening was drawing in and it would be getting dark soon. I questioned my own thoughts, trying to make light of my concerns. There was no need for concern. After all, Jesher was not a child, but a grown man, and patriarch of a family. He could look after himself.

Couldn't he?

My heart was not convinced; my mind wrestled with a strong desire to protect Jesher, along with the knowledge that it was not my place to do so. But I could not just stay here and do nothing. I must go and search for him. I must know why he was called to a meeting that I – or at least Moses – knew nothing of. I was readying myself to go and find Jesher, when I saw him making his way home through the jumble of tents that stretched out in front of us. I smiled and walked forward to greet him, but he did not return my smile.

'Joshua, I must talk with you,' he called out, panting from his exertions.

'*Abba*? Is it well with you?'

'No. No, it is most assuredly not well with me,' he muttered, reaching out to grasp my arm. 'I have need of you, my son. I received a message this morning about a meet – '

'*How could you?*' Shira's voice cut through the air.

Jesher swung around to see her stomping towards him, waterskins slung over her shoulders, her four granddaughters in tow. He stared at her, confused and somewhat annoyed. 'What do you speak of, woman?'

She dumped the waterskins on the ground and walked up to him, jabbing her finger in his face. 'Making a fool of yourself in front of the elders – in front of all the leaders – in front of *all of Israel*. How could you?' Mesha and Helah came outside to see what the commotion was; Hareph and Eglah joined them. Helah, seeing the scared looks on the girls' faces, picked up the waterskins, and she and Eglah took the girls inside the tent.

'Who told you this?' Jesher asked his wife.

'Word spreads fast among our people, as you well know! I was at the well – I heard what you did. Speaking out in front of all those people. How could you? I have worked so hard to make people think well of us. But no one will esteem us highly now. Because of your foolishness today, no one will esteem you any more.'

'*I will esteem me!*' Jesher bellowed, silencing Shira's abusive tirade. She cowered, her eyes wide with shock, and Hareph and Mesha froze. No one said anything. 'You know *nothing* of what happened because you have not asked me. Instead, you listen to the wagging tongues of those who would fill your ears with evil. I stood in the way of righteousness today, and my heart testifies to the truth I spoke before Yahweh!' He strode past her and then turned back. '*I* will esteem me,' he repeated, eyes blazing, his body shaking with emotion 'and Yahweh will esteem me, because today I upheld His name with honour.' He leaned into Shira. His voice cracked as he said, 'And in time, *you* will come to esteem me too.' Without looking back, Jesher swivelled round and strode away from the tent. Mesha looked at me, askance, then moved as if to follow his father. I motioned to him to stay where he was.

'I will go,' I whispered. He nodded. I ran after Jesher's rapidly retreating figure. '*Abba*? Would you be alone, or shall I walk with you?'

'Walk with me, Joshua. My heart is heavy,' he said, not looking at me. He halted where he was, in the middle of the pathway. 'No, my heart is not heavy.' He turned to look at me and whispered, 'My heart is broken. It is filled with such anguish.' He looked old and frail, as if he had just come off a battlefield, so I moved to stand close by his side and offered my arm for him to lean on.

'Speak your heart, *Abba*,' I responded. We walked on, much more slowly this time.

'I hardly know where to start,' he said, shaking his head. 'I was so full of hope yesterday, after our encounter with Yahweh at the foot of the mountain. So full of purpose, and . . . and joy! But now . . .' He sighed. I did not interrupt him, wanting to give him time to separate his muddled thoughts. He plodded on for a while, staring at the ground, until he was ready to speak. 'A messenger came this morning, summoning me to a meeting. The leaders of families were to meet to discuss what happened yesterday.' He looked up at the cloud. 'Ech, my heart was so stirred, I went with fire in my belly ready to discuss how we could become this kingdom of priests, the special treasure that the Lord God has called us to be. Hmph.' He snorted. 'I should have known when I did not see you or Moses there, what kind of a meeting it would be. There were no hearts lifted up in faith, only voices raised in dissention and fear.' He paused for a while, clarifying his thoughts. 'Eliab was the first to speak out. He addressed the congregation boldly, as if he himself was our chosen leader. Him? He is leader of but one tribe, and the tribe of Zebulun is not the greatest of our number, either.'

'What did he say?'

'He said they would not go again to the mountain of Yahweh or draw near to the fire and the cloud, and subject their families to such danger. Danger?' Jesher spat. 'What danger? There is only danger to those who disobey the word of the Lord. But perhaps he is such a one; perhaps he is right to fear Yahweh and hide from His presence.'

'What happened next?'

'Pagiel spoke out after Eliab. He said the tribe of Asher would not draw near again, that Moses should speak to God and tell us what Yahweh says, but they will not come before Him again, lest they and their children die.' Jesher recounted the list of elders who had spoken out: Gamaliel of the tribe of Manasseh, Ahira, leader of Naphtali, Elizur of the Reubenites – on and on, each elder lifting their voice in agreement, shouting out their approval of the decision to reject Yahweh.

A sickness rose in my stomach. This could not be. We could not let this happen.

Jesher continued. 'The meeting was to discuss the events of yesterday, but it was not a discussion: it was a proclamation. They had not called us there to discuss it, they had already made their decision, and purposed only to tell us what they had decided.' He turned to me, his eyes blazing with anger. 'It is not right, Joshua. What they have done is abhorrent. Their words were drawn swords, meting out violence with such arrogance. I could not abide it. How could I stand by and watch them defy the name of our God, treating His presence with such insolence? I could not do it.' Hot, angry tears rolled down Jesher's face. He brushed them away, stumbling on in silence until we came to a clearing. We sat under the shade of a tamarisk tree and I waited until he was ready to speak again. In truth, I welcomed the opportunity to be silent, as my own thoughts spiralled inside my head, like vultures over a rotting corpse.

When he had recovered enough to speak, Jesher told me what he had done. He spoke out against them. In front of all the leaders of Israel, he stood up and declared that what they were doing was wrong. He told them in no uncertain terms that they were leading Yahweh's people astray. He spoke Yahweh's words, reminding them of the promises that God had given them about being a kingdom of priests and a holy nation – His own special treasure. He pointed out that Yahweh had called *all* His people to the foot of the mountain, that He would speak to *all* of them, not just to Moses.

I looked on him as he spoke and my heart swelled with pride. The courage of this extraordinary man who I was now privileged to call father, was awe-inspiring. He was not a man of great physical stature or strength, or even a man whose tongue was skilled in eloquence. But the heart within him was as steadfast and brave as any of the great warriors I had known. To speak out in such a way, in such company – I had no words to express how much I esteemed him at that moment. So I kept silent and listened.

'I could see the disapproval on their faces – outright fury on many of them – but I could not stop speaking, even as their protests grew louder and louder. Then I saw Abidan making his way towards me.' Jesher looked up, as if searching the heavens for a sign of some kind. 'I was sure Abidan would stand with me. Although our tribe of Benjamin is one of the smallest, Abidan is revered, as you know, as a man of wisdom and knowledge. People listen when he speaks. I knew they would heed him.' Jesher sighed and stared at his feet. He scuffed the sand with his sandaled foot and, when he looked up at me again, his dusty blue eyes were brimming over with tears. 'But it was not to be so.'

It all happened so quickly. Before Jesher knew what was happening, he found Abidan at his side and felt himself being led out of the crowd and away from the meeting. Once Abidan had drawn Jesher far enough out of the crowd to talk without being overheard, he told him there was no point in speaking out. There was nothing they could do. It had all been decided the previous day at a secret meeting. For hours they had argued, back and forth, until Abidan was the only one left who opposed their decision. They chose not to listen to the voice of truth.

'Abidan said there were voices being raised that he had not heard before – new voices, voices of dissention. Very persuasive voices.'

'Who?' The hairs on the back of my neck stood up. I knew the answer even before Jesher told me.

'Men I have not heard of before – someone called Shimea, another named Rekem. They seemed to be the ringleaders. Abidan had not met them before yesterday, but many of the other men seemed to know them. He said their words were so persuasive, he found them hard to resist.' Shaking his head in confusion, Jesher frowned. 'He did resist and put his argument forward, time and time again, but he was overruled; the decision was made. There was nothing to be done.' His shoulders slumped in defeat. 'So I am never to hear His voice again. Because of the arrogance and fear of these men who purport to lead our people in the ways of Yahweh, I will never again hear the voice that called to me, so deep within my soul. He gave a sob of anguish. I can never know what it is to be His special treasure, or be part of a kingdom of priests. Joshua, it is more than my heart can bear.' He turned to me, his face a picture of utter desolation. Without thinking, I took him into my arms and held him as he sobbed like a child who had lost his greatest treasure. It was not so long ago that he had held me in his arms as I wept in grief at the death of my father.

Two days later, Jesher stood outside his tent watching Moses and I make our way through the camp to the foot of Mount Sinai. It was time. Yahweh had called Moses to come up the mountain to meet with Him, and I was to go with him. Jesher asked me how long we would be gone when I bade him farewell, but I could not give him an answer. Yahweh had not told Moses how long He would abide with him, only that he must come.

Mesha told me on my return that Jesher sat on an upturned stump, leaning on his stick, watching us. '*Abba*? What do your thoughts dwell on?' Mesha had asked him.

'I am pondering what it must be like,' Jesher had muttered, still gazing at the mountain.

'What do you speak of?'

Jesher did not take his eyes off us as he'd whispered, 'What must it be like to speak with Yahweh. Like Moses does. To speak with Yahweh face to face . . . as a man speaks with his friend. What must that be like?'

Mesha had sat down next to his father. They sat side by side in silence for a long while. Jesher squinted through furrowed brows as he watched us walk towards the mountain and start to climb. They did not move or talk at all until long after we had disappeared from their sight, swallowed up by the misty clouds that surrounded Mount Sinai.

36

Retribution

'*What have you done?*' Moses hurled Aaron's tent flap open and stalked into his tent. I followed close behind, checking that we had not been followed before entering and closing the flap.

Aaron sat up, petrified. 'Moses,' he stuttered. 'You are . . . you are back.'

'What have you done?' Moses asked again, glowering at his brother. I had seen him get angry several times in the course of the last few months, but never like this. This was not anger, this was rage. Fury. And it was terrifying. I stayed by the tent entrance, alert to the sounds of pandemonium that raged in the camp outside, but attentive to Moses' call.

Aaron cowered in fear. 'I . . . I . . . the . . .' he stammered, and then closed his mouth and just stared at Moses.

'Yahweh told me to come down. He said our people had corrupted themselves, but never would I have imagined these, these . . . *abominations* that I see before me. Have you seen what our people are doing in front of that idol? Dancing and gyrating and . . . I cannot even *speak* of the . . . the *wickedness* that is taking place. It is sickening, Aaron! Our people – Yahweh's people – are cavorting in front of that graven image. It is barbaric! How did this come to be?' he demanded.

Aaron lurched to his feet and pointed outside. 'The people – they are set on evil.'

'The people? They made this idol?'

'Yes! Uh, no . . . but . . . but it was their gold which formed it.'

Moses' eyes narrowed. 'It was their gold?'

'Yes.'

'They made this golden calf?'

'No.'

'Then who made it? Speak your mind, brother. I must know the truth.'

'Moses . . .' Aaron lowered his eyes. 'I did.'

'You did?' The veins in Moses' neck stood out. 'You made a golden idol for Yahweh's people to prostrate themselves before?' he roared.

'The people demanded it! They implored me to make it!' Aaron blurted. 'They said, "Make us gods to go before us, for we know not what has become of Moses." Seeing Moses' expression, he continued gabbling, 'So I said they should bring me their gold, I threw it in the fire, and . . . and . . . a golden calf came out.'

'A golden calf "came out" of the fire?' Moses questioned him. 'So you didn't *make* it, then?'

'I . . .' Aaron's eyes darted to me but, seeing no sympathy in my gaze, he looked back at Moses, and slumped in defeat. 'I did. I crafted it.'

Moses stared at his brother, incredulous. 'What did this people *do* to you, that you have brought so great a sin upon them?'

I watched the fear on Aaron's face turn to anger and defiance. He scrambled to his feet and pointed at his brother. 'You did not tell me how long you would be. I knew not when you would be back, or even *if* you would come back. Anything could have happened to you! You could have been dead, and how would I have known? I was not called to meet with Yahweh, was I? No.' He pointed at me and glared. 'Joshua went with you, but not me – your own brother. I had to stay here, with these people,' he gestured outside.

My hands formed fists. I longed to retaliate. But it was not my place and Aaron was not my kin. So I held my clenched fists tightly against my sides and held my peace.

'They wanted to leave here, to move on without the cloud of Yahweh's presence. I had to do something to find a way of keeping them here. That is why I made the calf.' Looking down at his feet, Aaron muttered, 'I did not worship it or bow down to it, and I did not sacrifice to it.'

Moses stomped to the entrance of the tent. I moved out his way and he flung the flap open. 'And that makes *this* lawful?' Moses closed the flap and walked back to face Aaron. 'Aaron, you must stop them. Now.'

'How can I stop them?' Aaron yelled. 'I am the one who gave this molten image to them! I am the cause of all this.' Aaron jabbed at his chest. 'Me! I led them down this path! I made that idol. How can I tell them to stop something that I started?'

Realisation flooded Moses' face. 'Well, if you will not restrain them, I will.'

'No!' Aaron's head shot up. 'Brother, it will not go well. These people are out of control, they will not be told what to do. I beg you – do not confront them!'

'I must, Aaron. Something must be done. Someone has to stop this great evil.'

'But they might kill you!'

Moses froze. I held my breath. Slowly, Moses turned to face his brother. Staring deep into his eyes, he sighed and then nodded. 'Then so be it. Where is Hur? Was he with you in this matter?'

'No. He . . . we . . . had a dispute.'

'Where is he now?' Moses asked.

'He went to try to restrain the people.' I could see Aaron hesitating. There was more he wanted to say, but was clearly fearful about saying it. Moses noticed it too.

'What is it? Speak your mind.'

'Eleazar. He went with him.'

I felt my chest constrict. Eleazar and I had become close friends and, although he was many things, a warrior was not one of them. He had no skill or training in warfare whatsoever – in fact, to my knowledge, I don't think he had even grasped a weapon before. I dreaded to think what a rampaging crowd of rebels might do to a gentle soul such as him. I glared at Aaron in disgust. How could he let his son go out there, unprotected? What kind of a father was he?

'What of Nadab and Abihu? Ithamar?' Moses asked.

'I have not seen Nadab and Abihu since this trouble started. It is Eleazar who has been at my side throughout this conflict, and Hur. I sent Ithamar a message two days ago to stay in his tent with his family until I sent word. I gave Eleazar the same instruction, but he refused.'

Moses turned to me. 'Joshua, send men to find Hur and Eleazar. Tell them to come without delay.' I ran from the tent to relay the message, and returned soon afterwards to see Moses setting two stone tablets down on the floor in Aaron's tent. He leaned them against a wooden chest. 'Do you know what these are?' Aaron shook his head. 'These are the commandments that Yahweh gave me to bring to our people. There are ten of them, written by the finger of Yahweh Himself, for His people.' Pointing to the engraving near the top, he asked, 'Do you know what this says?'

'No. I was not taught to read and write in Pharaoh's palace like you were.'

Moses held his breath. I could see the veins on the side of his neck pulsating; he did not look at his brother. He exhaled and spoke slowly, following the engravings on the first stone tablet with his finger. 'It says, "I am the LORD your God, who brought you out of the land of Egypt, out of the house of bondage. You shall have no other gods before Me."'[5]

Aaron looked at the engravings and nodded in acknowledgement. 'He spoke these words to us at the foot of the mountain.'

Moses ignored him and continued reading. "You shall not make for yourself a carved image. You shall not bow down to them nor serve them." He looked up at his brother, his eyes sparking with anger. '"You shall have no other gods before Me", Aaron. *No other gods*. I pleaded with Yahweh for our people. He wanted to destroy them – all of them – but I pleaded with Him to spare them. I interceded on their behalf – on *your* behalf – and I come down to find this . . .' He walked to the entrance of the tent and gestured angrily to the deprivation outside, 'this iniquitous debauchery and immorality – Yahweh's people flaunting themselves in pagan worship in front of a soulless god that *you* have made for them. The noise of their revelry was so great that Joshua thought you were being attacked! Listen to it!'

Moses grabbed Aaron by the arm and hauled him to the entrance. The sickening sounds of pagan worship assaulted our ears. Shrieks and cries, the sounds of wild music and revelry, along with the relentless pounding of drums. Aaron listened briefly, then yanked his arm away and slunk back inside the tent. Moses stared at him in disgust. He waited for some sign of repentance.

None came.

Overcome with zeal, Moses marched back inside the tent and hauled one of the stone tablets into his arms. He gestured to me to bring the second one and made his way to a high piece of ground.

---

5. Exodus 20:2-3, NKJV.

In full view of the carousing rebels, he lifted the first one high above his head, straining to hold it there. He shouted at the people, 'I am the Lord your God. You shall have *no* other gods before Me!' and hurled it to the ground.

I looked on in horror at the stone tablet smashed into fragments at my feet. What had he done? That tablet had been inscribed by the finger of Yahweh. What recklessness was this? Moses lifted his arms and pointed upwards, shouting again at the crowds, but most of them were too far gone to pay him much attention. '*No other gods!*' he roared. He turned to take the second tablet from me.

'Master, no!' I protested, but he ignored me, yanking it out of my arms. He heaved it up in the air and flung it to the ground, where it shattered into pieces like the first one.

Just then, Caleb arrived with Eleazar, breathless and grim-faced. Moses swung round to meet them and grasped his nephew by the shoulders. 'Eleazar, praise be to Yahweh, you are safe. And Hur?' he asked, looking behind him. 'Where is he?'

'It is . . . he . . .' Eleazar looked at Moses and then at me. I knew what he was about to say. 'He is dead! They murdered him!'

37

The Lord's Side

Moses stood tall. I could see tears glistening in his eyes, but he was motionless except for the shaking of his hands and the trembling of his lips. He clenched his jaw and said, 'Joshua, with me. Ready your sword.'

I nodded and unsheathed my sword, a deep sense of dread filling my heart as I followed him. Caleb and Eleazar joined us and, as we walked in the direction of the altar, I asked Eleazar how Hur had died. He said a rebel named Rekem had attacked Hur with a dagger while he tried to reason with them. He bled to death, surrounded by the mocking cries of his attackers. Rekem was known to me and to Moses, but only by name, by virtue of the fact that his name was linked to Shimea's. Darkness thrived in both of them, and I had no doubt we would encounter them at some point during this day.

I steeled myself for what I knew was to follow. I was no longer inexperienced in the ways of warfare, having plunged my sword into many a man. But I had never raised my hand against one of my own people, and the very thought of it made me sick to my stomach. Conflict raged within me; fury at what Yahweh's people had done, coupled with a fierce resistance to doing what I feared I would now be called upon to do. Arriving at the place where Aaron had set up the pagan altar, a wave of nausea washed over me as I saw close up the wanton debauchery that was taking place. My horror must have been obvious because many of the revellers pointed at me and laughed hysterically at my reaction, their eyes glazed over with a fiendish darkness.

I saw Shimea first. He was at the front, by the altar, sacrificing a goat to the bull god. Two men stood with him, holding down the struggling animal. Blood covered the makeshift altar and the ground around it was covered with the blood-soaked carcasses of animals. Shimea's robes and face were splattered with blood and he was chanting in a language I did not recognise, repeating the same words in a guttural tone, waving his arms in the air, knife in hand. His body gyrated and his voice swelled, climaxing in a shriek as he plunged the knife into the animal's body, not once, or even twice, but over and over again in bloodlust.

There were coals burning on the altar, but the flames that rose from the embers were unlike any I had seen before. They had a greenish tinge and the smoke surrounding the altar hung heavily in the air, like a thick smog. Eleazar pointed Rekem out to me. He was a small, wiry man with sharp, fox-like features; there was a restlessness about him that was unnerving. He moved from side to side as he stood, like a snake readying itself to strike. So this was the man who had joined forces with Shimea, stirring up trouble among the elders after their encounter at the foot of Mount Sinai. This was the man who had convinced them that Yahweh's people should not appear before Yahweh themselves, but let Moses talk on their behalf. This was the man who had murdered Hur.

He saw Eleazar pointing to him and sneered, obviously recognising me. Grabbing a handful of a dirty, powdery substance from a copper dish by the altar, he threw it onto the embers. Blazing green flames flared up, popping and crackling furiously. The idolators near the altar screamed, then shrieked with laughter when they realised where the noise had come from. Rekem stood in front of them, cackling with delight at my horrified expression. My heart started to beat wildly in my chest. What devilish evil was this? Zeal for Yahweh, and the desire to execute vengeance on His behalf, rose up strongly within me. I turned from the rabblerousers and looked up to the cloud.

Yahweh was angry.

His cloud was dark and heavy, its beauty shrouded by pain. Fiery shafts burst out of its midst and I could feel Yahweh's anger piercing my own heart. I stood behind Moses, sword drawn, and waited for my instructions. I was ready now.

Moses wasted no time. Stepping forward, he bellowed, 'Whoever is on the Lord's side, come to me!' Immediately, Caleb, Eleazar and I stepped forward to stand by his side. The revellers paused for a moment to look at us, then continued their carousing, screeching with laughter. Again, Moses shouted, even louder this time, 'Whoever is on the Lord's side, come to me!' Some of the revellers taunted him, imitating his words, calling out, 'Come to me!' in a grotesque mockery of his holy call. But others heard the call.

Those who had been watching and waiting responded to the call without hesitation. Three leaders – Eliasaph, Elizaphan and Zuriel – came forward and, with them, their brethren from the tribe of Levi. While we waited for more men to come forward, Eleazar told me how these three men had confronted Aaron about the idol the day before, refusing to have any part in the revelry. More and more Levites gathered to Moses, many of them armed with a sword or spear. Moses spoke to these faithful ones. He gave them clear instructions and, at his signal, we turned to walk in the direction of the revellers who were carousing by the golden idol, oblivious to the imminent attack.

I led the assault, the conflict within me now resolved. There could be no mercy for these idolators. They were too far gone; their eyes overflowed with the darkness which had overtaken their souls. They had made their choice – there could be no redemption for them now. We had to stop them from contaminating any more of Yahweh's people. My grip tightened on my sword. I scanned the crowds, looking for the man responsible for Hur's demise. Rekem saw me striding towards him, my eyes fixed, sword in hand. A flicker of fear shadowed his countenance, quickly replaced by a depraved sneer as he drew a dagger from the folds of his robe – no doubt the same one he had used to kill Hur. Crouching down, he cackled like a maniacal beast, readying himself for the attack.

It was a futile gesture. There was no fight. One blow and it was over before it had even begun.

Not stopping to revel in Rekem's death, I swung round in search of my next target. Eleazar had reached him first. Shimea's corpse lay in front of the altar among the carcasses of the beasts he had slain, blood oozing from his chest, his eyes open but unseeing. Eleazar's blade had given him a much more merciful death than he had given to the beasts that surrounded him. I moved to commend Eleazar, but he was not rejoicing in his triumph. He stared at Shimea's body and then at the bloody sword in his hand with a mixture of revulsion and anguish, and I remembered with a jolt that he had never killed a man before.

I grasped his shoulder with my free hand. Words were superfluous. Eleazar looked up at me. I nodded. He gazed back at me, frowning, his sword shaking in his hand, then returned the nod.

I walked towards the altar to find the object of their revelry. Lifting my sword with both hands, I gave a mighty roar and swung the blade, violently beheading the golden idol. Passionate cries of fury and grief filled the air as the Levites surrounded the idolatrous revellers, drew their swords and spears, and plunged them into their bodies. Sounds of revelry turned to screams of terror. Some of the rebels fought back, but most were too drunk on passion and blood to put up much of a fight. In truth, it was not a fight; it was a massacre. The revellers had come to carouse, not to make war so, although some drew swords or grabbed sticks and rocks with which to defend themselves, most were unarmed. They fell like ripe corn before a scythe.

There were women among the rabble.

I had never killed a woman before, but Moses had been very clear. None must live. This was not a time for delicate sensibilities. It was a call to radical obedience. I purposed in my heart to give them as clean and quick a death as possible, and aimed for the throat or heart, avoiding making eye contact with them. Many of the Levites, however, were not well versed in warfare; it took many blows before their victims found their final release. One Levite had an axe, which he used to hack open the back of a man's skull. Others swung their weapons like reaping scythes and had to strike again and again before the job was done. My heart shrivelled within me, but I closed my mind to the bloodshed that surrounded me and focused on the command of my master.

Many of the rebels tried to flee, and were brought down by spears or swords in their backs. Moses, who fought alongside us with surprisingly deadly aim, noticed those who were trying to get away. 'Let none escape!' he shouted to the Levites around him, pointing to the escapees. 'Follow them! Go throughout the camp. Leave none alive!'

The Levites gave chase, scattering in every direction, leaving just a few of us to deal with those who remained by the altar. Caleb fought by my side, driving a spear through a man's chest. The man sank to his knees and toppled over, revealing a woman crouching behind him. She screamed, clutching her torn robe around her shoulders, begging Caleb for mercy, sobbing and grovelling at his feet. She looked so much like his own young wife – the resemblance was uncanny – that he gaped at her. He turned to look at me, silently asking me for permission to spare her life. I locked eyes with him but, before any discussion could be had, we heard the hiss of a sword swinging, a scream cut short, and the thud of a body toppling over. Turning back, we saw Moses standing over her lifeless body.

'None shall be spared,' he whispered.

Caleb turned to battle two young men with daggers in their hands who charged him from behind. I ran to stand by him and, as my sword clashed with one of their blades, I recognised his face. He was one of the three men who had come to see Jesher and Azriel, when Joel's plan to marry Alya in secret had been discovered. This was one of Alya's brothers – and Caleb's opponent was her other brother. I remembered the look they had given me when they passed me that day. The look on their faces now was no less full of hate. We parried blows for a short while but, although both men were brawny and strong, their skill with a blade did not match that of ours. They died together, side by side.

The camp was in an uproar and the commotion continued for well over an hour. We could hear screams in the distance, the noise of clashing metal. The Levites had taken Moses' commission to heart – none would escape. The sounds of death started to fill the camp; weeping, wailing and the acrid smell of burning flesh.

I walked among the bodies that littered the open ground where the altar stood, ending the suffering of those who lingered with my sword. I recognised some of the faces of the dead. Some of these men had stood with me against the Amalekites. They had fought so bravely for Yahweh – what had happened to turn them so completely away from Him, in such a short time? The darkness. It had spread like a plague among our people, poisoning and deceiving. I grieved for the corrupted souls that now lay mutilated and lifeless on the ground. This was not the way they should have died.

There would be no honourable burial for these dead revellers.

Just a funeral pyre and premature death.

38

Numbness

More than anything, I just wanted that day to be over – to be able to return to my tent, eat a meal with my family and try to forget the bloodshed and brutality of what I had seen and done that day. But it was not over yet.

Moses asked me to talk to Eleazar to find out what had led up to this unimaginable slaughter. He needed to know and understand what had happened while we were away, and thought Eleazar might feel able to talk more freely to me than he would to his uncle. He was probably right, but I would rather have been anywhere else doing anything else at that moment.

We walked to the tent of meeting together and sank down inside.

'What is it you wish to know?' Eleazar asked me. His face was lined with weariness; the fire that had burned in his eyes earlier that day was gone, replaced by a glassy expression. I knew it well. I had seen it many times; the shock and stupor that assails all those who encounter their first battle. It clung to him. My heart condemned me for pressing him for information, but my head reminded me of my mission.

'What brought this about? What happened that Aaron would commit such transgression before the Lord?'

Eleazar sighed and looked down. 'It was not something that he planned, of that I am sure. He never purposed in his heart to create iniquity, but the fear in his heart had grown over the days and weeks, and ... it took him over.'

'Fear of ... ?'

Eleazar studied the ground, avoiding my gaze. He told me how, only days after Moses and I had been gone, crowds started gathering outside Aaron's tent wanting to know where we were and when we would return. At first they were polite enquiries and curiosity but, as the days and then weeks passed by, the crowd grew in size and in aggression. Sometimes two or three times a day, they would arrive unannounced, wanting to know what his plan was, when Moses would return and what Aaron would do if he didn't return.

'Shimea and Rekem were the ringleaders,' he said. 'They played the crowd with such skill, planting seeds of discord in the soil of their fearful hearts. I knew Shimea from that day we came across him, but Rekem was unknown to me until then. He was the second-born son of Abinadar, and he resented his brother, Jaren, who was the first-born, a quiet man, well thought of. From what I was told, he led his family with wisdom, but was not a natural leader.'

'So why did Rekem resent him?' I asked. 'He doesn't sound very threatening.'

'He resented the fact that Jaren was the first-born, not him, and hated how much people respected and admired him. Rekem always wanted to be in charge and to command respect. He was certainly strong enough to lead, but he was not a noble man. There was much evil in his heart. I saw it in his eyes – the darkness that Moses spoke of. I heard rumours about idols and talismans which he brought with him out of Egypt. They said he kept them hidden in his tent, but I never had sight of them myself.'

Eleazar went on to tell me how Shimea and Rekem denounced Aaron and Hur's leadership day after day, putting fear in people's hearts about what would happen if Moses never came back. They incited rebellion and encouraged the people to choose a new leader and move on without Moses – and without Yahweh's cloud. I stared at Eleazar, speechless. The fact that they would even contemplate doing that was so terrible, my mind could not conceive it.

But that was not all.

Shimea told the people they should choose a new god, one that would go with them, one that they didn't have to 'wait for'. He told them about the gods of Egypt, which were plentiful enough, and suggested the bull god, Hapi-ankh. The crowd roared their approval, and Aaron and Eleazar had watched, horrified, as they chanted, 'Hapi-ankh! Hapi-ankh!', dancing in celebration.

Eleazar sat back and looked up at me. Pain filled his eyes. 'I know what my *abba* did was unforgiveable, but if you had been here and saw what happened, you might understand what drove him to it.

Morning dawned and evening faded for nearly two score days, and the fear grew in him. He could not eat, hardly slept at all. Most nights I awoke to see him pacing the floor in his tent, wringing his hands, muttering to himself. He sent my mother, Elisheba, away to keep her safe from harm, and spent his days hiding in his tent. Hur and I kept vigil – at least one of us was with him all the time.'

'That must have laid heavy on you, my friend,' I muttered.

He nodded. 'I have never seen him like that before. You know my father – he is not a weak man. We saw Yahweh perform signs and wonders by his hands in Egypt. But they were relentless in their assault, and the darkness wore him down. It took hold of him, and when Shimea persuaded the people to move on without waiting for you and Moses, without waiting for Yahweh's cloud to move – it broke him.'

Tears came to Eleazar's eyes. 'He wept like one devoid of all hope, desperate to find a way of stopping them from moving on. That is why he made the bull idol. It was the only way he could think of to keep them from moving on without Moses – without Yahweh. He told them to bring him their gold, and he would make them an idol.'

I sat back and rubbed my forehead. My head ached, my body ached and now my heart ached too. Eleazar was silent. He sat hunched over; his head bowed as if waiting for a judge's verdict. But I was no judge. I was merely a messenger and I had no intention of passing judgement on anyone.

'What happened after that?'

'The crowd left to spread the word.' He grunted. 'They are a double-souled people. Only moments before, they had been baying for my *abba*'s death, and now they were singing his praises.' He shook his head and sighed deeply. 'Eliasaph, Elizaphan and Zuriel came to speak to him on behalf of the tribe of Levi. They pleaded with him to change his mind, but it was too late. It was done. There could be no turning back. The disbelief and loathing on their faces is something I can never forget. But I cannot sit in judgement over them, because ... because in truth, my heart agreed with them.'

Eleazar stood and walked away from me. When he turned to face me again, tears trickled down his cheeks.

'I hated him, Joshua. I was ashamed of him. My own *abba*! I hated him and yet there was still love in my heart for him.' Eleazar poured out his heart to me, holding nothing back. He had followed the Levites out of Aaron's tent when they left, and could not find it in himself to re-join his father. The conflict within him raged a fierce war. Hatred rose up inside him – hatred for this man who had given him life. He despised Aaron for what he had done, detested his father's weakness. Fury raged like wildfire in his heart.

'Everything in me wanted to walk inside that tent and rip him to pieces. I wanted to scream at him, to beat him with my fists,' he admitted. 'I was ashamed, so ashamed of him.' Then Eleazar had heard a groan, a whimper. It sounded like a wounded animal. It stopped him in his tracks. He stood outside his father's tent and listened to him howl like a creature in agony, hearing the noises of pounding and crashing – pottery and furniture being flung around. Still he stood, unmoving, outside his father's tent. Compassion started to melt the rage inside him, leaving in its place a brittle numbness. Time passed. Aaron's sobbing turned to low-pitched cries, groaning and whimpering. Then all went quiet.

Eleazar turned to face me, exhausted. His face was streaked with dirt and his arms hung loosely by his side. 'I could not go into him that night. But I could not leave him, either. I feared for his safety. So I slept on the ground outside his tent. When the dawn came and he awoke, I left.' Eleazar looked at me with dull eyes. 'That was two days ago. I have not spoken to him since.'

39

Restitution

'Aaron,' Moses shook his brother's shoulder. 'Aaron, wake up.' Aaron had fallen asleep, curled up in the foetal position on his mat, fully clothed. It was there that Moses and I found him the following morning. He opened his eyes, swollen from the previous day's outpouring of emotion, and looked up, blinking, to see Moses staring at him.

'Moses . . .' he mumbled, sitting up and wiping the strands of matted hair out of his face. 'Moses, I . . .' He looked at his brother with such remorse, but no words came out of his mouth.

'Come, get up.' Moses held out his hand, helping Aaron to his feet. He stood before us, unsteady and dishevelled, like a worthless prisoner on trial for his crimes. By now, Moses' anger had abated, and I saw sorrow in his eyes at the pitiful sight before him. He gestured to a clay basin and told Aaron to wash, which he did. Patting himself dry, he turned towards his chest of clothes, opened the lid and reached for a thick, woven material.

'That one,' said Moses, pointing to a plain, rough garment. Aaron looked at him in surprise. 'The camp is in mourning,' Moses said. I laid out the food and water we had brought with us, and Moses sat with his brother to eat. I stood by the entrance. I told them I had eaten earlier that morning but, in truth, it was more because I did not want to break bread with Aaron. I had no wish to talk with him. The rage I felt towards him still tormented me, so I avoided eye contact with him, not wanting him to see the thoughts I was wrestling with.

They ate in silence for a while and, after a few mouthfuls, Aaron turned to Moses. 'Moses – my sons, are they . . . ?'

'They are well, Aaron. They are all well.' Aaron breathed a sigh of relief and closed his eyes. Moses did not look at him when he said,

233

'Eleazar fought bravely yesterday, alongside your brethren from the tribe of Levi.' They continued eating, the unspoken accusation of 'but not alongside you, their leader' hanging in the air between them. The atmosphere was heavy and stifled. When they had finished, Moses brushed the crumbs off his hands and stood up. 'Come,' he said. 'Let us go to the tent of meeting and come before the Lord in prayer.'

Aaron stood up with him. 'Ah . . . with your permission, I will stay here.' Looking around, he gestured to the mess strewn all over his tent. 'I . . . I must set things in order.' He reached out to pick up a basket that had been tipped onto the floor, but Moses leaned forward and grabbed hold of his arm.

'Aaron! You cannot hide in this tent forever. You must face the people. Come,' he said, with a jab of his head. 'Strengthen your arms. There is much to do.' Aaron glanced around, trying to find some other reason to keep him holed up in his tent. He stared at me, hoping for a reprieve, but found none.

'Come,' Moses said, moving towards the entrance. I opened the tent flap and went out first. Checking to make sure all was well, I nodded to Moses. Aaron picked out a large rectangular piece of cloth, wound it over his head, in front of his mouth, and over his shoulders. He pulled it down to cover as much of his face as possible, took a deep breath and stepped outside. We walked on either side of him. Aaron kept his head down, peering out from under his headscarf as we walked. He grimaced at the desecration he saw, holding his head covering tightly over his nose when we passed the funeral pyres.

'Moses?' he muttered after a while. 'How many . . . how many fell?'

'I am told some 3,000.'

'Three . . . three thousand?' We walked on in silence until Aaron spoke again. 'Hur – how did he die? Who . . . ?'

Moses looked at me, indicating that he wanted me to answer that question. I acknowledged the request, still avoiding eye contact with Aaron. 'Hur died by the hand of Rekem. A knife to his ribs.'

Aaron grimaced and closed his eyes briefly, muttering a prayer under his breath. Turning to me, he asked, 'Is Rekem . . . ?'

'Dead.'

'How?'

'By my sword,' I said, looking straight ahead.

Aaron hesitated and then asked, 'And Shimea? Is he also . . .'

'Yes.'

'So you have avenged Yahweh fully.'

Moses turned to look at his brother. 'Joshua did not kill Shimea.'

'No?'

Aaron's eyes opened wide with shock when Moses told him. 'Your son, Eleazar, killed him.'

40

Deception

The atmosphere around camp was sombre and a sense of uneasy breathlessness hung in the air; we could not settle. People viewed their neighbours with suspicion and, at times, fear. Neighbours no longer gathered around their campfires together of an evening; the sound of chattering and laughter at mealtimes had all but gone. Brother had raised his sword against brother, and life as we knew it would never be the same again.

The slaying of our brethren was not something I could talk to Mesha or even Jesher about, so I hugged my guilt to myself and set my face like flint, trying to ignore the accusing glares of my people as I walked among them. I was just grateful that my brothers and father had not been involved in the massacre.

The days that followed were spent in meetings with the elders, making records of those who had been felled. Moses had learned the skills of reading and writing as a child in Egypt, so he scratched the names onto papyrus using a hard cane pen, and ink which he made from soot, resin, olive oil and water. It was laborious work and each name scribed on Moses's papyrus invoked torment in me. Although I knew we had acted in obedience to Yahweh's command, that knowledge did not help ease the burden of guilt that lay heavily on me. Nor did it take away the dreams that had haunted me every night since. The faces of those I had killed flashed before me as I slept, and the reproachful eyes of warriors who had fought with me against the Amalekites accused me throughout the watches of the night. I dozed fitfully and woke many times, damp with sweat.

I tried to let my mind wander as the names of the dead were read out, to distract myself, but was jolted back to reality when I heard the names Oren ben Eliphalet and Rami ben Eliphalet. My heart started to beat faster as I realised who they were – Alya's brothers. But the name that followed caused my heart to pound even stronger: Jamin ben Medad. Alya's betrothed. Dead! Jamin, dead? So Alya was no longer betrothed, then?

My thoughts raced. Did Joel know? Should I tell him? No, I could not tell him – Alya was not the right wife for him. Evil ran in her family. But how could I say nothing? If I held this knowledge back from him and he found out, he would despise me. Should I take counsel with Azriel or Jesher? Or remain silent? The rest of the afternoon was a blur. I heard none of the other names of the fallen but, by the time I left Moses and made my way home, I had come to a decision: I would speak to Jesher and Azriel and take counsel with them. As soon as I arrived home, I told them what I had discovered. My news alarmed them, my suggestion that we tell Joel even more so.

'No! He cannot know of this,' Azriel protested. 'He has accepted that he cannot take her as his wife, so let us leave it at that.'

'Has he accepted it?' I wondered to myself. Since the discovery of Joel and Alya's planned elopement and Eliphalet's vow to have his daughter stoned if Joel came near her, he had been like one who walked in his sleep. He woke unsmiling every day, ate just enough to sustain himself, went to work and returned home each evening. He lived, but the heart had gone from him. In truth, I would almost rather he had been angry – at least then we would have seen some signs of life and passion. Anything would be better than the empty shell we saw before us day after day.

'But what will take place if Joel finds out that we had knowledge of Jamin's death, and did not tell him?' I argued. 'That would cause great discord. He would not find it in his heart to forgive us.'

'Then we must pray that he does not find out.'

'Are you willing to risk this?' I asked Azriel, the memory of his past conflicts with Joel still fresh in my mind.

He paused, seeming to doubt his decision, then turned to Jesher. '*Abba*? What are your thoughts on this matter?'

Jesher looked at each of us in turn. 'I am not sure whether this knowledge would be helpful to Joel. What are your thoughts about Alya? Would she make a good wife for Joel?'

Azriel snorted. 'I have not met the girl, but we saw the wrath that beats in the hearts of her father, and her brothers, and we heard the venom that spewed out of their mouths. Clearly they are not a righteous family, and not true followers of Yahweh.'

'Joshua?' Jesher turned to me.

'Alya and Jamin's betrothal was purposed to align Eliphalet's family to Jamin's family through marriage. Unrighteousness runs through Alya's family, but it seems it was also in Jamin's family. I made some enquiries, and found out that Jamin is . . . was the nephew of Rekem, one of the leaders of the rebellious uprising. There is much darkness in his family and I would not have Joel align himself with that kind of iniquity.'

Jesher nodded. 'It would seem that we are decided, then. We say nothing of this.'

'*Abba*, I know it might seem good to us that Joel knows nothing of Jamin's death, but is it our place to withhold the truth from him?' I questioned Jesher. 'I do not feel we should hide this from him. What if he found out?'

We argued for some time, but Azriel and Jesher's minds were set in stone, so I submitted to them and resolved to say nothing to Joel, or anyone else. For three days, all was well. But on the fourth day, Joel burst into the family tent late in the afternoon, his face alight with excitement. His fellow apprentice, Dahn, had told him the news – Alya's betrothed had died in the massacre. She was free to marry another.

'No, Joel, she is not free.' Azriel stood up to face his son. 'She must fulfil her time of mourning and stay with her father and sisters.'

'Of course, *Abba*. When her time of mourning is over, I will speak to her father and we can make the arrangements.'

Jesher got up and stood next to Azriel. 'He will not favour you, Joel. Eliphalet will not give his permission for you to marry Alya.'

'I know he did not favour me in times past, but now that she is not promised to Jamin, I am sure he . . .' A thought occurred to Joel which stopped him in his tracks. He stared at Jesher, then at Azriel, searching their expressions. 'You are not surprised at my news. Why are you not surprised?' They said nothing. Azriel looked at his father, unsure of what to do, but Jesher held Joel's gaze. Joel's expression changed from confusion to anger. His eyes grew wide. 'You knew! You knew of his death, yet you said nothing to me. You told me nothing of this. Why?'

'Joel, Alya is . . . is not the right woman for you,' Azriel stuttered. 'You must not take her in marriage.'

'You have never even met Alya, let alone talked to her. How could you know whether she is good for me or not?' I could see Azriel was panicking. This was exactly what he didn't want to happen. He glanced over at me for reassurance, and Joel followed his gaze. 'You!' he spat. 'You knew too, and yet you said nothing to me? Why?'

'This was not Joshua's decision,' Jesher interjected, holding out his hand as if to separate me from Joel's hostile glare. 'It was your *abba* and I who chose not to tell you. We wanted to protect you.'

'From what?' Joel yelled. 'From the woman I love?' He swung around to face Hareph and Mesha, who were watching the discourse, somewhat confused. 'Did you know too? Does everyone know, but me?'

They both shook their heads, but Jesher interjected. 'No, Joel. No one else knew of this – and we would like to keep it that way, *nu*?'

I desperately wanted to tell Joel the truth about Alya – the truth about the evil that coursed through her family, about their alliance with Rekem and their rebellion against Yahweh, about how she was tainted and unworthy to be his wife. I wanted to tell him how she would lead him astray into the worship of other gods, despising his heritage. I wanted to tell him that I knew the pain that comes with thwarted love, that with all my heart I wanted to stop him from straying down that path.

I wanted to. But I couldn't. I couldn't tell him any of that. Instead, I watched as his countenance changed from anger to a cold, distant stare. No one said a word. We all held our breath, waiting to see what he would do next. He looked down at the ground.

'I lost her once,' he whispered. 'I cannot lose her again. I will honour her by waiting until her time of mourning is over. But when it is done, I will take her for my wife.'

'Joel, her father will not give permission.'

He looked up and stared at his father with steely eyes. 'With or without his blessing, I *will* take her for my wife.'

41

Lamentation

It was a quiet place. A peaceful place. Moses had moved the tent of meeting a short distance away from the camp. It was now near the foot of Mount Sinai, removed from the hubbub of camp life and the noise of the masses. I found great fulfilment in the time I spent with him there. I was always ready to deliver messages or help with tasks that needed carrying out, but the days I loved the most were those spent with Moses at the tent of meeting.

In the heat of the day we tied the sides up so the desert breezes could blow through the tent, unhindered. However, the hot summer months had finally come to an end, and the first rains had just arrived, so we had tied the tent sides down. These first rains were gentle; they teased the ground with their scattered showers, preparing it for the heavier rains that would follow.

We sat under cover of the tent looking out over the parched landscape, listening to the whispering sounds of the wind, the pattering of raindrops on the roof of the tent and the twittering of birds welcoming these much-needed showers. The earth rejoiced at their touch, embracing the showers with open arms, as did we. We breathed in deeply, filling our nostrils with the wholesome freshness of the scent of rain. The smell of rain falling onto the hard, rocky ground was earthy and robust; it carried the promise of new life.

The sound of the wind and rain, with the twittering of birds, made Yahweh's presence seem even nearer. I relished every opportunity to linger in that place. Then, of course, there was my beloved cloud. Whenever Moses went to the tent of meeting, the pillar of cloud would move with him. When he reached the tent, Yahweh's presence would settle at the entrance and stay there until Moses left. I sat and gazed upon the cloud, soaking up Yahweh's presence.

Since the golden calf incident, Moses spent most of his time in prayer, only coming away from the tent of meeting to eat or drink when Zipporah or I reminded him to do so. Even then, he just picked at his food, barely eating at all. Something was wrong, but I didn't know what. Some days Moses went to the tent alone, but today, I was with him, so I seized the opportunity to ask him. 'Master, are you still troubled by the idol worshippers? Do you mourn for those who died?'

'Hmm? No, no,' Moses replied, distracted. 'There will be no more mourning for the dead. That is behind us.'

I was relieved to hear that. 'That is good. Rekem and Shimea are ... gone, and we have rid the camp of their darkness.'

Moses peered at me, frowning. 'Joshua, the darkness has not gone. Rekem and Shimea are gone, yes, but their evil spread like poison among our people. There are many more like them who have hidden themselves away. They are lying low, out of sight, but they will rise again.' He stared into the distance and sighed. 'But I cannot think of them now. They do not occupy my thoughts.'

'What is it that troubles you, then?' I asked, frowning in confusion.

Moses hesitated. I knew this was not a time to push him for an answer, so I held his gaze and waited. Eventually he spoke. 'The Lord God has told me that we are to leave this place and travel towards Canaan, to the land flowing with milk and honey. He will send His angel before us to drive out the Canaanites, Amorites, Jebusites, Peri – '

'Amen!' I shouted, beaming at him. 'That is good, *nu*?' I could think of nothing better than to move on from this place, to leave behind the putrid stench of what had taken place here.

'Yes, but that is not all.' Moses cleared his throat and continued. 'Yahweh said ... He said ... He will not come with us.'

'What?' I gasped. 'No!'

'His presence will not come with us. He says we are a stiff-necked people and that, if He were in our midst, He might consume us. So He will not journey with us.'

'But ...' I stuttered. 'No! No, no!' I leapt to my feet and started pacing up and down. 'We cannot go on without Him. We cannot go *anywhere* unless He goes with us. We follow His cloud, His presence. We cannot go on without the cloud of Yahweh's presence.'

I pointed to the west. 'It would be better for us to go back to Egypt, than go on without Him.'

'Yes.' Moses' shoulders slumped and he put his head in his hands. 'I have spoken with Him, pleaded with Him. But . . . Yahweh will not relent. He will not come with us, lest He destroy His own people. We cannot go on unless He goes with us. But . . .' he shrugged.

I slumped to my knees and bent my face to the ground. A cry of lamentation welled up in my gut and poured out of my mouth with unbridled sorrow. Moses fell to his knees next to me and we travailed before Yahweh, deep into the night, until our throats were dry and our bodies spent.

Our labouring was not in vain. Moses told me the next day, tears in his eyes and a smile on his face. Yahweh had relented. He would go with us. He promised to give us rest. Relief and joy flooded my heart. I felt the stiffness leave my shoulders. Rest. That sounded good. So good. I had not realised until that moment how exhausted I was. The promise of rest felt like the first drops of rain in the heat of the day at the end of summer.

'Truly,' Moses whispered, 'the Lord God is merciful and gracious, abounding in goodness towards us. He forgives our iniquity and unrighteousness.' His voice broke with emotion and he closed his eyes. We stood together, master and manservant, soaking in the richness of that moment until Moses exclaimed, 'So! I must make ready to go back up the mountain.' He stood up, opened the wooden chest behind him, and drew out a patchwork shoulder bag which Zipporah had made for him.

'When do we leave?' I asked.

'Ah, yes.' Moses hesitated, then turned to look at me. 'Joshua, this time I must go alone.'

My heart started beating faster, my newfound peace dissolving in a flood of apprehension. 'Why, master? Have I failed you? Is the Lord not pleased with me?'

Moses reached out his hand and clasped my shoulder. Smiling at me with what seemed to me to be great affection, he said, 'No, Joshua. You have not failed me – and you have not failed Yahweh, either. It is because you have not failed me that I must leave you here in the camp.'

I was bewildered. 'I do not understand.'

'Joshua, I cannot leave Aaron alone. Not now. I am asking you to stay with him, to pray with him, protect him, help him lead this great people while I am gone.'

Aaron? I was to stay with Aaron, stand by his side? For how long must I endure it? I could not think of anything I would rather do less than that. My mind despaired at the thought of it, but I understood why Moses was asking me to do this. I also knew I could not refuse. 'Yes, Master. It will be my honour.' He knew how much it cost me to say that – I saw it in his eyes.

The following morning, we rose well before the sun. Clouds covered most of the mountain, and mist shrouded the paths as Moses, Aaron and I set off towards Mount Sinai. Silence fell as each of us wrestled with our thoughts. I wrapped my mantle around my body, trying to combat the cold but, thankfully, by the time we reached the foot of the mountain, the sun was rising. Without saying a word, Moses put his bundles down and turned to face the camp. Responding to an unspoken signal, Aaron and I did likewise. All three of us stood, watching in awestruck silence as the blazing tower started its transformation into the pillar of cloud.

The inferno lessened and the flames decreased in size, licking the sides of the glowing obelisk until only delicate tendrils of fire were left flickering on its exterior. The strength of the glowing embers within the pillar grew dimmer, soon to be extinguished altogether, replaced by a shimmering sheath of light that swathed the tower in flashes of silver, with the rainbow colours that I loved so much. Thin shafts of light peered through the clouds and the birds sang their song of welcome to the new day. A sense of newness, a fresh anticipation, filled the air.

Moses' voice cut through the silence. 'It is time.' He turned to face us, smiling at both of us in turn. 'Aaron,' he said. 'Look after Zipporah and the boys for me, yes?'

Aaron nodded. 'They will be safe, do not fear.' They embraced, holding each other close and tight, then Moses stepped back and faced me. Although I tried to hide it, I believe Moses could see the envy in my eyes. Putting his hands on my shoulders, he mouthed the words, 'Thank you.' I acknowledged him with a warm smile, was pulled into a bear hug, and received a resounding kiss on each cheek. I helped wrap the stone tablets which Moses had chiselled according to Yahweh's instructions, in cloth, and lifted them onto his back.

'Shalom,' Moses blessed us. 'May Yahweh grant peace to you, and bless His people Israel. Amen."

'Amen. *Shalom*,' we replied. Moses picked up his patchwork bag and turned to make his way up the mountain.

'Master,' I called to him.

'Yes?' Moses turned to face me.

'How long will you be gone for?'

He smiled. 'Yahweh has not told me that. But I will come back, Joshua. I will return.'

42

The Dream

He did return. He returned to find the camp at peace, and all as it should be.

Initially, my time spent with Aaron had been a struggle but, over the course of the days and then weeks that Moses was away, I had many opportunities to talk with him. He told me stories about his youth and upbringing in Egypt, and about what had happened when Moses and I were away, and I told him what it was like up Mount Sinai with Moses. We spent hours together, worshipping and praying in the tent of meeting and I grew to understand Aaron's heart. Although I still didn't agree with what he had done, I was able to forgive him. My relationship with him was restored; I could look him in the eye with no sense of judgement or anger.

I also spent a lot more time with Eleazar while Moses was away, and our relationship deepened. A shift had taken place on the day of the massacre, and our mutual respect had drawn us closer together. Not only did we have more time to spend in prayer, but we learned how to laugh. He, too, reconciled with Aaron, and we were both at peace.

It felt good. To be at peace. To laugh. To rest.

Moses returned from the mountain full of vigour and excitement. There was a gleam in his eye that made me think he was planning something. I was right! He called a meeting for the following morning, so I rose early and went to Eleazar's tent on my way. '*Shalom*, Eleazar.' I poked my head through his tent flap.

'*Shalom*, Joshua,' Eleazar answered. He rushed to put on his outer robe, tripping over the material that dangled down on one side. He groaned, yanking it up and tying the ends around his waist. I leaned against the tent pole, watching in amusement as he scurried over to the washbasin to splash water on his face. 'Brrrr!' He shuddered, patting his face dry with a cloth. Scooping some water up in his hands, he tried to wet his hair and smooth it into place, but it seemed intent on sticking out at right angles to his head. I laughed at the look of despair on his face when he glanced at his mottled reflection in a copper dish propped up on the wooden table. Eleazar shrugged. 'Ech!' Grabbing his head covering, he threw it over his head and shoulders.

'Come! We must make haste,' I chivvied him.

'Forgive me, my friend. My sleep was much disturbed,' he said, grabbing a few figs. He shoved a couple of the figs in his mouth, handing one to me as we hurried on our way.

'What disturbed your sleep?'

'I had a dream.'

'I dream each night – but that is not a good reason for being late for such an important meeting. You know Moses does not like to be kept waiting.'

'Yes, yes,' Eleazar protested. 'But this was not just a dream – it was a *dream*!'

'Really?' I laughed at him and cuffed him on the head. 'You will have to come up with a better excuse than that, you know.' I had taken on the role of an older brother to him, even though he already had two older brothers, Nadab and Abihu. They disregarded Eleazar and Ithamar, their youngest brother, much of the time, preferring to spend their days together without the interference of their younger siblings.

There was something about Nadab and Abihu that disquieted my heart, but I could not bring to mind what it was. It bothered me that they had not joined the other Levites when we took a stand against Shimea and Rekem, but I never mentioned it to Eleazar or Moses. They told Moses they were outside the camp at the time, and knew nothing about his call until after the massacre was all over. But I was convinced I had seen them in the camp, lurking behind a clump of bushes. I grew troubled whenever I thought of them. I knew something was not quite right but, since I had nothing definite to base my suspicions on, I could do nothing.

'Joshua!' Eleazar frowned at me. 'You are not listening to me.'

'Forgive me,' I said, putting aside my concerns about his brothers. 'What were you saying?'

'I was telling you about my dream. It was . . . it was like . . . I have never had a dream like that, ever. It was so . . . so real, so clear, so . . .' he sighed. 'So *beautiful*.'

My curiosity was piqued. 'What was it about? Who was in your dream?' I joked, 'Was I in your dream?'

'Just me.' He bit into another fig and chewed hard.

'Oh. Well, it cannot have been that good, then, if I was not there.'

'Joshua!' he snapped. 'Do not jest!'

'Brother, forgive me!' I held my hands up. 'I did not realise this laid heavily on your heart.' Over the past few weeks we had spent much time jesting and laughing. I had become used to it, but clearly this was not an appropriate moment for such light-heartedness – in Eleazar's opinion, at least.

'It does.' Eleazar brooded, his head down. 'It was . . . extraordinary. I have never experienced anything like it before.'

'Tell me what you saw. Was no one else in your dream?'

'No, just me . . .' His voice softened and he muttered, 'And Yahweh.'

'Yahweh?' Now he had my attention. 'Yahweh was in your dream?'

'Yes.'

'You *saw* Him?' I stopped walking and turned to face Eleazar, putting my hands out to stop him in his path.

'Well, no. I did not *see* Him, but He was there.' Pausing to think, Eleazar smiled to himself. 'I felt Him. I sensed His presence.'

I stared at Eleazar. I knew him to be kind-hearted, well-meaning, if somewhat clumsy, but of the two of us, I was usually the leader, the strong one. This fervent, passionate man that I saw before me unnerved me. I wasn't sure how to handle this Eleazar. Turning forward again, I urged him on. 'Come, we are nearly there. Make haste! We can talk more about your dream after the meeting.' We hurried on and, on reaching Moses' tent, found a strange group of people assembled. I had expected to see Eleazar's brothers and Aaron with Moses; however, I didn't recognise a lot of the other men gathered there. They were not elders or even leaders that I knew of, and they looked out of place and a bit overawed at being in his tent. There was no time for introductions, though. Moses greeted us and, when we tried to apologise for being late, he gestured to some spaces.

'Come, come. Sit. There is much to discuss, yes?' Moses gazed around the select group with an unusually boyish excitement and, to my surprise, I found a sense of anticipation rising in my heart. 'Thank you for coming to meet with me. I have gathered you together today because . . . Yahweh has spoken.' Every eye was on him, every ear open and each heart attentive to what he was going to say. 'Yahweh spoke to me on the mountain and said,' Moses paused for effect, looking around the circle of faces, his eyebrows lifted expectantly, '. . . that we are to make Him a sanctuary, that He might dwell among us here.'

Gasps came from all around the room. We looked at each other in shock, astounded by Moses' announcement. 'A sanctuary?' Aaron repeated, in astonishment. 'Here? Yahweh wants to dwell among His people *here*? Despite what happened with the . . .'

Moses smiled. 'Yes. Here. With us.' He made eye contact with each of us in turn, to make sure we understood the enormity of what he had just told us. 'He will dwell among us. His presence will be with us. We will be different from all the other nations and tribes.' Seeing our curiosity, Moses plunged straight on, eager to explain more. 'His sanctuary will be a holy place, worthy of housing the presence of Yahweh. We will use only the best materials, yes?' He began pacing in excitement. 'Yahweh has shown me all the details of how to design and craft this tabernacle. You,' he pointed to Bezalel, 'and your craftsmen will build it.'

Bezalel nodded, then frowned. 'Forgive me, Moses, but I thought we were to journey to Canaan and settle there. So why are we building a sanctuary for Yahweh here? Are we to stay here, by Mount Sinai?'

Moses shook his head and wagged his finger. 'No, no, Bezalel. We will settle in the land of Canaan, just like Yahweh promised us. No, the sanctuary we will build will be a *moveable* one – a tabernacle – one that we can pack up and take with us as we journey to Canaan. But one greater and more remarkable than any we have seen before.'

A flurry of excitement and anticipation echoed around the tent. Sighing, Moses stared into space. 'It will be truly magnificent, a fitting dwelling place for the Lord.' He continued, talking more to himself than to us. He spoke of asking the people to bring an offering for this sanctuary, saying that we would need threads of blue, purple, scarlet and fine linen for the curtains within the sanctuary. Turning back to us, he lifted his eyebrows and smiled. 'Royal colours, worthy of the King of the universe, *nu*?'

Moses continued his description, gesticulating as he spoke, as if marking items off an imaginary list. Rams' skins – they must be dyed red – badger skins and goats' hair to make a tent to cover the tabernacle, and wood (but only acacia wood) would all be needed. He swung round and gestured to the craftsmen among us, who agreed with him. 'Yahweh has been very specific about the design of His tabernacle. We must follow His instructions exactly,' he charged us. 'We will need fine oil for the lamps, and spices for the anointing oil and incense.' Turning to Aaron he said, 'The incense will be as the fragrance of heaven – made from sweet spices; stacte and onycha and galbanum, mixed with pure frankincense. *Pure frankincense*! Yes!'

Moses grew more and more excited as we started to grasp the importance and scope of this task. 'Gold, silver, bronze – we will need lots of this, and precious stones – yes! Precious stones, like those that our people brought out of Egypt.' Pausing for a moment, he shook his head and chuckled. 'Ay, ay, ay! I wondered at times why the Lord told us to ask the Egyptians for treasures when we left. Now we know, yes?' he looked around, grinning like a boy.

His enthusiasm was infectious; each of us found ourselves being caught up in the excitement of the vision that Moses was describing.

'Tables of acacia wood overlaid with gold – yes, gold!' he said to the group, nodding his head, chuckling at our expressions. He walked around, using his hands to indicate dimensions, as if designing the tabernacle within his tent. 'We will build an altar of incense for the anointing fragrance, and on one of the tables there will be a golden lampstand. Oy!' said Moses, closing his eyes and lifting his hands up. 'So beautiful. Six branches, three from each side, and the main shaft – all of hammered gold. The bowls for the oil will all be crafted in gold in the shape of an al – '

'Almond blossom!' Eleazar blurted out. Everyone turned to stare at him. He looked pale and I wondered if he was unwell.

'Yes,' Moses said, gazing at Eleazar. 'Almond blossom. How did you know this?'

'Forgive me, my Lord, I did not mean to speak out of turn.' Eleazar bowed his head, trying not to look at Aaron, who was obviously not much pleased at his son's outburst.

'Eleazar,' Moses said, crouching in front of him. 'There is only one Lord, the God of heaven, King of the universe.' Leaning forward with a twinkle in his eye, he said, 'and I am not He!' Eleazar smiled and nodded. I knew he had always been somewhat in awe of his uncle, and the miracles he had seen Moses perform over the past few months had served only to increase his admiration of this man of God.

'Now, tell me how you know about the almond blossoms.'

'I – well, last night, I had a dream.'

'A dream?' Moses was intrigued. 'Tell me . . . what was in your dream?'

'I saw everything you have described – the golden tables, the altar with incense burning on it, curtains of purple, blue and crimson, and the golden lampstand with almond blossoms . . .' he petered out, suddenly aware that everyone was staring at him.

Moses peered at him, fascinated. 'What was it like, in the dream? What did your heart tell you?'

Eleazar frowned in concentration, and lowered his head. He whispered, 'It was . . . the most . . . *wonderful* . . . in that moment, there was nothing else – nothing, no one but Yahweh. Such holiness, such beauty. My heart melted within me. I . . . it . . .' Eleazer exhaled in frustration and looked at Moses. 'I do not have the words to describe it.'

Silence fell. It was a holy moment. Yahweh's presence filled the tent.

Thick and weighty.

Rich.

Breath-taking.

Speech was superfluous. Humble hearts bowed before Yahweh, the great I Am, King of the universe – the one true God who desired to live among His people. His own people. His special treasure. His holy nation. I understood now. This was no ordinary dream. Yahweh Himself had visited my friend in the night watches. My heart started pounding as I pondered what that must have been like.

I saw Aaron staring at his son in disbelief. Nadab and Abihu stared too, frowning – not in wonder, but in envy. The craftsmen's eyes were closed, their heads bowed. Moses smiled at his nephew; the smile of one who knows and understands. Putting his hand on his heart, he whispered, 'This is wonderful, Eleazar. Truly wonderful. Yahweh has shown you in a dream what He told me on the mountain.' Shaking his head and smiling to himself, Moses walked to the other side of the tent. 'Marvellous are Your ways, O Lord,' he muttered, rocking gently on his heels. After a while, he swung around and pointed at Eleazar. 'You!' he said. 'You will help us build this sanctuary for Yahweh.'

'Me?'

'Yes, you, Eleazar.' Walking towards him, he held out his arms and raised him up. 'You have seen it, *nu*? You have *seen* this tabernacle in your dream, so you will advise us on how to build it. Yes!' Moses turned towards Bezalel and his team of craftsmen. 'Bezalel, go with Eleazar now – you and your men. Let him tell you everything he saw. Ask questions, yes? Draw it, mould it, let it take shape in your hearts and minds. We will meet tomorrow morning straight after we break our fast, to make plans. Yes?'

Eleazar glanced at me for reassurance before following Bezalel and the other craftsmen out of the tent. Nadab and Abihu stalked out without a word to anyone, and the rest of the men went on their way, chattering among themselves, leaving only Moses, Aaron, and me in the tent.

Aaron looked at his brother. 'Are you sure, Moses? Eleazar? Not Nadab or Abihu?'

Moses smiled and put his hands on Aaron's shoulders. 'I am sure. Yahweh Himself has chosen him.' Aaron nodded, but was clearly still not convinced. Moses turned to me. 'Truly, the ways of Yahweh are remarkable, yes? To give my nephew a dream, to show him this sanctuary, even while he *sleeps*?' Clasping his hands in front of his mouth, Moses whispered, 'Oh Joshua, it will be a marvel! A sign and a wonder! Like nothing we have seen before. The pyramids and edifices of Egypt were impressive, yes, but our tabernacle will house the very presence of Yahweh.' Tears started rolling down his cheeks. 'This will be a sanctuary for our God,' he whispered, eyes closed. 'Finally, He will dwell among His people.'

43

Tabernacle

'*Shalom*, Bezalel. *Shalom*, Oholiab,' Eleazar called out cheerfully.

'*Shalom*, Eleazar. Did you sleep well?'

'Very peacefully, thank you.'

'Have you had any more dreams?' Bezalel asked with a twinkle in his eye.

'No!' Eleazar laughed. 'Or at least, none that I can remember!' Eleazar's life had been irreversibly turned upside down. In the space of a single day he had not only become chief advisor for the tabernacle, but had been pushed into the forefront – a place where he'd never found himself before, and had never desired to be. Nadab and Abihu were strong, charismatic men, used to being well known as Aaron's sons and Moses' nephews. They had grown accustomed to the recognition afforded them. Aaron's youngest son, Ithamar, was happy to dodge all the attention and Eleazar had also been able to do so for much of the time – until now.

All of a sudden, the camp was alive with a feverish excitement. After the upheaval and tribulation of the previous weeks' events, the news of a glorious tabernacle to be built in the camp was greeted with almost hysterical enthusiasm. The Israelites threw themselves into donating the raw materials needed for the tabernacle. Wherever he went, Eleazar was mobbed by people asking questions about how the work was progressing, or wanting to talk through the intricacies of its design. Being thrust into a place of prominence was very difficult for him. He was very much like Moses, and Moses knew it. He had noted his nephew's increasing levels of anxiety. He drew me aside one day. 'Joshua, I have a new task for you.'

'Yes, Master?'

'I want you to assist Eleazar. Go with him on his visits to Bezalel's workshops, go to the meetings he attends, stay with him and make sure he arrives home safely, yes?' I nodded, oddly touched that Moses had thought to make provision for his nephew in this way. 'And report back to me every day on the progress of the tabernacle.'

So I mapped out the best route from Eleazar's tent to the workshops where Bezalel and his team laboured; we used the back pathways around the outskirts of the camp, thus avoiding contact with those who would bother him.

The workshop was his favourite place. There, he could forget he was Aaron's son, Moses' nephew, or the chief advisor, and simply be Eleazar. The men he worked with realised very quickly that he was not comfortable with formality or titles, and began to treat him as they would any other craftsman. He became one of them, and it delighted his soul. Eleazar made a point of spending time with each of the craftsmen individually, answering their questions and discussing their work, which meant I was able to spend time with them too. Our visits were a vital, joyful part of my day.

'*Shalom*, Joel. What are you working on today?' Eleazar asked.

'*Shalom*, Eleazar, *shalom*, Joshua. These are the crossbeams for the frame on the west side of the tabernacle.' Joel showed us how they slotted into the grooves that made up the frame. His enthusiasm was infectious and, even though to some the crossbeams might have seemed just an ordinary, necessary part of the structure, Joel crafted them with great care and pride.

'They will look magnificent when overlayed with gold.' Joel stroked the timber. 'Look at the grain in this wood – it is exceptional.'

'It is a thing of beauty,' Eleazar said, smiling. We walked over to Bezalel, who was by the fires, moulding silver hooks for the courtyard curtains. 'Joel seems to be doing well. Are you happy with his work?' Eleazar asked him.

Bezalel straightened up and stretched the muscles in his back. 'He is my best apprentice,' he murmured, looking over to where Joel was working. 'I have not found anyone who has a feel for wood the way Joel does. He sees the life in it and draws it out.' Lowering his voice, he whispered, 'He is even more skilled than my own sons, who have been learning under me for years. But do not tell them that – or him ,' Bezalel said, smiling. 'I would not want pride to cause his heart to go astray!'

Eleazar laughed. 'I do not think it would,' he said, watching Joel planing a beam. 'Joel does not craft for man's attention. He crafts because it is within him and he cannot stop himself.'

'That is true. He has changed so much since becoming my apprentice. He was quiet when he first came; unsure of himself – unsure of anything – trapped within his heart. But I have seen him unfold, like a plant whose leaves unfurl a little more each day in the light of the sun.'

I purposely stayed silent during discussions about Joel, not wanting to draw attention to his past struggles – or his current ones. However, Bezalel and Eleazar knew of my relationship with Joel's family, and it was difficult knowing how to respond when I was asked a direct question.

'He has days when he is not himself,' Bezalel continued. 'Many times in days past he has been withdrawn and unhappy, not unlike a caged animal. What happened to cause the change in him?' he asked, turning to me.

I paused before responding. 'Joel is ruled by his heart, led by his passions. Like most artists, his heart will affect the quality of his work.'

Bezalel grunted. He picked up his tools. 'Was he always good at crafting?'

'His father says that as a child, crafting wood or sculpting clay was his constant pleasure, but the day he was taken to the brick compound, it stopped. He did not whittle or mould after that, until he came to learn from you.'

'His skill is unrivalled for such a young man. What about sculpting stone?' Eleazar asked Bezalel. 'Is he good with stone?'

'I know not. He will not touch it.'

'Why?' Eleazar asked, intrigued.

'The stone quarries in Egypt.'

'Ah, of course.' Eleazar sighed. 'Well, he looks to have found his passion – see the way he touches that wood!'

Bezalel nodded. 'I am going to let Joel do some of the carving on the table for the shewbread, when he has finished the crossbeams.'

'Are you certain?' I questioned. 'That is quite a responsibility for such a young apprentice.'

'Yes, I am.' He pointed his moulding tool at us. 'But I have not told him yet, so restrain your words!'

Eleazar lifted his hands in surrender. 'As surely as I live, it will not come from my mouth! But is he skilled enough?'

'I believe he is,' Bezalel replied. 'Yahweh has placed a rare anointing on this one.'

I smiled, but my inward thoughts were not so harmonious. Yes, Joel was an exceptional craftsman. It was good that Bezalel recognised his skill and was drawing it out of him. But what would happen when Alya's time of mourning was over? What havoc would Joel wreak if he insisted on taking her for his wife? A shiver ran down my spine. It would not be too long now before we would have to find out.

44

In the Family

'Why? Why would Yahweh choose Eleazar, of all people?' The two brothers stood in my way, their arms folded, faces brimming with anger. 'Why would Yahweh give *him* the dream? As the eldest of Aaron's sons, He should have given the dream to me,' Nadab protested. 'Why choose a clumsy runt like him? How can he possibly know what to do? He is not a leader of people.'

Abihu guffawed. 'He is hardly able to direct the course of his own life, let alone lead a large team of craftsmen.'

'I know not why Yahweh chose Eleazar, but He did.'

Abihu spat on the ground. 'Eleazar is a fool. So clumsy, always tripping and dropping things. How can he be in charge of building a glorious tabernacle for Yahweh? It is foolishness!'

This was the last thing I needed. I was on my way to Moses to give him an update on Eleazar's meeting with Bezalel that morning when Abihu and Nadab ambushed me, demanding to know what was being said in our meetings, and questioning Eleazar's ability to carry out his role as chief advisor. I had never trusted them, although I could never understand why, and I purposely tried to avoid any interaction with them for that reason. It had worked up until today, but now I was cornered. 'We cannot question Yahweh's ways. We must trust Him and obey His commands.'

They scowled at me in contempt. 'You say that only because you are Eleazar's companion.'

I shook my head. 'That is not so. It was Yahweh who gave Eleazar the dream, and it was Moses who appointed him as chief advisor. It is by his instruction that your brother is doing this work. I seek only to obey Yahweh and serve Moses.'

Nadab lowered his voice. 'My uncle has been known to make mistakes before, you know. He is not unerring. We have heard the tales of what took place in Egypt before he took on the mantle of leading this great people. He is not the holy man you think him to be.' I looked into Nadab's eyes and my heart froze. No! It could not be! My thoughts scattered like grains of sand in a desert storm; I jerked my head down, breaking eye contact with him so he could not see my reaction. Trying to pull myself together, I muttered, 'That may be, but he is still Yahweh's chosen leader and we must honour his decision.'

Abihu unfolded his arms and leaned in closer. 'We are not the only ones who feel this way, Joshua. There are many others who see Eleazar's weaknesses – and Moses'.'

'We are not alone in this,' Nadab added, scrutinising my reactions. 'There are many who are not happy with the way things are. Many who want change. They want the freedom to walk their own paths, to follow their own ways, not always being told what to do by Moses.'

My heart was racing. I had to get away. 'That is as it may be,' I focused on the ground, 'but Moses is still our leader, and Eleazar has been chosen as chief advisor.' Backing away from the brothers, I glanced at them and said, 'With your permission, I will take my leave – I must make haste.' I turned around and hurried off in the direction of Moses' tent without looking back. My mind was a whirl of questions. I started running to avoid being pulled into conversation with anyone on the way.

'Joshua?' Moses looked at me in astonishment as I flung open his tent flap and stepped inside. 'What is it? What ails you?' I stood there, my heart beating so fast I couldn't breathe properly. I had run all the way to Moses' tent in my hurry to get there but, now that I'd arrived, I didn't know what to say. How could I tell him? What should I say? What would he say?

He stood up. Waiting until I had caught my breath, he led me to a large cushion. 'Come, sit.' I lowered myself onto the cushion as Moses poured me a cup of water. 'Drink.' I drank it in one go and grasped the empty cup in my hands. 'Joshua . . . what is it? Tell me,' Moses pressed me. 'What is it?'

'Master . . . it is Nadab. And Abihu.'

'What of them? Are they well?'

'Yes. No.' My thoughts were swirling; I felt nauseous. 'May it be that I am wrong. It cannot be true . . .' I mumbled.

'Wrong about what?' Moses was starting to get agitated, so I took a deep breath and started to explain. 'They stopped me on my way here to complain about Eleazar being made chief advisor for the tabernacle. They believe they should have been given that honour.'

Moses chuckled. 'I am sure they do, but Yahweh thought otherwise.'

'Yes, I told them that, but they continued to speak contemptuously, saying how stupid and clumsy Eleazar is and ... also how you ... make wrong decisions. They spoke about what happened in Egypt – when you killed the Egyptian.'

Moses looked surprised, then shrugged. 'Well, that is not a secret. I have never hidden it; but it is not something I like to talk about. I have put that all behind me.' He put his hand on my arm. 'I will talk to them. Do not fear, all will be well.'

'No!' I blurted. 'It will not be well. They seek your harm! They have ... their ...' I pointed to my own eyes. 'Their eyes! I saw it!'

'You saw what?'

'The darkness! I saw it. In their eyes. The same darkness that was in Shimea's eyes, and Rekem's.'

Moses stared at me, unblinking as the blood drained from his face. 'Are you sure of this?' I nodded. My heart ached at the vulnerability on his face. I hated the fact that I was the one to deliver this message. 'My own family,' Moses murmured. 'I wondered why I had not seen them around camp lately. They have been very quiet ever since the ... golden calf.'

'Yes. Master, I beg of you, do not reproach me,' I mumbled, 'but there is more I must say.' I knew that, now I had started this grim tale, I could hold nothing back. 'I know they told you they were not in the camp the day of ... the day we came down the mountain, but I believe they spoke falsely.' Looking into Moses' eyes and dreading what I would see reflected there, I spoke out, nevertheless. 'I saw them. I saw them when we were ... slaying the rebels. They were there. They were hiding behind a clump of bushes near Aaron's tent. I am sure it was them.'

Moses nodded but said nothing. He walked to the tent flap and stared out at the camp, scratching his beard.

'Master, forgive me.'

'For what?' Moses turned to look at me. 'You have done nothing deserving of forgiveness. It is right that you tell me these things, Joshua. I thank you for that. You have no reason to entreat me.'

Silence fell like a gloomy fog, wrapping itself around us as we struggled to make sense of the murky web of thoughts that muddled our minds.

'Master? What will you do?'

Moses stared at me for a while. 'I know not,' he whispered.

45

Ready or Not

As the day approached, I knew that Eleazar had experienced a growing sense of disquiet and, now that the day had arrived, his disquiet had spiked into full-on anxiety. Months of preparation, a workforce of hundreds, countless amounts of gold, silver, bronze, spices, fragrant oils, acacia wood and fine linen had gone into the preparation of Yahweh's tabernacle – and now it was ready!

I went to Eleazar's tent to help him prepare for the ceremony. He stood rigidly before me, dressed in his priestly robes, eyes tightly closed, hands clasped in front. He was a slim man and the ornate garments he wore were clearly much heavier than he had anticipated. He tugged at his breastplate and wiped a bead of sweat off his brow, knocking his turban in the process. He was shaking. I clasped the tops of his arms and held him steady. 'Eleazar, peace! Peace to you, my brother.' He nodded, breathed in deeply through his nose, and exhaled through his mouth. I squeezed his arm. 'This day has been long-awaited. Are you ready?'

Nodding, he drew himself up and held his head high. 'I am ready.'

'Mmm.' I scrutinised his form, adjusted his turban, pulling it down firmly on his head, then smiled. 'Now you are ready.'

We made our way through the crowds towards the tabernacle. As we neared the place where Moses, Aaron and his other sons waited, we saw that the craftsmen had been given the honour of lining the entranceway to the tabernacle. I glanced at Eleazar. I knew his heart was filled with gratitude and pride in these men who he had come to think of as brothers. He clasped their hands as he walked through the tunnel of bodies, thanking them for their service to Yahweh. Joel stood among them, his young face filled with pride. 'You have done well,' Eleazar said to him, putting his hands on top of Joel's. 'I look forward to seeing what Yahweh will create through these hands in time to come.'

Joel blushed and bowed slightly. 'It has been my honour to serve Him . . . and you.'

Eleazar moved on and stopped in front of Bezalel and Aholiab. Clasping their hands in turn, he shook his head and shrugged. 'I cannot express all that is in my heart, but I think you know what I would say if I could find the words.' Both men smiled, bowing in acknowledgement. Eleazar placed his hand on his heart and bowed, keeping eye contact with them as he did so.

Nadab and Abihu stood with Aaron, waiting for Eleazar. Nadab turned to his father and muttered, 'Is all this really necessary? Should we not just get on with the ceremony?' Aaron frowned at him and shook his head to indicate that further deliberation on the topic would not be tolerated. Moses and I stole a glance at each other. Concern flickered in his eyes, but we turned our gaze forward before anyone could notice. Eleazar joined the rest of his family, standing behind his older brothers, thereby giving them the place of honour. The musicians started playing; the worship began. Hearts overflowed with gratitude; voices lifted high in praise of Yahweh. Harps, trumpets, timbrels and drums sounded out as we worshipped the mighty God of Israel, led by the resonant voices of the priests. I nudged Eleazar and gestured to the pillar of cloud. It was moving.

Shimmering in the bright morning sunshine, the swirling pillar glided towards the entrance of the tabernacle. Ruffles of velvety swirls sparkled in response to the worship, and I saw within the cloud what looked like a thousand pairs of wings billowing in time to its rhythm. I stood transfixed as the cloud came closer and closer. I found myself holding my breath. When the cloud was almost upon us, Moses turned to Aaron and his sons.

'It is time,' he said. 'Eleazar, you will carry the anointing oil and accompany your *abba*.'

Eleazar stared at Moses. 'But . . . that is not my portion. I am the younger of my brothers. Surely Nadab must carry th – '

Moses smiled. 'You will carry the oil and assist Aaron in the consecration.'

There was no more to be said.

Eleazar looked at me. I tried to ignore the furious glares that were being hurled at us by Nadab and Abihu. Turning towards the sanctuary, Eleazar waited as first Moses and then his father entered the tabernacle. He took a deep breath. Holding the heavy curtain open, he squared his shoulders and stepped inside.

46

Transformed

He was changed. Transformed. The Eleazar that stepped inside that Holy Place was not the same man who emerged from it. Something had happened in there and I was desperate to know what.

The minute his duties were finished, I led him away from the crowds to his tent so we could talk. He was like a sleepwalker, struggling to wake from a deep slumber. I had to put my arm round him and steer him in the right direction. He said not one word. I took his turban and breastplate off, helped him disrobe and sat him down with a drink of water. Sitting opposite him, I stared into his eyes, trying to discern what was happening behind their glazed veneer.

'Tell me,' I whispered. 'What happened?'

He stared at me, dumbfounded. Shaking his head, he murmured, 'I cannot . . .'

'Try!' I urged him. 'Eleazar, what took place in there? I must know.'

He frowned at me and I could see he was trying to order his thoughts. He closed his eyes, concentrating hard. 'It was . . . the smell that touched me first. The incense – a heady, rich, sweet smell. It reached out and took hold of me as soon as I entered. Then I saw patterns reflecting light from the oil lamps, flickering like shadowy flames dancing, glimmering on the walls of the tent.'

He was silent, eyes still tightly closed.

'Yes? What then?' He opened his eyes and seemed confused to see me sitting in front of him, staring at him so intently. 'The shadows from the oil lamps?' I prompted. 'And then . . . ?'

'Yes. Shadows.' Closing his eyes again, a placid smile formed on his lips. 'The stillness. So quiet. So still. I could hear nothing but the swish of my robes. Everything outside of that place ceased to exist.

In there was everything. There was nothing else. Only Yahweh, His presence ... and me. Truly, such a holy place,' he muttered to himself.

Eleazar continued his discourse, eyes still shut. He started rocking gently backwards and forwards as he talked, telling me how his hands had felt clammy and his stomach tight, as if tied in knots. His breath came in uneven, shallow gasps. He had felt fear, but not the same fear that had assaulted him so often in times past. This was different. This was the fear of God; the holy, reverential awe of Yahweh.

'I have never seen anything so beautiful – so fresh, uncorrupted – and yet strangely familiar.' He opened his eyes and looked directly at me. 'You saw the furnishings when they were being crafted. We knew their beauty, watched them being fashioned day after day. I knew they would be beautiful to behold but I never expected that. In the light of the lampstand, their golden surfaces glowed with a glory that was ... unsurpassed.'

Tears filled Eleazar's eyes. 'Joshua, I had been there before. In my dream. I stood in that same place, sensed the same presence. I knew Him there. He was there – with me. He knew me. I was known.'

We were still for a while. I let my mind imagine what Eleazar described, picturing the furniture, the altars, the oil lamps, the glory of Yahweh's presence. I saw the flickering shadows from the oil lamp, smelled the pungent fragrance of the sweet incense; I was there, in the Holy Place with him. Eleazar gathered himself and continued, explaining how Aaron had given him the vial of anointing oil and invited him to accompany him. He had clasped the vessel with clammy hands and followed his father, walking slowly so as not to trip.

'I was so fearful that I might stumble,' he said. 'But I did not falter, until ... until ... I saw it.'

'What? You saw what?'

Eleazar's face broke into a joyous smile. 'The cloud! Yahweh's cloud. It was there! Inside the tabernacle!'

The cloud of Yahweh's presence had formed in that very room, in front of Eleazar's eyes. Feathery wisps had started to swell and multiply until they formed a lacy mist which hung in the air above his head. The mist descended until it covered his head, and then his shoulders, with a silvery hue. An unfamiliar weight had pressed down on Eleazar and he planted his feet firmly apart on the ground to try to steady himself, fighting the urge to fall to his knees with his forehead on the ground.

'My body was trembling, my hands shook. It was terrible – and wonderful – all at the same time,' he explained. '*Abba* was not well pleased when he saw the vessel of holy oil shaking in my hands. I believe he feared I would drop it.' He shook his head at the memory. 'That was my fear also.' As Eleazar tried to explain to his father why he was shaking, that he had been in that place before in his dream, that he was overcome by Yahweh's glory, his father's frown softened into a knowing smile. Aaron came close, put his hand on Eleazar's chest over his heart and held it there. He took the vessel of oil from Eleazar's trembling hands while Moses stood, silently watching the interaction between father and son.

'I saw no condemnation or anger in their eyes. They knew what ailed me. They knew that my languishing was of the Lord.' Eleazar took a deep breath. 'The hand of Yahweh was strong upon me. His holiness overwhelmed me.'

Eleazar had fallen to his knees in that Holy Place, crying, 'Holy, holy, holy, Lord. I am undone. Yahweh, I am undone'. He dared not open his eyes, or risk dissipating the beautiful holiness that drenched his heart. Profound grief struck him at the revelation of his own humanity and weakness, while he simultaneously overflowed with a sense of exquisite fulfilment.

He sighed. 'I have no recollection of how much time passed while I was there. Time had no meaning. I would have stayed there for ages to come, and never left His presence, if it were my resolve. I would give up this life and all that I have if, in turn, I could just stay in that place with Yahweh.' He shuddered with a euphoric contentment. 'For I have been in the presence of Yahweh. I am known by Him.'

47

Consecration

Looking out over the throng of men kneeling before Moses, I saw no smiles of satisfaction on their faces. Only immense sorrow.

'This is a holy day,' he declared. 'A time of consecration to the Lord.'

The whole congregation of the children of Israel had gathered together to witness the separation of the tribe of Levi for service unto the Lord. Aaron and his sons, with their brethren from the tribe of Levi, had been through a time of ceremonial cleansing. Sacrifices and offerings had been made on their behalf as atonement for their sins, in preparation for this day. Moses stood before the assembled crowd, staff in hand. I stood behind him. This was an auspicious moment for our people, but the atmosphere was not one of celebration; this was a hallowed time of sanctification which had arisen out of heart-breaking sacrifice.

The weather mirrored our hearts. The winter was now upon us and the gentle former rains had given way to heavy showers and gloomy days. Thick grey rain clouds rolled in; heavy laden, gloomy masses with darkened undersides. There were no flashes of lightning or rumbles of thunder to be heard or seen; these were not angry clouds; they were sorrowful and desolate.

'The Lord will bestow on you a blessing this day. For every man . . .' Moses' voice cracked; he swallowed hard before continuing. 'Every man has been set against his brother.'

The Levites knelt on the ground; many of them had tears silently streaming down their faces as Moses blessed them and set them apart before the Lord God of their fathers, Abraham, Isaac and Jacob.

The heavens opened in commiseration. The dense, sultry clouds dropped their precious cargo on these chosen ones. Many of them opened their arms and put their heads back, welcoming the cleansing rain, letting it wash away their pain and grief. The Levites' calling had been born out of death and sacrifice, but there were no swords or spears in their hands today. Purified and set apart, they would no longer join the ranks of those who went forth into battle. From today onwards, their hands would be used solely for the service of Yahweh and the work of His tabernacle.

'Yahweh has taken you for Himself,' Moses declared, 'to minister and do the work of His tabernacle before Aaron and his sons. From today onwards, you are separated unto Him, wholly given to Yahweh for His service.'

Aaron and his sons stood before Moses in front of the assembly of Levites; their hearts and voices joined with those of their brethren in a sacrifice of praise, their hands lifted in prayer to their God.

All except two.

Their eyes were boring into Moses. Nadab and Abihu were still seething over Moses' choice of Eleazar to assist Aaron with the consecration of the tabernacle. They knelt before him with the rest of the Levites, singing the words of the songs in time with their brethren, all the time glowering at Moses and Eleazar with undisguised malevolence.

48

False Fire

It had happened. It had taken longer than I thought it would, but it had happened. 'Master, make haste!' I gasped, bursting into Moses' tent. 'You must come!' Moses' head jerked up and he swallowed his mouthful of fruit. 'What is it?'

'Nadab,' I panted, out of breath from my frantic run to fetch him. 'Abihu.' Moses dropped his dish and followed me without questioning me further. There was no time for talk. He fell into step with me as we ran the short distance to the tabernacle. Already, a substantial crowd had gathered and we had to push our way through to gain entrance. Voices were raised in anger and Moses' eyes grew wide with disbelief as he entered the courtyard and saw his nephews holding censors of incense before the entrance to the Holy Place.

'What are you doing?' he bawled.

'Ah, beloved uncle.' Nadab sneered at him. 'I wondered how long it would be before you joined us.'

'Nadab, Abihu, what wickedness is this?' Moses said, gesturing to the censers they held in their hands. 'You know the commandments of the Lord regarding the tabernacle. You cannot offer incense before the Lord.'

'No?' Nadab asked, lifting his eyebrows in mock innocence.

'It is not for you to offer incense, you know this.' Moses stared at him in frustration. 'The high priest alone offers incense before Yahweh – and not in the middle of the morning or whenever he deems it so. Incense can only be offered at twilight and sunrise each day.'

'Aah, but the statutes of Yahweh do not apply to some people, do they?' Abihu stepped forward, his eyes glinting with venom.

Moses frowned in confusion. 'What do you speak of? I have not offered incense. Yahweh has not appointed me for that honour, it is for your *abba* alone.'

'Yes, but what about Eleazar?' Nadab spat.

'Eleazar?' Moses turned to Aaron for an explanation.

'Eleazar has not offered incense. I have told them this. He would not do such a thing. He knows the ways of Yahweh,' Aaron explained.

'Of course he does,' Nadab smiled at his father. A chill filled my heart when I saw the bitterness in his face – and the darkness in his eyes. 'Eleazar is the favoured son, is he not? The chief advisor, with authority over all the craftsmen, meeting with important people so he can instruct them in the way they should go. And why? Because he had a *dream*.' His face twisted into a snarl. 'When it came to the consecration of this glorious tabernacle, who was given the honour of holding the holy oil for the high priest? Not his first-born son who was loyal to him,' he said, pointing to Aaron, 'and served him faithfully for many years – the one who would follow after him as high priest. No! Eleazar was chosen!'

I was glad that Eleazar was not there to see this display of venom. It had never been his desire to overshadow his older brothers, in fact he had been more surprised than anyone when Moses appointed him chief advisor. Eleazar's heart was righteous in this regard and everyone knew it – everyone but his older brothers.

Moses stared at his nephews. He pleaded with them, reassuring Nadab that the sacred office of high priest would be his when Aaron went to be with his fathers, imploring them to stand down. Nadab responded by lifting his censer and swinging it in front of Moses' face. Moses wrinkled his nose up in disgust and covered his face with his scarf. Even though the incense had not yet been lit, the odour that arose from it was strong. 'What stench is this? What spices have you used in this incense?'

'None that you would know . . . or approve of,' Nadab sniggered, grinning at Abihu. 'A few select ingredients of our own choosing.'

'The Lord forbid!' Moses cried. 'Nadab, only incense made according to the measures and spices that Yahweh commanded can be offered. You know this! You cannot devise your own incense – that is an abomination before the Lord. Your own mouth testifies against you.'

'Why? Because you say it should be so?'

'It is not what I say but what Yahweh says that must be obeyed. Among those who approach Him, He must be seen as holy in the sight of all people. He will be honoured.'

Aaron stepped forward to look at the strange herbs and spices in the censers, also covering his nose with his headscarf. 'Where did you find these?'

Abihu looked at his brother, then his eyes darted back to his father. 'We found them. In Shimea's tent. After Eleazar killed him,' he spat.

'Shimea?' Moses stared at his nephew. 'Shimea used unholy concoctions to aid his worship of false gods. You cannot offer these before Yahweh. It is unholy fire! I cannot let you do this,' he said, lunging forward to try to take the censer from him. Nadab jerked his censer away and pushed Moses hard. He stumbled backwards, falling into my arms. I steadied him, drew my sword and stepped forward.

'What now?' Nadab scowled at me. Turning to Moses, he said, 'You are too cowardly to fight your own battles, so you bring your dog to fight for you?'

'Master, shall I stop them?' Out of the corner of my eye, I saw red flashes. Glancing up at the cloud that billowed above us, I saw glowing embers being fanned into flame by a fierce wind stirring in the heavens. Moses saw it too. We looked at each other and I waited for his response, but we both knew what was about to happen.

'No. It is too late,' he said with a strangled cry. 'Get back!' Not taking his grief-stricken eyes off his nephews, he instructed me to tell the people to move away from Nadab and Abihu. As I drove the crowds back, he pleaded with them one last time, begging them not to treat the Lord with contempt. His plea fell on deaf ears. Nadab gave his censer to Abihu to hold, while he drew out a flint from his leather belt bag and struck it. Within seconds, noxious green flames began to burn. Smoky tendrils, like skeletal green fingers, rose from the censers and a bitter stench filled the air. Moses staggered backwards, his knees buckling under the weight of premature grief. I caught him and held him up, my arms around his chest and shoulders, as he cried out, 'Yahweh, I beg of you, forgive them.'

We stood together, our hearts filled with foreboding, waiting for the retribution we knew was coming. Moses buried his head in my arm, distraught, but I did not turn away. I continued to shield him, watching through narrowed eyes as the embers in the cloud burst into flames, hurtled down, and consumed his nephews with a single thunderous roar.

49

Eldership

For days, Moses came out of his tent only to venture to the tabernacle to pray. Each day I went to him in the morning, as was our custom, but each day he gave me a sad smile and released me, preferring to spend time only with Zipporah and his sons. Moses, Aaron, Eleazar and Ithamar were not permitted to mourn Nadab and Abihu. Their bodies were carried outside the camp by Mishael and Elzaphan, their cousins, and Moses never looked upon them again. The Lord had decreed they should not tear their robes, uncover their heads, or perform any of the usual mourning rituals.

Although he obeyed Yahweh without question, in his heart I know that Moses mourned his nephews with a deep grief. He blamed himself for their deaths because he had seen the darkness in them but had not confronted it. So he cleaved to his family and they brought a much-needed healing to his heart. Zipporah was like medicine for him. She was a strong woman who knew her own mind, but her strength was coupled with tenderness and she loved Moses with a fierce passion. The preparations for the tabernacle had taken much of Moses' energy and so, having time to spend with his wife and sons was just what was needed. It was good for him. It was good for all of them.

As the days went by, I saw his countenance lighten and the heaviness of grief dissipate. The day came when he did not send me away as I arrived at his tent, but invited me in to meet with him. It was time to move on. He was ready. I rejoiced to be able to serve him again. I had missed our daily interactions and times of prayer. He gave me some messages to relay, and I was surprised to hear that one of them was a message for Jesher, inviting him to meet with Moses later that morning.

'Jesher? My Jesher?' I questioned, to be sure I had not misunderstood his instructions. Moses chuckled and confirmed that 'my' Jesher was the person he wanted to speak to, then asked me to join him at the meeting. He said nothing about what he wanted to speak to Jesher about, and I did not ask. I had learned over the last few months that if Moses wanted me to know something, he would tell me. So Jesher and I went to meet with him, returning home with full hearts and smiles on our faces. Shira was waiting for him when we returned, pacing up and down outside the tent.

'So, what did he want?' she asked him, totally ignoring me.

'Who?' asked Jesher.

'What do you mean, who? Moses, of course. What did Moses want with you?'

'Oh, Moses.'

'Jesher!' Shira scolded him. 'When the leader of the nation of Israel invites you to meet with him, he does not just want to discuss the condition of your tent, *nu*?'

'Well, in truth, we did talk about tents,' Jesher said, feigning nonchalance and giving me a quick wink. 'These ferocious winds have been causing the skins to rip on the coverings for the tabernacle. I told him – '

'Ech!' Shira rolled her eyes and put her hands on her hips. 'Must I drag this out of you by force? You know of what I speak. *What did Moses want?*'

'Well . . .' Jesher paused, a slight smile forming on his lips. His wife leaned forward and raised her eyebrows in anticipation. 'It seems there may be room among the elders of Israel for a man such as me.'

Shira gasped and her hands went to her mouth in shock. 'No! Truly? Jesher, do you jest?'

'I am not jesting, Shira. This is no lie. That is what Moses wanted to speak to me about. I have been asked to become an elder.'

'Even though you spoke out against them about what happened with Yahweh at the foot of the mountain?' Shira questioned, confused.

The smile went from Jesher's face. He looked at her with a mixture of compassion and pity, went and stood before her, arms by his side, head held high. 'It is *because* I spoke out at that meeting that I have been asked to become an elder.' He paused to give her time to think about that before continuing. 'Moses heard about what happened and made enquiries about me. They need another elder to replace Hur, peace be upon him, and they seem to think I have what is needed to help lead our people in these hard times.'

Shira was speechless – but only for a few moments. 'Well, I always knew you would become an elder,' she proclaimed. 'I knew it. I *always* said that you had a great future ahead of you!'

'That is not how I remember it,' Jesher mumbled, glancing at me sideways. I smiled and shook my head.

'That reminds me,' I said. 'Moses has heard rumours about more discontent among the people, another uprising – have you heard anything?'

'No,' Jesher replied in surprise. 'But, in truth, I have not heard much at all since that day I spoke out. It seems people avoid a "troublemaker" like me . . . even those I once called friend. Actually,' he added with a grin, 'it has been surprisingly peaceful.'

I laughed. 'Do not grow to like it! Once the news spreads that you are an elder, you will have a queue of people outside your tent wanting information, or asking for favours.'

Jesher raised an eyebrow. 'Shira will love that, *nu*?' he whispered.

Shira came outside, carrying her scarf and a small basket.

'Are you going somewhere?' Jesher asked her.

'I must go and tell Saadia our news.'

'But it is nearly midday. Will she not be resting?'

'Pshh! She will want to see me!'

To me, Shira and Saadia's relationship seemed to be tinged with an unspoken rivalry, an underlying sense of competition. Jesher being made an elder when Saadia's husband, Yacob, had not been, would be a significant triumph for Shira. Before she left, Jesher asked her if she had heard of any discontent in the camp.

'Of course!' she told him, apparently amazed that he knew nothing of it. 'There is much discontent, and who can marvel at why? All we have to eat now is manna. Manna every day. Manna when we break fast, manna at night. Our whole being is dried up, eating nothing but manna.'

Jesher looked at her, incredulous. 'This is what the discontent is about? Food?'

'Of course!' She gave him a scathing stare. 'We need meat to eat! We cannot live on manna day after day. We must have meat. I will see you later, yes?' Without another word she threw her scarf over her head and shoulders and rushed off to see Saadia.

50

Cravings

The winter rains were coming to an end, but there was still quite a chill in the air that evening as we sat around the fire. The evening meal had been a celebration of Jesher's appointment as elder. Many blessings were pronounced and we discussed the impact this could have on us as a family. The women took the children inside the tent to settle them down for the night, leaving us men to discuss the day's events. Joel and Yoram stayed with us and were included in our discussions, although neither of them would say much, usually choosing to listen and learn from their elders.

The aroma of the fresh herbs and spices which Helah had used in the sauce for our evening meal still hung in the air, mingling deliciously with the smell of burning wood from the fire. We sat in silence, listening to the buzz of cicadas and the crackling of the fire. As always, my gaze was drawn to the pillar of fire that hovered in the middle of the camp, near the tent of meeting, which was now located near the tabernacle. No matter how bad the day had been, or what problems were pressing on my mind, I could always find peace when I looked towards that great edifice of Yahweh's power and presence. Today, I drew strength from it – it had been a trying afternoon.

By now, my brothers knew that I had gone back to Moses in the afternoon to tell him about the disputes that were arising in the camp concerning the lack of meat.

'So,' Mesha asked, picking up a ripe fig, and biting into it with relish. 'What did Moses say when you told him?'

'He was much aggrieved,' I replied, keeping my voice low. This was not a conversation I wanted the women to hear – or our neighbours. 'I have only seen his anger burn fiercely a few times and it is terrible to behold – zeal for Yahweh seems to take hold of him.'

'What did he say?' Azriel asked.

'He spoke at length about this stubborn people who continue to rebel against Yahweh . . . what is he to do with them . . . how can he possibly find meat to feed all of them . . . why must they have such cravings . . . what more can Yahweh do to prove Himself to them, but still they will not believe in Him . . .' I grimaced and looked around the circle. 'His anger burned long and hard.'

'What did you say to him?' Azriel asked, pulling his outer robe tighter around his slim body. He did not welcome the cold winds that whistled through the camp in the evenings around this time of year.

'What could I say?' I shrugged. 'Besides, I have learned that it is better not to speak much when Moses is wrathful.'

'Ah, true,' Hareph agreed, his shoulder twitching. 'Very wise, yes. Hmm.' He cocked his head to the side.

I spoke in a whisper. 'Moses told Yahweh that the burden of leading this people is too heavy, that he cannot do it any longer, and that . . .' I paused, and they all leaned in closer, '. . . that if he must continue to do this, then he would rather Yahweh kill him now!'

Hareph gasped. 'No! In truth?'

Jesher leaned forward now, his eyes full of concern. 'Moses said that?'

'He did, *Abba*. But do not fear,' I reassured them. 'All is well.'

'How so?' Azriel asked.

'Yahweh has instructed Moses to choose seventy elders to help him bear the burden of this people. Eleazar and I are to seek them out tomorrow on his behalf.'

'Seventy?' Jesher looked at me with apprehension. 'Seventy elders? Am I . . . ?'

'Yes, *Abba*.' I grasped his hand in mine. 'You are one of the seventy who has been chosen.' Jesher sat back. He stared at me but said nothing. '*Abba*, Yahweh told Moses to bring the seventy elders to the tabernacle. He will take of the Spirit that is upon Moses and put the same Spirit upon the elders.'

Jesher shook his head slowly. 'The same Spirit that is on Moses? On the elders?'

I nodded.

'So, does that mean that *Abba* will be able to do miracles like Moses does?' Mesha asked, a cheeky grin on his face. 'Water from a rock, manna every day – because that would be a great blessing to us all, *nu*?'

Joel and Yoram stifled a giggle, but Azriel scowled. 'Mesha, how can you jest about such a thing? Your *abba* is an elder of Israel now. This is a great honour that has been bestowed on him – and on our family.'

'Aah, do not reproach me.' Mesha appealed to him with a charming smile. 'I rejoice that *Abba* has been honoured in this way. It is right and just. It was only that I thought . . . well, it might be useful to have a miracle worker in the family . . . *nu*?' Azriel glared at him. As Jesher's first-born son, the family honour was a matter of extreme importance to him and he was never well pleased when his younger brother belittled it in any way. Conversations like this often tended to turn into arguments, so I decided to put a stop to it before it could turn into a downward spiral.

'*Abba*, we all rejoice that you have been chosen for such an honour. You have brought favour to our family and we are esteemed because of your wisdom and faithfulness. May the Lord grant you long life and may Yahweh's footsteps be your pathway.'

Calls of 'amen' resounded. Jesher smiled, lifting his hands in acknowledgement of the blessing. Harmony was restored once again . . . until Mesha asked, 'Uh . . . Joshua? What about the meat? Will Yahweh give us meat?'

'Ech! Mesha!' Azriel hissed. 'We are discussing the honour and wisdom of our *abba*, and you ask about meat?'

'Why not? Meat is important!' Mesha argued. He looked at the rest of us. 'You would like to have meat to eat, yes?' Most of us nodded sheepishly, keeping half an eye on Jesher to see his response. He watched with a twinkle in his eye, then leaned back, roaring with laughter, clapping his hands in delight.

'Yes! You are right, my son,' he declared. 'Meat is good and we like to eat it. So,' he said, turning to me, 'Will Yahweh give us meat?'

'He will!' I replied, returning Jesher's smile. 'Yahweh told Moses that the people will eat meat. But,' I pointed one finger in Jesher's face, then two and then five, 'not for one or two days, even five days or twenty days, but for a month!'

'Ech! How is that possible?' Azriel did some quick calculations in his head. 'We do not have enough livestock to feed our people meat for a whole month. Even if we slaughtered all our flocks and herds, there would only be enough meat for a week or so, perhaps three at the most.'

'Most assuredly!' I said, laughing. I looked up at the blazing pillar. 'But Yahweh has spoken and He has told Moses that He will give His people meat.'

51

Same Spirit

My heart was pounding. I didn't know whether it was from fear or excitement – possibly both. The cloud rested over the tabernacle as the elders met with Moses to wait on God. Moses had asked me to be a watchman at the entrance to the tabernacle, which meant that although I was not one of the seventy elders who would receive the same Spirit as Moses, I would still be able to see what happened.

Neither Jesher nor I spoke as we walked to the tabernacle. We were consumed with our own thoughts and, if we were honest, our own fears. How would Yahweh meet with the elders? What if something went wrong? What if iniquity were found in us? There was no buzz of conversation in the tabernacle when we arrived, no long greetings or friendly welcomes, only the quiet murmuring of voices and fervent prayers of consecration.

Jesher told me afterwards that, as soon as Moses started praying, he felt heat spread from the top of his head down his body, coursing through his muscles with such power, he started to shake. Confused, he saw that the tent was filled with a cloud-like substance, although it was like no cloud he had ever seen before.

This cloud was *alive*.

I could see it from my standpoint by the tent entrance. It moved constantly, swirling and billowing. A myriad of colours shimmered within its form, most of which I could not have put a name to, and flickers of fire burst intermittently from its midst.

I looked over to Jesher, who had shut his eyes and fallen to his knees. As a watchman, I could not close my eyes, but I could still smell – and what I smelled sent my senses reeling. A sweet fragrance filled my nostrils, but I couldn't place its source. It was not incense. Of all the spices and perfumes I knew, none fitted its description. It was beguiling, yet not so sweet as to be sickly.

I mumbled to myself, 'What mystery is this?' I was desperate to sink to my knees in prayer.

I saw Jesher breathe in and out deeply; his face broke into an intoxicated smile. He obviously delighted in savouring the sweetness of that sensation. When we talked afterwards, he said it was then that something dropped on him, enfolding him in its grip.

'It seemed weighty,' he said, 'and yet feather-like at the same time. I could not fathom it.' He dared not open his eyes, but stayed bowed low, enveloped in the breath-taking peace and purity of the cloud that was Yahweh's presence.

All around, I heard gasps and groans, not of pain but of ecstasy; and then, out of the midst of the swirling cloud, I heard a voice. It spoke out with clarity and authority. I recognised it straight away: it was Abidan, leader of the tribe of Benjamin. He stood tall, shoulders back and head held high, declaring the word of the Lord in a loud voice.

'Yahweh alone is the Lord most high! *He* is your praise, and *He* is your glory! The one true God who has done great and awesome things which your eyes have seen!'

From the corner of the tent, another voice shouted out, 'He is the Lord our God; His judgements are in all the earth. He remembers His covenant, the word which He commanded generations, the covenant which He made with Abraham.'

He was followed by another and another and yet another voice, all boldly declaring the words of Yahweh. I watched and listened, enthralled at what I was hearing and seeing when, to my amazement, I heard Jesher's voice shouting out.

'The Lord has brought you out with a mighty hand, and redeemed you from the house of bondage, from the hand of Pharaoh.' I looked around and saw him standing tall, arms open wide, the word of the Lord gushing out from his mouth like a river that had burst its banks. 'The Lord your God says, "Now therefore, if you will indeed obey My voice and keep My covenant, then you shall be a *special treasure* to Me above all people; for all the earth is Mine. And you shall be to Me a kingdom of priests and a holy nation".'[6]

Jesher told me that the heat he felt when Moses first prayed had started to course through his body again – what felt like fire

---

6. Exodus 19:5-6, NKJV. Emphasis mine.

burned within his heart and flooded his being until he felt like he would burst. That's when he spoke – and what he spoke thrilled my heart and ignited a fire in me. I listened and watched as the word of the Lord poured out of each of their mouths, as leader after leader received the same Spirit that was on Moses. It was an unprecedented eruption of the anointing power of Yahweh, and it left every man indelibly marked with His glory.

52

Dark Cloud

'Jesher! Jesher, wake up!' Shira's shrill voice woke not only Jesher, but all of those in our family tent who had not yet risen.

'What is it?' Jesher asked.

'You have visitors! Quickly, get up. Get dressed!'

'Visitors? Now? It is too early for visitors. Ech! Who is it? What do they want?' I knew that the older Jesher grew, the more he enjoyed his sleep. He was never at his best when his slumber was interrupted. He said it was an old man's right to awaken only when he smelled the scent of manna cakes roasting on the coals.

'They want to talk to you about what happened yesterday.' I could hear the excitement in Shira's voice. 'They have heard that you are now an elder. They want to talk to you, to ask questions, to discuss what happened in the tabernacle!'

'Who is "they"? Ach, no matter. Not now, Shira. Tell them to come back later.' Clearly, Jesher was stubbornly clinging onto the vain hope that he might be able to sleep for a bit longer.

'I cannot. I have already told them you are coming out to talk to them.' I could hear an imperious quality to Shira's voice that was all too familiar: it meant she was building up to a lecture. 'I cannot tell them to go away. They are waiting for you. You have responsibilities now, Jesher. The people want to talk to you, so you must meet with them, yes?'

Jesher groaned. I roused myself, washed and dressed – it sounded like he might need some support. The rest of the family were also up – there were rumblings of conversation and whispered questions. I could hear Jesher splash water on his face, all the while engaging in an ongoing conversation with himself. I stifled a laugh. Jesher had a habit of doing this, especially when he was in bad humour, and these 'conversations' often took on a very humous tone – to us, at least, if not to him.

'A man cannot even have a good night's sleep. No! He must be woken up from the deepest night's sleep he has had in a very long time, because the people want to talk to him! But what if he does not want to talk to the people. *Nu*? What if all he wants to do is sleep for a little longer? He does not even have time to break fast. No – he must *talk to the people*. Hmph. If this is what it is like being an elder then perhaps it is not for me. Perhaps I am not cut out of the right cloth for being an elder. Perhaps I enjoy my sleep too much. Has anyone thought of that? No!' Jesher stopped suddenly and I froze when I heard my name. 'Joshua warned me. He told me this would happen.' He sighed deeply. 'Oy! What can I do? Nothing. So now, I will go and talk to the people, yes?' he asked, and answered himself straight away. 'Yes.'

I hid a smile as I stepped out of my curtained sleeping compartment. '*Shalom, Abba*. Did you sleep well?'

'Ah, *shalom*, Joshua. Yes, I did, very well . . . until I was rudely awakened from the best sleep I have had for many moons, to go and *talk to the people*. Ech!' He made his way outside, still muttering under his breath. Shira stood in the tent opening, lifted her arms to silence the smattering of conversation, and announced, 'Jesher is coming to talk to you now. Make room for him – here he is.'

'Shira, there is no need for that,' Jesher murmured, embarrassed. 'I am not our father Abraham, *nu*? *Shalom, shalom*,' he greeted the crowd, which I think was much larger than he had anticipated. 'Sit, please, sit,' he said to them. I stood around the back of the crowd, soon joined by Mesha and a rather rumpled-looking Hareph. Azriel went to stand behind Jesher, looking rather bemused at this surge of activity so early in the morning, but clearly feeling it was his duty, or perhaps privilege, to stand with his father. As Jesher started to lower himself to the ground, Shira hurried out carrying a large, rather ornate cushion, which she unceremoniously plopped under his bottom.

'Oh! Uh . . . yes, thank you,' he said awkwardly. Turning his attention to the people sitting around, he asked, 'So, what would you like to ask me?' Immediately, a barrage of questions was thrown at him, and he threw up his hands to fend them off. 'Oy! One at a time, so I can hear you, yes?'

Most of their questions were centred purely around their desire to know what had happened in the tabernacle the previous night. They asked who had prophesied, what they had said, and what the cloud was like. Jesher was answering their questions as best he could, when his discourse was interrupted by a colossal gust of wind that whooshed through the camp, throwing dust in everyone's face and blowing our clothing into disarray. It was closely followed by an unfamiliar sound, a discordant squawking and screeching and the steady drone of a vast number of beating wings.

I was at Jesher's side in seconds, shielding him as best as I could from the dust storm, and helping him to his feet. Azriel had been taken by surprise and was stumbling around, sand in his eyes. What was this? Sandstorms did not usually descend this quickly – they grew at a steady rate, and you could see them coming from far off. Besides which, this clattering noise was quite unlike any I had heard before and was definitely not the sound of a desert sandstorm. Questions about the previous day's events were forgotten in an instant as everyone rose to their feet, brushing the dust and dirt off their clothes and craning their necks to see where the noise was coming from.

'What is that?' said a woman, pointing into the distance.

'Where?'

'There – that dark cloud.'

'That is not a cloud, it is . . . it is . . . what is it?'

'Birds!' shouted Hareph, excited to be the first to identify the strange phenomenon. 'It is a flock of birds, but . . .' he peered up into the sky, 'there are so many. How can there be so many?' We watched in awestruck silence as the vast horde grew nearer and nearer. Conversation was pointless; the sound of the birds' cries and the beating of their wings was overpowering. We covered our ears with our scarves or our hands, watching with trepidation as the heavens grew darker and darker. The vast horde covered the sky, blocking out the sunlight for miles around. We watched, mesmerised, as the noisy throng passed over our heads.

No one moved until the sky grew lighter again and the sun broke through once more.

'What were they?' Mesha asked.

Hareph responded, still staring into the distance. 'Birds.'

'Oy! We know that, but what kind of birds, and why so many, this far out in the desert?'

Discussions and arguments broke out as to what and why and how. Jesher and I stood silently watching the dark cloud move further away. Just as we were about to turn our attention back to the crowd, we noticed the bottom start to drop out of the cloud. Narrowing our eyes, we squinted in the early morning sun and watched as dark swirls descended en masse to the ground.

Jesher realised before any of us what this strange phenomenon was. Clapping his hands and shouting, he called the crowd to order. 'Be still!' he shouted, lifting his arms high to get their attention. 'Joshua, Mesha, tell them to listen to me – I know what it is! That,' he said, pointing to the remains of the dark cloud as it descended to the ground in the distance, 'is *meat*!

53

Hunger for Holiness

A new smell besieged the camp that night, arresting our senses and capturing the attention of men, women and children alike: the tantalising aroma of roasted quail! It had taken hours for all the quail to be collected, brought back to camp and distributed. Our womenfolk wasted no time at all in plucking and preparing the small birds for a mass celebration.

Weaving, washing and cleaning were laid aside, and the air was soon filled with soft brown-flecked feathers blowing in the breeze. For birds with so little meat on them, they seemed to have an inordinate number of feathers! Some of our little ones had never seen quail before, but even those of us who were familiar with them were taken aback by the vast quantity that was now presented to us. Yahweh had been true to his word; we had meat to eat, and not just a little, either. This would be a feast like no other, and there was plenty more for the days to come!

The day-to-day business of camp was brought to an unusually early conclusion that day, as our people gathered round their firepits well before the time of the evening meal. Moses released me early so I could go home to join the family, who I discovered watching Shira with eager anticipation as she rubbed a mixture of herbs and spices into the quail skins.

'*Ima*, let me do that for you,' Mesha said, helping her to spear the quail onto thick sticks, cramming three or four onto each stick. The loaded sticks were then placed onto forked stands either side of the fire, so they hung a short distance above the flames.

Of all our women, Helah was the best at making sauces (although none of us would have dreamed of telling Shira that). Today, she had outdone herself; cooking the sauce on a slow heat until it was sticky and full-bodied. Leora was known for her bread-making, as she had a light touch with the dough, so she set to work on baking the bread cakes.

Normally when we roasted meat, one of the boys would be given the task of turning the sticks at regular intervals to ensure even roasting. Today, however, we all sat around, arguing over who would have that privilege. The flames licked the plump carcasses and the fire hissed as droplets of fat and fluids fell onto the flames. Conversation was strangely lacking as we sat around the fire, salivating at the aroma of roasting bird flesh which filled our nostrils. Our minds were focused on one thing alone: the mouth-watering, golden-brown fowls set before us.

They did not disappoint! The flesh was succulent and tender, the crispy skin crunching and flaking as we bit into it. Shira had done a magnificent job with the quail, and Leora's bread was put to good use, scooping up the sticky sauce.

It was a feast worthy of a king, and we revelled in it like royalty. There was not a morsel left: every last scrap of quail was eaten, the meat sucked off every bone, the bowls of sauce scraped clean and the dishes of olives and fruit emptied. Silence fell, apart from sporadic burps and sighs of appreciation, as we relaxed around the firepit and let our food digest. Even conversation was too much effort. The women stayed around the firepit for longer than usual, instead of clearing away the meal and washing up. I don't think any of us could have moved even if we had wanted to. We sat together, watching the glowing embers of the fire, relishing the opportunity to glory in Yahweh's miraculous provision for His people.

I smiled and lay back, putting my arms behind my head. I couldn't have eaten a single bite more – in fact, I couldn't remember the last time my belly had been so swollen with food. As always, my gaze was drawn to the fiery pillar in the distance. I let my thoughts wonder and waited for the sense of absolute contentment that usually filled me when I gazed upon it.

It didn't come. Rather than feeling contented, I actually felt restless and agitated.

'What's wrong with me?' I thought to myself. 'I've just enjoyed a delicious meal, eaten my fill, in the company of people I love. Yahweh has provided for His people yet again. The camp is at peace. We have water, we have food, Moses is happy – life is good.

So why am I not happy?' It bothered me that I didn't feel contented – today of all days, after such a celebration.

'What do you think on?' Mesha asked, staring at me. 'You have the look of one who is travelling to a distant land.'

I grunted and sat up. To my great regret, I had never been very good at disguising my feelings. I had always longed to be able to hide my emotions, to be like a rock, but it was not to be. My heart was as easy to read as the changing seasons. Brushing fragments of food off my robe, I stretched and yawned. 'My belly is so full; I think I will take in the night air and go for a walk.'

'In truth?' Mesha asked in surprise, rubbing his stomach as he gave a particularly boisterous belch. 'You want to walk now?'

I nodded and turned to Jesher. 'With your permission, I will take my leave.' Jesher smiled at me, but I knew those piercing blue eyes of his had missed nothing. I left quickly before he, or anyone else, could ask any more questions or offer to walk with me.

I wrestled with the thoughts that plagued me, my mind churning over the question of why I felt so discontented. 'I have so much to be thankful for,' I mumbled to myself. 'Why am I feeling so discouraged, and so . . . angry?' I realised with shock that I was feeling angry. *Really* angry. But why? 'I have nothing to be angry about,' I mumbled. I drew my head covering down over my face, pulled my mantle tight around my body, and trudged on through the camp, avoiding eye contact with any passers-by. The celebratory atmosphere around firepits that night only served to sour my mood further. I resented the fact that everyone I passed seemed so happy when I was not. I zigzagged in-between groups of tents, not concentrating on where I was going and, before long, I looked up to find myself standing at the entrance to the tabernacle.

I stood looking through the entrance into the tabernacle courtyard. What to do now? The evening offerings had ended and the Levites had gone home to be with their families in time to celebrate Yahweh's provision of quail.

'I should probably go home too,' I thought. But I couldn't move. Standing there, alone in the darkness, I closed my eyes. The buzz of campfire conversations dimmed. I became acutely aware of the crackling of the pillar of fire, and the swooshing of the flames that flickered around it. I breathed in, feeling the warmth of the fire permeate my body and, as I stood in the entrance, I felt an invisible hand reach out and pull me into that most holy place.

As soon as I entered the tabernacle, my thoughts turned to Jesher's account of what had happened when Yahweh had put the same Spirit from Moses onto the elders of Israel. I had listened afterwards as Jesher shared his experience with me; it caused my hunger for Yahweh to increase even more. My thoughts moved on to Eleazar's description of his encounter with Yahweh at the consecration of the tabernacle. My heart burned within me. I put my hand on my chest.

'I hunger for Your holiness,' I whispered. 'Yahweh, I hunger for you.' Anger welled up within me, and one word seeped out of my mouth, bristling with resentment and pain. 'Why?' I thought. Like a layer of dust being wiped off a copper mirror, it all became clear. That's why I was so angry. Anguish poured out of me and I fell on my knees before Yahweh, cries welling up and overflowing. 'Why?' I howled. 'Why not me?' I put my arms around my waist and rocked backwards and forwards, face to the ground. 'I am zealous for your presence. I have served You faithfully and done everything You have asked of me. So why do You not show Yourself to me? Moses hears Your voice. Eleazar has heard You. Jesher and the elders – they have all heard Your voice. So why will You not speak to me? Why do I not hear Your voice?'

The turmoil within me raged on, unabated, as I poured out my heart to God, laying bare my longing for His presence. After a while, my anger turned inward to self-doubt and shame.

'Am I not worthy?' I asked, still on my knees. 'What have I done to cause You to turn Your face from me? Why do You not look favourably upon Your servant? What have I done wrong? Is there iniquity hidden in my heart, that You will not speak to me?' The flow of words dried up and all I could mutter was, 'Why? Why?' until, exhausted, I turned to lay on my side on the floor, arms still around my waist. 'I am brought low,' I mumbled. 'The longing in my heart is too great. My heart is in anguish. I must . . .'

Out of the silence, I heard the faint sound of voices singing. I sat up, confused. Why would the choir be singing now, at this time of night? I peered into the darkness around me. Nothing. There was no one there but me. But the voices continued. Exquisite harmonies echoed in the tent as a chorus of voices joined together in a perfect symphony of sound. Their song was so beautiful it touched the deepest parts of my soul, like cool water pouring over my body in the heat of the day. I wept as each note washed over me, cleansing me of all my anguish.

Then I felt it.

A shiver ran down my back and spread throughout my body. My hands trembled and my legs started to shake. Within seconds, my whole body was quivering. I saw it. The cloud. My beautiful obsession, right there in front of me. Thin wisps of cloud entered the tent, joining together to form swirling feathery branches that glinted in the light of the oil lamps. They continued to expand, increasing in size and density until the tent was filled with infinite hues of rippling cloud.

Captivated, I held my breath and reached out a trembling hand. Immediately, feathers of wispy cloud wrapped themselves around my fingers, caressing them with such tenderness. I heard the faint sound of laughter echoing within the cloud. I sat absolutely still, for fear of disturbing the cloud when, near the other side of the tent, I saw what looked like a rainbow archway taking shape. It started a few feet off the ground and extended sideways, flowing gracefully down to the ground on either side. Its colours were rich and vibrant, even through the thick veil of cloud that separated it from me, and the archway shone with an ethereal glow.

I gazed at it, unable to tear my eyes away. As I watched, a figure formed within the archway. I frowned, squinting in an effort to see what it was. I couldn't see clearly defined features, but I recognised the form of a Man. The Man stretched out His arm; I plunged forward, prostrating myself before Him. A fresh gamut of emotions struck my heart. I was terrified and elated, simultaneously filled with loathing but also with thanksgiving. My heart was stripped bare, yet overflowed with every glorious virtue; defiled and yet, at that moment, incorruptible.

The Man spoke.

'Joshua!' His voice was rich and melodious. His words echoed, bouncing off the walls of the tent. I dared not lift my head. Speech defied me.

'Joshua!' the Man spoke again.

'L . . . Lord . . .' I gasped, my face still to the ground. He knew my name! I was known to Him!

'Lift up your eyes, Joshua, for you have found favour in My sight.' Every instinct in me told me not to move, but the lure of the Man's voice compelled me to respond. Fighting my fleshly instincts, I looked towards the figure within the arch, still shrouded in cloud. I could not see His face, but somehow I knew that the Man was smiling.

So I smiled back at him.

'Joshua!' the Man spoke my name again. This time I felt no terror, only an overwhelming sense of peace. 'I have called you by name. I have seen your faithfulness; your heart is pleasing to Me. I know your zeal for My presence. Your prayers have come before my throne.'

Tears flooded my eyes and overflowed. He called me by name. I was known to Him. Unashamed, I didn't wipe my tears away, but let them fall, unhindered, as the Man continued to speak.

'I am with you and My hand is on you to perform great wonders.'

My thoughts scattered in a myriad of different directions. Great wonders? Me? No. How? Surely He must mean Moses.

'What is the meaning of your name?'

'My name?' Why was He asking me this? 'My . . . my name means salvation,' I stuttered.

'You have spoken the truth,' said the Man. 'For through you, I will save many. You will be as a saviour to My people and you will lead them in My ways. No man will be able to stand before you all the days of your life. I will fill you with strength and courage and will be with you wherever you go.'

I tried to respond, but no words came. The Man stood there, beams of light pulsating around Him, radiating out from His form. The voices within the cloud were now joined by instruments: strings, all manner of pipes, bells and drums, the sound of running waters, wind, the rustling of leaves and the beating of wings.

Falling prostrate before the glory of the Lord, confronted with the mystery of Yahweh's Presence, I could utter but one word, over and over and over again.

'Holy, holy, holy . . . holy . . . holy . . .'

54

Waylaid

There was a new spring in my step, a confidence in my stride since my encounter with Yahweh in the tabernacle. I was changed. Transformed. I felt it. I knew it. I was known by Yahweh – He knew my name! That revelation caused shivers to go down my back; it was an extraordinary secret that I kept close, hugging it to myself. I had not spoken to anyone about that night. Not yet. I knew Moses suspected something, and I had seen Jesher watching me with a curious smile, but neither of them had asked what had happened to cause the change in me. They both knew I would tell them when I was ready. And I would. But not yet.

I smiled to myself as I walked through the camp, looking around me with great contentment, when I noticed a young woman staring at me. Although I did not like it, I was used to being stared at, especially since our victory over the Amalekites, so I muttered '*shalom*' and looked away. The woman continued to scrutinise me, then started walking towards me. '*Shalom*,' she said. 'My lord, may I speak with you?' I frowned at her, wondering at her assertiveness, but oddly impressed by her boldness. Women were strongly discouraged from speaking to men outside of their own families, and to waylay one in this manner was unconventional, to say the least.

'My lord, my name is Alya.' I froze. This was Alya? Joel's Alya?

'Forgive me, I cannot tarry with you, I have much to do,' I said, trying to walk around her.

'My lord, I beg of you,' she said, dropping the waterskins she carried and falling to her knees at my feet. 'Please hear my words.'

'Arise, woman,' I muttered, not wanting to attract attention. I looked around to see if anyone had noticed us, before moving off the pathway, gesturing to her to follow me. 'What would you say to me? Speak your mind.'

'My lord, I know you are a righteous man. Joel told me how you helped him in his dark times and he talks of your bearing in his family. He believes you to be trustworthy. I beg you please to take a message to him from me.'

A message? To Joel? No. Absolutely not! I could not get involved in Joel's affairs of the heart. It was not my place and I wanted nothing more to do with this woman or her family. The faces of her brothers still haunted me in the night, and I would be rid of them. I shook my head. 'Forgive me, I cannot do as you – '

'I beg of you, my lord,' she said. 'Do not treat me with contempt. I would not ask it if there was any other way. Please, hear my case.'

I hesitated. Alya was not what I had expected. I don't quite know what I had expected of Alya, but it was not this. This woman was modestly dressed, veiled, and bore herself with an air of humility. She did not have a haughty manner and I sensed no brazenness or defiance in her. In fact, she exuded a purity, a quiet strength. A nobility. Yes, she bore herself with a nobility that took me by surprise. I found myself responding, 'What would you have me tell him?'

'Thank you, my lord,' she said. Her relief was obvious. 'You honour me.' She spoke softly but clearly. 'I believe you knew of my betrothal?'

'I did. I am sorry that it will ... not come to pass.'

'Thank you, but my heart does not sorrow.'

I was surprised by her forthrightness. 'No?'

She lowered her gaze. 'No, my lord. Jamin was not an honourable man. My father only told me of the betrothal once the contract had been agreed. I begged him to reconsider, but he refused. My father and brothers and Jamin and his family were ... of the same mind ... and my betrothal to Jamin was part of their plan to unite our two families.' Before I could respond, Alya continued. 'My time of mourning has come to an end and ...' she searched my eyes, 'I fear for Joel. Please, my lord, tell Joel not to come to me or to try to take counsel with my *abba* until I send word to him. My *abba* has been ... his heart is much angered at the death of my brothers and he is not himself. If Joel comes to him, I fear what might happen. His life might be forfeit.'

'I understand. The news of your brothers' death must have been grievous to him.' I paused to give time for Alya to respond, but she only nodded. 'And you will send word to Joel when the time is right?'

'I will, my lord.'

'What would you have me tell him when he asks how long he must wait?' – as I knew he would.

'I cannot say how long. But I will send word. Please tell him he must trust me in this. He must not approach my *abba*.' When she spoke of Joel, Alya's face lit up, and a tenderness came to her eyes. I could see it without a shadow of a doubt; her love for Joel was steadfast. This was not a passing fancy, there was something much deeper at work. A knife sliced into my heart as I remembered the words of love, the promises that I had given. She had been about Alya's age when we . . . but it was not helpful to think on it, I reminded myself. I gathered myself, cleared my throat, and asked, 'And you will wait for Joel?'

'I will wait the course of time, my lord.' She looked up at me, silently begging me to believe her. 'There is only one man who holds my heart. If I cannot be his wife, I would rather die a virgin than be given to another.'

I searched her eyes for signs of darkness, a hint of pride or rebellion, but found none. Instead, I saw only light, something akin to purity. Her liquid green eyes were arresting; they seemed to bore into me. It was as if she saw me, she knew me. It was disarming. She was inviting me to know her heart; she had nothing to hide. The mistrust I had harboured towards her left me. I realised that I had been wrong – totally wrong – about Alya. I had judged this woman unjustly. I could see that in her was none of the evil that had resided in her father and brothers.

Taking a deep breath, Alya lifted her chin. 'My lord, there is something you should know. You have the ear of Moses, yes?' I replied, 'Yes,' although I was reluctant to admit this to her. I had not told Moses about Joel's struggles and I hoped she was not about to ask me to plead her cause with Moses.

She was not. My assumptions were wrong – again.

'My father has idols – many idols – which he brought with him when we left Egypt. He worships the gods of Egypt and indulges in their pagan rituals. He keeps them buried under the rug in our tent, near the waterpots. He thinks I know nothing of them.'

My eyes narrowed. 'Why do you tell me this?'

'Because we must rid ourselves of this evil that has poisoned our people and caused them to turn away from Yahweh.'

'You would betray your *abba* to me?'

She paused, clearly trying to discern how much she should disclose. 'My *abba* is a cruel man, my lord. His heart is dark and he does not walk in the ways of the God of Israel. He has brought dishonour to our family and . . . harm to many.' She lowered her eyes, drew back her veil, and I saw a bluish-purple bruise stretching across her cheekbone, down to her jaw. 'There is more, but it would not be seemly for me to show you.' She quickly covered her face with her veil, looking around to check that nobody had seen.

Anger welled up within me. I felt sick to my stomach, clenching my jaw at the abusive evidence I saw before me – it was abhorrent. I despised men who took their anger out on those weaker than themselves. An unexpected desire to protect Alya rose up within me but, when she met my gaze, I was amazed to see no self-pity in her eyes. Instead, I saw a transparency which I found unnerving. This was a woman who knew her own mind; she was not merely a puppet in the hands of her father. She was not the type of woman who was content to sit idly by while evil wreaked havoc around her. There was wisdom in her words and courage in her heart. Everything I had assumed about her had been wrong.

Alya looked around her. 'I must make haste. If my father hears that I have talked with you, it will not go well with me. You will tell Joel? Swear to me that you will give him my message.'

I paused, once again arrested by her passionate words. 'I give you my oath. I will give Joel your message.'

Relief flooded her face. 'Thank you, my lord. Thank you. *Shalom*,' she murmured, bowing her head. She picked up her waterskins and continued on her way.

'Alya?' She turned to look at me. 'If ever you should need help, send word to me. I will come.'

Her face broke into a grateful smile and she bowed her head. 'Thank you, my lord. You honour me greatly.'

I stood watching her as she walked in the direction of the well. How wrong I had been about this woman; my preconceived notions had blinded me to the truth. I felt a sudden urge to run after her and beg her forgiveness for judging her. Instead, I turned around and continued on my way to the tabernacle. Much of my day was spent in the tabernacle with Moses, which gave me a lot of time to think on my conversation with Alya. I felt conflicted about whether to tell Jesher and Azriel, or speak of it only to Joel. By the end of the day my mind was made up: the message was for Joel and I would deliver it to him, and him alone. I went to Bezalel's workshop to find Joel and, as we walked home together through the maze of tents, I told him of my meeting with Alya.

'You have spoken with Alya?' His eyes widened in a mixture of shock and joy.

'I did not seek her out,' I hastened to add. 'It was a chance meeting.' Or perhaps not, I wondered. Perhaps she had sought me out? Had she waited for me to pass? I could not be sure but, either way, my heart was glad that it had been so. I gave Joel Alya's message and told him what had taken place, intentionally leaving out the part where she showed me the bruise on her cheek. I feared it might propel him to act hastily. She would not want that.

Joel was like imbalanced weights on a set of ancient scales. One moment he was clasping his hands to his heart, mumbling about his love for Alya, the next he was worrying about how long he must wait, trying to conjure up a plan to rescue her.

'What must I do?' he asked me, grasping my arm to stop me from walking. 'Joshua, tell me, what must I do?'

In my mind, there was only one thing to be done.

'Heed her warning, Joel. There is wisdom in what she says. Wait for her. Wait until she sends word.'

55

Spies

Moses stood up, calling the meeting to order. The handful of elders who had gathered in his tent stopped their conversations and turned their attention to him.

'So! Our people have food and water. They have wise elders such as yourselves,' Moses gestured to the men sitting before him, 'to lead them and teach them the ways of Yahweh.' I looked across at Jesher and smiled. It was good to see him sitting in this congregation of elders. In a short space of time he had proven himself to be wise and honourable, and Moses seemed to value his input, at times singling him out to ask his opinion.

Moses walked towards the entrance of his tent, looking out on the tabernacle. 'We have a glorious tabernacle where we can worship Yahweh and call upon His name and,' he turned to me, 'we are busy training our men for war. Our armies are taking shape, *nu*?'

I nodded. 'Yes, Master.'

Moses turned back to the elders. 'All is well in the camp, yes?' The elders muttered their agreement, turning to one another to share their thoughts, but Moses interrupted them. 'So!' he declared, pausing to make eye contact with each of the men in turn. Leaning forward, he said, 'It is time for our next mission!' Jesher glanced at me and raised his eyebrows, but I shrugged. I was as mystified as everyone else. A buzz of questions arose, but Moses lifted his hands to silence them.

'We will soon be moving on from this place, taking the next step on our journey to the land of Canaan, and we must make the necessary preparations. I would ask you to help me choose one man from each of the twelve tribes to be sent out from this place.' He started pacing the room. 'They must be strong and courageous,' he flexed his arm, making a fist in front of his chest, 'men of wisdom, but not too advanced in years.' Pointing his finger in the air, he swung round and said, 'and they must not be recently married, nor have a young wife who has need of them.' Stopping to peer at the elders, he explained, 'They will be gone for many days.'

'One man from each tribe,' Abidan repeated. Turning to the other elders, he said, 'Erez, son of Dahan, is a good man, both strong and wise. He could represent the tribe of Benjamin – or Palti ben Raphu?' he said, turning to Moses.

'Yes, both good men.'

Before Abidan could discuss the virtues of the two men any further, Aaron asked, 'Will you have need of a man from the tribe of Levi?'

'No. The Levites will stay in the camp and do the work of the Tabernacle,' Moses replied. 'But we will choose two men from the lineage of Joseph – one from the tribe of Manasseh and one from Ephraim.'

'Elishama,' Moses turned to the leader of the tribe of Ephraim, 'I would like Joshua to represent the tribe of Ephraim, and to lead these men on their quest.'

'Of course, if that is your will,' Elishama responded. 'Joshua, will you agree to this mission?'

'It would be my honour to serve,' I bowed my head, wondering what I had just agreed to.

'I would also like Caleb ben Jephunneh to represent the tribe of Judah,' Moses said to Judah's tribal leader. 'I have been watching him for some time. He is a righteous man, brave and strong. Nahshon, will you speak to Caleb on my behalf?'

'I will,' he nodded.

'Uh . . . Master,' I said, stepping forward into the circle of men. 'It would be helpful to know what you would have us do, so we can prepare – and so that the elders can choose the right men for this task.' The elders murmured their agreement.

'Ech, most assuredly!' said Moses, hitting the side of his forehead with his hand. 'Sometimes I forget that you cannot hear all that is going on inside my head!' He turned to face me. 'Joshua, you and the eleven men chosen to go with you will journey into Canaan to explore this land that the Lord God has given us, and report back on the inhabitants of the land, how numerous their flocks and herds, the vegetation and the strength of their fortifications.' He leaned forward with a glint in his eyes. 'You will be *spies*.'

56

Reconnaissance

Sparks flew upwards in a burst of light as the freshly chopped logs on the campfire popped and spluttered. Twelve of us huddled around the fire, warming ourselves after our evening meal. The night sky was filled with stars, a flickering canopy overhead. It was a scene of such beauty, one to remember and treasure, were it not for the tense atmosphere and unnerving silence that hovered in the air.

Our mission had started well; we set off in high spirits, travelling north to Beersheba, then on to Gerar and Debir. We explored each town we came across, splitting into small groups of two or three so as not to draw attention to ourselves. Some of us walked through the marketplaces and backstreets, avoiding conversation as far as possible lest our accent led to suspicion, while others walked around the outskirts of the settlement. Two of our group always stayed near the camp to guard our belongings, watching from a distance the movement of people in and out of the town.

Our evenings were spent discussing what we witnessed during the days. Initially, our conversations were spirited and exhilarating, focused mainly on the lush landscape and the extensive range of fruit and vegetables which we sampled – especially those from a valley called Eshkol. We ate the fruit of that land until our bellies were fat like suckling lambs, all the while dreaming of the meals our womenfolk would cook with produce like this. But that all changed as we neared Hebron, the area around Moab where the Hittites dwelt. That's where we first saw them.

Giants.

Growing up, I had heard stories about the descendants of Anak who lived in that region, a people great and tall – but hearing about them and seeing them with my own eyes were two quite different experiences. I was considered one of the tallest and strongest of our people, but I was dwarfed by these giants of men. They stood more than twenty hands tall, as strong as bears and just as menacing.

Our conversation around the campfire the night we first saw them was subdued, at best.

Although the Hivites and Perizzites who lived in Jebus and Shechem were a strong race, we saw no actual giants among them, so I was hopeful that we could continue our mission with no more setbacks. It was not to be. The further north we journeyed, the more giants we encountered. They were numerous in the land of Ammon and even larger than those at Hebron, men of great stature and strong as oaks. We heard stories about a giant called Sihon who was the Ammonites' champion, and another called Og who dwelt in Bashan, famed for breaking the necks of his enemies with one hand. None of us had any desire to encounter these men.

We had been journeying for weeks and had just reached Beth Rehob. I hoped we would explore further to the north, but the looks on my fellow spies' faces (apart from Caleb, who had become my stalwart companion) told me that they thought otherwise. Caleb and I looked at each other from under our head coverings, heads bowed, eyes scanning the fireside area where our companions sat in sticky silence. Caleb lifted his eyebrows and bobbed his head at me, trying to provoke me to action. I frowned at him, so he rolled his eyes, cleared his throat, and said with a false sense of cheeriness, 'Oy! That was quite a day, was it not?'

The response was underwhelming. Most of the men continued staring into the fire and didn't look up at all. I tried to come to his rescue. 'It was indeed. Quite a day ... yes, it was ...'

'Shaphat, have you tried these pomegranates?' Caleb asked, holding one out to him. 'So juicy – they are like nectar on my tongue! Here, try one.'

Shaphat, the tribe of Simeon's representative, was sitting hunched over with his head in his hands. He turned to glare at Caleb. 'No,' he said frostily.

Undeterred, Caleb asked, 'What about you, Gaddi?', holding one out to his companion on the left.

Gaddi, looking flustered, replied, 'I have tasted one, thank you.' Gaddi was the youngest of our group, a man of few words with a gentle spirit. His eyes darted around and, seeing the faces of his companions, he lowered his head.

'Ah, yes. How about you, Ammiel? Would you like . . .'

'Oysh!' shouted Shaphat, sitting bolt upright, glowering at Caleb. 'Have you no understanding? We *do not want a pomegranate.*'

'Ech! Peace, Shaphat, peace!' Caleb lifted his hands, fending off the attack. 'I am just enjoying this fruit, and wanted to share it with you. I have never tasted anything like it – it is extraordinary! These pomegranates burst with flavour, and the grapes – have you tasted them?' he asked the group, looking around expectantly. 'Like little balls of pure – '

'Did you not *see* them?' Shaphat scowled at Caleb.

'See what?' Caleb shrugged his shoulders.

'*The giants!*' Shaphat stood up, gesticulating as he described them. 'Huge men with bulging arms and legs like tree trunks, holding spiked clubs the length of your body?'

'Yes, I saw them. We all saw them.'

'Then you should know,' Shaphat's voice increased in volume, culminating in a roar, 'that there is no way we can face them in battle without being utterly vanquished.'

'Shaphat, hold your peace,' said Sethur, a older man from the tribe of Asher. 'Sit down and let us take counsel together.'

'How can I hold my peace?' Shaphat shouted. 'Our people have been through much tribulation since leaving Egypt: plagues, war, starvation – death – and now all our plans come to nothing because the land that is promised to us is filled with stone fortresses full of giants. And all this fool can do,' he pointed to Caleb, 'is babble on about pomegranates and grapes!' He spat on the ground and sat down, shaking his head in disgust.

'Brothers, I entreat you!' I glanced around the group. 'Have you forgotten what Yahweh said? He said He would bring us into the land that He swore to give to Abraham, to Isaac and to Jacob. He said He would give it to us for a possession. Yes, we have seen some giants in this land, but Yahweh's promises still stand. He has promised this land to us; it is ours for the taking.'

'How?' Ammiel's brows furrowed. He was a practical man who liked plans and clear directions; he was not prone to dreams or speculation. '*How* do we take this land, Joshua? How do you propose we take a land that is filled with the descendants of Anak and Rephaim?'

I held his gaze. I would not lie. This was not the time for platitudes and false promises. 'I know not, Ammiel, but I believe our God will show us how. We can take this land. If we stand together and hold fast to His statutes, we can conquer these people and drive the giants out!' Ammiel did not look convinced, so I looked at Palti, the tribe of Benjamin's spy. I knew him to be a good man of strong character who was much respected in the camp, and my hope was that he would join his heart with mine and Caleb's.

'Palti?' I asked him. 'Let your voice be heard. What seems good to you?'

'What seems good to me?' Palti pondered for a moment. He stared at the group of men sat around the fire. 'I am wondering why Yahweh would promise this land to us if He knew we would be unable to take it.' Silence fell as we thought about what he had said. Since no one responded, Palti continued, 'I have seen things on our travels that I never thought I would see. This land is plentiful and fertile – it would be perfect grazing land for our herds and flocks. An abundance of streams and wells surrounded by plants and trees, most of which I have never seen before. The richness of this land and its fruit is remarkable, and – '

'You see!' Caleb shouted, pointing to Palti. 'He speaks truth! The fruit of this land is . . .' He saw me frowning at him and stopped mid-rant. 'Forgive me. Speak, please,' he gestured to Palti, who smiled at Caleb's exuberance.

'You are right, Caleb. This land is extraordinary and our people would thrive here – were it not for one thing.'

'Yes!' shouted Shaphat. 'The giants!'

Palti sighed and nodded his head. 'I have heard stories about giants before, but believed them to be tales for children, monsters that had long since perished. I never believed that I would see one, let alone large groups of them.'

'But we saw no giants when we first crossed into Canaan,' I argued, desperate to win Palti over. 'It was only when we neared the land of the Amorites that we saw them.'

'Few or many,' Ammiel interjected, 'their fortresses are impenetrable and even their women . . .' Ammiel paused to look around the circle of men. 'Well, we all saw the giants' womenfolk, *nu*?' Some of the men muttered in scorn, while others murmured with begrudging admiration for the magnificent female specimens they had seen.

'Brothers! I implore you!' I called them to order. 'Yes, there are giants in this land but, like Palti said, why would Yahweh have given us this land if He knew we could not take it? His arm is not short. Think on all the miracles we have seen by His hand. Moses is a fearless leader and he knows the ways of Yahweh.'

'Yes, but he will not be fighting the giants, will he?' Shaphat said. He stood up, walked to a clearing near the firepit, and turned to face the group. 'Remember what happened at Rephidim? He sent all of us to fight the Amalekites, while he stood in safety at the top of the hill with Aaron and Hur.' I frowned. Shaphat's voice was taking on a rasping, dissonant tone. It reminded me of something, but I couldn't call to mind what. 'So where will Moses be when we face the giants?'

I tried to defend my master. 'Shaphat, I am sure Moses will – '

'No, he will not! He will be standing on some distant hilltop again, watching us risk our lives in battle, fighting invincible giants in a land *he* led us to.' Shaphat was clearly trying to stir the men up with his rhetoric. 'Why do you think Yahweh led us to this land?' Shaphat walked around the fire, addressing each of the men individually. 'Why would He bring us here, knowing that there are giants in this land that He is supposedly giving us?' The men stared at Shaphat, waiting for him to answer his own question.

'To *kill us*!' he shouted. 'That is why Yahweh has led us here! He wants to kill us!'

'No!' Caleb yelled, standing to his feet. 'That is folly!'

Shaphat had no intention of stopping. A stream of venom spewed out of his mouth. 'Look at what He did to Shimea and Rekem, and all those whose hearts were joined with them – He killed them! You!' He swung round and pointed to me. '*You* killed them. They were your own people, and you killed them!' I could think of nothing to say in my defence. I did kill them, my own people, and I was still paying the price each night in my dreams.

Caleb saw the conflict in me and stepped forward in my defence. 'Joshua was obeying orders! Moses commanded him to do so, but he took no pleasure in it!'

'You see! *Moses* told him to kill them. What about Nadab and Abihu? Yahweh's priests, appointed by Him and consecrated to

Him – Moses' own nephews! But He killed them just because they wanted to offer up incense to the Lord.'

'No!' I cried out, appealing to the other spies. 'You know the truth. You know why they perished – they offered profane fire before the Lord! It was not theirs to offer incense before Him, and Shimea and Rekem were leading our people into the idolatrous ways of Egypt – the worship of false gods . . .'

'Who says they were false gods?' Shaphat challenged me. 'Why must there be just one God? Can our people not choose which god they want to worship? Why must we be slaughtered for wanting to make our own choices?' His shoulders were hunched in a bestial pose as he glared at me. 'Yahweh is a murderer!'

I froze in horror. My heart skipped a beat. Now I recognised the rasp in his voice. I stared into Shaphat's eyes. No! It couldn't be!

57

Shrouded

Sleep eluded me that night. I woke feeling hemmed in, trapped like a bird caught in a snare. Alive, but powerless. I roused Caleb early, signalling to him to be quiet, and we made our way to a clearing on the edge of the hill near our camp.

We stood in silence for a while, taking in the beauty of the landscape before us. The hill where we stood overlooked a luscious valley filled with row upon row of vines and fruit trees, as far as the eye could see. A stream ran through the middle of the valley, its waters glinting in the first rays of the sun. Over the last few months, I had become so accustomed to seeing brown wherever I turned – dirt, rocks, sand. To see so much green, like a fertile rug laid out before me, was refreshing, but my soul was too downcast to rejoice in it.

'Joshua, what happened?' Caleb asked.

I'd hardly spoken a word since Shaphat's attack around the campfire. My thoughts were like a tight mesh, trapping me inside their twisted strands of fear and doubt.

'Last night – what happened?' Caleb asked again. 'Shaphat?'

I nodded, still staring at the sumptuous spread of vegetation in the valley beneath us. I had no desire to talk, especially about Shaphat. I didn't know what to say, didn't trust my own thoughts. But I couldn't ignore Caleb's question. 'I trained him myself,' I muttered, 'and I made him a captain in the Simeonite ranks. He earned much respect from his people and it was on my recommendation that he was chosen for this mission. I thought I knew him. So why did I never see it before?' I mumbled to myself, forgetting that Caleb was standing next to me.

'See what before?' Caleb was frowning. I hesitated. Should I tell him? It was not that I didn't trust him. I knew Caleb's heart was

313

loyal to Yahweh and Moses – and to me. I just needed to be sure that he could restrain his words. His impetuous nature sometimes got the better of him; from time to time his tongue would lead him into trouble. What I was about to tell him could not be spoken of.

'What?' Caleb was squinting in the early morning sun. Turning around to stop the sun from blinding his eyes, he peered at me. 'What are you not telling me? Speak your mind.'

I crossed my arms and looked forward again. 'Darkness. An evil that fills the souls of those who rebel against Yahweh. It entices them away from their love of His ways and causes them to turn to other gods. It sullies everything it touches, stains it with filth. It is like a canker in a man's heart. It was within Shimea and Rekem.'

Caleb frowned. 'And it is in Shaphat?'

'Yes. I saw it in his eyes.' I sighed and turned to face him. 'Moses says that we can see what is in a man's heart through his eyes. He saw the darkness often in Egypt, especially in the priests and sorcerers. I saw it for the first time in Shimea.' I flinched at the memory. 'His eyes were dead and lifeless, like a darkened pathway with no light at the end. They were also strangely hypnotic.' I looked at Caleb, trying to put into words what my heart had not fully grasped. 'The darkness tries to pull you in, to control you; its poison spreads, unseen, like a plague. You see nothing and suspect nothing until suddenly, there it is, right in front of you, and you see it in their eyes.' I glanced away. 'By then, it is often too late. That same darkness was found in Shimea, and then in Rekem, and you saw how it poisoned the hearts of hundreds who joined them in their harlotry and all manner of evil against Yahweh. I saw it also in Nadab and Abihu.'

'That day at the tabernacle?' Caleb asked. 'When their hearts were set on offering false fire?'

'Yes, although it was some time before then that I first saw it in them. They were angry that Eleazar had been chosen over them as chief advisor for the design of the tabernacle. They allowed the darkness to poison them against their brother, against Moses, and evil found lodging within them. That is what I saw last night in Shaphat's eyes when he called Yahweh a murderer.'

Caleb stared at me. 'Is there no doubt in your heart about this?'

'No.' I met his gaze. 'I saw it. What concerns me is that we do not know how many Shaphat has infected. He is a man of great influence – he could poison many men. I must tell Moses. I must warn him.' I cried out in frustration. 'How has this happened? Shaphat was chosen out of so many. Why did I not see any sign of this before now?'

'You are not to blame. Clearly, this darkness has the power to stay shrouded until it reveals itself. No one can have seen it, not even Moses, or Shaphat would not have been chosen to join our ranks.'

I shrugged and shook my head. 'This land is truly wonderful. Everything about it is abundant and fruitful. We cannot let the darkness destroy the wonder of what we have seen. We have journeyed for some time and have only Beth Rehob left to spy out. I would go further into the north, to the territory of Mount Hermon, but I fear the men have lost heart and will turn back.' Voicing my biggest fear, I said, 'It will soon be time to go back, but I cannot return with a bad report. I cannot disappoint Moses.'

Caleb squared his shoulders. 'Then we must fulfil our mission and take a good report back to Moses.' Turning back to the camp, he said, 'Come! Let us break fast and be on our way to Beth Rehob.'

I could not think about food, not while my stomach churned so within me. 'Go. Eat. Attend to your needs, we will leave soon.' Caleb nodded and walked back to the makeshift camp, leaving me to my own thoughts. I turned to gaze again at the expanse of land which lay before me. It was lush and verdant, overflowing with every good thing. A gentle breeze ruffled my hair, so I put my head back, relishing the cleansing motion of the wind as it blew the dust off my robes and out of my heart.

'Truly, this is a good land,' I muttered to myself, looking out across the land. 'We would flourish here. To settle here, build homes, plant vineyards and crops – that would be good, *nu*?' I sighed and looked up at the sky. Puffy white clouds were scattered across its expanse, each outlined with a golden edge from the effects of the rising sun. I smiled. 'Even the clouds here seem to sing Your praises.' Closing my eyes, I whispered, 'But they are not as beautiful as Your cloud, my Lord.'

It had not dawned on me until we started out on our journey that Yahweh's cloud would stay over the camp where Moses was, and not go into Canaan with us. The realisation that I would have to travel for weeks without the covering of my beloved cloud was like a knife in my gut. My longing for Yahweh's presence increased with every day that passed, but it was the night-times that I found especially difficult. I sat alone by the campfire night after night after the others had gone to sleep, listening to the sound of the logs popping and snapping. I imagined I was standing by the pillar of fire and, for a moment, my soul felt the warmth of Yahweh's Presence.

But it never lasted. As soon as I opened my eyes, I would feel dry and forlorn. Yesterday's discovery of the darkness in Shaphat had only served to exacerbate my desperation for Yahweh's presence even further. I groaned and bent over. 'Yahweh!' I whispered. 'My heart longs for Your presence. I am thirsty for Your glory. I long to meet with you in Your sanctuary. My heart within me is parched, like a young gazelle in a dry land. When can I meet with You?' The longing overtook me. I knelt down and opened my arms wide. Putting my head back, I groaned. 'How much longer must I journey in this land without You?' The yearning in my heart overflowed; I bowed down. Crossing my arms across my chest, I swayed backwards and forwards in distress, until I heard it. The voice. The voice I had heard before.

'Joshua,' the voice whispered to me. 'I am with you.'

Unlocking my arms, I lifted them to the heavens. Tears rolled down my cheeks as I soaked in His presence, and the desperate longings of my heart were once again satiated by the grace and kindness of a gracious, omnipresent God.

58

Voice of Fear

The fear in my fellow travellers was intensifying. Shaphat's poison had spread, contaminating the spies, and all but Caleb were now firmly convinced that the 'land of milk and honey' was not the land of promise, but a certain invitation to an early grave. Our exploration of Beth Rehob that day was cut short – very short. In fact, we never went into the town at all. We surveyed its inhabitants and the land around it from a distance. The other ten spies had seen enough. They were done. That night, as we sat around the campfire, Caleb and I made one last attempt to persuade them to the contrary, but it was a foregone conclusion.

'I will not lead our people into this land to be slaughtered like animals.' Sethur looked round the group. 'I will not stand by and watch them die by the hands of these monsters.' Mutters of agreement broke out all around the campfire.

'They will not die!' Caleb's face was earnest in his appeal. 'Our God will fight for us. Brothers, Yahweh will not lead us to slaughter, He will fight for us! This land is ours! Remember how the Lord fought for us at Rephidim when the Amalekites attacked us? We had no trained warriors and few weapons, but we met them in battle nonetheless, and we were victorious!'

'Have you forgotten so quickly what Yahweh did?' I added. 'As long as Moses held up the staff, we were triumphant, but when he lowered it, the enemy overcame us. We defeated the Amalekites! Our band of inexperienced warriors defeated them! Yahweh fought for us then, and He will fight for us now.'

'You are crazy, both of you!' Shaphat glowered at us.

'It is true. Yahweh gave us victory against the Amalekites, but this is different – there were no giants in Rephidim, no huge fortresses.' Up until now, Igal from the tribe of Issachar had listened quietly, but now he sat up and addressed the men. 'These Canaanites are not like men; they are like gods. Moses neglected to tell us that there were giants in this land. We cannot defeat them and I agree with Sethur: I will not take my people into a land where these god-men live.'

'Next to them we are like grasshoppers, bugs to be crushed under their feet,' Gaddi muttered. 'I felt like a grasshopper when I looked at them. And we must look like grasshoppers to them.'

Shaphat nodded and snorted loudly. 'Grasshoppers to be crushed with a flick of their wrists. No, I will not do it. We will not go there.'

'Brothers, search your hearts. Think of all that we have seen,' I entreated them. 'This *is* a land of milk and honey, just like Yahweh said. Think of the . . .'

'Yes, and it is a land of milk and honey that does not belong to our people.'

'Shaphat . . .' Caleb stood up to challenge him.

'Brothers, I beg of you. Please do not rebel against Yahweh,' I pleaded with them, the knot in my stomach growing tighter by the minute. 'Do not do this. It will not go well with you.' They stood to their feet, arguing, and shouting their opinions, until Shaphat lifted his voice and cut through the noise.

'Be still!' he bellowed. 'We have talked long enough. We will discuss this no more. We have seen enough, yes? It is time to go back and report on what we have seen. So – we start on our return journey tomorrow. Yes?' Shaphat looked around the circle of men, noting their grim agreement. Pinpointing those who were not actively voicing their consent, he called them out by name – all except Caleb and me.

'Gaddiel? Are you one with us?'

'I am with you.'

'Nahbi? Geuel? Shammua? Are we agreed?' They nodded.

'Palti?'

Palti hesitated. 'Yes,' he muttered. 'I think it is time we journeyed home.'

'Good. We rest now,' Shaphat added. 'We have a long journey ahead of us tomorrow and we must set out before sunrise.' He threw a triumphant glare in my direction and stalked off. I was no longer the leader of our company. He had staked his claim and won. The men grunted in agreement and made their way to their makeshift tents, until only Caleb and I were left by the fire.

'What can we do?' I put my head in my hands and rubbed my temple. 'We must do something. Why can they not see it? They cannot see the might of Yahweh. It is as if the darkness has placed a veil over their eyes; they can see nothing except their own fear. What can we do?'

Caleb sighed. 'We can do nothing more than what we have done already – speak the truth and remind them of what Yahweh promised us.'

'I fear that will not be enough.' Silence fell. We grappled with the conflict that crowded our minds. I walked to the edge of the clearing. Looking up at the canopy of stars above us, I thought, 'After all we have seen, how can they not want to go into this land? Moses trusted me with this mission. How can I go back now and tell him that they refuse to go into Canaan?'

Caleb stood up and started pacing in front of the fire. 'We will tell the people about what we have seen; we will tell them about the land and the fruit and the hills, and the wells flowing with fresh water.' He turned to me, smiling with fresh passion. 'We will tell them that this land *does* flow with milk and honey and that the land Yahweh promised us is a good land. We will tell them that we are *well able* to conquer it, and that this land is ripe for the picking!'

'But will they listen to us?' I loved Caleb's unconquerable optimism, but I was unconvinced. 'The voice of fear speaks loudly, especially when the heart chooses not to hold fast to faith.'

We sat together, silent and unmoving, long after the coals of the fire ceased to burn, and the flimsy ashes were blown away by the night air. 'My heart is heavy, Caleb. I fear for our people. Not because of the giants, but for what will happen if they rebel against the Lord again. I fear what my heart is telling me.'

'What is your heart telling you?'

I spoke out of the gloom and darkness. 'That they will not see this land again.'

59

Death Sentence

I stood behind Moses, my body stiff, staring over people's heads into the distance. I avoided their gaze – even the gaze of my own family who had gathered with the rest of our people to hear the report of the twelve spies who had journeyed into Canaan. I knew that only my eyes betrayed the conflict that raged within me, as Moses declared to the people, 'The Lord your God says the carcasses of you who have complained against me shall fall in this wilderness, all of you who were numbered, from twenty years old and above, except Caleb son of Jephunneh and Joshua son of Nun.'

Gasps of shock and unbelief rippled through the assembled masses. There was more. I steeled myself, locking my jaw in anticipation of the grief and anger which I knew would be inevitable. 'Your sons shall be shepherds in the wilderness for forty years,' Moses shouted over the buzz of conversation. 'According to the number of days in which you spied out the land, forty days, for each day you shall bear your guilt one year. But your little ones, who you said would be victims, the Lord says the Lord will bring *them* into the land which He swore to you, which you have despised.'

All around me, blank stares turned into portraits of grief as mothers reached for their sons and held them close. Husband and wives clung to each other and families sobbed in a national outpouring of anguish. The entire nation of Israel was abruptly and painfully aware of the fact that none of their valiant men – brothers, sons, fathers, husbands, uncles, or nephews – would live more than two score years from that day. None of them would live to see the Promised Land, bar myself and Caleb.

The weight of that privilege lay heavily on my heart.

I listened with sorrow to two women standing nearby, as they realised the impact of this news on their lives. 'My Japhet reached his twentieth year and was numbered in the census. Does that mean . . . ?'

'Abishur also . . . twenty-one,' her friend stuttered. 'No! This cannot be.' With a jolt of realisation, she turned to her husband. 'No! Not you too, Mattias. Please, not you too!' I turned away, not wanting to watch their sorrow or intrude on their grief. I could do nothing now. It was out of my hands. The darkness had done its work and the sentence had been passed. The other ten spies, led by Shaphat, had given a damning report that even the most faith-filled of believers would have struggled to withstand. They put on a performance good enough to rival the greatest storytellers in the land and, by the end of it, not only were the children cowering in terror, but most of the adults, too.

Caleb and I tried desperately to counteract their report by sharing the many virtues of the land of milk and honey, showing the Israelites the samples of fruit we'd brought back with us. Gasps of delight and admiration were heard when we produced a huge bunch of grapes and a basket of ripe pomegranates. I studied the crowds when Caleb gave a long, animated account of what we had seen and tasted, but I knew in my heart that they would not be persuaded otherwise. Their fear of the giants far exceeded their desire to taste the sumptuous food that Caleb showed them.

'The land of Canaan is a land of abundance,' Caleb yelled. 'Do not gear the people who live there,' he roared, waving his fist in the air, 'for their protection has left them, and we will consume them like food!'

But they did. Fear had taken control, and Caleb's passionate exhortations fell on deaf ears. The crowd turned away, as one, refusing to go into the Promised Land. I looked away from the people as Caleb talked, gazing up at the cloud. It was heavy and dense and seemed flatter than usual. There were no spirals or silver edged plumes dancing in it today. No rays of sunlight passed through the cloud's form and the flickers of light that I loved so much were nowhere to be seen. It was not undulating – in fact, there was very little movement to be seen in it at all. The cloud of His presence was still and sombre.

I realised with a jolt of pain that Yahweh was mourning.

Grief and rage welled up in my heart. I bent over and picked up the bottom of my outer robe, ripping it with a loud cry. Caleb did likewise, and we stood before our people, bereft, in full mourning. A torrent of weeping began as the news spread throughout the camp. Men and women slumped on the ground, tearing their clothes, taking off their finery and throwing dust in their hair.

The time of mourning had begun.

The cries could be heard far and wide – cries of repentance, of sorrow and remorse. But it was too late. The time for mercy had passed and the sentence would stand. It was, in effect, a death sentence. They had chosen to listen to the voice of fear propagated by ten unbelieving spies, rather than Caleb's and my declarations of faith in our God. The men of Israel realised with horror that their decision would cost them dearly.

It would cost them their lives.

60

Inconsolable

As soon as Moses had finished his announcement, he withdrew to his tent and had no need of me. I could not go home, not yet, so I went to the tabernacle to pray, to think – to hide. Eleazar was there and, as soon as he saw me, my faithful confidant drew me aside and let me unburden myself.

'How can I face them? How can I look into the eyes of my family, knowing that I am the cause of their pain, that I have not done enough to stop the darkness from spreading among the spies – that because of me, most of them will never enter Canaan, never see the beauty of that land, or sample its delights?'

'Joshua, this is not your burden to bear. You and Caleb did everything you could to persuade our people to go into the Promised Land. You spoke valiantly, with much zeal, but their fear was too strong. You cannot lay this at your own feet.'

'Whose feet should it be laid at, if not mine?'

'This desolation is not due to one man, Joshua. It is the darkness that we must war against, not a man.'

'Yes, but it is men who will suffer the consequences. Righteous men who do not deserve to bear the pain of this iniquity. My *abba*. My brothers.' Grief welled up in me. 'They, who lived in captivity in Egypt for so long, must now live the remainder of their days wandering around this barren wilderness, never to enter into the Promised Land.'

I put my head in my hands, ran my fingers through my hair and rubbed my throbbing temples. My heart could not reconcile the fact that they would not enter Canaan with me. I could not comprehend going there without them.

'Hareph would have loved Canaan.' I gave Eleazar a weak smile. 'He has struggled to embrace the life of a sojourner. He would love nothing more than to dwell in a house again and raise up a family to continue his lineage.' I sighed. 'Neither of those are likely to happen now.'

Mesha. My heart constricted and my throat felt strangled as I thought of the effect this would have on him. 'Mesha has been my friend since childhood. He is so full of life and fun. Even when he married and fathered children, it did not change him. He laughs and loves and jests just as he always has.' Eleazar smiled at me, but said nothing. 'It is as if he has a gift of eternal youthfulness. But no longer.' My voice cracked and tears came to my eyes. 'His life will be cut short, because of me. Yahweh forgive me. How can Mesha forgive me? And Helah?'

Eleazar listened as I poured out my anguish but, as evening drew in, he said, 'Come, let us return home to our families.'

Home.

Guilt sat on me like a rock weighing down my chest; I could not be rid of it. I delayed as long as I could but, eventually, I knew I would have to go home and face them. It was dark and the evening meal would be over, but I had little desire to eat and even less desire to gather around the mat with my family after what had ensued that day. It was dark by the time I made my way home through groups of grieving families, but the darkness could not hide the resentful stares of my people as I stole by their firepits.

Even the pillar of fire seemed dimmer that night; its appearance was lacklustre. There was no vibrancy in its flames, no glowing spectrum of colours, and I saw no movement of wings in its midst. Truly, Yahweh was in mourning, just as His people were. I had hoped the family would be sleeping when I got back, but it was not so. The children were inside but everyone else, including Yoram and Joel, were sitting outside, huddled around the firepit. No one was talking. All of them without exception sat staring morbidly into the flickering flames of the firepit. Each wore mourning apparel and I could see by the redness of their eyes that the women had been weeping.

As soon as they saw me approaching, Mesha and Helah stood up and, without greeting me, Helah called out, 'Yoshi, is it true? What Moses spoke of – is it true?' A wall of faces stared at me, silently begging me to say the words, 'No, it is not true.' This was what I had feared the most. How could I tell them? Must I be the one to confirm that the death sentence must stand? Helah stared at me, her hopeful expression turning to confusion.

'Yoshi? It cannot be true. Not for Mesha. For those who refused to go into Canaan, yes, but not for my Mesha, surely?'

I stared at her.

She asked again, her voice wobbling. 'Yoshi? Is it true?'

Not trusting myself to speak, I just nodded.

'But . . . I do not understand. Mesha is a good man – as are all my brothers. They did not rebel against Yahweh – they stood with you and Caleb. They did not join with the other spies. They were ready to go into Canaan, to go to war against the giants. Why must they die? Why?' she pleaded with me, as if I could overturn the sentence.

'Helah,' Mesha said, putting his arms out to try to comfort her. 'This is not Joshua's decision, it is Yahweh's. We must accept His – '

'No!' Helah cried out, pushing his arms away. 'I cannot abide it. It is not right that you must die when you have done nothing wrong.' She turned on me. 'Why must he die? Why should *you* live when my Mesha cannot? Why, Joshua? Why?' she raged at me, accusation filling her eyes.

My heart ripped inside my chest.

'Helah!' Mesha barked at his wife. 'Be silent! This is not Joshua's doing. This guilt is not his to bear.' He turned to me, his brow furrowed with anxiety. 'Joshua, forgive her, I beg you. She is anguished. She is not herself. We rejoice that you will live to see Canaan. Truly. It is good you have found favour with Yahweh.'

I stared at him, then turned to look around the circle of those who stared back at me. I saw reflected in the faces of my family both pain and compassion, regret and fear, resentment and confusion.

'Forgive me,' I mumbled, stumbling backwards. 'I beg of you . . . forgive me.'

My voice broke, as did my heart. Clutching my chest, I turned from them and fled into the night.

61

Outcasts

I slept in the tabernacle courtyard that night, curled up behind the brazen altar for protection against the wind. The floor was hard and cold, but I welcomed the discomfort. It was my chastisement, the payment for my guilt. I lay there, listening to the ghostly call of owls as they flew overhead, and eventually fell asleep to the sound of their wings flapping. I woke early, cold and stiff, long before the Levites arrived to change the oil lamps and start the morning worship.

That night, I returned to the tabernacle to continue my lonely vigil. It was both my punishment and my comfort. I could not go back home. Not yet. I could not bear to see the blame in their eyes, the resentment that I knew would greet me if I returned.

The following day, I returned to the tabernacle again after dark to find a blanket rolled up behind the altar, and some food wrapped in a cloth. Someone must have seen me, but who? I scouted the area to see who was watching, but could see no sign of anyone. Whoever it was obviously did not want to be discovered, just as I did not want to be found. The blanket eased my sleep and the food filled my belly. I was grateful to my unknown benefactor, content for the moment not to know who they were.

The days that followed the death sentence merged into a colourless blur. I spent much of my time in the tabernacle, taking what comfort I could from being near my beloved cloud. Moses seemed very preoccupied and did not have much need of me; I wondered if he had become used to being on his own again, after my having been away in Canaan for so long. Whatever the reason, it left me with a lot of time on my own to ponder and to mourn. Too much time.

There was one person who I thought might understand the turmoil that churned inside of me, so I sought him out. Caleb was sitting outside his tent when I arrived, watching his first-born son playing a throwing game with some stones. He looked relieved to see me and greeted me warmly – I wondered if perhaps I was not the only one whose life was now in turmoil.

'They spit on me when I pass by,' he told me, bitterness clouding his features, 'and turn their backs to me. People who I have known for years are avoiding me. They see me coming and turn away.' He shrugged his shoulders. 'Or they glare at me. I can bear that; it is no great hardship. But yesterday, this happened.' He called his son, Iru, who threw one last pebble at the large rock he was aiming for, and came to stand in front of Caleb.

'Yes, *Abba*?' he asked, his eyes bright and inquisitive, much like his father's.

Caleb took Iru's face in his hands and kissed him on both cheeks. 'You, my son, are the joy of my heart. You know this, yes?' he asked, stroking the boy's tousled head and gently moving his curly hair to one side to reveal an ugly red gash on Iru's forehead. The wound was still raw and bruising was already forming around it.

Iru giggled. 'Yes, *Abba*.' He gazed at his father with what could only be described as pure adoration, and then said, 'Can I go and play now?'

Caleb gave him a kiss and said, 'Yes! Go, play your game while I talk to Joshua.'

Iru trotted off to continue his game. The smile on Caleb's face faded into a mask of anger. 'Stones. They threw stones at me, but their aim was misguided. They hit Iru instead.' He turned to me with a savage expression and whispered, 'They ran off while I tended Iru, before I could catch them. Cowards!' he spat. 'I can abide their hatred of me, it matters not, but I will not let them stretch out their hand against my son or my wife.'

'Where is Johanna?' I asked, not having seen Caleb's petite wife. 'Is it well with her?'

He sighed. 'She has gone to the well.'

'Now?' I asked. 'It is nearly midday.'

Caleb nodded. 'The other women scorn her openly. So she does not go to fetch water in the cool of the early morning now, or in the evening. Only at midday. So far she has been safe but if anyone should raise their hand, or their tongue, to my wife, I will answer them with fire!' I couldn't help but smile to see the familiar spark in my friend again. Caleb groaned. 'I feel ensnared here, staying by my tent all day. I must walk, breathe the free air.'

'Shall we walk together?' I offered.

Caleb turned to me. 'That would be good, my friend. But let me wait until Johanna has returned safely. I will not take Iru out with me again. Not now.' Johanna arrived back shortly afterwards; her trip to the well had been uneventful. I watched her embrace her husband and little boy, with a yearning in my heart. I longed to go home to my family, but I couldn't. It wasn't because I was angry. I understood why Helah had raged at me, and I harboured no resentment towards her. No, it wasn't anger that kept me away. It was guilt. I would live. They would not. It was an unexpected honour that I hadn't asked for and that, right now, I didn't want. It seemed it was the same for Caleb. We set off walking, avoiding the main pathways that snaked their way through the camp.

'Joshua, have you heard anything about Korah stirring up trouble in the camp?' Caleb asked.

I looked at him with alarm. 'You have not joined with him, have you?'

Caleb snorted. 'No, assuredly not. Korah has said nothing to me, but I have heard stories of a rebellion – it seems Dathan and Abiram are with him in this. This day past, when I was walking with Iru, I saw the three of them huddled together, whispering. They stopped talking when I came near.'

'Hmph.'

'I thought it might be because we . . .' Caleb sighed and ran his fingers through his unruly mop of hair. 'Well, there has been a lot of talk, *nu*? They resent the fact that I . . . or we . . . will not suffer death like them – or at least, not as soon as them. They have decided now that they do want to go into Canaan, but it is too late. Too late for them, at least . . .'

Caleb's theorising petered out and we walked in silence for a while, each thinking our own thoughts, trying to make sense of our struggles. 'Is Moses aware of it?' Caleb asked.

'Aware of what?'

'The trouble. You know – Korah?'

'Oh!' My thoughts were drawn back to the issue at hand. I refocused, pushing aside the feelings of guilt that plagued me, and the longing in my heart to see my adoptive family again. 'Yes. Yes, he knows. Some of the elders came to talk to him yesterday and it is true – Korah and his followers are stirring up all sorts of trouble.'

Since the day of the announcement, the majority of God's people had accepted their fate with a resigned sense of sorrow. There were those, however, who would not accept the consequences of their actions. It seemed that this rebellious faction was being unofficially, but most effectively, led by Korah – a Levite and a relative of Moses and Aaron. I was with Moses when the reports came flooding in – reports about the seeds of unrest being sown by Korah and his company, and of the plentiful crop of rebellion that was apparently ripe and ready for harvesting.

'But what do they hope to achieve?' Caleb frowned.

'I am not sure,' I replied as we continued our walk through the camp, 'but it . . . what is that noise?' I looked around, trying to locate the source of the commotion. We followed the buzz of voices and rounded a corner to see a large crowd gathered. There, in front of us, his eyes full of the darkness which I had come to loathe so passionately, was the man in question.

'Who are Moses and Aaron to tell us what we can and cannot do?' Korah yelled to the men and women standing before him. Caleb and I stopped dead in our tracks, unsure of what to do. This was a sizeable crowd and I recognised many leaders among it. 'Why should we stay in this wilderness and not go into Canaan?' Korah continued. 'We are free men, are we not? Each one of us is holy, and the Lord is among us all. So why do Moses and Aaron exalt themselves above the Lord's assembly? They have gone too far this time.' The crowd shouted their agreement, lifting their fisted hands in a show of aggressive solidarity as Korah went on, 'Yes, it is true that they are both great-grandsons of our leader, Levi. But I am also his great-grandson! I am from the direct line of Levi and, as such, I am holy, just as they are.'

Just then, Dathan, who stood with Abiram at Korah's side, pulled his robe to get his attention. He whispered in his ear, pointing to the back of the assembly. Korah's eyes searched the crowds and, when he saw us standing at the back, his face twisted into a snarl. 'And why should Joshua and Caleb be allowed to go into Canaan, when we cannot go in?' He pointed at us in accusation. 'Who are you, that you should go into this land of milk and honey, while we stay here and die in this wretched desert?' The crowd turned to stare at us and my heart sank when I saw the wall of angry, hostile faces and what my heart dreaded the most: the darkness. 'Why should you suffer a different fate to your people?' Korah yelled at us. 'You are no different from us! Who are you to set yourselves apart, as if you are favoured above us? You are nothing!'

Caleb's face filled with anger, and he took a step forward, ready to retaliate. 'Caleb, no!' I put my arm out to stop him. 'Not now,' I said with as much authority as I could muster. 'We must speak to Moses before we do anything.'

Caleb glowered at me, but stepped back. Korah continued his verbal attack. The rabble were now focused on us and everything inside of me was saying, 'Run!' But my instincts told me that if we ran, they would give chase. So I turned to Caleb and whispered, 'Do not run. Hold fast. Walk away, but do not run.'

We turned and walked away from them, hearts beating out of our chests. They didn't follow, settling instead for a barrage of jeers and verbal abuse. We breathed sighs of relief, walking faster and faster, finally breaking into a run when we were clear of them. So, it was no longer a rumour. It was true. Insurrection was once again rife in the camp, and the darkness had reared its ugly head to spit in the face of a holy, righteous God.

We found Moses in the tabernacle, kneeling down with his face to the ground, deep in prayer. When he finished, he rose to his feet and turned to greet us.

'*Shalom*, Joshua, *shalom*, Caleb.'

'*Shalom*, Master,' I replied. 'Forgive us for disturbing you, but we must take counsel with you.'

'Come.' Moses gestured to the entrance of the tabernacle, his face stern but peaceful. 'Walk with me and reveal what you have heard.'

'It is not what we have heard, Master, as much as what we have seen,' I responded.

'Oh?' Moses cocked his head to one side. 'So then, tell me what you have seen.' We set off together. I walked in the middle of Moses and Caleb and we told him of our confrontation with Korah. He said nothing, listening attentively while we spoke.

'Korah was speaking out against you and Aaron, questioning your leadership, and stirring the people up against you. He told the crowd that they were all holy and should all go into Canaan and that, since he is also the great-grandson of Levi, he is much like you and Aaron.'

'Hmm. Well, he is right about that, at least – he is our father Levi's great-grandson,' Moses mused.

'That may be,' Caleb muttered, 'but he is most assuredly *not* like you and Aaron.'

'We have no knowledge of what took place before we chanced upon them – as soon as Korah saw us, he turned on us.'

'Did they attack you?'

'No. We left before they could do anything, but . . . Master,' I hesitated. I felt a strong need to impress on Moses the danger that I sensed in the mob. 'This was not a mindless rabble like those who followed Rekem and Shimea. We saw many influential leaders among them, and their number was great. If Korah has men of that calibre standing with him, they could persuade many more to join them.'

'Mmm. Which is why we must take action straight away.'

'And do what?'

Moses didn't respond straight away. Having now arrived at his tent, we went inside and sat down. 'Joshua, I must know one thing.'

'Yes, Master?'

'Korah, Dathan, Abiram – did you look in their eyes?' I nodded. I knew what was coming. 'Did you see it? Did you see the darkness?'

'Yes. But not just in *their* eyes – I saw it in the eyes of many in the crowd. These are not just ignorant men who follow blindly. These men follow with purpose. They know what they are doing, they are not fools. The poison has gone deep into their souls and it shows itself under the guise of what looks like righteousness. Those who cannot rightly discern darkness from truth will be taken by them, like children in the night, unless we stop them.'

Moses sighed. 'Yes. This time, the darkness has attacked the root of our people's beliefs. It gnaws at the very fabric of our lives, at what gives us life and meaning – our worship of Yahweh.'

'Do you know what they want?' Caleb asked.

'Yes. They want the priesthood.'

'No! How can they think . . . ? The priesthood is handed down from father to son. It is not . . .' Caleb protested. 'And these are Levites? Korah is your relative, is he not? How can he do this?'

Moses sighed. I saw the ache of grief piercing his heart as he mumbled, 'This is not the first time I have had to deal with iniquity in my own family.' Leaning forward, he rested his arms on his thighs and closed his eyes. Silence fell for a while, and then he spoke. 'This darkness must be eradicated. I know what I must do, but it will not be easy and my heart takes no pleasure in it.'

'Will more of our people die?' I asked. He nodded. 'So many have died already because of this darkness. How many more of our people must die because of their own foolishness and idolatrous ways?'

'Yahweh does not long for a people who simply follow a crowd, walking blindly where they lead. He seeks faithful men who will follow His cloud. Yahweh is holy, and His people must be holy too.' Moses stood up and stretched, and we rose too. Turning to us, he said, 'Go together to the tents of Korah, Dathan and Abiram. Tell them and their followers to meet Aaron and I at the tabernacle first thing tomorrow morning. They are all to carry censers with incense in them. I will speak to Aaron, Eleazar and Ithamar – they will stand with us.'

Caleb and I glanced at each other. Censers of incense again? Moses ignored us, continuing his instructions. 'They are to bring their censers to the tabernacle and we will stand before the Lord together. Aaron will also bring his censer of incense, and Yahweh will choose which man He will cause to come near Him. The man the Lord chooses will be the one who is holy.'

'Yes, Master.' I paused. 'Master, in light of the size of this group, and their influence over the people, should we find some trusted men to stand with us tomorrow? Good men who are faithful to Yahweh, and to you?' I started making a mental list of the men I could call upon, but Moses smiled and reached out to grasp my shoulder.

'That is a good idea and I thank you for thinking of it – but we will not need them. The Lord God is our protector, and He will move on our behalf. However,' Moses smiled at us, raising one eyebrow, 'I would be glad to have you both stand by my side tomorrow, if you will?'

62

Censers

'Here we are again, *nu*?' Caleb looked across at me and grinned. 'Like the day we first met – do you remember it?'

'Like it was yesterday.' I returned his grin and turned my attention back to the crowd that was gathering outside the tent of meeting. Since our initial meeting, Caleb was now frequently at my side, especially when trouble was afoot, as it was today. My reputation as a warrior and leader of the armies of Israel was renowned, but Caleb was also becoming increasingly well known for his courage and skill with sword and spear. There weren't many who would willingly take on our formidable partnership in hand-to-hand combat.

I might have seemed calm and confident on the outside, but my heart was beating rapidly and my spirit was agitated. I searched the crowd for signs of trouble. 'This is not a small assembly – there must be close on 300 men here,' I thought to myself. 'And there are only two of us. Why did Moses not let me choose some men to stand with us?' I drew a deep breath, looking up at Yahweh's cloud which swirled above the tabernacle. 'As long as You are with us, we will defeat the darkness,' I prayed. 'Lord God, King of the universe, give your servants strength this day to overcome evil with good.'

As if in answer to my silent prayer, the cloud parted. Glistening rays of sunshine broke through, streaming down on the place where we stood. I closed my eyes, soaking in the warmth of the sun. 'Yahweh, You are with us,' I said. 'I sense Your presence.'

Looking back out over the crowd, it was easy to see who was with the rebels and who was merely a bystander; each of the rebels held a censer, as instructed by Moses. As I scanned the faces in the rebellious crowd, one stood out to me above the others: Eliphalet, Alya's father, stood near the front, glowering at me with open hostility. 'So you have decided to show yourself?' I thought. Perhaps I should have been concerned, but I felt only relief that this evil was now being displayed openly, for all to see.

On Korah's signal, the rebels lit their censers and, within seconds, a pungent odour permeated the atmosphere in front of Yahweh's tabernacle. I knew that smell; it was the same acidic stench that had fouled the air when Nadab and Abihu had offered profane fire before the Lord. Devilish flames started to flicker in their censers, wisps of smoke curled upwards, filling the air with a pale-greenish grey smog. I used my headscarf to cover my nose. I found the stench repugnant and had no wish to breathe in the toxic fumes.

'What ails you, Joshua?' Korah sneered at me, swinging his censer in my direction. 'Is our incense too powerful for your delicate nose?' The renegade crowd around him pointed at me and sniggered. I said nothing. Gritting my teeth, I wrapped my scarf around my head twice to stop the smell from penetrating, while leaving my hands free. Caleb and I stood, hands on the hilt of our swords, creating a human barrier to protect Moses from his own people.

Moses stepped forward, eyes watering from the acidic smoke that clogged the air. He shouted, 'You Levites have gone too far. Is it not enough for you that the God of Israel has separated you from the rest of the people and brought you near Himself to do the work of the Lord's tabernacle, to stand before the community and minister? But now you desire the priesthood as well? It is against the Lord that you have banded together.' Moses looked at the ranks of the rebellious assembly. 'Where are Dathan and Abiram?' he asked. Abidan stepped forward. 'We have just received a message from them.' He cleared his throat before continuing. 'The messenger said, "Is it not enough that you have brought us here to kill us in the wilderness, and now you also want to lord it over us? You have not brought us into a land flowing with milk and honey or given us the fields and vineyards you promised us. We will not be treated like slaves and we will not come."'

Moses nodded at Abidan, clenched his jaw, and barked, 'Joshua, Caleb – with me. Aaron, bring your censer.' We moved to stand on either side of Moses and Aaron. Caleb raised his eyebrows and looked across at me, as if to ask what was happening, but I shrugged and fell into step behind Moses and Aaron. When Moses was taken over by his zeal for God, no one could foretell what would happen. It was also best just to obey and not ask lots of questions.

As we walked, Abidan told Moses that Dathan and Abiram had moved their tents a few days ago, pitching them next to Korah's tent in the Levites' campsite, even though they were from the tribe of Reuben, not Levi. 'So, they flout the command of the Lord, by moving outside the boundary lines of their tribal campsite,' Moses muttered, leading us towards the Levite camping grounds.

I glanced up at the cloud; it was transforming. The glistening swirls that I cherished were dissipating and, in their place, dark, threatening clouds rolled in. Flashes of lightning flared, accompanied by rumblings of thunder. I had seen this before; it was not a good sign. Yahweh was angry.

Caleb and I, along with Aaron, his sons, and a group of faithful elders, accompanied Moses. The huge crowd of rebels trailed behind us, curious to see what would take place. Korah, however, was conspicuous in his absence, and I felt sure he had gone to warn Dathan and Abiram of Moses' imminent arrival. I was right. When we arrived at the site where Dathan, Abiram and Korah were camped, we found them outside their tents, talking, although it had hardly been necessary for Korah to warn them of our arrival. The murky green smog that hovered around the huge crowd of rebels accompanying us would have raised the alarm in plenty of time.

'Ah, Moses. We thought you might pay us a visit. *Shalom,*' Dathan said, inclining his head ever so slightly at Moses in a gesture of false deference. Dathan and Abiram both had short swords hanging from their belts, so I glanced at Caleb and patted the hilt of my sword. Caleb nodded. He had seen them too. I motioned to Abidan and the trusted elders to stand behind Moses and Aaron, creating a buffer between them and the huge crowd of rebels.

Jesher was among the elders standing near Abidan. I saw him and felt his eyes on me, but I did not look at him. I could not let myself be distracted. I had to fix my attention on Moses. 'Time enough for that later,' I told myself.

In a foolish show of bravado, Dathan, Abiram and Korah called their wives and children to come out of their tents and stand with their fathers. Moses grimaced when he saw them. Pain flashed over his face and he lowered his head, hesitating for a few moments.

When he looked up again, his face was like flint. He put his shoulders back, and took a deep breath. It was time.

Moses addressed the assembly. 'Yahweh is holy, and He will choose today which man He will cause to come near Him.' Turning to the crowds behind him, he shouted, 'Stand back! Move away from the tents of Korah, Dathan and Abiram! Do not touch anything belonging to them. Move away from their tents, all of you!' Caleb and I moved the crowd back while Korah, Dathan and Abiram, along with their families, stood glaring at Moses, stubbornly defending their right to challenge him. A buzz of voices cut through the uneasy silence as Korah's followers debated what to do. Most of them backed away from the tents, sheepishly avoiding eye contact with their mutinous leaders, while the onlookers who had come purely to witness what was happening stood a considerable distance away.

Moses joined us, raised his staff, and shouted, 'This is how Yahweh will show you who He has chosen to lead His people: if these men die of natural causes in the course of time, then I am not His chosen leader. But if the earth beneath them opens up, and swallows them whole, you will know that the Lord has chosen me to lead His people.'

What? I looked at Caleb. What did Moses say? Surely he couldn't mean that . . . ? We didn't have long to speculate. Within seconds of Moses' declaration, the earth started shaking and we were all thrown to the ground. I heard a noise, like the shell of a giant sea creature cracking open. The earth reeled to and fro like a drunkard, and we watched in horror as the ground under the rebels' tents split asunder, creating an ominous, pitch-black chasm. Korah, Dathan, Abiram and all their loved ones tumbled headlong into the black nothingness. Their tents, their families and all their belongings were obliterated in one fell swoop as the earth beneath their feet became their sepulchre.

The petrified spectators grovelled, screaming as the earth around the chasm once again shook violently. There was a hollow rumbling sound, a groaning and grinding, as the sides of the crevasse shifted once again, drawing together until the chasm was completely gone.

Almost immediately, the ground stopped shaking.

Stillness.

A frozen tableau of fear and disbelief.

I felt dazed. It had all happened so quickly. I wouldn't have believed anything had stood there before, were it not for the cries of terror that still echoed in my ears. As I looked at the bare expanse of ground I noticed a wooden tent peg, still stubbornly sticking out of the ground where the tents had stood. Incredulity sprang up in me. I felt the urge to laugh hysterically at the sight of that obstinate peg. But any thought of laughter was immediately crushed when I saw the charred remains of a firepit imprinted into the ground near the peg. A family had sat around that firepit. Their women had cooked meals for the family there. They had eaten together, laughed together, shared stories as they sat around the fire. Now they were gone. All of them. Women, children – gone. One lone wooden peg was all that remained of them.

A surge of grief and shock hit me as I sat crouched over on the ground; a groan of pain escaped from my mouth. More screams erupted behind me so I swivelled round to see a swarming mass of bodies: the rebel host had dropped their censers and were scrambled to their feet in a frenzy, shrieking as they tried to extricate themselves from the tangled mob of their fellow mutineers. Their cries were short-lived. Jets of fiery flames burst out from the angry cloud overhead – white-hot shafts, tinged with crimson and copper.

'Master!' I shouted, lunging towards Moses where he lay sprawled on the ground, covering his body with my own. I buried my face in the robes on his back but, even though that prevented me from seeing anything, it could not block out the shouts of the people behind us who were trying desperately to flee. I heard whooshing, whizzing noises and, within seconds, the cacophonous clamour of screaming stopped. I peered out from under my arm to see what was happening. What I saw would be imprinted on my mind forever.

Where the mass of rebels had stood, there was only bare ground, carpeted with some charred remains. Small piles of blackened embers littered the ground, wisps of smoke rising from them, like a landscape of burned-out firepits. For an instant, I smelled the pungent odour of burning flesh, before it was swept away by the strong winds that swirled around our heads, along with the piles of ash that had laid there.

A scuffling noise drew my attention to the edges of the clearing. A few rebel stragglers had managed to separate themselves from the others and were now trying to escape. They ran like drunk men, zigzagging haphazardly in-between the tents and clusters of stunned onlookers, who screamed and cowered when the fleeing rebels ran near them. Before any harm could be done, I saw individual shafts of fire burst out from the cloud. The flames incinerated the escapees one by one with deadly accuracy; they met the same fate as their friends. But that was not all that I saw.

Just before the blazing shafts came from the cloud, I saw groups of men appear, as if borne out of the air. The men were remarkably tall and broad-shouldered, similar in size to the Ammonite giants we saw in Canaan. They were robed in shining garments and armed with weaponry that was distinctive in both shape and design. Swords hung from their belts, or down their backs, held in place by the straps of their leather breastplates and armour. Some were curved like scimitars, others as straight and long as the length of a man's body, and each one was engraved with markings – possibly words? I could not tell – that sparkled.

The shining men moved with uncanny speed, standing shoulder to shoulder around each group of onlookers, facing outwards. As they lifted their arms, their long sleeves fell to the floor, forming a glowing canopy around their wards. They were glorious. The flames deflected off them like arrows bouncing off a stone wall. The runaway renegades were not so favoured. For them, it was over in a matter of seconds; the fiery shafts reduced them to piles of ash, just as it had their fellow rebels.

When the flames ceased, the shining men stepped away from their charges and lowered their arms. One of them stepped forward and looked directly at me. His hair was thick and dark, hanging down past his shoulders, and his eyes shone like burnished copper; I put my hand up to shield my eyes from the light that emanated from him. He held my gaze, regarding me with the recognition that one warrior gives another when the battle is done, then he acknowledged me with a slight bow of his head.

I sat up and stared at him through the slits between my fingers, only looking away when I heard Caleb stirring. When I looked back to the shining men, they were gone. I put my hand up to my head and ran my fingers through my hair, looking around me.

The faithful onlookers who the shining men had guarded were left stunned, but unscathed. I talked to some of them the next day.

They told me they didn't see any shining men. They also told me they didn't see the runaway rebels meet their fate. Some said there was a thick mist that blocked their sight – some said it was smoke. They saw nothing until the mist – or smoke – cleared. Caleb did not see the shining men.

But I saw them.

My eyes had not deceived me, I know what I saw. My heart was still pounding, but the terror had gone, banished by the flawless purity of the shining man who locked eyes with me.

Censers were strewn all over the ground, but the foul flames that had filled them, poisoning the air just moments before, had all but vanished. The flames of Yahweh's glory had extinguished them and, in their place, a sweet fragrance was filling the air. My beloved cloud was transforming again, the dense patches dissipating, being replaced by silvery swirls, as soft as the finest cloth. A sense of peace and comfort emanated from them.

Moses stirred next to me. 'Master – are you well?' I asked, helping Moses to his feet. He didn't answer. Staring around him in stunned silence, he leaned on his staff, tears flowing down his cheeks. 'Master,' I whispered. 'It is not wise for you to stay out here. Let me take you back to your tent.'

'No,' Moses replied. 'Thank you, Joshua, but I cannot go back to my tent. People will seek me there. I must be alone.' He reached out to grasp my arm. He was shaking. 'Will you walk with me?' I nodded and we set off, faltering at times, towards the edge of the camp. We made our way into the wilderness and headed towards a cluster of palm trees on a nearby hill. We spoke not a word. What would we say?

'Should I ask him about the shining men?' I thought to myself as we walked. But I knew the answer. No. Not today. Another time. Long into the evening, we sat silently together on the hill, praying, grieving, and pondering the ways of the Lord. Only when twilight had come, and the pillar of cloud transformed into fire, did we head back to camp together to face the agonising aftermath of the day's events.

I did ask him about the shining men, a few days later.

He had not seen them, either.

But I had. I saw them.

63

Survivor Guilt

'Joshua?' I jumped and looked up to see Moses peering at me from the other side of his tent. 'Joshua?' he repeated. 'Are you unwell? I have hailed you three times.'

'Forgive me, Master.' I shook my head to try to break the stupor I had been in. 'No, I am well.'

Moses put down the parchment he was reading. 'So, what is it that your thoughts dwell on? Are you oppressed?'

'No, no, all is well.'

Moses smiled. 'Joshua, we have known each other for some while now and I would like to think that I can tell when something is troubling you. I would also like to think that you know me well enough to trust me with your thoughts, *nu*?'

I shuffled awkwardly. 'I do trust you, Master, but I cannot speak of what troubles me because I cannot discern my own thoughts. I do not know what ails me.'

Moses nodded and chuckled. 'I understand your plight. The greatest angst is often found when our soul is brought low, but we know not why. Sometimes the only way to unravel our thoughts is by talking about them.' He leaned forward, hands resting on his legs, eyebrows raised. 'I have been told that I listen well.'

I heaved a sigh. 'I cannot find the words, Master.'

'Well, when did your soul start to feel sorrowful?'

I thought hard. 'I believe it was when we came back from Canaan ... all that took place ... the people rebelling against Yahweh, hearing His decree that we are to wander and die in this wilderness ...'

'Joshua,' Moses said. 'You must not fear. You and Caleb will inherit the land that Yahweh promised to our people. You will not die in this wilderness.'

'*I know!*' I blurted. 'That is what makes my heart sick.' I shook my head. '*Why?*' I started pacing up and down the width of Moses' tent. 'How is it that I will live when others will not? How can I embrace the joy of going into the land of promise, knowing that they cannot go there?' I stopped pacing and stood in the middle of the tent. 'I know there were many who rebelled against Yahweh and refused to go in, but there were also many who did not. He did not refuse! He did not rebel, and yet he cannot go into that land. He cannot come with me.' I turned to Moses, no longer attempting to disguise the agony that spilled out of my soul. 'Why? Why must he die? I cannot abide it. My soul is an anguish to think that he will never see the richness of that land, never get to taste of its fruit or bathe in the streams that flow down those hills – that he must live in a tent for the rest of his life and never build his own home or settle in the land of his ancestors. He will never grow old and full of years, or live to see his grandchildren grow up and wed.'

'He . . . ?' Moses asked.

The floodgates were open. I knew now what was causing me such angst, and there was no turning back.

'How can I rejoice in Yahweh's blessings to me when I cannot share them with him? He cannot go there. Through no fault of his own, he cannot go there. She condemned me for it. She said to me, "Why should *you* live when my Mesha cannot?" And she is right! I . . . I cannot get her words out of my head,' I hit the side of my head in frustration, 'because she is right. Why should I live a full life when he cannot? He is a good man, a righteous man who follows Yahweh fully.' My voice cracked and I rasped, 'He is the brother of my heart, and yet he cannot go where I am bound.' I glared at Moses and yelled, '*Why?* Tell me, why must he die while I live? Why must I go on without him, without all of them? *Why?*' My chest was heaving, and I stared at him with wild eyes, demanding an explanation – challenging him to defy me. I wanted a fight. I didn't get one. He said nothing. We stared at each other and I waited for a response. None was forthcoming. The frantic beating of my heart slowed and, as my rage abated, regret took its place. I had gone too far. I had spoken insolently, treated my master with great dishonour. I fell to my knees in front of him. 'Forgive me, I beg of you. My heart has gone astray. I spoke shamefully and . . .'

'Joshua!' I looked up. There was no anger or accusation in his eyes, only compassion. 'Come.' Moses gestured to the bench where he was seated. 'Sit.' I hesitated, then clambered to my feet and sat, hunched over, next to him, looking at the floor. 'I was still a young man when I discovered my true identity. I remember that moment so clearly. Do you know the first thing that happened after I realised I was a Hebrew, and not Egyptian?' I shook my head. 'The faces of the Hebrew slaves who I had abused over the years flashed in front of my eyes. Every one of them who I had mistreated – the men who I had watched being brutally assaulted or killed – their faces are what I saw. The faces of my own people, many of whom died in front of me with my consent. They died. I lived.' Moses sighed. 'Not only did I live, Joshua, but I lived a life of privilege; my every need was met, my every request pandered to. My own people died while I lived in the comfort of Pharoah's palace and looked on.' He stared down at his hands, clasped in his lap. 'So, yes, I know what it is to ask the question, "Why me? Why did you choose me?" Why did I live a life of lavish comfort, while my people suffered under the oppressive hand of Pharoah? Why should I live while they died?'

Moses waited while I digested that revelation. 'So what did you do?'

'Nothing, for a long while,' Moses answered. 'I knew not what to do, how to relieve the desolation in my heart. Guilt plagued my thoughts by day and my dreams by night. I was a man possessed, but I could tell no one. There was not one who I could talk to. After all, I was a prince of Egypt, the world was at my feet – how could there possibly be anything wrong?' Looking into my eyes, he said, 'There were times when I thought about ending my life. I felt I could not live on, knowing what I had done.' He gave me a rueful smile. 'I nearly succeeded – twice – but Yahweh protected me, stopped me both times. I did not know it at the time, but it was all by His design. He saved me for a reason. Now I know why but, back then, I could not comprehend it.'

'So, when did you come to peace with yourself?'

'Aah! Yahweh sent me into the remotest areas of the wilderness, where Jethro stood by me for many years while I grappled with the torment that gripped my heart. I could not have asked for a better father. He is a very wise, patient man.' He chuckled. 'He had to be, to deal with me, *nu?*'

I smiled. I had seen how Jethro dealt with Moses. It was true – he was a father that anyone would be privileged to have.

Moses grew serious again. 'Joshua – the darkness we have seen that poisons the souls of our people – I had some of that in me, too. But Yahweh used the love of a father to purge it from me and, in time, I began to understand who I was and what I believed. And, after He encountered me on the mountain in the bush that was on fire but did not burn – well,' he grinned at me, 'you know as well as I do what an encounter with Yahweh can do to a man, *nu?*'

I nodded, still trying to relate what Moses had shared with me to my own life and situation.

'Joshua! Yahweh has mapped out for you a good path – an important path. One day you will know why He chose you to go into the Promised Land. But, for now, until that time comes, you must choose to be at peace with His ways and His plans.' He grasped my arm. 'You must accept the fact that He has chosen you to live, without needing to understand why. That is the very nature of our faith. Our father Abraham left his home and travelled to a land he knew not of. That was faith! If you cannot learn to trust Yahweh, you will not be able to walk the path that He has chosen for you.' Moses stared intently at me. 'Can you do that?' he asked. 'Can you choose to be at peace with Yahweh's mysteries?'

I breathed in and out again before responding. 'I think so, Master.'

'Good!' Moses smacked my upper arm. 'This is good! Each new day is a gift from Yahweh. It is not yours to decide the future of another man, even your friends or family. But it is given to you to live every day that Yahweh gives you, to the full.' He stood, pulled me up and guided me towards the entrance to his tent. Standing there, he gazed up at the cloud in reverential awe. 'Look at it! It is a miracle, *nu?* Yahweh Himself chooses to be with His people every day, as we journey on through this desert wasteland. Every dawn that breaks, we see His cloud above us, and we know – we can see with our own eyes – that He is with us. That is a gift, Joshua. Such a gift!' He put his hand on my shoulder and pointed at me. 'Do not waste a day. Not a single one! Yes?'

I smiled. 'Yes, Master.'

'Good!' Moses let go of my shoulder, turned to walk back into his tent, then stopped and swung round. 'Ah, yes. There is one more thing I would say to you.'

'Yes, Master?'

'It is time for you to go home to your family.'

I could feel the colour draining from my face. 'How . . . how did you . . . ?'

A knowing smile crossed his face. 'Eleazar. He came to see me. He saw you in the tabernacle.'

'So, the food, the blanket . . .'

'Yes – he left them there for you. We thought it best to wait until you were yourself again, before telling you. It is time now, Joshua. It is time for you to go home.' Moses must have seen the reluctance on my face. He reached out to put his hand on my shoulder again. 'Jesher also came to see me.' My heart shrivelled. Why? Perhaps he had come to tell him that they did not want me back. Perhaps it was better that I moved away from the family.

'Joshua?' Moses looked at me in exasperation, seeing my reaction. 'Do you doubt what I say? Jesher is a good man – a wise man and a good father – and his heart is towards you.'

'In truth?'

'Yes. They have missed you, all of them. They long to see you – your family want you to come home. So go home. Now! Go!' he said, pushing me away from him, his face breaking into a broad smile. 'Go and see your family.'

64

Reconciliation

I set off with wings on my feet, longing to be reconciled with my family. But the further I walked, the more anxious I became. The thought of seeing them all at the same time was overwhelming. I started to feel like a captive walking to his execution rather than one who had just been set free.

Moses told me Jesher would welcome me back, but I wasn't convinced that everyone would be as happy to see me as he might be. I knew Shira would be unenthusiastic about my return, but I had become used to her disdainful ways and they no longer affected me. What about my brothers? Surely they would still resent the fact that they would not see the Promised Land. And their wives? Their husbands' lives would be cut short; how would they feel towards me? Fresh fears started churning around inside me. I thought about turning around and going back to the tabernacle, but I couldn't do that – Moses would ask me tomorrow how our reunion had gone. I had no choice but to face them, so I trudged on at a slower pace with heavier footsteps.

I stopped when I neared home, peering around the side of a neighbouring tent to see how many of the family were there. None of the men were present and, in fact, I could see only one person hunched over the firepit with her back to me – a woman. Her scarf was covering her head so I couldn't see who it was, but I guessed it was either Eglah or Helah. Where was everyone else, I wondered. Well, one person was a good start. I laughed to myself when I thought of the mighty captain of the armies of Israel hiding behind a tent in fear of his family. 'If my warriors could only see me now,' I thought, shaking my head in disbelief. I took a deep breath, gathered my thoughts and started walking towards the tent. The woman moved round the other side of the fire. Picking up her basket of palm fronds, she sat down, staring moodily into the embers of the fire. It was Helah. As soon as she saw me, she scrambled to her feet, knocking her weaving basket over and scattering fronds all over the floor.

'Yoshi!' She ran headlong into my arms and clung to me as if we had not seen each other for years. Her embrace took me completely by surprise, but I returned it with relief, if not a little shock. 'Yoshi!' she laughed, stepping back but still holding onto my hands. 'You came back!'

'Yes. I could not st – '

'Mesha said you would. I wanted to come and find you, but *Abba* said we must wait until you were ready to come back. I . . .' Helah paused. 'Yoshi, forgive me, I beg of you!' she said, bursting into tears.

'Helah, why do you weep?' I could not bear to see her so distressed. 'The Lord forbid that I have done anything to cause you grief.'

'No, no! You are not at fault, Yoshi,' she cried, staring up at me with her big brown eyes. 'It is I who maligned you with my words. What I said was unforgiveable. You had done nothing wrong and yet I treated you shamefully. Yoshi, my heart was false; I was not myself. I am truly happy that you will live to see the Promised Land. You are an honourable man who serves Yahweh steadfastly, and you deserve to be with our people when we go into Canaan.'

Tears cascaded down Helah's cheeks. I pulled her back into the comfort of my arms as the floodgates of her heart opened up again. Her head didn't even reach my chin. Her headscarf had fallen down, so I stroked her hair until her sobs became whimpers. Helah was a sister to me – the sister I'd never had, but always longed for. I admired her feistiness and joyful spirit, and found it hard to bear when her heart overflowed with sorrow.

As I held her in my arms, my own heart started to unfold. The pain that had clawed at my soul since that day started to loosen its grip and the tension in my shoulders began to relax. Although Helah didn't know it, her grieving was helping me to grieve. Her pain knew mine; her release became my release. After a few minutes she gave one last shudder and stepped back, wiping her face with her scarf.

'Come, sit,' I said. We sat down next to the fire and I listened as she told me of her shock at hearing Moses' announcement. She had not been able to grasp the notion of Mesha not going into the Promised Land. From the day she married Mesha, she had dreamt of growing old with him, of being surrounded by their children's children, and their children, and of one day going to be with their fathers' fathers, full of years. To find out that that wouldn't happen was more than her heart could bear. She started apologising again, but this time I cut her short.

'Helah, no. No more weeping. Reproach yourself no more. It is done. Yes? Let us put this behind us now.' I brushed away a stray piece of hair that had fallen in front of her eyes. She sighed and then nodded, blinking away some stubborn tears that still hung on her long eyelashes. I told her, 'I have learned much in the past few days about Yahweh's ways and I have chosen to trust Him – even when I do not understand.' I frowned. 'Helah – Mesha is going to die, but that will be so for all of us. The very nature of living involves dying; it is not something we should fear. We cannot choose the time of our death, that is for Yahweh to decide. Our seasons and our times are in His hands.' I grasped her hand in mine. 'I am coming to peace with that. I know now what I must do.'

'What is that?' she asked.

'Helah, we cannot let the fear of what might happen tomorrow rob us of the joy of today. We do not know when Mesha will die – it may be in two score years' time, it may be sooner. But what we do know is that today, he is *alive*. You are alive and he is alive, and you have five children who need their mother to live fully, and to love them.' Leaning forward, still clasping her hand, I said, 'I have come to realise that life is made up of moments – moments that capture our hearts. They are like . . .' I looked around, trying to think of a way to explain what I was thinking '. . . like beautiful jewels that sparkle in the sun. Those moments must be treasured. No one can take them from us. They stay here,' I put my hand on my heart. 'They are ours to keep, forever.' I felt an urgency rise up within me, a deep desire to help Helah come to a place of peace, as I had, so I urged her, 'We must find those moments. They are not always to be found in great exploits. Sometimes they are found in the small things, those which are easily missed, but they are there, nevertheless. Think of . . .' I tried to think of examples that she would understand, 'of . . . the expression on Shallum's face when he sees a worm crawling on a leaf, or . . . or how Shua's hair falls in those pretty little ringlets that curl around your finger! Those are moments to treasure, Helah. Capture them and hold them in your heart.'

As I talked, a curious expression came over Helah's face, akin to wonder. I realised she had not heard me speak like that before. I was not generally given to long speeches or much discourse, so for me to expound in this way was a revelation to her. It was to me, too! I found myself enjoying this unexpected flow of words that gushed out of me, so I continued, 'Look at how much Yoram is starting to look like Mesha – have you noticed? Even the way he stands, his mannerisms – he is his father's son. Arad's sense of humour, the way he mimics people – so naughty, but so funny! And Serah, when she closes her eyes to concentrate at prayer times – the little furrow in her brow,' I stroked the area between my two eyebrows. 'Have you seen it?' I smiled. 'What about the look of love on Mesha's face when he sees you coming. Now *that* is precious, Helah. That is worth living for, *nu?*'

Helah smiled. 'Yes. It is.'

'So let us live!' I opened my arms wide. 'Let us live fully all the days that Yahweh gives us with Mesha, with our friends and family. Let us make the most of every day He gives us, yes?' Helah nodded. She obviously needed time to think on what I had shared, so we sat in contemplative silence, staring into the flames that danced in the firepit. After some time, I heard her whisper, 'Yes. One day you will die, my love. One day.' She blew on the embers in the fire and watched them flare up into flames. 'But not today. No. Not today.'

65

Homecoming

To my relief, the rest of the family did not all return at the same time. Jesher, Azriel, Mesha and Hareph were the first to arrive back. They had been visiting Joel at the workshops where he practised his craft, to discuss a new potter's wheel and cart he was going to make for them. Their animated chattering stopped when they saw me. Mesha ran towards me, shouting and whooping, closely followed by Azriel and Hareph. I was welcomed back with a prolonged bear hug, along with much back-slapping.

When Jesher reached me, he held me at arm's length, peering at me from underneath his bushy eyebrows, his dusty blue eyes shimmering with tears, then pulled me into a tight embrace, whispering, 'My son. My heart has longed for this moment. You have come home.' His smile overflowed with love as he kissed me soundly on both cheeks.

The men were closely followed by Yoram and Arad, back from pasture, pulling the goats behind them and, thereafter, Joel's younger brother, Naim, with his younger cousins, carrying baskets of dung to dry for the fire. The youngsters seemed pleased enough to see me, but it was Yoram who flung himself into my arms. 'Yoshi!' he cried. 'You have returned! We have missed you so much!'

'I missed you too, Yori. Ech! I had forgotten how tall you have grown!' I said, looking at Yoram with pride. 'You have been eating lots of your *ima*'s delicious food, yes?' I punched Yoram on the arm, we laughed and embraced again.

Shira and Leora arrived back next – they had taken the girls with them to draw water from the well. I was relieved when Leora greeted me warmly, but it was Shira who surprised me. She kissed me on both cheeks, whispering, '*Shalom*, Joshua. It is good to see you again.' I sneaked a glance at Jesher, who raised his eyebrows and nodded at me. 'Perhaps I should go away more often,' I thought to myself, 'if this is the welcome I receive!'

Eglah returned to the tent with Shallum and his twin cousins, Ethan and Ephah. We exchanged warm smiles and embraces, but then, I would have expected nothing less from Eglah. I took Shallum from her and threw him up into the air, catching him and swinging him around as he shrieked with joy. Eglah told me that all Shallum wanted to do these days was run around on his chubby little legs. However, his newfound love of running had become somewhat problematic, as he had developed the habit of trailing after anyone who passed by our tent. Since there was a regular flow of people, Shallum was consistently getting 'mislaid', so Eglah had started taking him out for a long walk each afternoon before the evening meal, to tire him out and help Helah who, she said tactfully, 'had not been herself of late'.

I looked at the precious people gathered around me, and gratitude filled my heart. It was as Moses had foretold – everyone welcomed me home. I saw no resentful stares or sideways glances. No one talked about what had happened. It was done. We had moved on, and I was grateful. Joel was the only one still missing from our family circle, but he usually returned home from the workshops in time for the evening meal. I had need of a conversation with him, but it could wait.

Jesher clapped his hands and called his grandchildren together. 'Come, children, come!' he said. 'Would you like me to tell you a story while your *ima*s prepare a feast for us?' They all shouted, jumping up and down in excitement, and then sat around him, the little ones jostling for the best positions. 'Now,' Jesher said with a twinkle in his eye. 'Shall I tell you about Joseph, how he was sold as a slave and thrown into prison?'

'No!' they shouted with one voice.

'Not that one, *Saba*! You have told us that story many times,' Shua said, wrinkling her little button nose in a show of petulance.

'Have I?' he responded, knowing full well that he had. 'Well, who would you like to hear about, then?'.

'Abraham!' Naim shouted. 'Please tell us about Abraham, *Saba*. Tell us about the time he fought the Elamites and rescued Lot!'

'Abraham, hmm?' Jesher nodded his head. 'Yes, that is a good story, Naim. Did you know that we are very much like Abraham?

No? Well, it is true. Yahweh told him to leave his home and go to a land that He would show him. So, he left everything, and followed Yahweh. That is like us, *nu*? We left our homes in Egypt to journey to the land that was promised to us by Yahweh – the land of Canaan.'

The children were engrossed in no time at all. Jesher was a very skilled storyteller, putting on different voices for the various characters, and acting out the story as he told it. It was not just the children who enjoyed his stories, either; the adults would sit and listen just as attentively, when we had the opportunity. I smiled to see the wide-eyed faces of the little ones as Jesher told them about the time when Yahweh asked Abraham to offer his son, Isaac, as a sacrifice. Just as he was getting to the climax of that story, I saw Joel walking towards us, so I stood up and tiptoed around the back of the children's circle to go to greet him. His face, I was relieved to see, lit up when he saw me.

'*Shalom*, Joshua,' he whispered, giving me a firm hug. 'My heart rejoices to see you. You have come back to us, have you not?'

'I have, Joel. It is good to be restored to my family,' I responded. Deciding to make the most of this opportunity while we waited for the evening meal, I asked him whether he would like to walk a little way with me, as I had something to discuss with him. His eyes clouded over with anxiety – he knew there was only one topic of conversation that I would need to discuss with him privately.

'Is it Alya?' I nodded. 'Is she well?' He grabbed my arm. 'Joshua, tell me, is it well with her?'

'She is well, Joel. Her heart rejoices, as will yours when you hear my news.' As we walked, I wasted no time at all in telling him about Alya's father, of his involvement in the recent rebellion and his untimely demise. Joel's eyes grew wide at the news of Eliphalet's death.

'He is dead? But where is Alya now? She has not sent word to me. I have waited but I have heard nothing. She and her sisters – who will look after them?'

'Be still, Joel, all is well,' I smiled, squeezing his shoulder. 'Come, sit with me and I will finish telling you what has come to pass.' We sat down under a wide-spreading sycamore tree, leaning against its strong, gnarled trunk, and I told Joel what I had discovered. The day after the rebellion came to a head, and Korah's followers had been killed, I went to find Alya. When I told her about her father's death, she seemed neither devastated at his passing nor exultant that he would no longer be able to torment her. Instead, she emanated a quiet grief, a sadness that her family lineage had come to an end. We spoke about her relatives and she told me that she had an uncle named Amir.

'An uncle?' Joel interrupted, frowning. 'She has never spoken of an uncle before.'

'No, probably because she has not seen him since she was a small child,' I explained. 'It seems that Amir and Eliphalet did not agree about many things. There arose a dispute between them, whereby Eliphalet cursed his younger brother, turned his back on Amir's family, and did not see them or speak to them from that time onwards.'

'Will this uncle take Alya and her sisters into his household? What is his manner? Will he mistreat her? I must go . . .'

'Joel, be still!' I chuckled, reaching out to calm him. 'I made enquiries among the Simeonites and found out where Amir lives. I went to see him. He is a good man, and his wife a virtuous woman. They have children of their own – two sons and a daughter – but I spoke to him about Alya and her sisters, and he will take them into his family. I sensed no darkness in him – he is a true follower of Yahweh – and there was compassion in his heart for his nieces. It seems the breaking of his kinship with his brother was not of his doing, it was all Eliphalet's.'

'But does Amir know about me? Will he give consent to . . .'

'Joel!' I blurted. 'If you restrain yourself, I will tell you.' I smiled at his impatience. 'I spoke of you to Amir. He had no knowledge of you or your *abba*, but he has heard of Jesher, and of his place among the elders of Israel. He believes him to be an honourable man. I told Amir of your apprenticeship with Bezalel, the favour that Bezalel has bestowed on you, and I expounded on all your attributes.' I broke into a grin. 'Joel – he is in favour of your betrothal!'

Joel gasped. 'He is . . . so I can . . . we will be . . . oh, Alya! Alya! You will be mine! At last, you will be mine!' Tears came to his eyes as he tried to suppress the torrent of joy that surged up and overflowed.

I sat and waited, chuckling to myself at his reaction. Once Joel had calmed himself a little, I told him that although Alya was once again in mourning (this time for her father), as soon as her time of grieving was completed, Amir wanted to meet Joel and his family.

I put my hand on his shoulder and said, 'I am so happy for you, Joel. Alya is a good woman. My heart rejoices for you.'

'Truly?' Joel looked doubtful. 'You rejoice in this? I thought you did not want me to marry Alya.'

'No, that was not what my heart sought.'

'But that day when I spoke of her, you told me to restrain myself. You said I should let Alya go, that she would not be mine.'

'I did, but I spoke only . . .'

'Why would you say that if you did not wish me to take her as my wife?'

'Because . . .' I hesitated. Looking into Joel's eyes, I knew the time had come to tell him the truth. 'Because I did not want you to suffer the same pain that I bore. I could not bear to see you endure the desolation that I experienced when my heart's desire was unfulfilled – not after all that you had already endured. I could not abide it.'

Joel stared at me. 'You . . . have loved a woman?'

I gave him a sad smile. 'I have. But it was not to be.'

'Why? What hindered your union?'

I sighed. It had happened many years ago. I had not spoken of it to anyone since that time and I feared that speaking of it now would rip open a wound that had long been seared shut. But perhaps it was time.

'Her name is Merav. Her family are from the tribe of Asher. I came across her one day as I returned from the quarry. Some youths were troubling her, speaking insolently, dishonouring her. I stopped to help her and they decided to teach me a lesson.' I smiled at the recollection of what happened. 'It was I who taught them a lesson.'

Joel lowered his voice. 'How many of them were there? Did you . . . ?' he asked, clenching his fist as if to strike someone.

'There were three of them and yes, I confess that I did. It seemed fitting; I could not stand by and watch them reproach her in that manner. I was so taken with Merav, as soon as I saw her my heart told me that she was mine. There could be no other; she was my wife.' I frowned and stared at my hands. 'I believe it was the same for her. I saw it every time I looked in her eyes. They shone with love.' For a moment, I forgot that Joel was with me. 'Green eyes . . . like pools of still water. I could lose myself in their depths.'

Joel whispered, 'Alya has green eyes.'

'Yes. I saw them when I spoke with her. Her countenance is much like Merav's.'

We shared a cherished moment of silence, then Joel asked me, 'So, what happened? Were you betrothed?' His question cut through my thoughts like a shard of ice.

'No.'

'Why not?'

I looked at Joel, no longer trying to conceal the agony that I had carried for so long. 'Because she was already promised to another.'

Our stories were joined, like branches on the same vine but, whereas his vine would now flourish and grow, mine had been cut short. The scarred wound in my heart ripped open again, but there was no point in trying to conceal it. It was time to uncover it, to let the light and fresh air bring healing to its ragged edges. I would tell Joel my story and find consolation in knowing that this young man knew my pain and would understand me like others who had not been broken by love could not.

'When she was yet a girl, she was pledged to be married to a boy from the same tribe – her uncle's son. They played together as children and grew up knowing that one day they would be joined in marriage. She liked him well enough and was content to be his wife – until she met me. Only then did she realise that what she had known with him was only friendship, companionship and duty ... but not the deep love that grows between a man and woman. Our hearts were bound together from that first moment and, over the next few weeks, I begged her to turn her back on her family and deny her intended. But Merav is an honourable woman. Although she could not deny her love for me, she would not bring dishonour to her family or disavow her betrothed.' I cringed. 'I, on the other hand, did not behave so honourably. My heart was enamoured of her; if I could not have her, my life would be over – or so I thought. So, I pushed my way into her home, uninvited and unaccompanied, and challenged her father. I laid aside all honour, trampling on our ancient traditions because I could not conceive of life without her.'

Joel's face creased with concern. 'What did her *abba* do?'

I shrugged. 'What any righteous man would do. He listened to me, then had me thrown out of their home. He banned me from seeing Merav, or speaking to her, again. She was given in marriage soon afterwards.'

'Is that why you have never taken a wife?' Joel asked after a while, although I suspect he already knew the answer.

'There is no room in my heart for another.'

'Where is Merav now?'

'She is here, in the camp.'

'Here?' Joel looked surprised. 'Have you seen her?'

I nodded. 'I have seen her twice, although I did not seek her out on either occasion. The first time was in Egypt. I turned a corner and there she was, standing in front of me, as beautiful as ever. She was with child, her belly curved and full with new life. We spoke briefly and I asked her if she was content. She said, "Well enough." Her husband is a good man; he looks after her and treats her well. She held her head high and smiled bravely when we said farewell, but I saw the tears she tried to hide.

'The second time was when we were camped at Edom. I was delivering a message for Moses and saw her playing with a little girl. She had not seen me, so I stayed hidden and watched for a while, unbeknown to her. The child had waves of curly hair and a smile like rays of sunlight. I knew just by looking at her that she was Merav's daughter. She was a beauty, just like her mother. They looked so happy together. I did not approach her. I have no desire to cause her pain.'

I sighed. This time, however, it was not a sigh of pain but of relief. A cleansing was taking place, a releasing of the ache that had throbbed within me for so long. It felt good to speak of it – to speak of her – and in my heart I knew that although Joel was still a young man, there was a depth of understanding in him. I knew I could trust him. When I turned to him, there were tears in his eyes. He wiped them with the back of his hand and muttered, 'Who else knows of this?'

'Only Mesha and Helah, of our family – and possibly Jesher. I believe my *abba* took counsel with him during that time, although Jesher has never spoken of it to me.'

Joel groaned, putting his head in his hands. 'That night when we found out that Alya was betrothed: I accused you of knowing nothing of love, of not knowing what it is to feel passion for a woman burning in your soul. Joshua, forgive me. I beg of you, forgive me for my arrogance and pride.'

The memory of that day had burned in me since it happened, but I realised as Joel was speaking that the embers of my anger had cooled. I no longer felt the pain of his accusation. I was able to say to him with a true heart, 'Joel, be at peace. You did not know what you were speaking of. All is well, truly. Be at peace.'

We stood up and embraced, for the first time as brothers in heart; warriors who had fought the same battle and understood the cost of both defeat and victory. I pulled back and said to Joel, 'Come, we had better not delay – the night is drawing in and I believe there is a feast planned for tonight. You know what Shira is like when we are late to break bread! Besides – you have some important news to share with the family, yes?'

66

Celebration

It was a celebration that Abraham himself would have been proud of! Platters and baskets full of manna cakes, herb bread, grains, green leafy salads, green olives, dates and oranges, sticky baked figs and clusters of raisins covered the surface of the mat, along with dishes of vegetables cooked in Helah's delicious sauces.

Joel could not hold his peace; he told them the news about Alya as soon as we arrived back home. His news was received with great joy (and more than a little relief for Azriel) and the sounds of celebration filled the air. We feasted on food and love, until our hearts and our bellies were full to overflowing.

Conversation dimmed for a while when we noticed Yahweh's cloud starting to sparkle. No matter how many times I saw it, it never ceased to warm my heart and take my breath away. I watched its transformation into a spluttering, crackling pillar of fire with a sense of great contentment. I felt as though I had been gone from my family much longer than I had actually been away; as if I was seeing them anew, with fresh eyes. I found myself looking for moments to treasure – and I found many. As I looked around the family circle, Helah caught my eye. We smiled at one another, a smile of mutual understanding, of a secret treasure, a love shared.

As soon as the transformation was complete, Mesha stood up and went into the tent, returning with a bulging skin in his hands. 'No good celebration is complete without the fruit of the vine, yes?' he said with a flourish. 'And I have been assured that this one is a particularly good wine!' Yelps of excitement exploded from all around the circle, and the dregs of water in our cups were quickly downed to make room for wine.

'Where did you get this from?' Jesher looked at his son in amazement, sniffing the contents of his cup with obvious anticipation.

'From Itzhak,' he said with a smug smile. 'I traded it for a set of new waterpots. Apparently his daughter is most clumsy and keeps breaking them!'

'But we do not have any new waterpots to trade,' Azriel said, looking both confused and concerned.

'No, not yet. But we will soon have plenty, when you start to work at the wheel, *nu*?' Mesha grinned at his older brother.

I turned to Azriel. 'Is this true? You are going to sit at the wheel again?'

He shrugged. 'We were going to wait until we settled in Canaan, but *Abba* and I took counsel together and decided that, since we are to wander in this wilderness for many years, this would be a good time to start crafting again. *Abba*'s hands are no longer steady enough to mould the clay, but he will guide me and teach me all he knows. Hareph and Mesha will gather the clay, dig the pits for the ovens, turn the wheel for me, and do the trading. *And . . .,*' he declared loudly, 'my son Joel is making a new wheel for us, and a cart big enough to carry the wheel and all the fine vessels we will make!'

'That is wonderful news!' I lifted my cup of wine and shouted, 'Many blessings on your new potter's wheel. May Yahweh establish the work of your hands and give you the skill to craft many, many vessels in the years to come!'

'So that we can trade them for more wine!' Mesha added, to the sound of laughter and shouts of 'Amen! Amen'!

'A blessing on my son and his young wife-to-be!' Azriel held his cup out towards Joel. 'May your marriage be fruitful and your strength plentiful! May the Lord God give you rest from adversity and grant you an abundance of children!'

'Amen! Amen!'

'May . . . may wisdom be a garland to grace your head, and may He increase the days of your life . . . for many generations!' Hareph added, getting carried away in the moment.

We all laughed and agreed, then Jesher lifted his cup towards me and said, 'And to Joshua: we welcome you back into the arms of your family. May you live to be 120, and flourish in your old age! May Yahweh send you abundant peace from heaven and deliver you from all your troubles!'

'Amen! Amen!'

Hareph looked like he was readying himself to declare another blessing, but was cut short by Joel, who started playing his reed pipe. Yoram ran to fetch his animal-skin drum and joined in, beating out a distinctive rhythm. Ululating and whooping abounded as children and adults alike stood up and formed circles, dancing and whirling in time to the music. Neighbours came to see what the celebration was in aid of, and were dragged into the circles.

Mesha hoisted Shallum onto his shoulders. He squealed with joy, clinging to his father's head, bouncing up and down when Mesha danced. Jesher could not dance as fast as the other men, so we formed a circle around him. He tottered around in the middle, arms lifted high, clapping and kicking in time to the music as best he could. In truth, he was a better dancer than Hareph who, no matter how many times he tried, still always seemed to be moving in a different direction to everyone else!

The women formed a circle around Shira, who protested about being singled out. However, she soon succumbed to the persuasive powers of her children and grandchildren, and started dipping and twirling with the rest of them, waving her headscarf in the air. After a few minutes, she pulled her little granddaughter into the middle of the circle with her, as Ephah was struggling to keep up with the bigger children. Ephah tried to copy Shira's movements, flicking her hands and stamping her feet, swaying and twisting, beaming with excitement at being allowed to dance in the middle of the circle with her grandmother.

The festivities continued into the night, helped along with generous amounts of Mesha's wine, until we all collapsed, exhilarated but exhausted, and sat panting around the fire. I lay on my side and looked around at the extraordinary people I was blessed to call my family. Little Shallum had fallen fast asleep a while ago, and now lay curled up in Mesha's arms, dozing with his mouth open, tiny lips quivering. Azriel and Leora's twins had also fallen asleep, lying side by side on the mat, their arms intertwined, as was their way. Hodesh sat in Leora's lap, almost purring with satisfaction. Although she was nearly thirteen, she still loved it when her mother stroked her hair, twisting the curly strands around her fingers.

Naim and Arad sat together, drawing patterns in the dirt with their fingers, while Yoram and Joel lay on their backs, staring up at the twinkling canopy of stars overhead, exhausted after playing their instruments for so long.

Jesher, Azriel, Hareph and Mesha discussed their plans for their pottery trade, arguing about what they should charge for the different vessels, as well as which vessels would be most in demand. Helah and Eglah smiled at each other, listening to the men's animated conversations, before taking Shua and Serah inside the tent to sleep. Shira was inside already, cleaning and preparing the bed rolls for her family.

'I am at peace,' I thought to myself. My heart glowed with contentment. 'I am home. I may not have a wife, but I have a family. This family that the Lord has given me. These are my people. My family. I am come home.'

67

New Pathways

'So! Did you see them?' Moses asked me the next afternoon.

I smiled; a peaceful, contented, almost smug sort of smile. 'I did.'

'And . . . ?'

I grinned. 'It was as you said.'

'Ha!' Moses slapped his leg. 'I knew it would be so! Tell me, what took place?'

I told him about my homecoming and how I was welcomed back into the family fold. I told him of the feast we had enjoyed, and of my brother's decision to start trading in pottery again. I also told him things I had never spoken of before. For some reason unbeknown to me, I knew that I had to tell him everything, holding nothing back; everything about me, about my family, my struggles, my desires – and my heartache. I told him about *her*. He listened without interrupting as I shared the story of my love for Merav.

I told him about Joel's love for Alya, about his impetuosity and rebellion, even his plans to run away with her. I spoke of her family, the evil that blighted her lineage, but also of the hope and future that she could now look forward to, with Joel.

I told him about the dreams that had haunted me every night since the slaughter of the golden calf idolators, and of my hope that they would grow dull and disappear over time.

I told him how my heart still ached for my father, how I grieved his death and thought of him every hour of every day, longing for him to be with me on this journey; but also of how grateful I was for my new family. I spoke of Jesher and his great wisdom, his love and acceptance of me. I told him of the anger I felt when Shira did not honour Jesher as she should, and of her callous treatment of me.

I told him about Mesha, the brother of my heart, and of Helah – what happened the day of the great announcement when she realised

Mesha's life would be cut off early. I spoke of the cutting nature of her words to me, of our reconciliation and the understanding that now existed between us.

I told him about Hareph, about his clumsiness, his love of discussing the ways of Yahweh, and of his virtuous wife who was barren and yet bore her pain so nobly.

I told him about Azriel and of the seriousness of being Jesher's first-born son. I shared with Moses my thoughts of what kind of a patriarch he would be when Jesher went to rest with his fathers, and how I believed Leora would be a good matriarch, standing calmy by his side, helping him to lead this family when it was their time.

He smiled when I told him of Yoram, of the bond we shared and the name he had called me since a child. I spoke of my love for him and the light which I saw in his heart and his eyes.

I spoke to him of Caleb and of Eleazar, of how important these two men were becoming in my life. I told him of my overwhelming passion for Yahweh's presence, His cloud and fire, and my fear that the darkness would come back to poison our people and turn them against Him once again.

I spoke of the contentment that had started to flood my heart, and the peace that I now carried.

I didn't hold back. I told him everything; every thought that entered my head came out of my lips. The afternoon passed and the shadows lengthened, but I spoke on and on. Moses said not one word and asked no questions of me. He just listened, nodding or smiling from time to time. When the overflow of my heart finally came to a standstill, he grasped my hands and said, 'Thank you, Joshua. Thank you for honouring me, for trusting me; for revealing your soul to me.' It was a significant moment, a shift in our relationship. He had seen me. He knew me, in truth. He stood up and stretched, groaning as his back clicked. 'I have been sitting in this tent all day, I am in need of a walk.'

'My need is like unto yours,' I said, grimacing as I stood up. 'The meal our women prepared for us last night was as a feast for the eyes as well as the stomach. I had not eaten such good food – or drunk wine – for quite some time and I fear I lacked restraint.' I rubbed my belly and frowned. 'I ate far too much.'

Moses roared with laughter. 'That is a just price to pay for such delights, *nu*? Come, let us hope our bodies heal as we walk.' We picked up our waterskins, slung them over our shoulders, put our headscarves on, and headed out. We walked in companionable silence until we reached the outskirts of the camp, then Moses said, 'Yahweh has spoken to me.'

'Yes?' I looked expectantly at him.

'Mmm-hmm.' Moses nodded. 'He has spoken to me about what He would have us do.'

'And ... ?'

'Oh, there is much to do, and so much to learn, Joshua. We will be wandering these lands for many years, and Yahweh does not want us to be idle. There is much that He would teach us, and we in turn must instruct our people in His ways. We will teach them His laws and His commandments.' He gave me a mischievous smile. 'You and I will be very busy!'

'Doing what, Master?'

'Well, for a start,' he said with a grin, 'I am to teach you how to read and write.'

'Me?' I was appalled. 'But I have never ... I fear I may not be able ...'

'You will.' Moses glanced at me with an air of confidence. 'Yahweh has spoken. You will need these skills for times to come. We will leave this place soon and move towards Rithmah.' Moses drew in a big breath and exhaled. 'There are many adventures waiting for us, Joshua, I know it in my heart. I believe Yahweh is leading us on new pathways. We will not enter Canaan for quite some time, but He is with us and His presence will go before us as we travel.'

We both looked up at the velvety canopy of cloud that hovered overhead and took a moment to express our silent gratitude to Yahweh for the miracle of His presence with us. 'There.' Moses pointed to a rocky outcrop near the bottom of a hill. 'Let us tarry there.' Turning to me, he said, 'It is nearly time.' We clambered up to a large, flat rock that protruded. We sat down, side by side, looking out over the vast expanse of tents that littered the landscape in front of us. Twilight was falling.

'Master?'

'Hmm?'

'The darkness . . . has it been vanquished? Is there more to come?'

Moses frowned and thought for a while. 'Darkness will always seek to capture the hearts of those that bow to its dominion,' he said, still focused on the camp. 'Our enemy will not relinquish his hold easily, but as long as Yahweh is with us, we have nothing to fear. His presence is more powerful than any darkness we could encounter. If we cling fast to Him and follow His ways, the darkness will never defeat us.' He grasped my arm. 'Never seek to follow the crowd, Joshua! Never follow the crowd – follow only Yahweh's cloud, yes?'

I nodded and looked back to the magnificent pillar of cloud that towered over the centre of the camp. 'Look! It is starting!' I cried. We leaned forward in eager anticipation.

Silence fell. This was not a time for talking.

We sat, completely mesmerised, as fiery sparks started to flicker within the silvery swirls of cloud, rapidly multiplying into what looked, from our vantage point, like a swarm of fireflies encircling the cloudy tower. The sparks morphed into dancing flames, then we saw the glow of embers. Shimmering shards of red, burnished copper and amber increased in intensity until the whole tower burst into a blazing column of fire.

A sense of awe hung heavy in the air. We watched as the celestial dance began; the mysterious flickering of fire-tinged wings, swooping and diving within the flaming tower in a perpetual celebration of Yahweh's glory and power.

We watched in captivated silence, master and manservant, as Yahweh's mighty presence kindled in our hearts a blaze that would never be extinguished.

Book 2
in *The Wilderness* series

Desert Wanderers

Sentenced to forty years of wandering around the wilderness because of their stubbornness and rebellion, the newly born nation of Israel must now battle the elements, learn how to survive life in the desert, and see their families torn apart by conflict.

Journey with Joshua and witness heart-warming moments of joyful celebration, alongside the agonising pain of death and loss, as he reluctantly prepares to take on the mantle of leading this mighty nation, while facing his own fears and battling his greatest adversaries yet . . . giants!"

The hairs on the back of my neck stood up. My heart started pounding; my body trembled. Something was behind me. A shiver ran down my spine and a sense of dread filled me.

Everything in me screamed, 'Don't turn around!'

I did.

The need to find out what was behind me was stronger than the fear of what I might find. I crouched low, ready to run, and swivelled in what felt like slow motion. Raising my head, I saw two tree trunks. 'What?' The tree trunks moved. Not tree trunks. Legs! Huge, hairy, muscular legs. I stared at them with morbid fascination, tracing the sinewy contours of calf muscles up past the knees, to a set of leathery thighs.

'Whoosh!'

My warrior instincts told me, 'Duck!' Dropping to the ground on all fours, my hair wafted in the current of a huge wind. Cowering on the floor, I craned my neck to see a huge wooden club, covered with rusty metal spikes, held by a hefty, fisted hand. My eyes followed the patterns of muscle up a beefy arm, to a thick-set neck, and into the glowering face of a . . . giant!

Available Autumn 2023

Printed in Great Britain
by Amazon

25630658R10208